ALTER EGO

K. A. MASSON

BELLENDEN PROJECTS

JOIN THE KAT CLUB

K. A. Masson's 'Kat Club' members will receive a free novella-length epilogue of *Alter Ego*, and behind-the-scenes photos to accompany the book.

Members are always the first to hear about new books, and have the opportunity to become an advance reader.

See the back of the book for details on how to sign up.

 facebook.com/kamassonwriter

 instagram.com/author_kamasson

twitter.com/kamasson_writer

For 'M'

PROLOGUE

'Mum, wake up. Mum, there's someone at the door.'

I was dreaming, surely. My son had finally passed the age where he woke up at five every single morning. Still, the arrival of parenthood brought with it an end to uninterrupted nights and, for me anyway, the ability to sleep through anything.

Except for on this occasion. It wasn't a dream. Ned was shaking my shoulder, with all the strength his whippet-thin, seven-year-old frame would allow.

'What is it, darling?' I asked, not quite managing to open my eyes.

'There's someone at the door... can't you hear?'

I hadn't, but my fuggy head was a reminder that I'd taken a couple of sleeping pills at two in the morning. Banging, then the metallic clatter of the doorbell for six or seven seconds, more banging. I leapt out of bed and grabbed my dressing gown.

'Stay there, I'll just be a minute.'

As I darted down the stairs, I could see blue lights flashing through the first-floor window.

Another round of pounding, accompanied by a low bellow through the letterbox. 'Police, open up.'

As I ran down the last flight of stairs, two thoughts formulated in my head.

One: something similar to what had happened one night a few months ago. A man, trying to escape from a criminal gang, I found out later, had got cornered in our back garden. He'd pleaded with me to let him in through the patio doors. Yes, he did have the fear of God in his eyes. But he must have been nuts to think I was going to invite him in. Instead I'd picked up the phone and called 999. He spat on the glass, told me I was a 'fucking bitch', and shinned over the fence into our neighbour's garden.

Two: Sean, Ned's dad, my ex, had killed himself. Or attempted to. It wouldn't have been the first time. Or the second. For the last few years, I'd kind of expected it to happen at some point, a knock at the door from the police, just like this.

As I reached the bottom of the stairs, the internal debate I was having over which scenario was more likely was brought to an abrupt halt by more hammering. I tried to turn the Chubb key in the bottom lock, my hands shaking uncontrollably.

'What's going on? You're going to break the door down.' I finally managed to open it, forgetting the chain was still on.

'Alexandra Kendrew?'

The chain stopped the door opening by more than a few inches. All I could see was the upper body of a man, taller than me, around thirty, unshaven, wearing a short-sleeved white shirt underneath a tight, thick bodywarmer.

I answered through the small gap. 'Yes, that's me, what's going on?'

Without warning the hallway erupted with the shrill screech of the burglar alarm. I ran to turn it off.

'Take the chain off immediately or we'll force entry,' he barked.

I could just hear Ned's voice above the noise. 'Who is it? Why are they shouting?'

I turned round for a moment and saw that he'd appeared at the bottom of the stairs, hands covering his ears, his blue furry penguin held tightly by one foot. As I undid the chain, I turned to him again. 'Don't worry, it's nothing. Go back upstairs.'

The door was flung open. The young officer I'd seen through the gap in the door grabbed my arm and pushed me against the wall, using one elbow to pin me in place. I winced, my shoulder muscles screaming as he pulled my wrists together behind my back and closed the handcuffs around them.

I was facing Ned, who stood on the bottom stair looking at me in disbelief. A dark patch appeared and grew on his pyjama bottoms. His face crumpled and he buried it in the body of his penguin – I knew he was crying, too afraid to make a noise, too embarrassed at what had happened.

'Go back to your room, honey, please.'

He turned and ran upstairs.

The more senior male officer, in plain clothes but wearing a stab vest, marched up to me. 'Alexandra Kendrew, I'm arresting you on suspicion of the attempted murder of Malcolm Russell.'

I felt simultaneously light-headed and heavy-limbed. Blood rushed in my ears but somehow wasn't reaching my brain. I knew it so well, the feeling just before fainting, and I pressed my weight against the wall to stop myself collapsing to the floor, the cold metallic ridge of the radiator digging into the top of my thigh.

He continued. 'You do not have to say anything. But it may harm your defence if you do not mention when questioned something which you later rely on in court. Anything you do say may be given in evidence.'

'Mal? What's happened—'

'I'm Detective Sergeant Lambert, Lambeth CID; my colleagues here are Detective Constable Noble and Constable Grayson. Please be aware that Constable Grayson is wearing a Body Worn Video device and will be filming throughout.'

I stared at the red light at the top of the tiny square camera on the uniformed officer's stab vest. They were all wearing them, not body warmers as I'd thought; large, rectangular Metropolitan Police badges emblazoned on the left.

'You said attempted murder... so, what, Mal... he's alive?'

'I can't tell you anything more at the moment.' The man who'd cautioned me, Lambert, was the eldest; I assumed he was the most senior. I directed my question at him, with as much authority as I could muster in the circumstances. 'Are you a parent? Do you have any idea what psychological harm this could do to my son?'

The female officer, Noble, led me along the hallway, turning left into the lounge.

Lambert answered. 'I'm sorry your son was present during your arrest. Your son's father isn't here?'

I was shaking uncontrollably; it was difficult to concentrate enough to speak. 'No.'

'Does he live here?'

I took a moment to calm down, closing my eyes and

taking a couple of deep breaths. 'We've been separated for about four years. We haven't seen him for a few months. He lives just outside Oxford with his mother.'

'Is there anyone nearby who could look after your son now? You'll be taken down to the station for questioning. We'll need to get in touch with your son's father so he can come and look after him while you're in custody. Do you have his phone number?'

'Yes, on my phone. It's in the kitchen I think.'

The female officer, Noble, tightened her grip around my arm momentarily before standing up.

'Stay there please, Mrs Kendrew, I'll get it.' She got up from the sofa and returned a minute later with my mobile.

'There's no passcode on your phone, Mrs Kendrew?' she asked as she sat next to me.

I closed my eyes for a second, hoping it would help me to compose myself. 'No, my son kept typing in the wrong number and I got locked out so I took it off.'

She pressed the home button on my phone again. The screen showed the text conversation I'd had with Mal the night before, that I'd read and re-read before I'd gone to bed. A one-way conversation, all blue boxes. I'd left the phone downstairs, knowing I'd be checking it all night to see if he'd called or texted if I'd taken it to bed.

The only officer in uniform, Grayson, appeared in the doorway with Ned. He ran towards me, his little arms instinctively wrapping around my neck. 'Sweetheart, don't worry, it'll be fine.'

He was sobbing. I felt Noble unlock the handcuffs. I swept Ned up onto my knee, and felt his hot, wet cheeks against my neck.

'So, Mrs Kendrew, is there anyone who could look after

your son now?' Lambert asked, an impatient tone barely concealed.

'God, I don't know, how early is it... five?'

Noble glanced at her watch. 'It's a few minutes before six.'

I could see now, through the gaps in the thick velvet curtains, that there was daylight behind them. I tried to think who could look after Ned. My head felt blank, like wading through fog; the zopiclone I'd taken only a few hours ago still had a hold.

DC Noble was scrolling through my phone. 'The people you've contacted in the last few days are...' she paused for a moment. 'Mal, Ingrid, Agnes, Itsumi, Denny.'

God, why hadn't I thought of Denny? I'd always joked with her that she was my get-out-of-jail-free card. Ned moved for the first time and looked up at me. 'Is Auntie Denny coming?'

'Maybe, darling', I whispered back before replying to Noble. 'Yes, Denny, Denise Coleman; Ned knows her very well, she's only round the corner.'

Noble was already pressing the green button. Four rings, five, then Denny's voicemail message – I must have heard it a thousand times. 'Hello, Denny here, leave me a message, when I get a bit of time I'll call you back.'

Noble spoke after the beep, explaining the situation, and asking her to call back as soon as she could.

'What time does your son start school?' Lambert asked.

'Ten to nine – it's the school opposite,' I replied.

'If there's nobody else who could look after your son, he will have to come down to the station with us and someone could pick him up from there. We can probably organize for a social worker to stay with him while you're being questioned.' The two detectives exchanged glances. Noble turned and walked into the hallway and I could hear her talking in a quiet murmur with her colleague. Were they discussing the logistics of taking a young child to a police station? One of them opened the door and the conversation continued outside, one of them talking into their radio and a crackly response from it.

I tightened my hold around Ned and kissed his right temple. He stayed absolutely still, his gentle, silent breaths warming the small cavity between our bodies.

I felt a sob rising in my chest. I looked up at Lambert. 'This is barbaric – he's only seven for crying out loud. There must be some kind of...'

Noble handed the phone to Lambert who briefly looked at it.

'You sent Mr Russell four or five text messages last night, all unanswered.'

I nodded, impatiently. 'It isn't like him really, but I realised when I heard the news on the radio before I went to bed that Arsenal played a friendly last night and I just...'

I stopped mid-sentence. They probably didn't need to know all this. TMI. Lambert kept looking at me. Just to break the silence, I continued.

'... I just assumed he'd either gone to the match and hadn't mentioned it to me or he'd been watching it on TV at home or at a pub and that's why he hadn't replied. Surely if I'd tried to kill him, d'you think I'd have gone to bed like it was just a normal night?'

'People act in all sorts of strange ways in these situations, Mrs Kendrew.'

Noble came back into the lounge. Lambert continued. 'DC Noble will accompany you and your son upstairs so he can get dressed. Can you also show her where the clothes you wore last night are?'

I nodded as I stood up, Ned's body still wrapped around me, like he'd done when he was a toddler and had fallen asleep in my arms.

Upstairs, I showed Noble the linen basket in the corner of the bedroom. 'Everything I wore yesterday is in there, on top.'

I asked if I could get dressed but was told my dressing gown would be treated as evidence. 'You'll be given some clothes to change into when we get to the station. Forensics will be searching the property for the rest of the day, and may take some items away for analysis, particularly any computer equipment you may have. We'll need to keep your phone too,' she added, holding it up – she'd already put it in a clear, plastic evidence bag.

Ned came out of his room. I checked his trousers and polo shirt weren't inside out. 'Is it okay if he cleans his teeth?' I knew this probably sounded ridiculous. 'It'll only take a minute.'

She nodded. We walked downstairs to the bathroom. Noble held the door open while I squeezed some toothpaste onto Ned's brush.

'Do I have to clean them now? I haven't had breakfast yet.'

'Yes,' I whispered back.

I joined Noble on the landing.

Downstairs there were voices, outside in the street, dogs barking, and a familiar voice. Denny, bless her.

'Alex, you okay, darling?' she called up the stairs. 'What's going on? I was walking past with the dogs and saw all this kerfuffle outside. I went to text you to find out what was going on and saw you'd called. And then I heard this message from the police. Is it something to do with Sean?'

Lambert appeared in the doorway. 'Come inside please madam, and I'll explain.'

Ned finished in the bathroom – we filed downstairs. Spotting Denny, Ned ran towards her. 'Come here, sweetness.'

Denny, or more accurately, her family, had already had a few run-ins with the police – she had a pretty dim view of them. Her son, now in his early twenties, had been stopped and searched on numerous occasions, without ever being found with a knife or drugs, or anything else they assumed might be in his possession. Just for being mixed race and in Brixton or Peckham after 10 pm.

'Mrs...?'

'Coleman,' Denny said.

'Mrs Coleman, we need to take Mrs Kendrew down to the station for questioning.'

'Questioning, about what? Have you got a warrant to come barging in here?' She looked at me, searching for a clue.

'They think I tried to kill Mal.'

'What, that's ridiculous.' Denny turned towards Lambert. 'Are you serious? Alex wouldn't hurt a fly, look at her.'

'Mrs Coleman, are you able to look after her son while she's in custody?'

'Yes, but—'

'That's all we need to know for the moment, thank you. Our colleagues at the station will call you.'

'Alex, shall I take Ned to school this morning?'

Ned turned to look at me optimistically.

'Yes, definitely. I want to keep things as normal for him as possible.'

'Has he had any breakfast?'

I shook my head. Ned buried his head in Denny's fleece. She stroked his hair – it had grown long, falling in loose curls over his white school polo shirt.

'Come on then, sunshine. What's it going to be? Toast or CocoPops?' she asked, trying to make it sound like an exciting choice.

I stood, like a school kid in front of two teachers deciding what length of detention would be most fitting, while Lambert and Noble exchanged a few words. Noble took notes in a small, flip-over pad which struck me as ridiculously analogue.

'Let's go,' Lambert said.

Noble handcuffed me again. As they walked me into the hallway, I mouthed 'love you' as I met Ned's gaze, tears pricking the back of my eyes.

Lambert conferred with the more junior, uniformed male officer in the hallway; when the SOCOs would be coming, when house-to-house enquiries would start, here and at Mal's. As I waited, I couldn't understand why I felt so calm; somebody had tried to kill Mal and I didn't feel anything. Now that Ned was being cared for, for a moment my mind was empty of thought.

As we waited for Lambert, I scanned the wall of happy snaps I'd recently framed and hung, adding to photos already there; Ned when he was a baby and a toddler, his first day at school, stirring the Christmas cake, camping with the other Ned and his mum in the New Forest. And then one more – the only one not of Ned – was of Mal and me, when he'd taken me to the Emirates Stadium to see his team play Manchester City. He was in his red Arsenal gear, hat, scarf, ear-to-ear grin. He'd used it as his Facebook profile photo ever since – I'd been really touched that he was finally acknowledging, maybe to himself, that we were an item.

Before I could stop myself, I felt my chest tightening; a huge sob rose up and exploded, tiny droplets flying out and landing on the detectives' black stab vests.

'Jesus Christ,' DS Lambert shouted. Noble renewed her grip around my upper arm and the others wiped the spit away with the back of their hands.

I couldn't stop a steady stream of tears coursing down my cheeks, nor the small, hiccup-like sobs that broke out from deep in my throat. The two men looked embarrassed, like they'd never had to deal with a hysterical woman before, though surely they must have, hundreds of times. I couldn't stop myself blurting out, 'Look, I need to know what's going on. Where is Mal? In hospital? God, I'd never do anything to hurt him. You have to believe me. This is just mad.'

Noble spoke as soothingly as she could manage. 'Mrs Kendrew, our colleagues down at the station will be able to give you more details. You'll be interviewed fully but before that takes place, you'll have the opportunity to call a solicitor, either someone you know, or you can appoint one of the duty solicitors.'

I kept my head bent as we walked towards the marked car; I didn't want to see anyone. Although, I was sure some neighbours must have been watching from their windows to see what was going on, a bit of juicy local gossip. DS Lambert opened the door and motioned me to get into the back of the car. As I bent down, I glimpsed my neighbour opposite, Rob. He was standing in his open front doorway, with an expression changing quickly from curiosity to concern. I reddened and looked down, not knowing how to respond.

We made off down the street, Noble driving speedily but adeptly, nimbly moving into spaces to allow other cars to pass. I'd always felt car sick if I wasn't driving; as we skimmed over speedbumps without breaking, I felt a strong surge of nausea. To counteract it, I tried to concentrate on the small section of road I could see between the two front head-rests.

I caught blurred glimpses of Brockwell Park and Herne Hill; the familiarity of the surroundings making the journey all the more surreal. Half way along Railton Road, instinctively I turned my head to look for Mal's street. I closed my eyes; I could picture his face but his features kept disappearing. Instead, the question I'd evaded formed in my mind: who had tried to kill Mal?

My heart pounded, echo-like, in my chest. As the car turned several sharp corners and came to a sudden halt in front of a solid metal gate, I threw up all over myself and DS Lambert sitting next to me.

PART I

FOUR YEARS EARLIER

CHAPTER 1

Hi, I'm grabbing five minutes between meetings so I thought I'd send you a quick message! Love your profile – I'm a fellow Scot – I was born in Glasgow but no longer have the accent, unfortunately! Anything more you'd like to know about me, please feel free to drop me a line. Mal.

Three days after unhiding my dating profile, I was already beginning to feel the onset of online dating fatigue – man shopping should be as fun as it sounds. But the kid-in-a-sweetshop appeal of trawling through profile after profile quickly subsides when you begin to suspect the photographs are ten years old, before the men have lost their hair and gained a beer belly. And they start their 'bit about me' with 'Hello, thanks for stopping by. I consider myself a gentleman with integrity, am genuine, caring and thoughtful. I've been told I'm good looking, charming, well-mannered, interesting, interested and engaging, fun loving with a good sense of humour.'

Anyone who feels the need to mention they possess a sense of humour clearly doesn't. What stops me throwing the towel in completely is the prospect of being single for the next forty years, gradually drying out and becoming increasingly wrinkled and grey and crotchety.

On the whole I could scan pages of profile photos of men that had appeared as my 'matches', with no danger of my heart racing. Occasionally, some square-jawed, raven-haired, dark-eyed lovely would cause it to skip a beat, providing a brief interlude from the real world. Until reading his profile where he would undoubtedly prove himself to be a narcissist, only interested in women twenty-five years younger than him, with dubious beliefs, religious and political, providing too much information about his hobbies, terrible taste in music or a lack of interest in anything that isn't sport-related.

Sometimes all of these traits are missing, but I had grown to assume there must be some unspoken rule, that if someone is not only extremely attractive but also appears to be sane, intelligent, successful and solvent, they pretty much can pick or choose from the entire site. I had learned that, in the interests of self-preservation, they were best avoided.

The odd profile made me laugh out loud though, spraying coffee all over my keyboard, as had happened earlier that morning.

'Recently I've looked around and realised I'm the last one left on the dance floor and if I'm not careful, I'm headed for an undignified single existence, probably involving silver leather jackets and some kind of white sports car.'

Sadly he fell into the above category, so I decided not to darken his inbox.

I remembered this guy though. He'd 'liked' me a few days ago, and had looked at my profile a few times. He sounded just my type, mainly because he said he was obsessed with music – he'd listed a few bands that would get into my top ten too. His profile stated Brixton as his location which was handy; I lived not too far away. He had a line about wanting to meet someone who'd like to go to gigs with him so that he no longer look like a record company executive; on his own, in a suit and twenty years older than the rest of the crowd. His photos were a little uninspiring though; his main one a selfie taken on a train – no one is going to look their best under the harsh strip lighting of public transport. But there was one – he was in profile, sitting on a bench with a lake behind him, wearing a really good suit, tanned, expensive sunglasses, hair coiffured with just the right amount of care and product. And, I noted with delight, a slight chin cleft. A true sign of a flirt, they say. Ned, then four-years-old, had one and he was already in training.

Anyway, I had been preoccupied over the last few days with messaging a cute investigative news reporter, with dark almond-shaped eyes and floppy black hair that framed his face to perfection. He sent me a message the first evening I'd been on the site. *Hi Leica, I love the way you've written your profile. Mmmm... you seem so perfectly lovely... why haven't you got a handsome boyfriend to kiss you goodnight?*

Good start, I'd thought. His profile was succinct and self-deprecating, with a funny retelling of meeting a girl on the tube a few weeks earlier. I'd asked him in one message what had happened to the girl. *I don't know. I allowed her to kiss me for a few seconds before I got off at the next stop.* That struck me as odd, probably not the whole story. We continued to exchange messages for a few days, but I was well-versed in this endeavour, and knew putting all my eggs in one basket was not the sensible approach.

So it was with promiscuous haste that I moved a few into Mal's. I replied. *Hi Mal, nice to meet you. So what was your last gig? Mine was Nick Cave – he's a genius. Alex.*

I went online half an hour later, and saw by the small green dot next to his profile name that he was too – a few minutes later I got another message. *Hi Alex, yes, Nick Cave, totally love him, seen him loads of times and have everything he's ever done, even all the Grinderman stuff which is pretty difficult to listen to. So, you obviously have great taste! Do you fancy meeting for a coffee or a drink sometime? If so, when is good?*

We continued emailing for a few days, exchanging top ten lists of our favourite artists, and talking about the difficulties of co-parenting. I said to him that it was to his credit he spent so much time with his son. I'd come across dads who rarely saw their children – something I found extraordinary. But over time I also realised that spending little time with their offspring allowed men to do pretty much what they wanted, when they wanted. After a spell of domesticity, they reverted to a bachelor lifestyle, albeit with a significant portion of their salary going to their ex-spouse. Dating a woman with kids is probably not going to be an attractive prospect for a guy who doesn't spend any time with his own.

We decided to meet sometime on Friday. A few days before we swapped from messages on the dating site to texting.

Hi, it's Mal, just so you know I'm a modern man, I'm ironing my work shirts as I type! Your work sounds very creative, I'm impressed!

I replied. *Yes, well, these days everybody thinks they're a photographer so our days are numbered... I'll make the most of it while it lasts. Got a shoot for a new client tomorrow. So what about your work? I know you work in the financial sector.*

I got a message alert a few minutes later. *Yes, I work for a German investment bank, in their corporate sector. My department is responsible for managing risk across the business, so we're involved in analysing performance and giving support to our international finance teams... I could go on but I imagine your eyes might have glazed over by now! I really admire people who work for themselves. So, are you free on Friday morning? The café at the Ritzy?*

The exchange of messages had happened quite late that night. The next morning when I woke, I turned over and reached for my phone on the bedside table. I was pleased to see there was another message from Mal. *Hi, good luck with your shoot today.*

Getting Ned ready for school, and myself prepped for the shoot, I didn't get a chance to reply. Also, if I'm honest, maybe I sub-consciously wanted to give the impression I was a busy, professional woman; not always available.

On the way home after the job was finished, I replied. *Thank you, it's gone really well, just a few simple shots of a gallery – plenty of natural light which I love. Tomorrow morning is great – 10ish? Can't wait!*

Yes, me too... so, have you shown my profile to any of your friends (he asks, cringing slightly).

I replied. *No – I did once when I started internet dating – a year ago I guess. Not many of my friends have done it so they think I'm totally mad anyway. Oh dear, I daren't ask – have you shown mine to any of your friends? "What does she want – the moon on a stick?" might be a measured response...*

LOL! I did show yours to a friend... he said if we don't hit it off he'll leave his wife for you!

This was how it always started – an optimistic exchange of messages where both parties are pretty certain they're about to embark on the romance of the century. The trouble is after that it often goes tits up.

CHAPTER 2

The next morning was resolutely grey as I searched for a parking space. My stomach lurched with last-minute apprehension. I knew it would disappear as soon as I met Mal, but for those few minutes, I knew I was going to feel queasy.

I jogged as fast as my low-heeled boots would allow across the pedestrianised square in front of the Ritzy cinema; I hate being late. The doors to the café were blocked by abandoned buggies; it must have been 'Watch with Mother' morning. I had to step over a huge double Bugaboo. Mal spotted me before I managed to regain my composure completely. He had the merest hint of amusement on his face as I approached him, causing the little crows' feet and dimples to appear that I'd seen in one of his profile photos. Mmmmmm, I thought. Cute. A suit. But a cute suit. I might have struggled to recognise him from his profile photo, had he not been the only middle-aged man sitting alone.

He was dressed in a light grey, light-weight wool suit –

Reiss or Ted Baker. White shirt, trendily wide, black knitted tie, thick, black-rimmed glasses. He looked comfortable in his own skin – every inch the finance guy, though he could easily have passed for the record company exec he'd mentioned in his profile too. I'd never gone out with anyone who was likely to wear a suit to work.

He stood up as I reached the table. I was expecting an awkward *do we shake hands or do we shake hands and kiss on the cheek, or just a kiss on the cheek* routine that dates always start with. None of that – very naturally we kissed, just left of each other's lips.

'So, how has your morning been so far?' I asked him as we sat down.

'Oh, not bad. I've been here for about an hour, just organising stuff for some meetings next week. How about you?'

'I'd forgotten it was Reading Half Hour in Ned's class, so I went to school with him. That kind of thing must seem a long time ago with Ewan?'

'Yeah, it does I suppose. It goes quickly though – Ned'll be at secondary school and a regular stroppy teenager before you know it.'

He asked me what I'd like to drink and went to the bar, having more luck circumnavigating the buggies than I did. The yummy mummies all seemed to notice him and obligingly moved them out of his way.

When he returned, he sat back, slightly defensively, in his chair. 'Alex, one thing I've got to get out of the way first – I've lied about my age.' He lifted his hands in mock surrender.

I snorted involuntarily. 'Ah, I see, by how much? I'm not sure I remember exactly what you said anyway.'

'I said I was 42. I'm 46, just! I had my birthday a couple of weeks ago. How did that happen?'

'Look it's not a deal-breaker. Anyway, you could easily pass for 42.'

'And you could easily pass for 22.'

'Yeah, right. You must have special lenses in those frames that blurs out all my wrinkles.'

Mal took his glasses off, and for a few moments we looked at each other, not smiling, just taking in the little details. He had a Scottish look about him – I'm not sure I could really describe what I meant by that in words. In the same way as Daniel Auteuil looks French or Vladimir Putin looks Russian. Something about his colouring – pale freckly skin, dark hair and eyes, or at least I imagined he would have been. He was now firmly in the 'salt and pepper' camp. I tried not to think how drop-dead gorgeous he must have been when he was twenty-five.

Neither of us had mentioned the music playing in the café. As we'd been talking, I'd been only vaguely aware of it; Beck, Massive Attack, then a dubby track I didn't know – not the kind of thing I listened to, but I liked it, and it suited the atmosphere perfectly.

A six-month-old baby broke the silence with a high-pitched shriek of delight, balanced on his mum's hip as she one-handedly packed her changing bag. It was impossible not to smile back at him when he gave us a gummy grin.

'So,' I began, both of us still watching the baby as his mum navigated her buggy between the tables and out of the café. Knowing what I wanted to say but not quite finding the right words, I just blurted it out. 'What happened with your marriage?'

He looked down at his cappuccino.

'I'm sorry, that's a very personal question. But I guess we wouldn't be sitting here if you were still married.'

He smiled, a slight pink tinge spreading over his cheekbones. 'Well, I had an affair.' That made sense; he totally looked like the kind of man who would. He looked at me, gauging my reaction. I raised my eyebrows a little, perhaps with the faintest smile, prompting him to continue.

'With my cousin's wife.'

'Wow, that's pretty heavy duty.'

'Yeah, it was. Both our marriages broke up. Carnage.'

'How did the family take it?'

'I'd always been the golden boy... you know, with the fancy job in banking. Overnight I turned into the black sheep. I'd always been very close to my cousin, Stewart; I persuaded him to come down from Glasgow after he left university, and I helped him get a job. We spent a lot of time together... he'd come and stay with my wife Mel and me. He met this girl, Louise, and then the four of us went out together, all the time.'

'But what happened with your wife? Did the affair just happen? I'm not sure affairs ever just happen, do they?'

'No, you're right. After we had the baby, I was bored, to be honest. I was bored with her, with our life. We'd stopped doing anything together, you know, as a couple. We never had...' He hesitated.

'You never had sex. I get that,' I responded.

'And when Ewan got a bit older, occasionally we booked a babysitter and went out, often with Stewart and Louise. Lou and I got in the habit of sharing a sneaky fag out the back of the pub. Even at Ewan's Christening, in a couple of the photos, everybody else was looking at the camera and smiling, and us two were deep in conversation, like two naughty school kids not paying attention.'

'It must have been exciting, when you finally got together?'

'God, yes, it was amazing. I mean, it'd built up, the tension between us. It was inevitable, looking back. But we were both grief-stricken by the damage we'd caused everyone, and to the family. I was anyway, still am if I'm honest.'

'So what happened, in the end?'

'Well, we've had an on-again, off-again thing for the last five years. She kept going back to Stewart in between, or rather he persuaded her to go back to him and she broke up with me. But we decided last time it was over, and that we both needed to move on. That's why I'm here.'

He smiled, waiting for my response. There was a sorrowful look in his eyes, even when he was smiling. I'd seen it before with guys whose marriages had broken down. Nobody expects to find themselves single after a twenty-year relationship – I put myself in that camp too. And with the men I'd met on dating sites there was often this same sadness, perhaps caused by the sudden transition from being a full-time to part-time dad; finding yourself redundant. Sure, it gave men the freedom to do all the things their wives or partners stopped them doing. Some men embraced this and started going out drinking five nights a week, and watching their football team at every match, or buying a built-to-your-exact-requirement off-road bike that cost as much as a family car, and wearing the obligatory neck-to-ankle black Lycra while riding it.

I checked with myself whether I really wanted to ask the next question, but again I heard the words spilling out. 'So how long ago was that, that you both decided it was over?'

'A couple of months.'

I raised my eyebrows a little.

'I know what you're thinking, that's not very long.'

I was resting my head on one hand, looking at him intently. During dates I often had an internal discussion. *Yes, he's great, but he's not interested in me. No, definitely no, who would turn up at a date with protruding nasal hair, for fuck's sake? Yes, he's quite nice, go with it. Or no, let's face it, you're never going to see him again if your life depended on it.*

I wasn't having any of that. I knew I wanted to see Mal again, but I was worried that he wasn't over Louise, though perhaps it wasn't the time to say it.

'So what happened with your marriage?' He took the opportunity to divert the conversation to me.

'Actually, we were never married.'

'Why not?'

'I don't know, it never really occurred to either of us I suppose. He never asked me. And I was never interested in looking like a gigantic meringue for a day.'

'Why did you split up?'

'It's a long story. We'd been together for years, but he was always depressed. I mean, seriously depressed. It took a few months after we met for me to really understand what was going on. I'd never known anyone who had depression, and it just wasn't talked about like it is today. I mean, from his behaviour, and piecing together bits of what he said, it gradually dawned on me.'

'So what made you realise he really had a problem?'

'We went out one night, with a group of my friends from college, my best mates, and I was looking forward to them meeting him, me showing him off.' Mal smiled, a flicker of recognition of the sentiment.

'He could be really charming when he felt like it. But not this time. He just sat there, scowling, answering any questions with a curt 'yes' or 'no'. It was excruciating. Half-way through the meal he got up and said he wasn't feeling up to

it. I didn't hear from him for about a week after that. It was
in the days before mobiles – they were just starting to
appear, you know, the Dom Joly type ones. I called him at
home a couple of times a day, and his flatmates just said he
was in his room and hadn't come out.'

Mal kept looking at me; I guessed he wanted me to
continue.

'I should have dumped him there and then. But, I'd
started to fall in love with him, I guess. He was tall, dark and
handsome and through my 25-year-old eyes, perhaps being
a bit fucked up made him more alluring. I dunno. Funny,
when I saw the date on the parking ticket earlier, I realized
tomorrow it'll be fifteen years since we met.'

'God. How does that make you feel?'

'Sad, actually. Sad it turned out the way it did. And sad I
wasted all that time, if I'm honest. My life would have been
very different if I had finished it, but then I wouldn't have
Ned. And he's amazing. I just never had myself down as a
single parent.'

'What made you, in the end? I'm guessing it was you
who finished it?'

'It was the stark realisation that he was never going to
change. That no matter what I said or did, whatever
approach I tried... carrot, stick, carrot and stick, unless he
wanted to climb out of the pit he'd dug for himself, my
efforts weren't going to make a blind bit of difference. I had
hoped, having a baby, him having a dependant, he'd finally
have to sort himself out. But of course, if anything, having
that extra stress only made matters worse. So, there was all
that, and then the fact that I was about to hit forty. I thought
to myself that I could be hitting fifty or sixty and in exactly
the same position if I didn't do something about it. After
that, there was no turning back. It took me over a year to get

him to move out of the house. But blimey, the relief when he did was incredible.'

'How did you finally get him to go?'

'That's another long story.' I paused. Mal didn't need to know about my ex's suicide attempts ten minutes into our first date. 'Anyway, all we've talked about is how crappy our previous relationships have been. Tell me about Ewan.'

And he did. He showed me photos, and I showed Mal ones of Ned, scrolling quickly past the odd shot of men I'd met in the last few months and who had somehow ended up on my phone's camera roll.

We talked inevitably about music, and found that we had almost exactly the same taste, with a few exceptions. He had a lifelong and abiding love of The Fall whereas I had an equally passionate hatred of them. Nick Cave we knew about, and we discussed what it was like being a teenager and feeling the disconnectedness that comes with that age.

He explained that he rented a room from a colleague, Sally, between Brixton and Herne Hill, but that his son Ewan lived with his mum in Brighton where he had a flat, and spent most weekends with his son. 'How I became her tenant is a funny story. We ended up on the same table at a Christmas do, about four or five years ago. It wasn't long after Louise and I had split up for the first time... Sally made a bit of a play for me; I was paralytic and didn't fight her off.'

I looked down at my coffee; I wasn't sure I wanted to know the details. Mal must have sensed that. 'Well, long story short, the next morning we both agreed that getting involved with a colleague was a bad idea. I told her about Louise too, pointing out what a nightmare my lovelife was, which was why, when I asked around to see if anyone had a friend with a spare room, she offered, knowing we'd got all that out of the way already. We've become mates, over time.

I even give her free advice on dating – she shows me profiles and I give them marks out of ten.'

Did I like the idea of him living with a colleague, potentially one that still had a bit of a thing about him? That, and living some of the time down in Brighton would change the dynamic of any potential relationship. Not wanting to dampen the mood, I didn't ask why he hadn't mentioned it earlier, or quiz him about his colleague. Instead I jokingly asked him if he ever walked round Brighton in the hope he'd bump into Nick Cave.

We talked about Scotland and how the sound of bagpipes had both of us reduced to tears. His parents had met at a dance hall in the east end of Glasgow in the fifties.

'Wow, that's so romantic,' I said.

'I don't think it was. I mean, they were in love, I'm sure, but my father was a typical Glaswegian with a fiery temper. And a drinker, of course. He worked in the shipyards all his life – he was an electrician. My mother was a saint, looking back, having us three kids and him to look after. She had a couple of part-time cleaning jobs, but she was always there when we got home from school, tea on the table. And then one day we had a knock on the door. Our dad had been killed in an accident at work... he'd been electrocuted.'

'Oh God, Mal, I'm sorry, that must have been terrible, especially for your mum. Was the accident investigated? Did she get any compensation?'

'No, nothing like that. My brother was fourteen, my sister twelve and I was six. Mum decided there and then that we needed a new life, away from Glasgow, away from Scotland. A few weeks later her brother drove us down to Brighton in his Transit van. She'd wanted to get as far away as she could, so the south coast it was.'

'And what did you kids think about it?'

'Dermot and Katriona weren't very happy. I don't remember, I was too young, but they've talked about it a lot since. They were leaving all their mates behind, Dermot had a girlfriend by then. I think they've come to see how hard it was for our mum and she did what she thought was best. But they blamed her for a while.'

'Did she ever remarry?'

'No, I think she was mourning for a long time, years probably. It wouldn't have occurred to her to think about finding someone else. It was her role to bring us kids up. And she did a braw job, on the whole.'

'That's a very Scottish word. I remember my granny using it. Do your brother and sister have an accent? I can't hear one in your voice at all.'

'Yeah, my brother Dermot does. My sister a little. I was too young I think. What about you? You don't sound Scottish either. You sound southern and posh!'

'Oh, I don't know, I still cling on to my hard vowels. I'll always say 'bath' and 'fast'. I was about nine when we moved from Scotland to the north-east of England and we were there until I went to art college. I still sound the same as I did when I was eighteen. Actually, I sound just like my mum. And sometimes I catch sight of my reflection in a car window as I'm walking past and I see her looking back at me which is a very frightening thought.'

Mal looked puzzled by this. 'You're not close?'

'No. I really envy people who have a close relationship with their mother. It's complicated, I can explain another time. Talking of which, I could happily sit here all day, but...'

Mal looked at his watch. 'It's just after twelve. Of course, you must have work to do.'

'Sadly; you must too.'

We both stood up. Mal was taller than I'd expected. He'd

put six foot in his profile, though, as with age, people often lie and, with height, men especially. I'd deliberately worn low heels, so as not to be taller than him.

I think we were both having the same thought, as the first bars of *Modern Love* began filling the café, but it was me who said it.

'Bowie, God, how could we have not included him in our pop icons pantheon earlier?'

'But it kind of goes without saying, no?' He turned towards me and winked. 'I'll walk you to your car,' he added, as we pulled on our coats.

'That'd be lovely, if you're sure. I'm parked a little way off though.'

Our stride fell into the same rhythm and, as I glanced down at our feet in step, realized we had almost-matching black raincoats. I felt a pang of sadness that it was coming to an end. I'd learnt to accept that even if a date had gone brilliantly, sometimes I wouldn't hear back.

Mal asked me what I was doing over the weekend. I told him Ned and I had a packed weekend of shopping and soft play centres with his friends and their mums. 'Sounds really rock 'n' roll, doesn't it? What about you?'

'I've got Ewan this weekend, so I've got a couple of meetings this afternoon and I'll get on the train to Brighton as early as I can. I think we'll probably go Christmas shopping at some point; he hasn't got anything for his mum yet.'

We turned the corner, and I was disappointed to see my car was only a little way along the street.

'Well, this is me.' I was embarrassed at my car. Ten years old, filthy on the outside, and the seats covered in the detritus that comes with chauffeuring a small child around. 'Don't look, please, it's a complete tip.'

Mal came and stood next to me. For a moment I think

we both contemplated whether we were going to snog, but instead he gave me a very soft kiss on the lips.

'It's been great.'

'Yeah, really good.'

I was determined not to be too pushy or appear needy, and though I considered texting Mal a few times, I didn't. But he did. *So, would you like to get together again?*

I replied. *Er, let me think about that ;)*

I waited for a minute. *Go on then, twist my arm! Are you free on Monday evening? You could come over for dinner... 7.30?*

He replied a few minutes later.

Cool! It's a shame we had to leave when we did – could have happily chatted all day! My friend texted earlier – the one I showed your profile to – asking how my 10 am meeting had gone! I told him that perhaps you're not too good to be true after all!

Just after three, I walked over the road to school, taking my place in the loosely-formed queue outside the classroom door. Ned was in Reception, and though we knew a few other kids from toddler groups and nursery, most of them we didn't. As a result, I didn't know most of the parents. We chatted briefly at drop-off and pick-up, but during the first term I hadn't yet got to know anybody well. A few days earlier, we'd had a Christmas afternoon in the classroom, with singing and craft activities. The singing was so sweet, I had tears rolling down my cheeks, as did a mum standing next to me. Afterwards we laughed about it and introduced ourselves – she was Jess, Millie's mum.

I spotted Jess as we waited outside; tall, thin, blonde, gorgeous, at least five years younger than me. I felt quite intimidated by her, though she'd been very friendly that afternoon in the classroom. I was just plucking up the courage to go and say hello to her when Ingrid, a mum that had been in our NCT antenatal class, appeared in front of me. She was heavily pregnant, with only six weeks to go before her second baby was due. Yet she looked ridiculously elegant, in layers of cream knitwear and navy leggings, in the way all Danish women pull off effortlessly. I put it down to hygge or lagom or lykke, or a combination of all three.

'Sorry, I was miles away.'

'You look like you've been up to something!'

I felt my cheeks redden. I always knew I could rely on Ingrid for the truth, whether I asked for it or not.

I was debating whether to tell her what I'd been doing earlier and possibly leave myself open to criticism, but the door opened and the children spilled out, flinging coats and glittery crowns and red book bags in the general direction of their parents.

As Ned grabbed my hand and pulled me along, I looked back towards Ingrid. 'Come round in the holidays – the boys can play and we can chat over a cuppa.'

We got back home and Ned immediately got his Lego out and sat down on the lounge floor with it. Knowing he was occupied and wouldn't miss not having my attention for a few minutes, I checked my phone. Mal had sent another message. *On the train back to Brighton now... glad it's Friday! I'm assuming you prefer Alex to Alexandra, Lexie or Sandy?*

I took the opportunity to reply. *I'm Alex to everyone apart from college friends (they seemed to all adopt Sandy which I loathe but twenty years on it's way too late to mention it) and my mum calls me Alexandra. Are you always Mal?*

Mal at work, usually. My ex-wife still calls me Malcolm, and all my family... I answer to both, take your pick! How about Mal when I'm watching Arsenal and Malcolm when I'm taking you out to dinner?

Okay, well I think I need to get to know you a bit better before I can tell which suits you best. Might have to be Malcolm if you're being naughty!

A few minutes later, his reply made me feel slightly uneasy, though its intention was clearly the opposite. *You are lovely, Alex. You've caught me off guard a bit to be honest... you have my word I won't be dating anyone else while we're together.*

CHAPTER 3

Monday evening arrived. I'd been too busy for the last couple of hours, getting Ned's tea ready, him into the bath, into bed, everything going to plan without any hiccups, to notice that the excitement that had built during the day had given way to anxiety. What if we didn't get on as well as we had on Friday? What if we didn't fancy each other enough? What if he didn't like my body if we got to the point of taking our clothes off? Mine didn't look too bad fully clothed, but stripped bare it had the tell-tale signs of age and pregnancy – silvery stretch marks on my stomach and thighs. I'd got used to that, but being confronted by a new lover in my early forties was not something I'd thought I'd ever need to do.

Mal texted me when he arrived. *Didn't want to wake the littl'un by pressing the bell. But I'm here!*

I took a deep breath and opened the door, wishing I'd had the foresight to down a tot of whisky – Dutch courage. He was wearing a slim-fitting leather jacket and dark jeans; very different to how he'd been on Friday morning. I flung my arms around his neck, his enveloped my waist, and we had a lingering kiss on the lips, both anticipating what would happen later.

'Come in, let me take your jacket.'

We walked through into the lounge, and I could feel his gaze on me. 'You look great, Alex.'

He glanced around the open plan ground floor, the over-filled bookshelves, photos and art on every wall. 'Lovely house. And the road looks nice too.'

We locked eyes and he raised an eyebrow, the faintest smile appearing on his face. The little crows' feet appeared again.

'You look pretty good too – I like you casual. And thanks, the area is nice and neighbourly. Kid-friendly as well.'

'I'm sure it is. Talking of kids... I know you said not to bring anything, but I brought a little something for Ned.' He passed me an Argos carrier bag. Inside was a Lego box – a Star Wars spaceship, and a bottle of Montepulciano.

'Wow, thank you! I love Italian reds, and it'll be perfect with dinner. I think we might have seen the spaceship in Hamley's the other afternoon – he'll love it! Maybe I should keep it for Christmas?'

'Whatever you think.'

'Thank you, that's really sweet.'

I left Mal looking at my music collection and walked into the kitchen to check on dinner.

'Something smells good. Shall I open the wine?' He walked over to me, put the bottle down on the worktop, wrapped his arms around my waist and softly kissed me on the cheek.

'Are you hungry?' I asked.

'Ravenous' he answered as he held me tighter, bending down to plant little nibbles on the side of my neck. I laughed and kissed him back.

'The corkscrew's in that drawer.' I gestured to the wooden unit on the other side of the kitchen. 'And the nice glasses are just above.'

He handed me a large glass – we clinked. 'Cheers.'

'So, what is Ewan up to this week?' I asked.

'Well, he's in Year 8 now, so it's all getting a bit more serious at school. They had some tests a few weeks ago, and he did really well. And he seems to have a real aptitude for acting – he's so confident. He definitely doesn't get that from me.'

'I don't believe that – you seem very comfortable in your own skin.'

'No, it's true. Perhaps that's an unwise thing to reveal on a second date.'

'I love the fact that we've been very honest with each other so far. It's very refreshing. Online dating, I dunno, some people treat it as an opportunity to create a fantasy persona for themselves.'

'I don't think you have though.'

'No, I haven't. I've been brutally honest, too much perhaps. I thought long and hard about alluding to my ex's depression in my profile. I just know I don't want to meet somebody else who was ravaged with it as much as Sean is.'

'I get that. I thought your profile was very insightful. And of course, I may have been swayed by your photos.'

'Well, likewise, I can't deny your photos played a part in my replying. If you'd been dressed head to foot in stuff you'd bought in Sports Direct for a fiver, I might not have replied, however brilliant your profile was. Not that I'm shallow or anything.'

My female black cat appeared in the kitchen. Just as I knew she would, she started rubbing herself against Mal as he sat down to stroke her. Had a female friend arrived, she wouldn't have budged from my bed.

'I think she likes you. This is Maisy.'

'Hello Maisy.'

Maisy, quite vocal as cats go, made little grunty noises, voicing her pleasure at being fussed over.

We ate at the kitchen table, which was more like a breakfast bar – tall and narrow. Mal was in the middle, in Ned's usual spot, and I was on the end. I berated myself for not checking that Ned hadn't dropped any peas on the chair and hoped Mal didn't now have one or two squashed into the seat of his jeans.

We talked about our previous dating experiences. I gave him a few details about the men I'd met. The ones I could remember anyway. Pierre, an equities trader who lived an hour's drive north of Paris, with a typically French open marriage; Grant, a fellow photographer – that was never going to work, too competitive; Colin, the sociologist, though I omitted the only thing I missed about him. As a teenager, he'd learnt a technique or two from his dad's porn videos. Recalling the details sent a shiver up my spine.

Mal topped up our glasses, and soon I began to feel the first wave of tipsiness take hold.

'This is lovely, Alex, thank you for cooking. I'm a meat and tatties man through and through, but this is really good. You might turn me into a vegetarian yet.'

I stood up and started to clear away the plates.

'Are you happy here or shall we move to the lounge?'

'Let's stay put – it's nice and cosy. And the lighting probably doesn't show up my wrinkles too much.'

I moved over to him, as if to take a better look. 'Nope, can't see any. How old did you say you were again?' I leant over and gave him a kiss on the cheek, just where his crows' feet kept appearing.

'So Mr Russell, you've heard all about my dating disasters – are you going to tell me about yours?'

'Well, there's been no-one long-term. I seemed to have a run of French women getting in touch with me. I met one a while ago – she was a teacher, really pretty. We only met twice. The second date, we went to the cinema, and had a drink before in the bar, and I realised she just didn't get my humour at all. She kept looking at me like I was mad every time I tried to say something funny. So we sat in silence watching the film. No canoodling in the back row that night!

'And then I met one woman who I thought was going to be great – you know, she had a really funny profile, looked pretty hot in her pictures and everything. She sounded sane too. It was May or June – a really warm evening. We'd arranged to meet at a pub, and she'd arrived before me, and was sitting at the bar with her back to the door, wearing a short-sleeved dress. She had these enormous arms, like the size of my thighs.'

'Was she nice though?'

'Yeah, she was but I couldn't get the image of those sumo shoulders out of my head for the rest of the evening. I just made an excuse that I was busy when she texted me to see if I wanted to meet up again.'

'And what about Louise? Presumably you and her have got together a few times too, between your internet dates.'

'Yeah, I'm not proud of it, and I'd understand if you thought getting involved with me was a bad idea because of it. We've just got so much history together, you know? But each time we decided to split up, or to be more accurate, she decided to go back to Stewart, I just tried to get on with my life, see Ewan as much as I could, try not to feel too guilty for all the carnage I'd caused to everybody. And part of that was trying to meet somebody else. But Louise had this amazing knack of getting in touch with me, just when I'd met someone.'

The wine gave me the confidence to ask the next question. 'Are you still in love with her?'

'God, I don't know. Probably, a little, I can't change that. But we both acknowledge it's become completely toxic. We blame each other for all the shit that's happened. And when we did get back together, the time we were happy and couldn't wait to see each other... that got shorter and shorter.'

'So what happened the last time?'

He ran his index finger along the rim of his glass. 'Well, I'd met this woman. She'd recently split from her husband – they had a couple of young kids. I'd been seeing her for a few months I guess. But I knew it wasn't going to be a long-term thing. And then Louise got in touch again, and that was it, I finished it.'

'Why?'

'I don't know. It just didn't feel right, I suppose. We didn't have a huge amount in common. And her kids were so much younger than Ewan... I felt I'd been there already, and didn't want to go back there again. Her ex had them every other weekend – you know, the usual set-up. And we saw each other quite a bit those weekends. But I also have a lot of mates I like seeing. And Arsenal of course. She just got a bit naggy, always wanting to see me. And then when Louise called me one night, I don't know, I just ended it. I told her my ex had wanted us to get back together and that was true, and I suppose it stopped me having to tell her I was going to finish with her anyway.' He paused for a moment and took a swig of wine. 'And then, when I went back onto the site, a couple of weeks ago, she saw I was on there and got in touch.'

'What did she say?'

'She asked if Louise and I had broken up again. And if we had, why hadn't I got in touch?'

'Because you hadn't told her you knew it wasn't going to work in the long run.' I paused but he didn't fill the silence. 'Have you replied?'

'No, I've deleted my profile.'

I raised an eyebrow. He hadn't been entirely honest with this other woman. I felt like I should be taking this all in, perhaps making myself more wary of getting involved. I just liked him too much to allow myself to process it fully.

Mal must have sensed this. In what I took as a mock gesture he started to get up from his stool. 'I can leave now if you like.'

I kept his stare, raising my right eyebrow for a moment, waiting for him to explain. He just continued to look down at me as I tried to work out what he might be thinking.

'Sit down.'

I'd never met a man before who was able to smile with his eyes, not quite like Mal could. As he sat, and our gaze was level once more, he dropped his – thick, straight lashes obscuring his eyes. An almost imperceptible colouring in his cheeks appeared, together with the crows' feet. I was falling in love with those bloody crows' feet.

'We've finished the wine, haven't we? Lagavulin or Laphroaig?' I asked, wishing I'd had the foresight to expand my very small collection of single malts before a fellow Scot visited.

'Now you're talking my language.'

As I stood up to get the whisky glasses from the shelves behind him, he pulled me towards him. I leant over and we kissed; gentle, separate, quick kisses. He stood up, holding me round the waist with one hand; with the other, he held the back of my neck, pulling me towards him. I moved my hands to his shoulders, feeling the shape of him beneath the thin wool. Over the last few days, I'd tried not to think too much about what he might look like without clothes on; the prospect of now finding out was intoxicating. Our mouths found one another again. A few more kisses on the lips, becoming longer each time. My hands moved down his arms to his hips, then up his back.

He had the most amazing way of kissing – very gentle, breaking off for a moment to look at me. I ran my fingers through his closely cropped, thick hair. He was still firmly holding the back of my neck, but he moved the other hand under my sweater, his fingers gliding over my back, moving to the front, brushing over my breasts, beneath the lacy edge of my bra. Our kisses became deeper, still gentle. I let out an involuntarily gasp of delight as he tweaked my nipple. In response, I moved one hand down over his jeans. Beneath the thick, dark denim I could feel his hard-on. In response, my body stirred. Don't they say the more sex you have, the more you want? And if you don't have any, you forget about it altogether?

That had definitely happened to me, I thought, as Mal one-handedly undid my bra, moving his hands round to the front. I waited a moment, enjoying the sensation, then found his belt, managed to unbuckle it, and fumbled, expecting a zip fly, but found buttons.

'Didn't you offer me some Lagavulin?' he whispered into my ear, in such a perfect, throaty Glaswegian burr, I shivered in delight. I'd always been a sucker for a Scottish accent.

'Shall we take the bottle upstairs?'

I didn't wait for an answer. I picked up the whisky

glasses and, holding them in one hand, held Mal's in the other and led him into the lounge, grabbing the bottle of whisky.

As we passed the mirror in the hall, I glanced my dishevelled reflection, with my bra undone, my hair tangled and covering most of my face. We didn't say a word as we ascended the stairs, not quite breaking into a run. I could see Mal looking into each room as we passed them.

'You're not going to give me a guided tour?'

'This is the 90-second version,' I said as we reached the last flight, up to the second floor where my bedroom was. And Ned's. As a precaution, I closed his door. I'd left the fairy lights on in my room – in lieu of a bedside lamp they gave just enough soft illumination for reading. I had draped them over a few picture hooks as a short-term solution when we moved in – eight years later, they were still there. One friend had commented they looked like an art installation, but I did worry they made my bedroom look more Teenage Girl than White Cube.

Both cats had arranged themselves on my bed, curled up in circles, a few inches apart and mirror images of each other. Soft and sleepy, they weren't too happy being moved. I picked them up and deposited them on the landing, closing the door.

I stood in front of Mal and we kissed again. I unbuttoned his jeans and pulled them down with his underwear, over his ankles and feet, and tossed them theatrically on the floor. I took his hand and led him over to the bed. He sat on the edge and I kneeled in front of him. I glanced up and as I did so, held his cock between my thumb and index finger, making a ring that circled it, and began to move slowly up and down. He kept my gaze, but I broke it by dropping my head and taking him in my mouth, the full length, to the point where I almost gagged, but then taking a moment to breathe, holding him in my hand, circling the tip with my tongue. I went back to sucking, more quickly, one hand travelling up over his stomach and chest to his neck. I raised my head to his, and he kissed me urgently, lifting me up as he did.

'Jesus, you're really good at that.'

I whispered 'thank you' as he pushed me onto the bed, lifting my sweater up, pushing my bra out of the way and began sucking my nipples, alternately rubbing them against the palm of his hand. I could feel myself becoming wet. He stood up and pulled down my jeans and knickers, tossing them aside. He began licking me gently. I gasped, and looked down at him, running my fingers through his hair.

'You're very good at that too,' I said, as he paused for a moment. 'I'll pour us some whisky.'

I sat up and leaned on one elbow. I opened the bottle I'd left on the bedside table, silently wincing as I cut the edge of my index finger on the torn foil seal. I wasn't lying at the best angle for pouring, and the golden, viscous liquid sloshed out, almost filling the glass as I tipped the heavy bottle too far and it slipped out of my hand, crashed against the bedframe and onto the floor.

'Ooops,' I said, bursting into a girlish giggle; I must have been more drunk than I realised.

'We can share it,' Mal said as I passed the glass to him. 'Cheers.' He took a large gulp and passed the glass back.

I raised the glass and took a sip. It burned the back of my throat, but I took another and the pain subsided to a familiar heat that spread through my chest. 'To new beginnings. And to not dwelling on the past.'

I handed the glass back to him. He took another large gulp. I reached over and pulled his sweater and t-shirt off above his head, leaving his hair a little dishevelled; very cute, I thought to myself. I had a full-length mirror on the back of my door; instinctively the movement of our bodies caught my eye as we embraced. Mal did the same. For the first time, we observed each other undressed, our middle-aged bodies in profile, flattered by the warm glow of the yellow fairy lights, further softened by the alcohol.

I suddenly shivered. Mal held me closer. 'Are you thinking what I'm thinking?' he whispered in my ear.

I fell backwards on the bed, pulling him with me.

I twisted my upper body round so that I could open the bedside drawer. The tips of my fingers felt around for the condom packet I'd put there earlier. All I could detect were blister packs of ibuprofen. I reached a little further, while Mal planted a diagonal trail of hot, wet kisses from my hip bone to shoulder blade.

'Mummy, I heard a loud noise.'

I looked towards the now open door. Ned was standing there. I turned to look at Mal who had an expression of total horror on his face. I couldn't believe neither of us had heard him open the door.

'Darling, get back into bed, I'll just be a minute.'

Mal instinctively pulled the duvet up, covering both our bodies.

'I'm so sorry, he never wakes up in the night. I'll just get him settled – it'll only take a minute.'

'Don't worry, take your time, it's fine.'

I grabbed my kimono that doubled as a dressing gown and as I tied it closed, rushed into Ned's room, stubbing my little toe on the corner of his door. I swore under my breath; 'fuck, fuck, fuck'.

'I'm sorry I woke you.'

'Who's that man, mummy?'

'Erm, he's just a friend, a new friend, he came round for dinner earlier.'

'What's he's called?'

'Malcolm.'

'What were you doing? He didn't have any clothes on. I saw his bottom,' he said, sniggering.

I was lost for words – I guess I'd been lucky this hadn't happened before. He'd never even seen his dad and I in bed together, we'd been sleeping in separate bedrooms long before Ned could walk.

'Anyway darling, go back to sleep. Malcolm brought you a present – if you're a good boy, perhaps you could open it in the morning.' At that moment, having resorted to bribery, I hated myself more than anyone in the world.

'Okay, sweet dreams.' I bent down and kissed his forehead.

Before I saw Mal, I could hear he was getting dressed. I stood in the doorway, suddenly feeling ashamed. The kimono had a habit of sagging open – I tucked the green silk more tightly in at the waistband so that he didn't think I was showing off my rack on purpose.

'Stay, please,' I said with as much dignity as I could muster.

'Look, Alex, it's been a great evening but it's late, I should be getting home.'

'It's not that late; we were just getting...' I walked towards him, laying my forearms against his chest, and looking up at him, eyes pleading, head cocked several degrees to one side, pulling out all the stops.

'Look, we can do this another time.'

And achieving an erection after being caught in the act by a four-year-old might be difficult, I thought but didn't add. He turned away, looking round the far side of the bed to see if he'd left anything on the floor, more to extricate himself from my grasp than to spot any stray item of clothing.

'God, Mal, I'm sorry. I can't believe he—'

'Look, don't worry, it happens. We've had fun, that's all that matters.'

We walked downstairs in silence. I asked if I could book an Uber but he said he'd just hail a black cab. He kissed me on the cheek, turned and walked up the road. 'I'll call you tomorrow, okay?'

I nodded, not wanting to speak; I knew I'd start crying if I did. I shut the door quickly. Fuck.

The following morning, Ned woke me half an hour before my alarm; I staggered out of bed; three seconds of consciousness and I was already aware that I had a stinking hangover. And, as if I needed reminding, my feet landed on the sticky patch where I'd spilt a third of a bottle of whisky.

Ned didn't mention the previous night and it occurred to me he might not even remember it. Since he'd started school a few months earlier, our mornings had taken on a routine – breakfast, ten minutes of children's TV while I made his packed lunch, getting dressed, teeth cleaned, out the door. The normal, easy, relaxed chat between us was replaced by bad-tempered, monotonal orders from me as I rested my head in my hands, sitting at the kitchen table. Every time he said or did something more loudly than necessary, I jumped down his throat. Ned picked up on my mood, of course. His replies were equally grumpy, and it was a relief to him as well as me when we reached the door to his classroom, the fresh-faced NQT Miss Renoir there to greet everyone with a winning smile.

I bent down and kissed him on the cheek and he avoided my gaze. 'I'm sorry, sweetheart, I'm just a bit tired and grumpy this morning. Have a good day.'

I spent all day feeling guilty about putting Ned in that situation. Mal too – perhaps I should have waited until the following weekend when Sean was due to pick up Ned. But he had cancelled at the last minute a couple of times recently, so there was no guarantee it would happen. I had probably unconsciously factored that in.

I made coffee and sat at my desk, failing to focus on anything. I tried to imagine what Mal would have made of last night. He would have been embarrassed, surely. Putting myself in the same situation – at his place with his son finding us naked in bed – I'd have been mortified. On top of that I couldn't help but remember what he'd said about the woman he'd met who had young children. 'Her kids were so much younger than Ewan... I felt I'd done all that, and didn't want to go through it again.'

If Mal had decided it was a non-starter, there was nothing I could do. We'd made a vague plan to go to the cinema later in the week – that would give us both a chance to recover from a late, drunken night. But I realised it would also give him time to weigh up the pros and cons in the cold light of day, stone cold sober but with a hangover to concentrate the mind. As morning turned to afternoon without a word from him, I convinced myself I'd never see him again.

CHAPTER 4

ey, how are you? It was the most innocuous thing I could think to write in a text, yet I imagined between the words the unease I'd felt for the last few days, had been displayed.

Thirty minutes' wait. I knew there was a chance Mal would be in a meeting. When the phone lit up with the cheerful iPhone 'ting' I jumped five feet in the air.

Hi Alex, I'm on the train. Starting a text with my name wasn't a good sign. He hadn't done that since our very first messages. *I'll call when I get to Victoria. Sorry for the radio silence. To be honest I've been thrown by something. I've had a message from Lou.*

My chest tightened, the top of my nose fizzed. I wasn't going to cry, not yet.

It was Friday morning, over three days since I'd seen him. It had been torture not getting in touch, and finally I'd caved in. I knew he must have decided that it was a no-go after Monday night. Only a tiny part of me clung onto the hope I was wrong. It was crazy to have started to fall for him so quickly, but still, the thought of losing him was too much.

I felt like a complete loser, sitting and waiting for him to call to tell me I was being dumped. So, I did what I was planning to do anyway, what I always do in times of stress. I gathered my headphones and keys, filled my water bottle and put on my running shoes. Just as I was heading out the door, he called.

I answered with a breezy 'Hi,' but already my voice wavered in my throat.

'Hi. How are you?'

No baby.

'Oh, okay.' Tears pricked the back of my eyes. 'Or at least I was until I got your text.'

'God, I'm sorry, it's completely out of the blue. I wasn't expecting to hear from her.'

'And you said you'd both decided it was over, didn't you? When you came to mine the other night. I looked you in the eye and asked you if you were still in love with her.'

'I know, and we'd both decided we needed a fresh start. But we've got all this history. Years of it. Both our marriages have broken up as a result. It was me and her against the world.'

'I know, I remember you saying that. But, I also remember you saying it was over. Done and dusted, that it'd become toxic. We got on so well together; the thought that it's come to an end before it's even begun...' I'd been keeping calm and holding it together until this point, but saying those words I felt my throat tighten again and my eyes filled with tears. I started sobbing.

'Look, I haven't talked to her yet. I said I'd call her later. I dunno, we've argued so much, every time we've got back together. But I just need to hear what she's got to say. I'm really sorry, it's just bad timing. I'll call you later.'

'Okay.' I pressed the red button to end the call. I didn't

want to prolong the agony for either of us. But also at that moment I didn't want him to say goodbye.

My chest ached. I felt sick. Everyone's been dumped, of course, I'd just forgotten how raw the pain was.

I picked up my keys and headed out. Within a minute or so the rhythm of running had taken over, and I lost myself in the act of putting one foot in front of another. Nowhere does bitter, grey, still, dry, midwinter mornings better than south east London. Each breath in felt like my lungs were filling with tiny shards of glass. Every breath out yielded a swirling cloud of white that dissipated just as quickly as it appeared.

I ran through Herne Hill towards Brixton. It hadn't occurred to me when I left home that the route took me past the end of his road. I came to a stumbling halt, leaning on a parking ticket machine to stop myself collapsing on the ground. I glanced along the road. Perhaps Mal was at home, having breakfast before work, and would appear any moment.

Get a grip, I told myself. He'd been on the train from Brighton when he called. I needed to make a promise to myself that I wasn't going to start looking for him everywhere I went, turning up at places he might be. That way madness lay.

But for the rest of the run, I allowed my head to fill with thoughts of him. I knew I was going to feel completely fucking miserable at the end of it, but I couldn't help myself. A slideshow of images of him, accompanied by passages from our conversations I'd already committed to memory, shuffled inside my head. With no conscious intention, I'd been logging everything, more precious because there was so little.

I diverted from my normal route that took me into Brixton. Instead I ran along Effra Parade and paused for a moment at the spot where Mal and I had said goodbye after we left the Ritzy. There should be a blue plaque on the wall of the house. *Here Mal Russell and Alex Kendrew first kissed during their short-lived romance.*

The last leg of the run was one long road, unusually wide for London, and flanked on both sides by huge, detached three-storey Victorian villas. I knew every drive-way, every view into ground floor living rooms, a split-second glance into spotlit Bulthaus kitchens as I sped past. Approaching home, I was consumed with a sinking feeling. Jesus, this was really happening. A few minutes later, glad to shut the door on the real world for a while, I stumbled into the lounge and collapsed onto the sofa.

I was vaguely aware of message alerts on my phone as I lay in the foetal position. It wasn't until it rang that I summoned enough energy to get it out of my pocket. It was Agnes – was it still okay for her to come round mid-after-noon to go through Monday's shoot? I tried to sound as upbeat as I could; we agreed on 2pm. I was thankful I'd have something concrete to focus on.

I'd had a text from Jess. *Hey sweetie, you still okay to come round for dinner next Wednesday? Are we going to meet your new man?*

I was going to have to start telling everybody. Accepting their pity, listening to them tell me not to worry, that I'd meet someone else just as lovely. Maybe I should just post on Facebook; *Mal has dumped me to go back to his girlfriend.* Get it over and done with in one fell swoop.

I was on the verge of crying for the next few days, though I knew I couldn't. Not in front of Ned. So I stored up all the emotion until he'd gone to bed and let it out in big, body-shaking sobs. I'd catch my reflection in the mirror and be perversely satisfied at how shit I looked with red-rimmed eyes, rivulets of mascara staining my cheeks.

And all the time I checked my phone just to see if Mal had called or texted or emailed and I'd somehow not heard the ring or beep. No, just a deafening silence from him and, as the days went past, his name moved further and further down the list of messages on my phone.

On some level I willed myself to become even more miserable so I could hit the bottom. At least then I could begin the slow ascent back to normality. I hadn't been that unhappy, had I? That lonely? I couldn't remember any more. Lying awake at night, I conjured up images of him as I replayed parts of our conversations in my mind, those few moments of pleasure. I put together a playlist on Spotify, entitled 'M'; comprised of Scottish bands and singer-song-writers we'd talked about, melancholic songs by a couple of my favourite artists, interspersed with Nick Cave's most devastatingly lovelorn songs.

I didn't change the sheets for a couple of weeks after we'd spent that night together. Part of the night, I should say. His DNA was on them; how could I part with that? Until one morning I woke up and realised how ridiculous I was being; that was not the way to get over him. I leapt out of bed, strip-ping the sheets, and bunged everything into the washing machine.

CHAPTER 5

I made a decision; I was going back online. Find another Mal. Someone just like him. Someone completely unlike him. I just needed to get him out of my head, one way or another.

I opened up my profile. It must have been six weeks since I'd logged on but familiar old faces grinned back at me. Could I face doing this again? Probably not. Could I cope with being this miserable? I unclicked the 'hide my profile' button, then had a quick look at new members. One or two interesting-looking men. Lots more uninteresting. I'd only ever sent a handful of first messages. My default position was to wait for men to message me. Sure enough, a few minutes later my inbox filled up with new 'likes'. It was pathetic, but I did get a momentary rush of excitement.

Gentle Jim sent a message. *Hi, I read your profile and thought you seemed like a really nice person.* Unfortunately he looked like a teddy bear. Gino T 'liked' me. The thumbnail profile photo that appeared on my screen looked like it had been taken from a laptop, all chin and nostrils. NSR1 was next. In his profile photo he wore a blue and white broad-striped shirt. He looked tanned and relaxed and smug and completely the kind of man I wouldn't be interested in if my life depended on it. He had flown a helicopter over a live volcano. He had a very successful business career and worked internationally as a managing director for large corporations. He was financially comfortable, with his own successful business. Blah, blah, blah.

It wasn't going well, but it always took a few days for someone interesting to come along. I would just have to bide my time.

And anyway, I was busy. I had a shoot in a few days that I needed to prepare for. And tomorrow was the weekend and Sean had texted me to say he wasn't in a fit state to have Ned. I didn't tell him, but having Ned around would be a blessing in the circumstances. I needed to organise some child-centred activities to keep me from going crazy.

I sent a message to Ingrid, who I'd met at antenatal classes. Ned and her son Johan, only a week apart in age, had played together since they were toddlers. They were at the same school but in different classes, and they didn't see that much of each other at play time. He was a nice boy, and I wanted to keep their friendship going. Ingrid had become a good friend too, in the way you do when you have small children; Sunday mornings spent together at a children's farm or zoo, or toddler splash sessions at the local swimming pool, at a time inconceivably early for any non-parents. We reminisced how, pre-children, we'd usually not surfaced until midday at weekends. After babies that was the middle of the day, by which time we were sleep-deprived, craving coffee and already longing for bedtime.

Ingrid agreed to a soft play centre date the following day. We picked her and Johan up after breakfast. She was from Copenhagen but had lived in London for 15 years. I never asked her why she'd come to London, when Danish society seemed so perfect. Perhaps that was the reason – there was nothing to rebel against. She was tallish, thin, beautiful, with high cheekbones and perfect skin, almost white blonde, blue-eyed. She never wore make-up. She didn't need to. I always felt like an oaf in comparison and avoided joint photographs for fear my relative plainness would enhance her beauty, and vice versa. I'd joked to Mal when she came up in conversation that she was drop-dead gorgeous and I wasn't going to ever allow him to meet her.

Now he never would.

'Gosh, Alex, how old do you think you are... twenty-three?' she said, looking up and down witheringly at my outfit as I got out of the car. I grabbed the carseat from her and put it in the back, next to Ned.

I didn't really know how to answer that. I could have said *I'm feeling really shit because Mal has dumped me, and I thought I'd make a bit of an effort to cheer myself up.* So instead I just laughed it off.

We got to the soft play centre, with fifteen minutes to spare before tickets went on sale, joining the huge queue of hyper-active toddlers and bleary-eyed dads. Inside, Johan and Ned's shoes and socks were off within seconds and they disappeared into the primary-coloured archway that led to the ball-park and slides.

'I'm so glad they're grown up enough now that we don't still need to follow them round,' I said, as I scanned the top floor for them. I couldn't remember what Ned was wearing. Most five-year-old boys look the same as they run past at twenty miles an hour.

'Absolutely, and especially now.' Ingrid looked down at her perfectly-shaped but ever-growing bump. 'Though I'll be back to clambering after a toddler pretty soon. Shall we get a drink?'

'I'll go. What do you fancy?'

While I queued, I checked my emails. More messages from men, mostly no-gos but a few interesting ones. My heart wasn't really in it, but I had to make the effort to stop feeling so lousy.

'So how is everything going with your new man?' Ingrid asked when I got back with the drinks.

'It's all over. He got a call from his girlfriend and he's gone running back.'

Ingrid looked shocked. I'd already told her all about Mal and she was excited I'd met someone nice. I'd shown her his photo after our first date. There weren't many of my female friends whose opinion on such things I sought but Ingrid was definitely one of them. He'd got the thumbs up.

'So I'm back on the website, I just feel too crappy to be on my own again. It's only been a couple of days but so far it's the usual mix of old, bald, fat men getting in touch.' I showed her my phone and let her flick through their profile photos.

'I see what you mean. Oh, wait, this one's okay.' She showed me the photo of one. He'd caught my attention too and I'd 'liked' him a few days ago and he'd 'liked' me back. It was a black and white photo; he was looking straight at the camera with a hint of a smile, wearing a tight t-shirt and he looked like he was in good shape. He had pleasantly messy, slightly spiky hair. His profile was succinct and witty; he said he was a lawyer and wanted to meet someone who would challenge him intellectually, physically and emotionally. He also alluded to being polyamorous. I wasn't sure that was my thing. But still, he was cute.

'I'll message him later.' I'd made a plan to respond to the best five and limit it at that.

Feeling a bit self-conscious, I tried to move the subject away from my love life and asked her about her birth plan. She told me all about the scans she'd had, how she was hoping to have the baby – a girl -- at home. Though Jim, her partner, wasn't into the idea at all.

The boys came back to the table a few times, hot and sweaty and downing several glasses of water each time and having a bite of a sandwich or cookie. We'd been at the play centre for a couple of hours, and were acclimatised to the deafening and constant high-pitched screeching that is the norm at soft play centres. Everything we said we'd had to shout to each other and my throat ached.

Half an hour later, Johan came back crying.

'Ned isn't playing with me,' he said.

Oh shit, I thought to myself. The two boys hadn't been as close since they'd started school. I wanted to them to stay friends as they'd known each other almost their whole lives.

'Oh darling, what did he say?'

I saw Ned skulking at the entrance to the soft play frame. I gave him a hard stare and motioned for him to come to the table. He ran back inside.

'Sorry sweetie, I'll go and find him. Maybe we should think about making a move?'

Ingrid agreed. Johan was sitting on her lap, crying. I went to the entrance and, not spotting Ned in the ball-park, or anywhere else on the ground floor, got on my hands and knees and climbed up to the first level, shouting his name as I went. I eventually found him right at the top, queuing for the zip wire.

'Hey, what's going on with you and Johan? We've come to have a nice time and play together.'

'He didn't want to go on the big slide, just the little one. It was boring. So I just went off to the big slide on my own. And then he came and said he was going to tell his mummy.'

What could I do? I agreed with him, partly – if he wanted to go off and do something more exciting, why shouldn't he?

'But he's your friend, honey, it's nice to do things together. Anyway, we're going home in five minutes. One more time on the zip wire and then come back to the table, okay?' He nodded and disappeared behind a padded plastic red and yellow striped wall.

The boys sat in silence on the way back. When we reached Ingrid's she turned to me.

'You know Alex, Ned's behaviour is getting worse. You let him do as he pleases, all the time. Perhaps you should spend less time on dating sites and more on parenting forums.'

CHAPTER 6

By the time Ned was in bed, I was ready for a glass of wine. I sat down with it and logged onto the dating site.

I dismissed all those who lived in Manchester, Devon, North Yorkshire – I'd tried long distance and it didn't work for me. All those with silly names. All those where their profile photo was taken on a boat. Or in Lycra on a bike. Or skiing. Any twenty years younger than me – I didn't want to be anyone's MILF.

After the filtering process I was left with five. There was 'Joyrider'-- the one whose profile I'd shown to Ingrid earlier; 'All_Tomorrows_Parties' – a tall, thin guy with a floppy fringe who said he lived in Soho. In his profile he said friends described him as looking like he could be the lovechild of David Bowie and Brett Anderson of Suede. That got my vote. One guy who I'd had a brief conversation with a few months earlier, before Mal – 'Silly Boy Blue.' I liked the Bowie reference. Another photographer, who also had the name of a camera manufacturer as his profile name – a lens manufacturer which was even more esoteric – 'Zeiss'.

And 'Skærbæk' – a man I'd 'liked' at the same time as Mal but who hadn't 'liked' me back. Though I seemed to remember he'd looked at my profile quite a lot. Time waster. Anyway, he was quite cute, though sounded pretty arrogant in his 'about me' bit.

I sent a one- or two-line reply to those five and then logged off and went to bed.

The next morning I'd had three replies – nothing from 'Joyrider' who'd been my favourite, or 'Skærbæk'. 'All_Tomorrows_Parties' had sent a message saying he wasn't currently subscribing. Of the two that did send proper messages, 'Silly Boy Blue' was probably the more promising. He said, *Hi Alex. All good here, thanks. We never quite made that lunch date… to be honest I started seeing a woman – a friend of a friend – it was going well but about a month ago we decided to call it a day, hence being back on here. I saw you were too, what's been happening in your world? Paul.*

Paul, that was it. I'd forgotten. I sent a quick message back. *Hi Paul, yes, something similar, good while it lasted! What have you been up to?*

We had a frenetic email exchange that morning. He had a daughter who lived in Paris with her mum, so it wasn't often he saw her, but he spent a big chunk of the school holidays in Paris, or with her in London, or taking her away on what sounded like ultra-luxurious holidays. He said he had a busy week ahead and was about to go to Paris to bring her back for half-term. It would be next week before we could meet. Fair enough, I thought. And the French school holiday was a week earlier than ours – the following week was our half-term so it might be difficult for me to meet him then unless I got a babysitter.

Don't put all your eggs in one basket, I thought. Look what happened with Mal. So I replied to the photographer guy, even though I was reluctant. I'd met another photographer six months before and the competitiveness had got in the way.

Zeiss had remarked at us both having camera-related usernames. *There's got to be something in it, surely?* he said. *Pleased to meet you, I'm Bill.*

Something in it, or we were both equally unoriginal and/or pretentious. *Pleased to meet you too, I'm Alex.*

Perhaps it was inevitable that we'd show interest in each other's work – we swapped website addresses. He was mainly a portrait photographer and shot quite a lot of famous people – authors, actors, musicians, a few corporate clients which I guessed paid the mortgage.

I wasn't sure I really fancied him. The pictures in his profile, ironically, weren't great, but he seemed very keen in his messages, and asked if I'd be free to meet in the next few days. I said I was, for a quick coffee.

Two days after we started messaging, we met in the Photographers' Gallery café. I was there first and managed to let my nerves get the better of me. He arrived after ten minutes or so, and I was pleasantly surprised. I'd had him down as potentially friend material and nothing else, but he had a nice face, dressed well, seemed normal. As I queued at the bar for coffee, I had to rethink what I was going to say to him.

The conversation flowed easily and we talked about the usual things. Children; he had two grown-up ones. Relationships; two failed marriages. Work, of course. Art, books, music.

'So where are you based?' I asked. He'd said east London in his profile.

'I'm in Leyton... do you know it?' he replied, taking a sip of coffee. 'It's one of those up-and-coming areas, according to estate agents. In reality it's still got a way to go. And you're south?'

Leyton was miles away, though I didn't mention that the distance might be a problem. 'Yeah, south-east, it's nice and residential, good for bringing up kids.'

'Leyton is the same. My ex-wife, the last one, she has a daughter. We'd been together all the time she was at school.' He looked away, tears forming in his eyes. 'It's still quite...'

'Bill, I'm sorry, you don't have to talk about anything you don't want to.'

'It's okay. In a way it helps.'

I searched around in my head, trying to think of anything that would sound sympathetic, but failed. 'It must have been tough when you split up. Do you see your step-daughter much?'

'I did, to start with, but her mum has made it clear I can't have anything to do with her. At first I used to go round to the house to see them, have dinner once a week, or take Tamsin to the cinema. My ex has put a stop to it all. I've sent a few messages to Tam and she hasn't even read them.'

That struck me as a bit odd; surely it would be damaging for any child to lose contact with a step-parent when their relationship had been so good. His ex must have been a complete cow.

He seemed sensitive, and he'd had a long marriage with a woman who already had a child, as well as his own two. It struck me as completely different to Mal's reticence to date women with kids.

Bill seemed totally cool when I said I had to get back to pick up Ned. As we walked towards Oxford Circus station he explained he was driving down to Kent the next day.

'Even my own kids don't need me, really, they're both in their twenties, they've got their own lives now.' He looked at me, a rueful smile forming. 'I've got a morning's teaching at a college near where they live with their mum. I'm hoping to see them while I'm there. Just an idea... I could drive via south-east London on the way home, if you're free?'

'Er, sure, I'll see if I can get a babysitter.'

We said our goodbyes in the tube station ticket hall; him going east, me south. I texted Denny to see if she could babysit, but her daughter had a few college exams that week and Denny was looking after her baby grandson so her daughter could revise.

I couldn't think of anyone else that would babysit at the last minute. Why not just ask Bill to come round for a drink? I thought. Mal had come round for dinner on our second date and I hadn't thought anything of that. I sent him a message asking if he'd like to pop round for a cup of tea.

A few minutes later, he got back to me. *Sounds great, Alex, text me your address, I'll call you when I'm leaving Tunbridge Wells.*

The next day Bill texted me quite a few times; links to exhibitions he thought I might like, information about bands we'd talked about, the site of a friend of his who had a studio in Hoxton. I'd mentioned I had a job coming up which I probably needed to hire a studio for. I sent a quick *Thanks, those look interesting.* He sent a couple saying *Can't wait to see you tonight,* or variations. At one point I looked at my phone and there were twelve new messages from him. And I had a Facebook friend request from him too.

Around 7pm he called as Ned was having a bath. It would take him about an hour to get to me, so Ned would be in bed before he arrived.

I tidied the house a bit, nipped round with the vacuum

cleaner, put the dishwasher on. I decided to stay wearing what I'd been in all day, but put on some make-up and changed into heeled boots.

When he knocked on the door just after 8pm, I was beginning to feel a bit apprehensive. Was it just the over-keenness on his part, shown in the abundance of messages? Whatever it was, I was on edge.

He was driving so I assumed he wouldn't want to drink, but when I offered him a choice he opted for a beer. We leaned against the worktops as we drank, talking about what we'd been up to during the day. He still did some part-time lecturing in photography at a college in Kent, from the days when he'd lived there with his first wife, when their kids were at school.

It felt a bit too formal, standing in the kitchen, so I suggested we go through to the lounge. He sat on the sofa while I chose some music.

'Nice place you've got here.'

'Thank you. There's quite a lot needs doing to it but for the moment it's fine. I love this house, I'm very happy here.'

He was sitting almost in the middle of the sofa. I didn't want to appear too stand-offish and sit at one end, but at the same time didn't want him to think I was giving him the green light, so I sat towards the other end but facing him. Perhaps I was starting to feel more comfortable. He was a nice guy, just a bit too eager, but I knew that often put me off.

'I'm quite handy round the house. Is there anything I could do to help you?'

'Oh, no, don't worry. That's very kind though.' I smiled at him.

Yes, too keen.

'I really like you,' he said, as he put his beer bottle down on the coffee table. He leaned over to kiss me, his face close to mine, waiting for me to respond. If I didn't, he'd think I wasn't interested. I wasn't sure I was interested, but at the same time, I hadn't yet decided I was totally uninterested.

There were some things I liked about him. Part of me wanted to just get Mal out of my system, and date as many men as I could to make that happen. I kissed him back.

He pulled me on top of him. He ran his hands down my thighs, up my back, my shoulders, momentarily holding the back of my neck and pulling me closer to him. I did the same, skimming over his arms, shoulders, chest, stomach. I couldn't feel a single bone or muscle and tried not to imagine what he'd look like with no clothes on.

'You are gorgeous,' he said as he grabbed the bottom of my jumper and raised it over my head, my camisole top along with it. He was looking at my breasts in that way some men do – like they're a separate entity. He undid his belt and jeans, pulling them down over his backside. He grabbed my bra strap and pushed it down, over my shoulder. He grabbed my wrist, pushing my hand under the elastic of his boxer shorts.

Smeg. Oh my God. I gagged, a reflex action at the back of my throat. I'd only ever encountered that odour, reminiscent of sour milk and just as vile, once or twice in my life but it was unmistakable. It took all my concentration not to burst out laughing. I felt a gag forming again and disguised it as a cough.

I would have been more turned on watching Newsnight; any modicum of sexual desire I'd had before was snuffed out. I'd chosen a PJ Harvey album to listen to; *To Bring You My Love*, with an ironically-named track. Polly was plaintively calling, "Come on, Billy".

Was it my imagination, or could I hear Ned's voice

mixed in with Polly Harvey's? No, just wishful thinking. Bill threw me down onto the sofa, pulling my jeans and knickers down to my knees.

I couldn't do this. A get-out plan had formed in my mind. I slid onto the floor, landing on my hip bone. I hastily pulled up my jeans and grabbed my jumper.

'Sorry, Bill, I think I can hear my son upstairs.'

'Oh, really, I didn't hear anything... are you sure?'

'I'll just be a minute'.

I ran upstairs, as quietly as I could. I didn't want to wake Ned up by accident. I sat at the top of the stairs, peering down to check Bill wasn't following me. I could hear him moving around, whistling along to "Down By The Water".

I counted to a hundred, and then slowly walked downstairs. In the lounge, Bill, thankfully, had got dressed and was perusing the bookshelves. He was flicking through a book of photographs by Josef Koudelka. I'd bought it when Sean and I had been in Prague about ten years before, at an exhibition of Koudelka's work. It had been a rare happy period and I didn't want to associate that book with Bill instead.

'Listen Bill, I'm sorry, he's really not well. He feels sick and he's got a bit of a temperature.'

'Oh, that's a shame, I was really enjoying myself.' He raised an eyebrow and smiled at me, returning the book to its space on the shelf. He came over, putting his arms around my waist.

'Yeah, me too. Another time, eh.'

'Okay, I'll call you tomorrow.'

We kissed briefly and said goodbye.

'Okay, safe journey home.'

As he walked away, he kissed his fingers and blew them towards me. Now all he needed to do was text me in the next few minutes saying 'missing you already' to make the whole episode full quota cringe-worthy.

Flooding with relief, I sank onto the sofa, head in hands. What the fuck was I doing? Why hadn't I just said no? Why couldn't I have said to him as he left that I didn't want him to call me tomorrow, or ever?

CHAPTER 7

Over the next few days, Bill continued to email me with links to galleries, reviews of films, a gin festival at some listed house in Finchley. It was painful. I had to put an end to it. One evening I texted in response to a text about a gig the following week. *I'm really sorry Bill, this just doesn't feel right. Perhaps it's just that I'm not over my last relationship yet. I don't know.*

Most people would see this as code for 'I'm not interested'; I hoped he would too.

Well, I can wait. You're a fantastic woman, Alex, why don't we stay in touch, meet up as friends, see how it goes?

The number of messages did reduce, thankfully. I hoped they'd dissipate completely. What had happened that night didn't make me feel particularly proud of myself on several levels. I tried to convince myself that I'd decided it was a no-go before I realised he had a serious hygiene problem.

I recounted the events over the phone to Agnes one morning, when we were talking through the details of a job we were doing together later that week.

'Oh my God, Alex, he sounds creepy, not to mention

dirty. Get rid of him once and for all. Some men never get the message.'

I knew she was right. I just needed the right moment. I'd had a couple of messages a day from him. I'd ignored them, but then one gave me the perfect opportunity.

What was the perfume you were wearing the other night? He went on to explain he'd inadvertently picked up my camisole top with his clothes. *It smells so good I took it to bed last night*, he confessed.

I replied. *Bill, I'm sorry, I've been thinking over the last few days. I'm not sure it's ever going to work between us. You've swamped me with messages and it's been overwhelming. I think I'd feel very claustrophobic in a relationship with you. I'm sorry. I hope you find someone nice. All the best.*

Fifteen minutes later, he replied. *Okay Alex, I'm sorry, I know I've been a little over the top. I sensed you were backing off and I didn't want to lose you completely. I'd like to think we could be friends in time as we have so much in common, especially with our work. You have my number. Take care, gorgeous.*

That felt quite final. I'd been cowardly and hadn't handled the situation well, but I'd come off lightly. I couldn't allow myself to get into a similar situation again.

Was it comic or fortuitous timing that the next morning I saw I'd had a message from 'Joyrider' overnight, the defence lawyer?

Alex, thanks for the enthusiastic message – it's great to be appreciated! You look rather nice too. Wanna hook up sometime soon? Neil.

.   .   .

The rest of the week I had a shoot with Agnes art-directing. Early in our careers, when she was a junior designer and I was a photographer's assistant, we often worked on projects together. We'd gone travelling around India a few times in our mid-twenties which cemented our friendship. There's a special bond between two people who've had Delhi Belly together. For hours, travelling between Mumbai and Kerala, we'd taken turns heaving into the open hole in the floor of the train's toilet, holding each other's hair out of the way as we bent over.

Twenty years later, we knew each other's way of working so well, it often felt that we communicated telepathically. That's not to say we agreed about everything – we didn't – but she was usually my client and in that situation, if she wanted the shots to be lit in a certain way, or to use a background that I didn't think was quite right, my job was to make the best of it and not throw my toys out of the pram. There were times when the atmosphere between us would be a little edgy but usually we found a way to settle our creative disagreements without it affecting our friendship. Often the best way was to just not speak for a few weeks, by which time we'd both calmed down.

We were photographing an elegant Georgian house in Hoxton that had virtually been rebuilt brick by brick by the looks of it and, on paper, should have been easy. My client Nigel, the architect, had agreed with the owners of the house that the shoot would happen, but they had either forgotten or hadn't seen the need to tidy up or vacuum beforehand. Nigel negotiated with them which rooms we could photograph that day. We lost half the morning cleaning but by lunchtime we were ready to start shooting.

The front of the house was east-facing, so the garden had sun in the afternoon. The kitchen had the now-obligatory sliding glass doors onto a decked area, dominated by large raised flower beds. We photographed the space with and without the doors open. When closed, the doors allowed the sculptural plants from the garden to be reflected in the glass and I loved how they softened the sharp angularity of the interior.

We moved onto the master bedroom, where the decor and interior design was more in keeping with the original architecture. The walls were wood-panelled and had been painted a dark blue, not quite midnight. The silk curtains in almost the same hue, hanging in luxurious swathes at the windows, stopped the room feeling too much of a pastiche. Lighting the shots was going to be tricky; it could easily look dark and funereal.

While Agnes and I sat in the garden, agreeing shot angles and weighing up the lighting possibilities, I checked my messages. Neil had replied, confirming meeting that evening.

'Please tell me it's not the bad hygiene guy again?' Agnes eyed me wearily.

'Nope.'

Neil and I had agreed to meet in a pub in Brixton, on a quiet residential square off the main drag. I arrived first and ordered a glass of wine and sat at a table where he'd be able to spot me easily. He arrived after a few minutes and ordered a non-alcoholic beer.

'So what's with the non-drinking, if I'm not being too nosey?' I asked, wondering whether he might be an alcoholic, and therefore on the wagon. I hoped not.

'I like to be in the moment, you know. Alcohol clouds everything, especially sex.'

I had expected him to be a bit arrogant and self-opinionated, but he wasn't. We talked about our previous experiences and situations; he had an 'open' relationship with his wife.

'How does she feel about it all?' I asked, trying to get my head around the whole idea of polyamory.

'She's quite cool about it. We fell out of love a long time ago, but we wanted the most stable environment for our daughter, and we both agreed that having separate private lives would be a way to do that.'

I understood that part. 'So do you have your partners round to the house?'

He must have thought this was a dumb question. 'No, never. We agreed Sienna mustn't be exposed to any of it. She's nine now, and when she's old enough, we'll explain it to her.'

Neil told me about his current relationships; he was quite serious with one woman he'd known for a couple of years. One with a much younger woman who had really fallen for him but wanted kids. Neil knew he didn't want to go down that road, but they both enjoyed each other's company. Another relationship he described as FWB; I made a note to Google it when I got home. He also talked about the sex parties he went to and was a little surprised I'd never been to one. I felt momentarily prudish but added in my defence that I'd never been invited to one.

'And does your wife have several partners?' I asked, in an attempt to move the conversation away from sex parties.

'No, not usually, just one at the moment. I think she liked the idea but she found all the organisation too much... there's a fair amount of planning involved.' He looked at me, ready to gauge my reaction. 'What about you? Would you consider going poly?'

I shrugged. 'I don't know. It's not something I've thought about. I can see the whole idea has its advantages, but I can't help imagining it depends where you are on the ladder. Some people are likely to get hurt along the way.'

'Yeah, you're right, it's not for the faint-hearted.'

Neil asked me about Ned's dad, and I gave him more detail about his depression than I normally would on a first date. We talked a bit about work; he frequently represented terrorists and criminals. It made photography feel very trivial in comparison, but he was interested in what I had to say and the conversation flowed easily. It felt completely un-date like though; I didn't think there was any chemistry and half-way through the evening I put it down as a one-date thing.

We left the pub just after ten. He said he'd be in touch, and I was expecting us to have a slightly awkward hug or peck on the cheek, but instead he kissed me; a full, throaty snog. It was nice. I responded, still slightly taken aback.

We said goodbye and walked in separate directions; I needed to go the same way he was going but that would have been awkward after the kiss. I still thought there was a good chance I wouldn't hear from him. But I waited for the bus feeling pretty happy. Perhaps I needed to rethink what I wanted. Could I just enjoy dating and not get too bogged down in finding something long-term?

The job for the architect was pretty full-on; the next few days disappeared and we made up time after the semi-disastrous first day. The weather was kind to us, staying dry and the last few hours of the final afternoon we spent shooting the garden, the view of the back and front of the house, and some of the street and surrounding area.

On the way home the traffic was appalling. I realised with a rush of guilt that it was Ingrid's due date. We'd exchanged a few short texts, since the morning at the soft-play centre and I hadn't seen her for a few weeks. I'd thought perhaps Ned and Johan just needed a break from each other. While creeping forward a few feet at a time trying to cross Tower Bridge I sent her a message saying I was thinking about her and offering to look after Johan if it would help.

I hadn't heard from Neil and, as each day passed, I thought it was less likely. Perhaps it was best I wouldn't see him again. Sex parties were probably a step too far for me, weren't they?

I realised I needed to have someone to think about if, as I suspected, nothing was going to happen with Neil. I knew I was being ridiculous, but to stop me lurching back into thinking about Mal, I had to keep moving forward, making steps to meet someone else. I went back onto the site, had a look at a few profiles, skim-read new messages. But I'd made a deal with myself; limiting potential dates to five. Any more and I'd have to put together a spreadsheet. I'd had a message from Silly Boy Blue aka Paul, who said he was back from Paris after bringing his daughter over to London for half-term. *Tell me again where you're based... I'm Fitzroy Square,* he added at the end.

Fitzroy Square; swanky. I replied. *I'm in south-east London but getting into town is nice and easy. I'm pretty flexible time wise. Were you able to enjoy a little of Paris or did you have to come straight back?*

An hour or so later, he replied. *Sadly just a quick turn-around this time but I sometimes stay for some shopping and a cheeky bouillabaisse. Any thoughts on where would be halfway for us? I'm a member of a few clubs in town if you wanted to meet there?*

I'd also had a message from Skærbæk, one of the five. He'd not replied at the time. *Hi Leica. Nothing cooler than an esoteric camera manufacturer for a profile name. Is it more profound than that though? Are you German, perhaps? Or, pronounced in a certain way, 'Leica sounds a bit like 'Like her'... is it actually a subliminal message?*

I couldn't remember much about him. I went onto the site and clicked on his profile. Six foot, two. Brown hair, brown eyes, slim, divorced. He was fairly ambivalent about what kind of relationship he was looking for. His profile photo showed him in a bar, at the ICA on the Mall. I recognised the bars on the window. There was a bottle of Danish beer on the table. He was dressed in black and had that classic square-jawed look I loved. Dark eyes, quite close set, a touch of sadness in them.

I replied. *No, nothing really profound, other than loving their cameras, though I don't use them for work. Talking of esoterica... Skærbæk... is it your surname? Alex.*

Five minutes later, I got a reply. *Hi Alex, I'm Nate. Or Nathaniel to my mum. No, not my surname, it was my grandmother's who was Danish. So, would you like to meet for a drink or a coffee sometime?*

I'd also had an email from Caroline, an old college friend who lived in Cambridge. *Hi there, just wondered if you'd had any news from Mal? Have you discussed any more with Sean what's going to happen long term? And also I wondered if I could pop down to London and stay with you in a couple of weeks? Lots of questions! Speak to you soon. PS Am seeing Carl again on Monday... he's not free until then, he's probably fitting in lots of dates!*

Poor Caroline. She'd been dating for so long, and never

met anyone who wanted to stay with her. In the morning I replied, saying it was fine for her to stay.

I'd also had a message via the dating site from Bill. It had been sent just after 3am.

Can't get you out of my head, Alex. And to make it worse I can see you've still been logging onto the website... so much for still getting over your ex. I feel betrayed and hurt and angry. Women like you are bitches, you lead men on and change your mind and think you can treat us like shit.

I wasn't expecting that. I did feel guilty but I'd been as kind as I could without being brutally honest and that would have hurt more. But still, the message left a nasty taste in my mouth.

CHAPTER 8

I spent the Monday at Agnes', planning the following few days' shoot. Her client had sent her the products; Japanese bowls and vases, all in beautiful iridescent blue and green glazes. I'd brought my camera and a couple of lights to take a few test shots. We tried out a few different backgrounds; a dark, smooth wood, a rough linen and some tatami -- Japanese mats, she told me, that were traditionally used as flooring.

As we worked on the shots Agnes asked me about dating and what was happening in general. I always felt a little reticent talking to her about men. I felt she was judging me, along with a handful of other friends. Her twenty-year marriage was rock-steady, and though she understood how difficult life with Sean had been, still questioned whether I should be dating at all. In general my approach with her was to keep any details to a minimum, and try and change the subject. I got the perfect excuse when I got a call from Ingrid, but I suspected the conversation was going to be even more uncomfortable.

'That sounded a bit fraught?' Agnes asked when I finally came off the phone.

'It was Ingrid, one of the mums I know from the NCT group; all of a sudden Johan and Ned aren't as friendly. Also Johan has a brand new baby sister; I can't say it to Ingrid without fear of having my head bitten off, but I think that might be partly why he's more sensitive than usual.'

'Has something happened?'

'They were playing football at break time yesterday. Ned didn't pick Johan for his team.'

'That's it?'

'He didn't pick him last week either. When Ingrid picked Johan up from school yesterday, he must have told her all about it. She called me, but I was driving and didn't answer so she left a message. She sounded hysterical.'

Agnes raised her eyebrows. 'What did she say?'

'She couldn't believe what a terrible parent I was, allowing my son to behave so disgracefully. I had no idea what she was talking about at the time, and texted her to say so. I told her Ned was still at after-school club, I was working, and I'd ask him about it when we got home. When we did, he told me they'd had this argument about football... just a normal, playground tiff.'

'She sounds... pretty highly strung.'

'You can't micro-manage every single thing children do or say. So I sent her a reply saying that this was all a storm in a tea cup, and that I was drawing a line under it. But Ingrid sent one back to say that she thought I wasn't taking Ned's bad behaviour seriously, and had it occurred to me that it was because I work too much, and I don't give Ned enough attention?'

. . .

On the way home from Agnes', I got a text from Neil, the lawyer I'd met for a drink about a month before, apologising for the silence; he'd been busy with work. He said he'd been surprised we'd talked about sex that evening. At the end he asked me if I'd had any thoughts about what to do next.

Driving through the south London rush hour, I weighed up my options; I didn't really have any. As the days passed, it seemed very unlikely I'd hear back from Skærbæk aka Nate, who'd sounded promising. What did I have to lose by seeing Neil again? He'd told me he was in an open marriage. He lived nearby. He had children. Perhaps a casual 'Friends with Benefits' thing was just what I needed. I decided to reply. *I'm thinking why don't we find a date to swap more stories...?*

The road was choc-a-bloc when I got home, and I had to park quite a way down. With a couple of minutes to spare before the finish of after-school club, I ran past the house to pick Ned up. I read Neil's next text as I was buzzed in and I walked towards reception. *Sure. Just stories? I thought you might be up for a practical demonstration...*

Walking along the corridor towards the main hall where I could hear all the children were playing, I texted him back. *A practical demonstration sounds enticing. I'm sure we can work something out...*

It was dark by the time we reached home. As I was digging around in my bag, looking for the house keys, Ned jumped onto the low brick wall.

'Get down darling, I've told you before, it's a bit wobbly.'

Another job I hadn't got round to fixing. At one end the wall had slumped forward, at the same angle as the Tower of Pisa.

'Mum, what is 'B... I... T... C... H...?'

'What? Where did you hear that word?'

'It's here, look.'

Sprayed across the front of the house, half on the bay windows, half on the brickwork below, in red capital letters, each around two feet high.

'Come in, please, that's a horrible word. I don't know why somebody would say that. They must have sprayed our house by mistake.'

Even as I said it, I knew that was untrue. Bill; it had to be. He'd used the word in a text, hadn't he? Could I report him on the dating site? I still had all his texts.

As I cooked pasta for dinner, I Googled 'graffiti removal.' I found one company in Croydon and left a message. I decided I'd take photos of the front of the house in the morning when it was light and report it to the police. Would they take it seriously? Would they investigate at all? I doubted it.

The pasta needed a minute more; Ned was not an al dente fan. Neil had replied. *How about meeting in a hotel? A classy five star establishment in Mayfair, or a sleazy no-star joint above a Chinese takeaway on the Old Kent Road – take your pick. I'm thinking about kissing you with my left hand on the small of your back and my right firmly between your legs. I'm thinking about easing my fingers in between your lips and slowly starting to tease your clit.*

I hadn't really done sexting. I wasn't averse to the whole idea, but this was nought to sixty in under three seconds. If I didn't respond, he'd think I was boring or frigid.

A few minutes later, he sent another message. *PS I'm curious about fucking you. How do you like it?*

There was a chasm between my present, very domestic situation, and the fantasy sex being played out on the screen of my phone. But still, the words had turned me on. Part of it was down to a drought of much action, save for the odd, sporadic interlude. And, of course, the interrupted night with Mal. Even though we hadn't actually had sex, it was him, without question, I wanted and yearned for.

After getting Ned bathed and ready for bed, I returned to my phone, realising an hour or so had passed. I knew that to keep the momentum going I would have to respond, though my mind stayed resolutely blank about what to say.

After starting and deleting various scenarios, I remembered a text conversation I'd had with Colin the sociologist, six months before. It had worked for him. I copied and pasted the relevant part, and checked through it, removing any references to Colin. As I read, Neil must have seen I was on WhatsApp. He sent a short message. *I wondered whether you'd be sliding your fingers onto your clit anytime soon.*

I typed a quick response. *Perhaps. What about you?* A moment later, he said *Already handled so to speak.* I replied. *Next instalment forming in my head...* This quickfire messaging, I had to admit... there was something sexy and exciting about it.

But did I fancy him? Physically, he was cute. Not my usual type which I'd realised was tall, thin, beautiful and complicated. Neil was shortish, only a little taller than me, quite stocky, nicely messy grey hair. Steely blue eyes, I remembered those. And a great kisser. I knew if we did meet in a hotel room, it was unlikely we'd have boring sex.

After I'd vetted the text one more time, I pressed send. *I text you to tell you I've booked a room at a hotel near London Bridge station. I've arrived first, and when you knock on the door, without speaking, I lead you by the hand, through to the bed. I loosen the tie of my silk kimono; underneath I'm wearing an all-*

in-one black body, with stockings and high-heeled boots, lots of
dark, smoky eye make-up. I won't allow you to get undressed;
while we kiss I want the contrast of you being fully clothed, while
I'm almost naked.

After Ned was in bed, I went upstairs to my studio to get
ready for the next day's shoot. I charged the camera
batteries and checked all the memory cards were empty.
The shoot was happening at home which made life easier,
but Agnes and her client were coming at 9 am so I wanted to
be completely ready, and Agnes had a habit of arriving half
an hour early. I cleared the space so that there was room for
several set-ups at once – we had a lot to get through in the
following few days.

I glanced at my phone and saw that Neil had texted a
response. I was slightly annoyed that this interlude was
happening, mostly at myself that I'd allowed it to. The next
few days were going to be too busy to write long messages
about what it might be like to fuck him.

As I sat on the toilet and cleaned my teeth I sent him the
next paragraph. By the time I got into bed, my phone screen
showed a short message. *I like undressing...*

Instead of reading my book in bed that night, I decided
to write the long sex scenario text he'd been waiting for. I
was using my iPad as it was quicker to type on than the
phone. As I sent the message, the Wifi icon disappeared
from the top of the screen. I didn't have 4G on the iPad and
when I restarted the app the message had disappeared. It
had taken twenty minutes to write; I couldn't face writing it
again. It felt a bit like a chore. I'd have to write it in the
morning.

I woke at around 3 am and saw that Neil had sent
another one, an hour or so before. *I was thinking about you*
lying on your back with your arms above your head, my hands

on your wrists. Your knees are slightly lifted and spread and I'm hard – in between your legs. I let go of one wrist and reach down taking my cock in my hand and use it to part your lips. I'm pressing against you.

I could see on WhatsApp that he was online. I texted him. *You can't sleep either, huh? Hang on, I sent you a really long message... did you get it?*

As soon as I sent it, the two grey ticks turned blue. *No.*

I replied. *I tried to send it from my iPad while the Wifi was down. I'll have to retype...*

He responded a second later. *Tease. Did you end up reliving any of those moments, with a finger or two on your clit?*

I hadn't. It's true, the long messages had been a turn on; reading his and writing mine. But I'd had to get on with doing something else every time, like making Ned's supper and reading bedtime stories. Lying in bed, with my head full of thoughts about sex, I decided I would. My vibrator was too loud to use in the middle of the night, with the risk of waking Ned. And it was a while since I'd used it. Turning it on and finding it was uncharged would be frustrating, and a turn-off.

I went back over Neil's messages, and found the one I was looking for, where he pressed against my G-spot with his finger. I closed my eyes and conjured up an image of Mal in my mind's eye. I started to feel myself soften, moisten, tingle. I used two fingers to circle my clitoris, sweeping over the small rosebud of flesh. The feeling was already there; I knew it wouldn't take long. I kept up the pace – the same, exact circles. Twenty times, thirty times, the last few speeding up, the circles becoming a little smaller every time. The waves spread from that point outwards, familiar yet still exciting. The knowledge of how it felt, knowing I could get it again so easily, was addictive. Inside, I could feel the contractions, as regular as a heartbeat, but with each one, they lost a little power until my body lay still.

I picked up my phone. *Yes, just now. What about you?*

Straight away he texted back. *Yes.*

I settled into the foetal position and fell into a deep sleep.

CHAPTER 9

Sean had agreed, more or less, to come and stay for a couple of days; he hadn't seen Ned for months. I knew guilt-tripping wouldn't work and giving him an inkling that I wanted him to come because I was dating wasn't a good idea either. Forget taking his responsibilities seriously, he didn't get that. I couldn't rely on him turning up, even if he said he would.

I'd arranged a date with Nate. Denny was going to babysit if Sean didn't turn up. I didn't believe he'd really come until he knocked on the door just after four on Friday afternoon.

On the train journey to Victoria, to stop pre-date nerves getting the better of me at the last minute, I checked my emails. There were a couple of work things. I checked LinkedIn; someone I'd been at art school with, Adrian Evans, had looked at my profile. He'd been a bit of a hippy back then; long, curly hair, leather wristbands, scruffy clothes that hung elegantly on his skinny frame. He smoked a bit too much dope for my liking but I think we might have got off with each other at a couple of parties.

I hadn't thought about him for years. I sent a message. *Adrian Evans? THE Adrian Evans??? How the devil are you?*

Nate and I were meeting in Soho, at a place I'd been to a couple of times. He had taken the only space round the bar that was free; right by the door so he saw me immediately. We kissed on the cheek, and ordered drinks, him a Moscow Mule, me a Negroni. Nerves must have got the better of me because I knocked it back in a few minutes and began to feel pleasantly tipsy quite quickly. Every twenty seconds, the door opened which brought with it a blast of chilly spring evening air, stopping me feeling too woozy.

We talked about previous dating experiences, our families, work, being self-employed. London and how it had changed over the previous twenty years. Nate noticed a couple getting ready to leave and grabbed the table while I bought more drinks.

Sitting opposite him, I was finally able to look at him properly. Perhaps it was the alcohol now flowing through my bloodstream that gave me the confidence to gaze at him, taking in all the tiny details.

His face was quite long but broad at the same time, with high cheekbones, made up of thirty or forty carefully chiselled planes. His eyes were dark, and deep set, and even when he smiled they retained the sadness I'd seen in his profile photos. This guy had been through the wringer, it was etched on his face.

We'd worked our way through a bottle of Montepulciano, and I felt blissfully unaware of everything around me. Apart from Nate. Eventually he looked at his watch and said, 'God, it's 11.30. We're almost the last people in here.' He looked me up and down. 'And I really want to kiss you.'

We both leaned forward as much as we could without sending our wine glasses flying, our lips only just touching.

The table was in the way. I stood up and stumbled between the eight-inch gap between our table and the empty one next to it. Our first kiss; it should have been gentle and delicate, but it was the kind that happens in the middle of fucking.

I was shocked at how I'd become so completely lost in the moment. I had Sean at home looking after Ned. I'd been very non-committal about when I'd be back, hadn't given him any information about where I'd be or with whom. Between kisses, we negotiated what we were going to do next.

'You've got a babysitter, you need to get back, I guess,' he asked, more a statement than a question.

'Well in the end my ex -- my son's dad -- has come to stay for the weekend.'

'D'you want to come back with me?' he asked as he kissed me again.

'I don't do this kind of thing any more.'

'No, neither do I.'

Nate ordered an Uber. We walked out onto the street. It had started raining. Waiting for the car to arrive, we sheltered under the bar's awning. We kissed again. His hands covered my body; round my waist, squeezing my breasts, feeling between my legs.

'The cab's here,' he whispered in my ear. He grabbed my hand again, we ran across the street and he opened the car door. He undid the belt on my coat and pulled it off my shoulders. We kissed continually, our hands roaming over each other's bodies. He had told me he did a lot of cycling. I could tell how fit he was by the shape of his chest, and the strength in his shoulders and arms.

I glimpsed Friday night Camden through the diagonal streaks of rain on my window as we sped up the High Street.

We went back to kissing. Nate's hand rested between my legs and I remembered with relief that I'd waxed my bikini line earlier. Had I really thought the evening would turn out like this? No, but I knew I never felt very sexy with several weeks' growth. I felt sorry for the cab driver. I guessed he got this quite a lot on Friday and Saturday nights, but most couples making out on the back seat were probably half our age.

The next time I looked up, we were driving past Kentish Town tube station. A few minutes later we'd arrived. Nate led me by the hand down the stairs to his basement flat.

Alone together for the first time, I dropped my handbag and coat on a chair at the small dining table. He grabbed me around the waist, showing his strength and we kissed. Knowing the sofa was behind me I bent backwards in response, thinking if I leant over too much at least I'd land on the sofa. Wrong. Possibly not helped by my silky dress which must have offered little resistance, I fell backwards onto the sofa momentarily and then slid completely off it, banging my head on the hardwood floor. A fractured skull was not what I needed. Nate rushed over and helped me to my feet.

'What happened there? You okay?'

'I don't know. I totally misjudged it.'

The back of my head was throbbing but I tried to ignore it. We kissed as Nate deftly undid my bra at the back, and moved his hands round to the front. The ties of my dress had come undone and it slid off my shoulders into a heap.

'Your tits are perfect.' I'd always hated that word, but is there a good alternative? He leant down and sucked one nipple after another, so hard I screamed out. I undid his belt – he was wearing skinny jeans that fitted him like a glove. Add to that a massive hard-on, removing them did not appear as effortless and nonchalant as I hoped and I couldn't pull them down any further than his thighs.

'I don't remember the last time I had a cab ride home where I didn't see any of the journey,' I whispered in his ear.

'I know, yeah, must be twenty years.'

With his jeans impairing his movement, he crab-walked me into his bedroom and threw me onto the bed.

He deftly peeled his jeans off, holding my gaze. I didn't think anyone's had ever bored into me quite as deeply as his did. I tore myself away to take in his body. He joined me on the bed. I held his cock firmly between my fingers and kissed him. He reached inside my underwear, pushing fingers into me; one, two, three? I couldn't tell. I gasped and our eyes locked. I knew he would want to see my reaction as he did it.

We kissed, tongues wrestling. He pushed me down onto the bed, and kneeled, parting my legs. He started to lick my clitoris, pushing fingers inside me again, one arm reaching up to my breasts and squeezing, then finding my nipple and pinching it, moving to the other side. I glanced down at him but his eyes were closed. I moved my hand down to run my fingers through his hair. My whole body writhed in time to his thrusting fingers. He looked up and I gave him the slightest smile which he must have taken as a sign of approval, because he started to push even more deeply into me, against my G-spot. Pleasure and pain in equal measure.

He looked up at me again. He had a dispassionate look on his face, his eyes narrowed.

'That good?'

'Jesus, yes. But…'

'Mmmmm?'

I pushed myself up onto one elbow. 'I want to suck you too.'

We kissed for a moment and then he stood up, and I took him in my mouth. He held the back of my head and pushed me towards him. I couldn't breathe to start with, it took a moment to get into a rhythm. I held the base of his cock in one hand, he moved his hands down to my breasts and rubbed his palms against my nipples. I looked up at him.

'Fuck me.'

With what I imagined was only a fraction of his strength, he pushed me down onto the bed.

'But I haven't got any condoms with me,' I added.

This was all completely unplanned. He sat up and, holding my gaze, opened the drawer in his bedside table where he must have kept a stash. He expertly put one on and, in a moment, he was inside me, his body on top of me. We kissed deeply and urgently. Instinctively I ran my fingers up and down his spine, digging my nails into his skin. Nate felt for my hands and with one of his, held both of my wrists above my head. I looked up at him; his face was red and contorted with concentration. He sucked my nipples and I cried out. Pain and pleasure again.

It must have been three or four in the morning by the time we decided to sleep. Around that time the back of my head had started pounding from falling off the sofa earlier that night, and my system was too full of adrenaline and alcohol to sleep properly anyway.

I became aware of a familiar rumbling underground. It lasted for twenty seconds or so at a time, then a few minutes later, the same sound. It took me a while to work out that it was the tube; the Northern line tunnel must have run underneath his flat. The ground shook ever so slightly, running up through the legs of his bed, through the mattress, into my sex-weary body.

I lay there, trying not to change position and waken Nate who had managed to fall into a deep sleep as soon as his head hit the pillow, that way men do after sex. His lower arm was resting on my hipbone, long, slim and rectangular. His hand gently weighed against the lower part of my stomach where the skin, post-pregnancy, was like crêpe paper.

He had beautiful hands, long, fine-boned fingers, masculine in size and shape but still with the finesse and elegance of a pianist. I could see a rusty-brown deposit under his fingernails, and here and there a sweep of russet red on his fingers. Menstrual blood; my period must have started. Some men were a bit squeamish about that sort of thing but somehow I didn't think Nate would be among them.

I must have drifted off to sleep; next time I opened my eyes I was facing away from Nate and milky, grey daylight had seeped into the room. He was awake and, with a single fingertip, was lightly tickling my inner thigh. 'I wondered how long I'd have to do that to wake you.'

We fucked again – energetically, frantically wrestling with each other, all with a clarity that comes with being totally sober. We finally collapsed, covered in each other's bodily fluids. My head found a resting place on his chest, and there, arms wrapped around each other, we lay in silence, listening to each other's breathing, his heart beating slowly beneath my temple.

Nate ran a bath and, lying end-to-end with our legs entangled in the middle, I studied him intently as he told me about his family, especially the competitive relationship he had with his older brother. They both took part in a bike race in the south of France the summer before and his elder brother stormed ahead of Nate after 10km, along a downhill part of the course. Nate didn't take the bait. He knew the course well, had done it before, studied the changes from the previous year, read all the blogs. When he passed an ambulance at 30km, around the half-way point of a gradual but punishing uphill stretch, it didn't occur to him that the cyclist lying prostate on the stretcher as he sped past was his brother. He'd had a heart attack – a mild one – but serious enough to warrant a two-day stay in a Toulouse hospital. Nate had finished the race in a decent time, and despite calls from the paramedics, he went back to the hotel and showered before visiting his brother. 'It was his own fault; he didn't train, thought he was better than me. I was teaching him a lesson.'

'What's your relationship like with your brother now? He doesn't blame you?'

'No, he's just really annoyed, still, that I beat him. Cycling's always been my thing, he just thought it would be piss easy. His wife hasn't forgiven me though. From her perspective I'd left him to die by the side of the road.'

His face looked completely different to how it had the night before. Perhaps it was lack of sleep; mine or his or both, the cold light of day. Maybe it was his wet hair lifted from his face too – it looked broader, his gaze more intent, his manner less open, more guarded.

It was midday by the time we were dressed. I expected Nate had stuff to do. I didn't want to outstay my welcome, so I gathered my belongings, strewn around from the night before.

'Wanna grab some brunch?' he asked.

'Yeah, that'd be lovely, if you've got time.'

'Sure, there's a place along the road that's good.'

I hadn't looked at my phone and, as we walked along

Nate's road towards Fortess Road, I pulled it out of my bag. Nineteen missed calls from Sean, a dozen texts, variations on a theme. *Where the fuck are you?*

We reached the café and found a table towards the back, in a covered garden. Nate went to order and I took the opportunity to send a curt reply to Sean. *None of your business. Home mid afternoon. Out tonight too.*

I'd had a LinkedIn message from Adrian Evans, the guy I'd been at college with. He was trying to organise a reunion. A date had already been decided, in a few months' time. *Would be great to see you if you can make it, Alex. Are you still in touch with Iona Ferguson and Hugh Matthews?*

And a text from Ingrid telling me that Johan and Ned were friends again. *I should just let four-year-olds sort out their issues themselves*, she added at the end.

As Nate walked back to the table, I was struck by his coolness, how his clothes fitted him perfectly. As he weaved through the tables, he swaggered, holding my gaze, enjoying the attention of me and a few other women who'd clocked him.

After we'd eaten, he walked me to the tube station. We'd studiously avoided talking about seeing each other again. I fumbled in my bag, pretending to look for my Oyster card to prevent myself blurting out something dumb. I can't remember the exact words we used when we parted, but it must have been along the lines of 'Yeah, it was fun.' Or, 'See you.' What I did remember was how he kissed me. I was left gasping for breath. Gasping for more. He'd eaten Steak Frites at the café, the meat rare, and his mouth tasted metallic, of blood, and English Breakfast tea. He released me, turned, and walked away. I managed a mouse-like 'bye' as I watched him disappear along the road, not looking back.

CHAPTER 10

*G*ood afternoon, sorry for the radio silence. I was thinking about you in bed this morning... in high heels and no knickers (you, that is, not me) bending over slightly against a wall so I can lift up your skirt.

Paul, the guy who lived in the centre of town. We'd seen each other a few times. He'd been desperate to take me to one of his fancy member's clubs. I'd met him there one evening, a sprawling converted warehouse in Shoreditch covering four floors with a swimming pool on the roof. We'd agreed it was too soon for him to meet Ned, and after the incident with Mal and the close shave with Bill, I was adamant it wasn't going to happen again. After we'd had a couple of glasses of champagne, he leant in towards me. 'I've got an idea,' he whispered.

He led me across the open plan bar towards the stairs. On the next floor down he opened the door to the ladies' loos. He had a quick look round the corner to make sure no-one was there, and led me into the cubicle at the end. He pinned me against the closed door with his body, kissing me hard on the mouth. He undid the belt on my coat, running his hands over my body, holding me round the throat with one hand, with the other he reached up my skirt. 'Mmmm, stay ups, very nice.'

He kissed me again. I unbuttoned his coat, pushing it down over his arms. He grabbed my elbows and held them up above my shoulders, against the toilet door. I locked eyes with him. I didn't want to be a bystander. With his body pushed against mine, I could feel him unzipping his jeans, the metal of his belt cold and hard against my skin. He raised my left leg and held my thigh in place while he used his other hand to guide himself into me. I cried out as my skin caught. He stopped for a moment as I reached down to readjust myself. He grabbed my hand and held it back in place. His thrusts were slow and rhythmic, gradually gathering pace. He held my left leg in place, partly taking my weight.

'You're so wet,' he whispered. 'It really turns me on.'

I had to admit I was enjoying it, the novelty of it, the unexpectedness, but at the same time knew this was mainly for his benefit.

Afterwards, readjusting my clothes and smoothing down my hair, I wondered if any other couples in the club had been doing the same. It occurred to me he'd done the same thing before.

That was about a month ago. Until this message, I'd heard nothing and guessed he'd met someone else. After a month, it was perfectly possible he had and it had come to an end, and that was why he decided to get in touch. Fuck him, I thought. I didn't bother to reply.

I ran around, tidying up before Caroline arrived. She had an interview at a photo library in town the next morning and was staying with us overnight. Only a few days before had the guy from Croydon finally come to remove 'B.I.T.C.H'. For some reason, I hated the idea of Caroline seeing it. When Sean had stayed he milked it for all it was worth, but I didn't rise to the bait.

The doorbell rang as I was dusting the mantelpiece. Caroline and I hugged in the hallway and I took her bag upstairs to the spare room. She'd arrived early so she could see Ned, so we picked him up from school at home time rather than him go to after-school club.

As Caroline helped Ned build his Lego spaceship, the one Mal had bought him, I filled the dishwasher, emptied the washing machine, and started chopping vegetables for dinner. She supervised Ned's bath and after she'd read him stories, joined me in my studio. I knew from her expression she was going to ask about Mal, so I got in first. 'Tell me more about the photo library... what's the position?'

'Oh, nothing special, just a senior researcher. They're mainly wildlife and nature...'

'Sounds just up your street,' I added enthusiastically.

'We'll see. It's not going to give me the opportunity to do much photography myself, but I guess I should accept I'm unlikely to have a career surge at my age.'

'I'm sorry, I don't know what to say. You're happy enough, aren't you? I do worry about you.' I reached over and squeezed her hand.

'On the whole. I've made a real effort to make new friends recently. I've started going to a ceramics class once a week, and pilates. And a book club once a month. The trouble is at all of them, it's nearly all women.'

'Perhaps you should take up snooker, or cycling... how about that? There must be hundreds of cycling clubs around Cambridge. They're all going to be guys.'

'Actually, that's not a bad idea.'

We Googled 'cycling club Cambridge' and the iMac screen filled with photos of cheery groups of Lycra-clad men. Caroline's face lit up.

'Go on, send a few messages,' I said, already clicking on links to websites. 'You could sign up in time for a ride this weekend. You've got a bike.'

She clicked on a few of the photos, scanning the faces. I stood up to look more closely at the screen; they were nearly all men, ranging in age from early thirties to late seventies. 'Look, some of them have one or two women members... that's perfect.'

She nodded, but her initial enthusiasm seemed to have waned. 'So what happened with that chap you were seeing... what was his name again? Mark? You said in your text he'd gone back to his girlfriend.' She said, head tilted to one side in concern.

'Mal. Yes, it was one of those things. He was lovely, really lovely. I have to accept I didn't mean anything to him.' I paused, shocked at how open and frank I had been, not showing my usual bravado about such things. 'I know I'll go mad thinking about him, but I just need to get him out of my head, so I've adopted a scattergun approach. Dating a few guys at the same time. That's what men do... if you can't beat 'em, join 'em.'

She looked at me, questioningly. I wasn't going into the details with her; I knew she wouldn't approve. Instead I kept looking at cycling clubs' Facebook pages, hoping a photo of Nate clad in black Lycra wouldn't somehow appear.

'Ooooh, can I see some photos?' she asked.

'Of what?'

'The guys you've met recently.'

'I don't have any... only on the dating site.'

'Oh, go on, let me see some. You know how much luck I have. There's got to be a much bigger dating pool in London than Cambridge. If I get that job tomorrow, it'd be easier to meet someone in London.'

I smiled weakly, and sighed quietly enough for her not to hear me. I'd done this once before with Caroline, when I first told her I was dating.

'Brace yourself,' she'd said, 'it's a rollercoaster'.

I logged onto the site, and then clicked on 'people I like'. The screen filled with thumbnail images. I hovered the cursor over one. 'Okay, this one is Neil. He's a defence lawyer, lives in Clapham.'

'He looks quite nice. Does he have children?'

'Yes, one daughter.'

'Have you met him?'

'Once.' She didn't need to know about our ongoing sexting. I moved the mouse to sit over Skærbæk's photo.

'And that one's Nate, I met him on Friday night.'

'Wow,' she peered at the thumbnail. Subconsciously she took the mouse and clicked on his profile to make the photos bigger. 'He looks like... '

'Sean. Yes, he does a bit,' I said.

I turned round to glance the time on the clock behind me. Caroline was pressing the forward button so she could view each profile in turn. She stopped at one. 'What about him?'

'That's Tim. He's an academic, works at Imperial. A few messages in we worked out he was the 'Tim' my friend Fran had dated for a few months. That was a non-starter, but it's a shame, he seemed like a nice guy.'

'This one?'

'Not him. He looks cute but he's too much of a player.' I took the opportunity to shift the conversation. 'What about the guy you were seeing, Carl? You had a second date with him, didn't you?'

'Yes, that was a week ago. I texted him the next day and haven't heard back from him.'

'Are there a few more you could try? You could show me your 'favourites'?'

She looked away. 'No, don't worry, I'm finding it all a bit depressing to be honest.' She turned back to the screen. 'What about him?'

'I've met him a couple of times.' I hesitated. She'd be appalled to know I'd had sex in the toilets. I decided to keep a positive spin on it. 'He's a writer for TV. His ex-wife is French and she lives in Paris with their daughter. He's shown me photos – both are beautiful.'

'What happened with his marriage?' she asked.

'He said they were totally unsuited. She was very fiery, typically French. She's a TV director, that's how they met. He said he was completely seduced by her, that even listening to her read out the contents of the fridge would give him a massive hard-on. He didn't realise what a terrible mistake he'd made until Mathilde was pregnant with their daughter.'

The hard-on comment shocked Caroline into silence. I'd included it with the intention of bringing the conversation to a close. I stood up.

'Let's open a bottle of wine.'

A few days later I met Neil at a hotel. Could I sum up the experience in a few words? Soulless. Formulaic. Or, possibly, predictable. The sex? Yes, I can't deny it was great; strenuous, athletic, adventurous. We pretty much followed the scenarios set up in our text conversations. But it lacked any intimacy or passion. The excitement I felt had all been in the build-up. As soon as he knocked on the hotel room door, it fell away. It was purely a chance to fuck someone's brains out.

Neil left shortly afterwards, and I followed half an hour later, after showering in an attempt to make myself look presentable, so I didn't look like a hooker who'd just visited her punter as I walked through the hotel lobby. Part of me, a small part, did feel empowered and in control and all the other things modern women are supposed to feel, but the larger part just felt a bit grubby. Used? No. I used Neil as much as he did me. In retrospect I would, by a considerable margin, have preferred to spend that Friday evening at home, cuddled up on the sofa watching a film with Ned, catching up on household chores after he'd gone to bed.

When I got home I opened a bottle of red wine and watched *Drive*. I'd had a conversation with Mal about the film – we'd both missed seeing it at the cinema – and he'd commented on how easily Ryan Gosling had become the new thinking woman's crumpet. I'd bought the newly-released DVD, imagining we might watch it together one evening. That wasn't going to happen now, so I consoled myself with the Tempranillo and Mr Gosling. When I'd finished the red I moved on to whisky.

The next morning Ned gently woke me. 'Are you okay, mummy? Are you feeling poorly? Would you like some toast? I'm hungry.'

He sat next to me and I hugged him tight. I said I was fine, just tired and that's why I'd fallen asleep on the sofa. Even to a four-year-old, he must have realised something wasn't quite right. I remembered my own father and his relationship with alcohol. Even at Ned's age I had recognised the smell of beer and whisky and uncleaned teeth the morning after he'd been out on a bender, spending his entire week's wages at the Vane Arms along the road.

I couldn't easily describe the look on Ned's face. If he'd been a few years older, there would have been disgust, surely, or embarrassment. I was lucky, I suppose, that he was too young to understand, and I hoped with all my heart that in time he would forget finding me drunk on the sofa one Saturday morning.

That was all I needed; I vowed that I was going to put him first. I thought that was what I'd done, but it hadn't been nearly enough. My desires and wants and needs had to take a back seat for the time being. Every day I spent, each decision I made, any relationship I had, they all must have a common purpose – to be the best mother I could be.

CHAPTER 11

A couple of months had passed since the night I'd met Neil in the hotel room. I'd had a text giving me the all-clear after an STI test. We'd used condoms but all the same, I wanted to be sure.

I was enjoying my dating-free period. I wasn't drinking much either. For the first time in at least a year, my time and energy were devoted to Ned and work. It suited me.

I was half-way through a week-long job – photographing around a hundred pieces of ceramics. A friend of a friend had recommended me for the job. The client, the wife of a retired heart surgeon, had come to ceramics fairly late in life, but her work was stunning and showed a great deal of technical skill. The glazes she'd used on simple, solid bowls and plates gave them a shimmering, metallic sheen. Others -- tall and thin vases and jugs -- were more delicately made. The rims were paper thin and translucent. I grouped the pieces according to how they needed to be lit; I wanted to capture all of the detail. I'd always found solace in my work, and being able to envelop myself in this project was stopping me thinking about what a car crash my personal life had become.

My memory card was full after a couple of hours shooting, and I transferred the images onto the Mac. I had a few email alerts and checked those. They were mainly from retailers, a few about gigs that had just been announced. And one from Adrian Evans, the guy I'd connected with on LinkedIn a few months back, and who was organising a reunion. I'd pencilled it in my diary realised with a sinking heart that it was in a couple of weeks' time. The email had been sent to around twenty people. Some names I recognised, some were vaguely familiar.

His ex-wife, Antonella, was on the list. Her family was Neapolitan, though she'd been born in London and had always lived in the UK. Tall, thin, with a mass of auburn, curly hair, and unbelievable green eyes. Antonella was very intimidating at college. After she'd bagged Adrian in the second year, she made it clear he was off bounds for every other female. But we had a mutual friend from college and over the last few years I'd seen her at various parties and private views, and she'd been much more friendly. She hadn't been with Adrian at the private views and I'd never asked her about him during our short chats for fear mentioning him might stir what she might perceive as a long-standing interest in him, though the friend we had in common had told me Antonella and Adrian had recently separated. Yes, Adrian and I had got off with each other at a couple of parties in the first year, before they were an item. I definitely wouldn't have taken her on after that.

Could I bear going to something like a college reunion on my own? Properly single for the first time since my early twenties and possibly with everyone else in couples, I'd feel like a total failure, wouldn't I?

Having mulled over the invitation during the day, in the evening I emailed Adrian back. *Hello Adrian. Good to hear from you, the reunion sounds like fun. Please count me in, and thank you for thinking of me. All the best, Alex Kendrew.*

Over the next couple of days, perhaps because going to the reunion had brought into stark focus my singledom, I lurched from feeling quite acquiescent and pragmatic about what had happened with Mal, to having an anger so overwhelming one evening I threw a glass at the wall. It was true, I admitted, that the other flings I'd had over the last few months were no different, in essence, to what had happened with him. Yet, there was something in our conversations, a closeness that had developed very quickly, the fact that immediately we just 'got' each other; that hadn't happened with the others. I was angry with Mal, but more so with myself for being stupid enough to fall for him so quickly.

The day of the reunion arrived, and I'd really given it very little thought since the email exchange.

Denny arrived to babysit Ned, with her usual Cockney Sparrow cheerfulness. I hated myself for occasionally finding it irritating. She'd saved my bacon so many times. *You're such a cow*, I told myself.

The reunion was at the same place I'd been to with Nate. Adrian had booked a private wood-panelled room off the main bar with burnt orange and sage green velvet chairs, artworks by Keith Tyson and Peter Blake adorning the walls, and heavy ornate silverware on the table. Most of the light came from the abundance of tall, white tapered candles, all in individual brass holders, which wouldn't have looked out of place had Samuel Pepys turned up for dinner in Soho with his contemporaries.

Almost everybody had arrived and there were only a couple of chairs round the table not taken. There was a buzz of excitement, partly fuelled by the aperitifs being consumed. I ordered a Negroni from the waiter who'd shown me to the table. Thankfully I recognised most people and I weighed up in my mind which of the two positions, which likely conversations with the surrounding people, would be less uncomfortable. I opted for the spot on the long green banquette sitting diagonally opposite Adrian, next to Dinny Jamieson who'd been a Fine Art painter at college, but was now the owner of a bar on Upper Street. On the other side was someone I knew well; Matt Beetson, who'd been a photographer in my year. We'd remained good friends, and we'd lived together with another friend, Jenny, in house-shares when we both moved down to London after college in the early nineties. We'd given each other work over the years too; if a new client had got in touch and we'd been too busy, we'd put the other in touch.

I don't know if art courses have a higher intake of privately-schooled children than the average degree. Our year, I remember thinking at the time, seemed to be at most thirty per cent state school kids. I always felt in the minority. This evening was no exception; there was much talk of Daddy helping out this way and that, or of taking over the family business after Daddy retired.

One woman, Sorrel, who'd been prime potential gold-digger material even when she was nineteen, had married a banker. This, it seemed, allowed her to continue painting, after a brief hiatus having three children which I'm sure all had the perfectly-ringletted blonde heads of their mother.

Didn't her final show consist entirely of watercolours of fairies? Perhaps I was being unkind.

In sharp contrast, sitting next to Sorrel was Andy Markham, another trustafarian. He'd lived in the same house as Adrian for the last summer we were there and you'd see them skateboarding together around town. Andy became something of an anti-hero when he failed his degree after his final show consisted entirely of naked self-portraits. The photographs were close-ups of his penis in various states of arousal, his whole body caked in white paint.

While we waited for our desserts, as the fine artists discussed agents and their astronomical fees, Matt nudged my elbow and, sitting further back in the generously deep balconette, whispered 'They're a different species, aren't they?'

'Yeah, I know. I don't think it's a coincidence that they were all born with silver spoons in their mouths,' I whispered back.

'So what's happening with you?' Matt asked.

'Oh, I can't complain. Work's okay, Ned is wonderful and enjoying school. How about the girls?'

'Oh, they're fine, thanks. Fiona was going to come tonight but our babysitter couldn't make it. That's what she told me anyway. I have a sneaking suspicion she thought it was going to be a bit la-de-dah and decided she'd give it a miss.'

'She was right.'

As we chatted I caught Adrian's eye. He'd been looking at me, maybe trying to catch some of our conversation as the two people each side of him talked across him. His gaze made me slightly uncomfortable, I don't know why. But I smiled back at him while Matt was talking to me about work and his eldest daughter's piano exams.

'So how's life with Sean not around? You'd met somebody when we saw you before Christmas, I think you said.'

'Yeah, I had. It all went tits up though. He'd had an affair with this woman, on and off for the last five years or so. They kept splitting up and getting back together. We only saw each other a couple of times, and then the woman called him and he went running back to her. End of story.'

'Oh, Alex, I'm sorry. What an arse.'

'Yeah, well, it was fun while it lasted. And then I met a few other people after that; each time it was equally short-lived. So for now I've put my wild side on ice and enjoying a life of abstinence and sobriety, except for this evening, obviously.' I paused as I glanced round the table. 'I don't think I could've got through it without drinking, could you?'

We chinked glasses. The desserts arrived and, as I wasn't having one, I took the opportunity to duck out and leave early, using the excuse of needing to get home for the babysitter. Half true. I glanced down at my watch – it was late enough. I said my goodbyes and, as I was leaving, I realised I hadn't paid so grabbed the maître d'. As I was putting my purse away, somebody placed a hand on my arm. Antonella.

'Don't get involved with Adrian, I'm warning you,' she snapped, before turning on her heels and walking back towards the table.

'What are you talking about?' I managed to blurt out, but it was lost in the busy chatter of the restaurant.

I travelled home, relieved to have got the night over with. I was also trying to work out why I'd found Antonella's warning so irritating. Not that it was any of her business, I knew I didn't want to start a new relationship; I had promised myself Ned and work were the only important factors in my life for the time being.

At college she was intimidating; she even had a couple of henchwomen who accompanied her everywhere, like she was some kind of D-list celebrity. Occasionally I'd accidentally catch their eye and they'd stare back accusingly. As a result I wouldn't have dreamt of going anywhere near Adrian.

Around lunchtime the next day I got a text from him. *Hello Alex, lovely to see you last night. I'm sorry we didn't get a chance to talk... I didn't realise you'd left! It all got a bit messy – somebody decided it'd be a good idea to order brandy! What are you up to over the next few days? Got any time free... maybe we could have lunch?*

I had to go into town to see a client briefly and I put off replying to him until I got back. What could I say? I didn't want to jump to conclusions. Perhaps it was work-related and if I didn't reply he'd think I was rude.

On the train home from Victoria, I sent him a quick text, trying to sound as laid back as possible. Fuck Antonella. *Hey, Adrian, sounds like I had a lucky escape! Where are we today... Thursday? How about tomorrow lunchtime if that's not too soon? South Bank? Or next week?*

An hour or so later he replied. *How about meeting at the BFI bar tomorrow lunchtime – the one that spills out onto the riverside, under Waterloo Bridge?*

CHAPTER 12

Friday morning; reading half hour with Ned in the classroom. It was always so sweet and special and it helped me to take my mind off meeting Adrian later. I remembered with a slight lurch of unease that I'd done exactly the same before meeting Mal.

I arrived at the BFI bar before Adrian, ordered a glass of sparkling water and found a table outside. This stretch was always busy, with the usual booksellers' tables taking up most of the space on the pavement under the bridge.

I spotted him first, scanning the tables for me. He was dressed well, in a grey linen suit with a dark shirt underneath. It was a look I liked, though realised it was very different from the way either Mal or Paul or Nate would dress. Their tastes were similar, I realised – Ted Baker, Paul Smith, All Saints. Adrian was a different type of man. He came from a privileged background and had been successful as a painter, and that somehow translated to the way he dressed, consciously or not.

I stood up and waved as he spotted me. We kissed on both cheeks and sat down.

'Let me get you a drink,' I said.

'What are you having? Just water?'

'Yes, for the moment anyway. What do you fancy?'

'I'll have the same, please. I've booked a table at Tate Modern for 2 pm – I hope that's okay with you?'

'Sounds great, thank you. I'll just be a minute.'

When I returned from the bar, we soon began catching up on the last twenty years or so. I asked about his work, and he showed me his website on my phone. He was proud of the fact he had an ancient Nokia. I was really impressed with his painting; beautiful, graphic landscapes, some were quite realistic, others more abstract. I asked him how he went about selling them, and he told me he had an agent and mainly sold pieces through him. He'd had numerous solo and group exhibitions, and he now also had a few loyal patrons who regularly commissioned him.

As we left the BFI, I realised we'd been talking about Adrian the whole time; he hadn't asked about me at all. That was fine, I suppose. I guess he saw my work as quite commercial, without the artistry or creativity of his. He had no idea how hard I worked, and how difficult it was to get clients. Antonella, his ex-wife, was a fine art photographer, a completely different ball game. Though it felt a bit intrusive, stalker-like even, I'd looked up her work after the night of the reunion. All studio shots of flowers and cabbage leaves and shells, not a million miles from what she'd done at college. Still, with a rich man to support her, I guess she could churn out pretty photos, sell the odd one and convince herself she was an artist. I realised I was being ultra-cynical.

'So how are your daughters? Have they come out of your separation intact? It must have been tough on them.'

'They seem to be doing fine; they're very close to

Antonella, always were. I suppose I was away a lot when they were little. It seemed very natural to them when I moved out.'

'And how about Antonella? I didn't get a chance to talk to her at the restaurant the other night.' Almost true. 'She still looks amazing.'

Adrian snorted. 'Yes, she's got good genes. And the perfect bone structure that all Italians seem to inherit.'

I laughed. 'Yes, she does, I always found her very intimidating at college, I have to admit.'

He looked at me as we walked along by the river, under an avenue of young plane trees.

'Really? I find that quite hard to imagine. You were pretty intimidating at college too, I think.'

'I was always pale and I wore a lot of black eyeliner. I never thought of myself as a goth but I guess that's probably how I appeared to most people.'

'No, I don't think so. You just looked very individualistic. Maybe a bit serious. You were the best photographer in your year. And you worked hard, you were quiet, a bit shy, quite enigmatic I think.'

'Blimey, really?' I stopped myself adding *and look where I am now. A jobbing photographer, all my high ideals dead and buried.*

We'd reached Tate Modern and were walking down the ramp of the Turbine Hall. The entrance near the lifts was busy and as we waited to get through, I turned to Adrian.

'So what happened with you and Antonella?' I blushed and after a moment turned my gaze to the slowly-changing numbers illuminating above the lift, realising it was a question he might not want to answer.

'We both strayed. I know it's sad and regrettable but I think we wouldn't have stayed together as long as we did without having done so. We were very discreet and we both silently acknowledged that we'd come to an agreement, without us uttering a word. But for me anyway I felt like I was living a lie.'

We gave up on waiting for the lift and started walking up the large oak staircase. A couple of times Adrian said hello to people, Tate staff, a man at least ten years younger than us who didn't have an orange Tate lanyard round his neck. I asked him who it was. 'Oh, Jay Agnew, do you know him? He's an installation artist, mainly outdoors. Wonderful work.'

My installation art knowledge was quite limited. 'Gosh, I don't think so. I might recognise his work if I saw it. I'll look him up.'

'Yes, he's a rising star. Nice chap as well.'

I made a mental note to myself. Mal wouldn't ever use the word 'chap.' I tried to banish any thoughts of him. We continued walking up the stairs and to break the silence I asked another question.

'Why did you finally decide your marriage was over?' I paused, stopped walking and looked at him. 'Sorry, I'm asking too many questions.'

'Not at all. It was me who wanted us to separate and though she'd never brought up the subject, I think she was as unhappy as I was.'

'What finally brought it to a head, with Antonella?'

'Oh, I don't know. There wasn't one specific incident. I just realised I was constantly finding ways to avoid her. You know, going for a cycle ride at 10pm, knowing that by the time I was back and showered she would be in bed asleep. And so as not to wake her, I'd sleep in the spare room. It was very gradual. But when you stop sharing a bed with some-one, stop hearing their breathing, forget what their skin smells like, how it feels. When you have no idea what they're reading or what they dreamt about... I think it's quite easy to withdraw. And you miss that, you realise it's happening and that you set it all in motion in the first place, but you don't want them enough to reverse the process. And before you know it, you slip out of love with them completely.'

'I get that. It happened with Sean too.'

'That's your son's father?'

'Yes. I met him a few years after we left college. He was seriously depressed, still is actually. But I fell in love with him and we'd been together so long, I couldn't imagine finishing it. I look back and just wish I'd been brave enough to get rid of him earlier. But, like a lot of female friends, I just didn't have the courage to go it alone. I'd always wanted to have children and I'd got to my early thirties... thinking about finding someone new that I liked enough at that age, and stay together for long enough to want to have a baby with them. I don't know, if internet dating had been around then... I mean it was, but it wasn't the norm like it is now. Perhaps I would have cut my losses and tried to find someone new.'

'You didn't meet anyone in the meantime? Neither of you had an affair?'

'No, not as far as I know; I didn't anyway. But Ned was only about two when I caught Sean on the phone trying to organise a date with a stylist who I'd worked with a few times. She was completely innocent, I didn't blame her at all. But I just thought, okay, that's enough, I've put up with all his shit all this time, his inertia, his irritability, his misanthropy. He didn't work the whole time we were together. That was the moment I thought... I'm done, enough's enough. We never slept together after that, and though it took a year to get him out of the house, my mind was made up.'

'Gosh, good for you. It must have been difficult, starting again. How long ago was that?'

'Well, Ned was only about 18 months, he's nearly five now, so three and a half years ago, give or take. I've never looked back though. It's been really tough. But one of the main factors was thinking what would be best for Ned. I realised, in the months before we separated, that he had become quite withdrawn, wanted to stay at home rather than go out and see other children. I'd read a lot when I was pregnant about how depression can be inherited, genetically but also through learned behaviour, and I could see it happening before my eyes. I just couldn't do that to Ned. And almost overnight, when Sean finally left, Ned's mood lifted, he became more outgoing and laughed more. I've got millions of photos of him around that age, with big cheesy grins, head cocked to one side. You can see he's happy and relaxed. And I knew I'd made the right choice.'

We'd reached the restaurant on the sixth floor, and were shown to our table by a neat, suited French maître d'. The whole room had an almost overwhelming smell of fish that momentarily made me feel queasy.

'Gosh, you must have friends in high places... this is the best table in the whole place.'

'Well, let's just say I can namedrop if I need to. The art world is an incestuous one.' He turned to the waitress as she swept past. 'Excuse me, can we have a couple of... gin and tonics?' He looked at me to check that was okay. I nodded.

'That'd be lovely.'

'And what about you – has there been anyone special since?' Adrian asked.

'Well, I've done a bit of online dating. It's a bit embarrassing to admit but on the whole it's been fun. I've kissed a few frogs. But special... well, yes, one man, quite recently, I thought he was. But he ended up going back to his girlfriend, and that was that.'

'Oh, that sounds quite painful. Were you together for quite a while?'

'That's the strange thing – not long at all. But we just kind of...' My voice wavered in my throat. I stared at the salt and pepper pots on the table. 'We just seemed to understand each other.' I looked up at him, with what I imagined was a rueful half-smile.

A different waitress came back to take our order. She was Eastern European, though my knowledge of different accents was too limited to work out where from. Not Polish, I didn't think. Maybe she was Estonian or Latvian. She was beautiful in an elfin way, very cropped blonde hair and pale blue eyes. While Adrian asked about how the steak was cooked and pondered over the wine list, it gave me a few moments to think about where the conversation was going.

I looked down to the river; it was very high, muddy, choppy. I'd never noticed many seagulls on the Thames before, but it looked like they'd moved into Bankside, big time. They circled and swooped, flirting with the crows that perched in the silver birches outside the gallery. I couldn't bear the sound of seagulls, but even without the floor to ceiling glass window, the chatter of diners would have resolutely drowned them out. On the wide pavement next to the water a man was making huge bubbles between two lengths of string. It was such a pointless exercise, I'd always thought, when I'd seen him on this stretch before.

The waitress and Adrian were both staring at me.

'Sorry, I was miles away.' I glanced down at the menu

and chose the first thing I spotted with a 'V' for vegetarian at the end.

After the waitress took our order, and the gin and tonic began to give me some courage, I blurted out my next direct question for Adrian.

'So, why have you asked me to lunch?' I looked at him, straight in the eye, aware that his facial expression might answer me better than anything he said. 'I mean, it's not like we've stayed in touch all this time. We don't really have any mutual friends. I'm sure our lives are very different.'

He looked puzzled, and then slightly embarrassed, and his gaze shifted from me to the salt and pepper.

'Alexandra, I suppose I always held a torch for you. You were a bit of an enigma, as I said earlier, and I've always found mysterious women very attractive. But Antonella was very forceful and to be honest I kind of stumbled into a relationship with her. I know it sounds very weak-willed, but it was almost like I had no say in the matter.'

'I suppose my question is... why now? What's changed?'

'Well, I'm single. Properly single. But I'm only forty-five, and I don't want to spend the next forty years on my own, or be a serial monogamist. I want to be with someone significant.'

'Earlier you mentioned there'd been affairs... have any of those women been important to you?'

He reddened slightly. 'I suppose I thought so at the time. But looking back they were more just a means to escape my marriage, albeit temporarily.'

We were interrupted briefly by the waitress pouring the wine.

'And you think you might be able to have something significant with me? I mean, maybe, but we don't really know each other very well, do we?'

'No, of course not, but I know, from what I remember of you from twenty years ago, and what I've seen already today, that you're the kind of woman who I can imagine being with.' He sat back in his chair. This time it was him gauging my reaction.

His gaze was too much. I looked down to the river again. A tourist boat moved diagonally over to Blackfriars pier on the north bank.

'I don't know what to say, Adrian. I think I just need a bit of time to think. As I said, it's not long ago that I broke up with someone and I'm still a bit emotionally bruised from that. It's probably not wise to jump into something new straight away.'

Adrian kept looking at me intently. I smiled back at him. I was trying to remember what he'd looked like when he was twenty-one. Now his hair was grey, his skin a little ruddy. I guessed he probably drank too much – most men his age did, all those I knew anyway. I knew I had a few photographs of him somewhere, in a big box of photos I'd kept from school and college. I should look for them.. Would I find seeing pictures of him from over twenty years ago a bit depressing?

Our food arrived and I took the opportunity to change the subject. I asked him about his daughters, Isabella and Giuliana. He told me they were eleven and eight, both quite musical and artistic and I got the impression they were bright girls. In his wallet he had a few photographs of them; performing on stage at school, skiing in the Italian alps at Christmas, some with their mother. They both looked like her, though Isabella, Issy, the younger of the two, was much fairer than her mum or sister. I showed Adrian a few photos of Ned too.

I was quite relieved the conversation had moved on. He

didn't press me further. But even as we talked about other things, I was mentally making a pros and cons lists about him in my head. He was the kind of man I should be with – solid, reliable, a family man. Arguably, Mal wasn't. Adrian was safe, gentlemanly. I liked the fact he'd ordered wine without asking me what I wanted. He was a bit old-fashioned. He dressed nicely; not trendily, but expensively. I think he knew what suited him. He seemed comfortable in his own skin. His daughters weren't that much older than Ned. Perhaps if we were together it'd work because of that. And he was rich. I'm not proud of that being a factor. He wasn't interested in music other than classical which left me cold on the whole. My mother was a diehard classical music fan and had always berated me because of my non-appreciation of it.

I'd warmed to Adrian during lunch, partly helped by the white wine. Alcohol affected me much more during the day, but this was a special occasion. We had coffee before we left, and I hoped its effect would in part counteract the Albariño.

We walked eastwards along the south bank towards London Bridge station. Adrian was going into town to pick up some books he'd ordered. I was going home to get on with some retouching on the ceramics shots. I was going to need more caffeine.

By the ticket barriers for the Jubilee Line, Adrian took my hand and pulled me towards him. We held each other for what seemed a long time. I breathed in his smell; skin, fresh cotton, wine, coffee, L'Eau d'Issey. His linen jacket felt rough against my cheek, he had the beginnings of five-o'clock shadow. His shoulders felt solid and substantial and I liked the way my body felt small and delicate in comparison. His arms enveloped my waist, his huge hands felt weighty as they rested in the small of my back.

I turned my face towards his and kissed him on the cheek.

'Thank you for a lovely afternoon,' I said.

His hands moved up my body and he held my face, kissing me softly on the lips. 'Thank you, Alexandra, it's been lovely to see you. Think about what I've said.'

CHAPTER 13

It was May; the light had begun to seep into early evenings, so that by eight, dusk was only just beginning. Ned was tired after a day spent shopping, his school shoes looked like he'd been rock climbing in them. Despite his protests, a trip into town to get a new pair was necessary. To balance out the shopping, I agreed to take him up to the park when we got back. An hour running around wore him out completely and he was bathed and ready for bed before eight.

Over the last few months, evenings had mainly been spent at home with Ned. I was sticking to my decision not to meet anyone new. I was still sickened by the memory of him having to wake me up on the sofa that Saturday morning.

Yet, as spring turned to summer, the prospect of months of long, warm evenings stretching out in front of me without another adult to share them, was depressing.

Over the last week, Adrian and I had been exchanging long emails. He'd been in Paris with his agent and they were due to travel back earlier that afternoon; he was going back to his cottage in Wiltshire. We'd discussed art, architecture, music. He told me he'd sold his pop record collection for a pound when we were at college, having decided classical music was the way forward.

We both talked about our past relationships. Adrian talked a little more about Antonella and I couldn't decide whether I pitied her or envied her. Without explicitly saying it, his successful career as a painter had afforded her a very comfortable lifestyle. She'd given birth to the two girls at home, a doula on hand for a month afterwards, and then a succession of nannies had been in place once Giuliana reached six months. According to Adrian, Antonella always had one or two projects ongoing. I didn't mention to him that I'd had a look at her website and that, on the whole, her work was self-indulgent crap.

I'd been fairly non-committal with Adrian, but as we'd opened up to each other I'd begun to lower my guard and not completely rule out the possibility of something happening. After Ned went to bed I sat on the two steps that led from the lounge down to the kitchen, the light gradually fading as an inky blue cast descended. I had a glass of red on the go and at some point Marmaduke, my ginger male cat, came to sit with me. As I stared into space, the phone rang, making me jump several feet in the air. A landline number with an area code I didn't recognise.

'Hello.'

'Hello Alex, it's Adrian.'

'Oh, gosh, hello. How are you?'

Why had I suddenly started using the word 'gosh'?

'I just thought, when you said 'call any time'... well, I just thought I'd take the bull by the horns.'

'I'm glad you did.'

We chatted for a couple of hours and I soon began to relax, just as I had when we'd met on the south bank. For the first time we talked about our upbringings. I'd always been under the impression he came from a very wealthy background but I was wrong, like me his childhood had been very modest, living on a council estate with his mum and siblings and very little money. From his voice I would never have known it. All those years ago at art school he'd been well-spoken, and I'd always assumed he was one of the trustafarians that made up at least half the alumni. No, he was a normal kid from Swindon.

I told him, hesitating beforehand, that I was taking Ned to stay with his dad for the remainder of the bank holiday weekend, and that I'd be free to meet up if he was. We agreed to meet on the Sunday morning – he would come to mine for breakfast, and I'd suggested we could go and see a few exhibitions.

Sunday morning. I got up early and had a run. The weather had turned warm and for the first time that year I arrived home covered in a sheen of sweat. I showered quickly, made coffee, shortlisted three summer dresses, draping them on the bed so I could ponder them. I opted for a figure-hugging white and black geometric patterned dress, mainly because I had some wedges that went well with it and I couldn't think of a good footwear match for the other two.

I sat in hair rollers drinking coffee, reading emails and having a quick look on Facebook. A text from Adrian appeared on my phone screen. *We've just had a monumental downpour on the A303 – I'll be arriving in south-east London wearing water-proof trousers and wellies!*

In contrast, Gipsy Hill was bright and warm. I got dressed, put on make-up and finished my hair before walking along to the shops to buy croissants, fruit and yogurt. I was pleased with my choice of outfit – the dress was just right but I wished I'd had the foresight to put on some fake tan. My legs were milky white after months of winter.

I got home and set the table in the garden for breakfast. My stomach lurched, as I imagined Adrian driving ever closer. Inviting him round for breakfast probably, seemed like I was giving him the green light. I had tried to banish the niggling questions from my thoughts – why was I doing this when I'd agreed not to get involved with anyone? And did I fancy him as much as I had Mal? That was the benchmark.

I couldn't think like that; Mal had dumped me after all. Adrian was a good man, I was sure of it. He was a father, he had an amazing career, he seemed to be very sorted. He would be good for me. When the doorbell rang I took a few deep breaths; this was going to be one of those life-changing moments. Perhaps.

We didn't make it to the exhibitions. We didn't even manage to eat breakfast. When he arrived I made coffee and Adrian spotted my vinyl collection, sat down on the floor and started leafing through my LPs.

I sat down to join him with a brimming cafetière and cups. A pile on the floor was growing; albums he either owned, or had liked and never bought. It included the Pixies' *Surfer Rosa* and The House of Love's debut album, New Order's *Technique* and The Stone Roses début, all released within the first couple of years after selling his collection in the second year of art college.

I poured the coffee and enthused about the music, recalling some of the gigs I'd been to in intimate venues.

Bands who would, only a few years later, be selling out stadium tours.

'I can't remember if you came to any of our infamous house parties, did you? Rob, a guy on our course, was always the DJ. I remember vividly him playing the twelve-inch of *Fools Gold*, the first time I'd heard it. The whole house shook with the bass pumping out of Rob's huge speakers. I think it was the same party where the police were called... some of the lads had lifted up a camper van and blocked the road with it. Hilarious.'

Adrian didn't answer. He took my coffee cup and placed it gently on the floor, leant over and kissed me. I wasn't expecting it at all, and I hated myself for enjoying the feeling of being small and delicate again, succumbing to his greater physical strength as he pushed me down onto the thick rug on the lounge floor.

We kissed urgently as he loosened the tie at the back of my dress and lifted it over my head. I undid his belt and the buttons on his trousers; he was wearing boxer shorts and the thin cotton strained under his hard-on. He pulled my knickers down and they landed in a twisted knot inches from my face.

In a split second he was inside me. He gripped my wrists above my head with one hand, and with the other he pulled a bra strap down. He sucked my nipple for a second before returning his mouth to mine. His thrusts were urgent and fast and brutal, and I don't think I'm exaggerating when I say within thirty seconds he'd come.

He collapsed on the rug beside me, his face and neck red, little beads of sweat forming on his temples.

'Sorry Alex, I'm a little rusty.' He sighed heavily and turned towards me, elbow bent, resting his head on his hand.

I was lost for words. Without having to think too hard I knew this was the least egalitarian sex I'd ever had, even more so than the episode in the women's loos with Neil. No expectation from Adrian that I would want to participate. No expectation that I might want to orgasm. And, I observed, feeling more angry at myself than him for letting it happen, not even a fleeting notion that perhaps we should have used a condom.

'Don't worry, it's fine,' I said, as I sat up and untangled my knickers.

He reached up. His hand felt warm and weighty on my shoulder.

'Please, come here,' he whispered.

I turned to look at him, his expression full of hurt and trepidation, his sea-green eyes glassy with tears. It was impossible to reconcile this vulnerable middle-aged man with the arrogant student I'd known, who swaggered around the college acting like he owned the place. I couldn't help thinking that his arrogance had just been displayed in a very different way.

I rested my head on his chest, and he wrapped his arm around me. Despite what had just happened there was something about him that felt more solid than all the other men I'd met recently. Perhaps it was simply because we'd known each other for a long time; he hadn't appeared in the ether, with the distinct likelihood of disappearing into it just as quickly.

CHAPTER 14

The week's shoot had gone according to plan. Though I should have really started work on the image files, I'd spoken to Adrian the night before and he'd asked if I was free the following lunchtime, so I mainly spent the morning getting ready.

It didn't matter how many times I went to west London, it always seemed foreign to me. As it did when I emerged from Notting Hill tube station. I had a vague idea where Adrian lived and that I needed to walk up towards Portobello Road. I found a florist and bought some peonies, and a fancy wine shop where I picked out an expensive Chablis. Expensive for me. Adrian had already told me about his wine collection, so I could hardly have turned up with a bottle of Echo Falls.

I meandered for a while, not wanting to arrive at Adrian's early. I had thirty minutes to kill. It was a million miles away from our local shops; we had a greasy spoon in place of the plentiful chi-chi cafés, but, as I took in the boutiques and artisan butchers and yoga studios, I could imagine getting very used to the new surroundings. I had to stop daydreaming. I was getting ahead of myself; imagining moving with Ned to live with Adrian. I knew how dangerous that could be. We'd only met a couple of times.

I lost track of time in Rough Trade and I was a few minutes late as I turned into Adrian's road. The house numbers decreased in inverse proportion to my heart rate. I was nervous; I was on his territory. The bravado I'd felt earlier had all but left me and I felt completely out of my depth.

His house was almost exactly as I'd imagined it – a large, imposing stuccoed villa. It was huge compared to my house. Ned's eyes would be on stalks if he ever saw it.

Adrian and I kissed on the doorstep. He led me down to the kitchen on the lower ground floor. The walls were covered with paintings and I recognized his style in around half of the ones displayed. Some others were female nudes – beautiful, young girls. His website had only shown land-scapes, as far as I could remember. I felt an involuntary flinch of jealousy as my eyes surveyed their nubile flesh.

I was expecting the interior to be a combination of tradi-tional and contemporary, but it was resolutely modern. Not a reproduction Chesterfield in sight.

'Let's go outside, Alex, I want to show you this house's pièce de resistance.' He took my hand and walked me through the garden, up a few steps to a gate, and into an enormous communal garden. Huge horse chestnut trees dominated the space, just in leaf in mid-May. their creamy-white blossom had been blown off by the wind and were photogenically piled against the edges of footpaths and flower beds.

'This is incredible, like a secret garden,' I said, taking it all in. Adrian reached up to pull off a sprig from a lilac tree and passed it to me. The heady scent transported me back twenty years. I hadn't smelt it since my Nanna had died. My grandparents had a lilac tree in their garden, it had been her favourite scent.

'I've only come in here a handful of times. I moved here six months ago, and the weather so far has been pretty appalling. But I'd quite like to get a dog; the girls have been badgering me about it since I moved out. Antonella's allergic to them. But this is a perfect spot for a quick walk with a pooch, early morning or last thing before bed.' He looked at me as though waiting for me to tell him what a great idea it was.

We walked back to the house. Adrian had already laid the garden table for lunch and there were three or four large bowls of salad covered with cloths.

'Help yourself, I'll get the champagne.'

I took off the cloths covering the food and was relieved he'd remembered I was vegetarian. He'd made some Ottolenghi salads – I recognized the combination of ingredients. Red rice with orange and pistachio, chargrilled broccoli with chilli and a sprinkling of flaked almonds. I was impressed, and when Adrian came back out to the garden, told him so.

'Oh, you know, I just threw some ingredients together,' he replied, looking bashful.

Adrian asked me about my work. He'd looked at my website and seemed to have remembered quite a lot about some of my recent projects. I was glad. I didn't want him to think I just did a bit of photography on the side, like a hobby. I was the only breadwinner, always had been. My work wasn't art, like his was, but it paid the mortgage.

The champagne had taken hold and, at one point, Adrian had moved round the table to sit next to me. We started kissing. It felt good, but I knew where this might lead and I was worried about the time.

He leaned into me and whispered into my ear. The vibrations of his voice against my skin gave me goosebumps. 'Come upstairs.'

He took my hand and led me up to his bedroom. The bed was huge, with an ornate wooden headboard and abundant pillows and cushions arranged too artfully for a middle-aged, straight man to have done himself. I wondered if his cleaner had been working earlier, or whether he had a part-time housekeeper. It wouldn't surprise me.

I was determined not to have a repeat performance from the morning at mine; I took control. Slowly but purposefully I undressed him and ushered him to sit on the bed. I started to suck him, resisting his attempts to touch or kiss me by pushing him away. He moaned; little deep, throaty bursts of pleasure. Eventually I sat astride him, bending down to kiss him as I moved rhythmically, toying with him, just the end of his cock inside. One, two, three, four, and then I thrust the full length of him inside me and quickened the pace until he was gasping and almost crying.

'Wow,' he said afterwards. 'That was...'

I raised an eyebrow.

'Payback for Sunday?'

I needed to get home. I resisted his attempts to keep me there by suggesting he took me shopping or that we went to the Serpentine Gallery. In the back of my mind, I remembered what he'd said about being an enigma; I needed to keep him keen.

He adopted a comedy grump when he realised none of his tactics were working. He was still in bed, propped up on a mountain of pillows. He was in good shape. So far I'd only seen him wear loose shirts, never anything that really showed his physique, but his shoulders were broad and strong, his arms well defined and he had a light tan that enhanced it all. I leaned over and kissed him.

I skipped down the stairs and picked up my bag from the kitchen. Adrian had brought the bottle of champagne in from the garden. I put it in the fridge so he could enjoy a chilled glass of it later. There was a large paper bag from Ottolenghi on the middle shelf. Peering inside I saw four or five almost empty food cartons. Sweet, I thought, trying to impress me with his prowess in the kitchen, but not wanting to mess up.

Later, when Adrian called, he said he'd like me to meet his daughters, and for him to meet Ned. His brother was coming down to stay with him from Manchester with his wife and kids at the weekend.

'It's a bit early though, isn't it? I don't want them to feel awkward.'

'No, not at all, they'll be fine. And with Peter there, and their cousins, I think it'll be a really natural way for you to meet them. I can just introduce you as my friend, and gradually over time, I'm sure it'll dawn on them that you're more than that.'

His brother's family arrived on the Friday evening and we arranged to meet at the Museum of Childhood the following morning. Earlier in the week I'd agreed to look after the other Ned for Nicole – she dropped him off at nine – we were meeting Adrian at eleven so I decided to leave straight away.

I texted Adrian to let him know we were in the park next to the museum. He replied to say they were on their way and he was picking the girls up from his ex-wife's. I wondered whether he'd said anything to Antonella about me since the reunion. I was pretty sure he hadn't seen her talk to me at the end of the night.

The boys had been running around and were hungry. I'd come armed with snacks, enough for lunch if the boys didn't like the look of the museum café food. My Ned was extremely picky, the other Ned less so. They were finishing off carrot sticks and humous when in the corner of my eye I caught a group of people approaching; Adrian and his family.

I waved and called to the boys to come back – having refuelled they were ready for more running around. Good to get some of their excess energy used up before the museum, I thought.

Adrian and his brother Peter didn't look at all alike. Peter was shorter, a bit stockier. Most interesting of all was that he still had quite a strong West country accent from growing up in Swindon. Adrian didn't have it at all. Peter was an art teacher in Hale on the outskirts of Manchester and his wife, Lucy, worked for an arts charity in the city, organising workshops for underprivileged kids and their families. They were both very welcoming; nice and friendly and completely normal. I couldn't work out if Adrian had told them about our burgeoning relationship. Perhaps he was keeping that under wraps.

Adrian introduced his daughters to me. I said 'hi' in as relaxed a way as I could. They smiled briefly, looking slightly embarrassed and shy. Peter and Lucy's youngest, a boy called Max who was a little younger than Ned, spotted the older boys making a hole in the mud of a flowerbed with a stick and ran over to them to join in. The girls followed; Adrian's two and Peter and Lucy's oldest, Maddy, who looked about twelve.

We made small-talk. It turned out Peter and Lucy had met at the same art college that Adrian and I had been to, only four years ahead of us. We chatted about our time there. We got onto the subject of halls of residence, and Lucy and I worked out we'd had exactly the same room, four years apart.

The museum was busy. We soon got separated as the girls were interested in seeing the dolls' houses and the collection of childhood objects. The boys made a beeline for the cars and Lego. Max wanted to stay with the other boys, so Lucy came with me. We found it easy to chat. It became apparent that Adrian had told her and Peter about me, but I kept the conversation away from Adrian, and asked about their lives, and she mine. It struck me how different her and Peter were from Adrian and Antonella, as couples, as people.

We had lunch at an Italian on the main road. Adrian skillfully managed to sit us next to each other, with all the kids at the other end of the table. Within a minute of us sitting down, he put his hand on my knee, gradually moving it up to rest between my legs, but showed no outward sign of affection which was just as well as his elder daughter, Giuliana, kept looking over at me with an expression of curiosity if not outright suspicion. She wasn't anything like I expected her to be. Antonella was stunning, even at forty-five; her Italian genes serving her well. She still had the same air of nobility and privilege that she'd had in her late teens at art college. But Giuliana hadn't inherited her mum's good looks. Similarly, her face was long and almond-shaped, with high cheekbones and a slim nose. In Antonella, they were framed by a mane of dark red hair and Sophia Loren lips that were naturally the shade of dark pink that looked like she'd just eaten a bowl of raspberries.

Giuliana had mousey brown hair, too frizzy to do anything with, her chin too small, and with what seemed to be an almost permanent frown.

Isabella, or Issy for short, was altogether different. She was younger by a couple of years. Her face was softer, rounder, her hair darker and almost completely straight. Her personality seemed, after this one meeting, to be lighter too; she was completely absorbed in the game of Wink, Wink, Murder that the kids were noisily playing at the other end, and couldn't have been less interested in me.

After lunch we said goodbye, Adrian kissing me on both cheeks in a way that didn't arouse any suspicion from his daughters or anyone else. It might have been different had they known he'd had his fingers in my knickers for the last ten minutes as we finished our coffee and he'd paid the bill, one-handed. Ned, rather bizarrely, threw his arms around Adrian's legs, just above the knee.

'I love you, Adrian,' he declared, which made everyone laugh, apart from me and Giuliana, who immediately scowled and looked in my direction. I couldn't think of anything I'd said to Ned earlier that might have resulted in him telling Adrian that he loved him. I'd just told him to behave and be nice and polite and not fart.

I didn't talk to Adrian that evening. We just exchanged a few short texts and I apologised for Ned's display of affection. He said he thought it was funny and that there was no need to apologise. He'd invited his aunt and uncle over for dinner; it had been a while since they'd seen Peter and his family so he was glad to be able to get everyone together. He'd signed off – *Such a shame you're not here too… next time…*

The next morning I saw Adrian had called when I'd been in the shower, leaving a long voicemail message. He'd taken the girls home after dinner and they'd immediately told Antonella that they'd met 'Daddy's new friend, Alex'. Antonella put two and two together and rang him, telling him under no circumstances was he to meet me when he was with Giuliana and Issy. It was far too soon after their break-up and, whether he did or didn't become involved with someone else, their daughters were to be left out of it.

I kind of agreed with Antonella. It was too soon. I hadn't really got my head round how I felt about him. Maybe in a week's time I'd decide that actually I'd enjoyed being single over the last few months and that it was better for Ned too if I stayed that way.

CHAPTER 15

Three missed calls from Caroline. Two texts. We were going to be late. I'd picked up Ned as soon as school finished and we'd set off in the car. The Friday afternoon traffic was horrendous. As we neared Elephant and Castle I remembered I hadn't picked up the prints from the specialist film processors in Bermondsey that I'd promised to take up to Cambridge with us. Instead of crossing Tower Bridge I had to veer off east along the Old Kent Road and negotiate back streets of industrial estates, clogged with white vans making deliveries. It took an hour to cross Tower Bridge and another hour to get to the M11.

We made up some time on the motorway and rush hour had subsided by the time we reached Cambridge. Ned watched *Up* for the dozenth time on the iPad, and fell asleep at some point. I was grateful he woke in a good mood.

I lifted Ned up so he could reach Caroline's doorbell, and she buzzed us in. We hugged, as always I was immediately enveloped in her scent. I'd always been completely promiscuous when it comes to perfumes but she had worn the same one – something sweet and floral – for as long as I'd known her. She couldn't possibly change it now.

I apologised for being late as I left our bags in her spare room, and she opened the bottle of wine I'd picked up at the shop nearby.

As we sipped the wine, we leant against the oven, gleaning a little bit of extra warmth. It continued to be rainy, miserable and cold for June. As Ned tipped up the plastic box and started playing with the Lego we'd brought, Caroline asked how he was doing at school, how I was coping, and how work was going. I told her everything was great.

'Are you sure? You've had a lot to deal with... I'm worried about you,' she said, tilting her head in concern. I had wondered before if she was hoping for me to tell her my life was a complete disaster so that she would feel needed, have a role to play. Perhaps there was a tiny element of Schadenfreude too, though I felt mean thinking it.

'Honestly, I'm absolutely fine, never been better.'

'You didn't ever hear back from that chap... Mark?'

'Mal? No, that's all over, he went back to his girlfriend. It's a shame, I really liked him, but it was his decision. I just had to move on.'

'Oh, gosh, Sandy, I'm sorry, I thought he sounded really promising. I thought there was a chance he might get back in touch.'

Ned called me over to look at the tower he'd built and I rushed over to look at it before it toppled over. I was glad also to escape having to talk about Mal, and also was reluctant to tell her about Adrian. The session at my computer a few months earlier had been uncomfortable and I didn't want to do it again.

Caroline had set the small table in the kitchen rather than the larger one in the lounge. With a lurch of guilt I recalled that, two visits ago, Ned had dropped tomato sauce in the middle of her lounge carpet. Caroline's flat was always clean and tidy. I wondered whether she'd have become more chilled if she'd had children.

As we ate I asked Caroline about her family. I first met her parents when we were at college together and they seemed to have such a perfect marriage. Caroline's happy, normal upbringing had been in such contrast to my own, I'd always been very sketchy about mine. Her father had died a couple of years earlier, losing his footing on a gravel path when Caroline, one of her sisters and him had taken a short walking holiday in the Peak District. The trip had been six months or so after her parents had divorced and, ever since, Caroline had become reluctant to talk about her dad. She was very close to her sisters, though they were at least seven or eight years older than Caroline, and had children already at university. Photos of her nieces and nephews were dotted all around the flat, but I suspected these visual reminders only made the fact of her own childlessness more acute.

'And how's your new job?' I asked her, very happy to keep the conversation steered away from my love life.

'Oh, you know, it's okay. Not very exciting really. I spend a lot of time commissioning other photographers and all I'm doing really is managing them and cataloguing all the shots on the library website. It's not what I thought I'd be doing 20 years after graduating.'

Ned got down from the table and nagged me to put the TV on. I agreed he could watch one episode of In The Night Garden or Octonauts but then it would be bedtime. I helped clear away the dishes and ran a bath for him.

While Ned cleaned his teeth, I got his pyjamas out of my bag and noticed the photos I'd picked up earlier. I hadn't looked at them at all. They were from Caroline's birthday party at her parents' house. They'd been taken a year or so before her dad had died, so it must have been shortly before her parents had announced they were divorcing, five years ago at least. At the time I'd clung resolutely onto using film but, along with everyone else, had finally given into digital photography as film processing costs went through the roof. The roll I shot at the party had been one of the last.

I grabbed a couple of Ned's story books from my bag and handed the pack of photos to Caroline.

'These are the shots from your birthday party... I only picked them up this afternoon so I haven't looked at them but I hope there are some nice ones of your dad. He was so sweet that day... I was a few weeks' pregnant with Ned. I didn't want to make a fuss and it was too early to tell everyone anyway; I didn't want to raise suspicion because I wasn't drinking, so he found a bottle of alcohol-free bubbly for me.'

'Thank you, I'll have a look at them while you're getting Ned ready for bed.'

Caroline went to bed early, complaining of period pain. The next morning she still felt unwell. Ned and I walked into the centre of Cambridge and did some shopping and on the way back we stopped at a kids' playground. I texted her to see how she was feeling and to ask if there was anything I could pick up for her. I didn't get a reply and assumed she'd fallen asleep. She said she'd been awake half the night with stomach cramps. Instead of going back to her flat we turned round and had lunch in town. A few hours later, when I rang her buzzer, she opened the door for us but she was back in bed by the time we'd walked up the stairs and reached the door of the flat. I said I thought it was best if we went home, expecting her to protest, but she didn't. I packed all our things away and we went to say goodbye to her in her bedroom. It was so unlike her to not want us to stay, but she had always had painful periods, and had finally been diagnosed with endometriosis in her late thirties. Years of menstruation and never a pregnancy; I'm sure she felt the bitter irony of it.

On the way back to London, I had a text from Ingrid. After the football debacle, I hoped she would let things rest for a while, but judging from the text, that looked unlikely. I read it in sections as we stopped at traffic lights along the A12. She accused me of letting Ned get away with everything, that I had no control over him, and at the end, adding that she could see plainly that Ned's behaviour was due to me not paying him enough attention, because I was spending so much time dating... blah, blah, blah. I'd seen for a while that there was a definite parting of the ways beginning between the two boys. Johan was one of Ned's oldest friends, but kids change and make new friends when they start school. I was just accepting it more than Ingrid was. I wrote a reply, in short bursts as we stopped at traffic lights, pointing out that perhaps her and Johan were feeling a little emotional with the arrival of the baby, but deleted it. It would only have made matters worse. If there was any truth in her accusations, I was well on the road to redemption.

CHAPTER 16

In the three months I'd been seeing Adrian, we'd more or less spent the time together, either with Ned at home or out for dinner, seeing an exhibition or going to the cinema. I'd been reluctant for Adrian to meet my friends, and I struggled to acknowledge to myself that I was worried he would look down on them. But, in equal measure, that my friends would think he was a bit posh, even though I knew he wasn't.

My fears on both sides subsided over time, and it seemed sensible to introduce him to my closest friends to start with. I'd been invited round to Nicole's one evening as Ned was having a sleepover there with the other Ned. I asked Nicole if she'd mind if I brought Adrian too. *Of course, darling, I'll enjoy interrogating him... I mean meeting him!* she replied in a text.

I told Adrian that Nicole was picking Ned up from school, and he jumped at the chance of us spending a few hours alone. He arrived around five. The weather had settled into midsummer, and by late afternoon my bedroom at the top of the house was bathed in an orange glow. We had sex; we were still at the stage where it was a given. Afterwards we lay in each other's arms, me resting my head on his chest as we always did.

Adrian had a few calls to make so was going to head over to Nicole's a little later. Perhaps it was just as well he'd miss dinner; though I knew she'd be embarrassed if she knew I'd said it, Nicole was not the world's greatest cook. I glanced at the time on my bedside clock. 'I need to start getting ready to go to Nicole's.'

'Don't go, wait a few minutes.' He looked injured, that puppy dog face he'd perfected. As I rested my head against him again, he whispered into my hair, 'I love you.'

Tears in his eyes, he repeated those three words, a pained expression on his face.

I had no choice but to reply, 'I love you too.'

At Nicole's, we opened a bottle of white wine at the small table in her garden and I soon began to feel tipsy on an empty stomach. Nicole hadn't started cooking. When the boys complained they were getting hungry I offered to make dinner instead, but Nicole begrudgingly went inside to start chopping. It would seem nigh on impossible to make a hash of a simple tomato sauce, but she managed it. To top it off, the spaghetti was undercooked. We all laughed about it, Nicole especially. The boys had hastily-prepared cheese on toast instead.

Adrian arrived around ten when it was almost dark, and we were well into our second bottle, though I'd been carefully drinking plenty of water too. We'd been discussing our last sexual encounters and I'd assumed Nicole would change the subject when he arrived but, if anything, she turned up the dial. Her most recent on-again, off-again fling was with another German she'd met through work. She was a psychotherapist and he a GP, so they had a lot in common. She explained they discussed their sex life, at length, including former partners. Perhaps it was impossible for her not to, given her profession.

Adrian sat back in the garden chair with his arms folded, listening intently and nodding in agreement as she recollected details of their most recent foray into role-playing. He no doubt felt like the outsider; he was meeting Nicole for the first time, and he was stone cold sober. Nicole had drunk considerably more than me and was slurring her words. I could feel Adrian bristle every time she forgot what she was saying mid-sentence.

The boys were still up, though I knew it was well past bedtime. I suggested we leave, mainly because I wanted Ned to have a decent night's sleep; the next day was Saturday so no school but he was still at the age where he could turn into a monster if he was tired.

I didn't need to ask him what he thought about Nicole. She was fun and irreverent, and I enjoyed her company. Adrian was just a bit too starchy to appreciate her. I made a mental note to avoid them meeting again for a while.

The next morning, as Adrian left to go home, he suggested we go away for a few days. 'You choose the time and location, darling, I'll do the rest,' he said as he left.

The school summer holidays were about to start and, for the last month or so, I'd been panicking about how I'd be able to keep Ned occupied over the six weeks. There was a holiday club at one of the larger nurseries not too far away. A couple of his friends from school were going and he seemed to be keen to join them. I wanted to go away with

Ned at some point too but, as usual, work dictated when and if that might happen. If I were to manage a few days away with Adrian, Sean would have to come and stay. I didn't relish asking him.

Italy was always my default holiday destination. I'd fallen in love with the culture and architecture and everything else when I went back-packing after art college. But the uncertainty and upheavals of the last year had left me feeling adrift and I couldn't ignore the yearning I felt to visit Scotland. Somehow, I thought, going back to my roots might help.

There was a glen in the Cairngorms I visited with my dad when I was a kid; he loved salmon fishing and probably would have preferred to have had sons rather than two daughters, so he could share his passion. Every summer holiday we would visit my Scottish granny. I don't remember how it started, but I was nine or ten, and when he asked if I'd like to go fishing with him, I agreed.

There had been a hotel, where at lunchtime my dad would go and have a few pints, me sitting in the car with a Coke and bag of crisps. I Googled the hotel; it was still there. Recently, it said on the website, the area had received European Union money to develop tourism, and the hotel had built a handful of luxury wooden lodges, scattered picturesquely in the woods at the back of the hotel. Each lodge had a sauna and hot tub. Adrian would approve. I sent him the link.

CHAPTER 17

The few days we spent at the lodge in the Cairngorms were the happiest I'd had all year. We did a huge supermarket shop, supplemented by a visit to a cheesemongers in Edinburgh that I'd read about. We picked up a hire car from Waverley station and headed north, over the Forth Bridge into Fife and then over the Tay Bridge into Angus. I knew the area well; my father's family had lived there and I had a surge of nostalgia as the signposts showed towns I'd known as a kid. I scrolled through Spotify to find an album I loved, Everything But The Girl's 'Idlewild'. In *The Night I Heard Caruso Sing*, Ben Watt recalls taking his father to revisit his old haunts. He mentions Montrose, a small seaside town where my granny used to play lawn bowls on Sunday mornings.

Our mornings started with a run along the almost-deserted track further up the glen, then breakfast, sex, ten minutes in the sauna, a long shower, and finally a nap. In the afternoon we explored the area on foot, spotting golden eagles one day, circling high above us. In the evenings we cooked simple dishes and drank wine and talked about our hopes and dreams. Though we didn't vocalise it, I think we both acknowledged that spending a few days together had been exactly what we'd needed. We began to fall properly in love.

On the final night we both got dressed up. I wore a simple shift dress and heels, with a new pair of Wolford tights. Adrian's default was a linen suit, so he was dressing down a little in jeans and a smartish shirt.

Adrian made his favourite dish, his take on carbonara; though he normally added pancetta, he was making a veggie version for my benefit. I found a recipe online for Cranachan, something I'd never done before but I remembered my granny used to make it. I wondered if she'd put aside a non-alcoholic portion for my sister and I, and then remembered she'd advised my mother to put whisky on our gums when we were teething. It felt fitting to choose something traditionally Scottish.

'I can't believe the last few days have gone so quickly,' I said as we finished eating and moved to the sofa with our wine glasses. 'I'm going to miss this place. And spending so much time together.'

We hadn't quite touched on what the future might hold for us, but I could feel it might be on the cards. The last few days had acted like a catalyst; our relationship felt much more solid. I no longer felt reservations, and I could see the positives of being with Adrian far outweighed the negatives.

He studied me; was he thinking the same? I poured us another glass of wine.

'It's been lovely waking up with you every morning. I know it's very early but perhaps we could start to think about how we could live together. I need my studio though. I know I'm being selfish but it would be difficult for me to move in with you. There's not quite enough space.'

'Well, it's a lovely thought; let's not rush into anything. If we moved to west London to live with you, Ned would have to change schools, so it'd be a huge upheaval for us too.'

'Okay, at least we both think it's a possibility. We can see how things progress. I just know I can't think about anything else but you at the moment, and after this week...' He broke off, leaned over and kissed me. 'I really want to fuck you.'

He knelt on the floor to undo the straps at the back of my shoes.

'My God, your legs look fabulous in these tights,' he said.

'Don't you mean my stubby legs?'

I've no idea why I said it. For a few seconds I could have rescued the situation and turned it into a joke, but I didn't. We were both quite drunk, me especially. Perhaps the honesty and the exposed emotions had risen to the surface too quickly. I had absolutely no reason to want to spoil the mood.

He looked up at me, perplexed. 'Alex, what are you talking about?'

'Don't you remember? The Sunday of the Artists' Open House weekend? We were walking from one house to the next. I made some comment about my legs and you said they were stubby.'

'Don't be ridiculous, I said nothing of the sort.'

'You did.'

Yes, I'd brought this up at the worst possible time, but I wasn't going to allow him to deny he'd said it.

'You're wrong Alex, you've imagined it.'

I staggered to my feet and slammed my empty wine glass on the table.

'You were just being a shit, admit it.'

I stormed off to the bathroom, locked the door and burst into tears. I sat on the toilet waiting for him to come and apologise but he didn't. Eventually I stood up and looked in the mirror above the basin; rivulets of white streaked my face where tears had washed away my make-up. I looked like shit. I undressed. I'd been saving my best underwear for the last night, and, if I hadn't fucked it up, Adrian would have been taking it off instead, at this very moment. I dumped it in a heap on the bathroom floor and had a long, hot shower.

I felt stupid as I got into bed next to Adrian. His bedside lamp was out and his eyes were closed, facing away from me. I doubted he was already asleep. After a few minutes he turned round and held me.

'Sorry,' I whispered.

His grip around me tightened for a moment before he kissed my forehead. 'It's okay.'

The next morning we didn't talk about the previous night. It was our first proper argument, brief though it was, and I guessed it was good to have passed that milestone. I felt a niggling unease that he hadn't admitted to saying what I know he did. At the same time I had to find a balance; it was a tiny little thing, said in a teasing way, and not worth damaging our relationship for. But he had said it. I berated myself for not picking up on it at the time rather than leave it to simmer in my mind.

We didn't put a date on when Ned and I might move to Westbourne Grove. We still talked about it in an abstract way, but Adrian occasionally dropped into the conversation how long the drive took from his to south-east London, and how convenient it would be if we were living under the same roof. I usually went over to see him in west London one morning each week, and he came and stayed with us one night midweek and every other weekend when he wasn't seeing his daughters. Antonella was still insisting that they had no contact with me. It annoyed Adrian, but he acknowledged it was a battle he wasn't going to win.

Within the space of a few months, Adrian had met my mother, I'd met his, and his aunt and uncle. My mother came to stay one weekend in September. As she was a classical music fan, I had taken her to a concert, or one of the Proms, once a year for the last fifteen at least. I'd bought tickets a few months before Adrian and I were in touch, for my mum and I to go to see a Prom that featured works by Elgar and Rachmaninov. I later bought Adrian a ticket, though it was for a seat in a different part of the hall, high up in the Gods. I suggested they sat together during the concert as they'd appreciate the music much more than me.

I knew my mother would approve of Adrian. The next morning she talked endlessly about how handsome he was, how cultured he was, how nicely he spoke. She'd always found something wrong with all my boyfriends, but he ticked all the boxes. He was just the kind of man she thought she should have married.

The following weekend, Ned and I went to stay with Adrian at his cottage in Wiltshire. He'd spent the week painting down there; his studio was much larger than the one in London, and he said he always felt more relaxed there.

The cottage was picture-postcard pretty; grey-green stone with a Wisteria twisted around the door, the leaves just turning. Adrian had booked a table at his favourite local pub a few miles away. I offered to drive so he could drink, and ran upstairs to change. His bedroom was in sharp contrast to his London one; much smaller, with a tradi-tional-looking iron bedstead, painted floorboards, floral bedlinen and simple, well-crafted furniture. It was all very much in keeping with the house, and I wondered if, at some point, Antonella had chosen everything to be perfectly English rose garden.

I heard Adrian and Ned talking in the garden. Looking down at them, Adrian was bending down and showing Ned some photos. I hadn't yet managed to persuade him to buy a smartphone to replace his ancient Nokia.

I glanced in the mirror; my skin was shiny after the jour-ney. I took my make-up out of my bag and powdered my face, touching up my eye shadow. I dropped my mascara and I heard it roll under the bed, so bent down to retrieve it. I noticed a small piece of fabric rolled up. A sock, I thought. I grabbed it and the mascara and was momentarily horrified to see how dusty it was, before acknowledging that under my bed was probably the same.

I stood up and took the fabric to the window, expecting to unravel one of Adrian's socks. I shrieked and dropped it when I realised it was a pair of knickers. Lejaby, one of my favourite brands. They were black, lacy, I wasn't altogether sure they weren't mine. Perhaps Adrian had taken a pair from my underwear drawer as a memento. That thought vanished as quickly as it had formed; these were someone else's. How long they'd been there was the question. I got the tweezers out of my make-up bag and picked the knickers up with them, and put them in the plastic bag I'd packed for our dirty laundry. I didn't really think about what I was going to do with them, or whether I would confront Adrian, but I knew the knowledge of them sitting under his bed would niggle away at me all evening.

We had a table in a book-lined room to one side of the

pub. After we'd eaten, Ned spotted a stack of board games and brought over the Scrabble box, and we all played, though I felt oddly removed and struggled to hide it. Ned and Adrian exchanged conspiratorial glances. It occurred to me that they'd hatched a plan when I'd gone to the toilet and that they were collaborating to beat me at the game, but I was glad that a bond was developing between them.

I tried to blank out my memory of the knickers as I let Adrian fuck me that evening. He didn't seem to notice that I wasn't entirely engaged.

The next morning he drove us to see a local ruined castle. Ned loved the great hall, the information board and illustrations of what it would have looked like sparked his imagination. Adrian held Ned up so he could look over the parapets and way in the distance they spotted a handful of hot air balloons.

After lunch, we went to visit Adrian's mum in Swindon. I would normally be quite nervous about meeting a new partner's parent, but Adrian downplayed it. 'Honestly Alex, don't worry at all, she's very normal and she'll love you.'

He was right. The council estate she lived on, where he'd lived before leaving for college, was very much like the one I'd grown up on. All the houses were neat and tidy, with only the odd one that looked like it might be the home of the local drug dealer. Hers was a bungalow with a newly-painted high fence that screened a neat garden with a large paved patio, surrounded by flower beds populated with rose bushes and lavender.

Adrian's mum, Maureen, had bought Ned some Lego. He opened it as Maureen and Adrian disappeared into the kitchen to make some tea.

'Mum, I've got this already.'

I looked at the box; the same spaceship Mal had bought

only a few months ago. He was slowly growing out of Lego, but I didn't want Maureen to think Ned and, by default, his mother, was ungrateful.

'You can play with it now darling and say thank you.'

He nodded as he opened the box and carefully placed all the separate tiny cellophane bags on the garden table.

I immediately warmed to Maureen. She was unassuming, and seemed very content with her life. Adrian sat back and let us both talk. I asked her what Adrian was like as a boy and mentioned that I'd met Peter too. She mentioned a 'Nicola' and I asked who that was. Maureen told me she was Adrian's sister.

'Let me show you some photos,' Maureen said, suddenly animated and running back into the house.

'I didn't even know you had a sister,' I whispered to Adrian.

'He smiled. 'She lives round the corner. We're very different though.'

I could identify with that; my sister and I not only looked completely unalike, our lives, interests and politics were poles apart.

Maureen's photo albums were full of carefully-labelled square photos, all with a border, and faded to shades of warm browns and oranges after thirty years.

She had thoroughly catalogued her children's early years and was clearly proud of all of them. As we leafed through she explained that, after she'd split up from the children's father, they lived for a few years with her own parents. We had done exactly the same when my mother decided she'd had enough of my father.

I spotted one photo Adrian had sent me when we'd first been in touch. He was wearing a flowery orange shirt, with a neat bowl haircut, those sparkly green eyes and a mischievous grin. I called Ned over to look at it; he was roughly the same age. Maureen patiently went back through the album with Ned, pointing out snaps of the Eiffel Tower, a family holiday to Paris in 1976, giraffes at Whipsnade Zoo, all the time asking Ned questions about where he'd been on holiday, and what his favourite animals were. It struck me how much more engaged she was with Ned than my own mother, and at the same time how good it would be for Ned to have a step granny like Maureen.

Strange thoughts floated in and out of my mind. Adrian's mother, and his upbringing, seemed completely incongruous with the person he had become. Even when he was at college, his personality and demeanour were a million miles away from the humble start in life he clearly had. I struggled to imagine Antonella sitting chatting to Maureen about mundane family memories. She would have looked down her nose at Maureen, I was sure.

We said goodbye to Maureen and, as we got back in the car, I noticed Adrian wink at Ned and he giggled in response; they were definitely planning something. Ned started bouncing up and down in his booster seat, something he did when he was very excited. He had almost grown out of it, I thought with a mixture of sadness and relief.

On the way back to the cottage Adrian said he'd forgotten he needed to pop in quickly to see a friend who lived nearby to pick something up. We turned off the main road and down a series of small country lanes, barely wide enough for one car, never mind two. We climbed a small incline in the road, and past open iron gates and along a tree-lined driveway, which opened up to reveal an imposing Georgian country house.

A woman in late middle-age, with a striking resemblance to Theresa May, met us, surrounded by five or six dogs of varying sizes, but all the same breed. Ned had always loved dogs and he immediately started playing with them, letting them jump up at him, and chasing round the courtyard with them.

'Your timing is excellent, Adrian. The puppies have just woken up and are feeding. They'll be finished in a minute and we can take them out for a play in the garden.'

I glanced at Adrian, puzzled. He smiled back, putting his arm around me.

'I'm sorry, this was all a bit clandestine.'

Ned looked up at me, searching for a reaction, hoping it would be positive.

The dogs were lurchers, Theresa aka Suki, told us. A few generations back, the cross had been a whippet and a flat-haired collie. The crossbreed was now recognised as a golden lurcher; the fur was short and flat, mostly a mid-brown. There were three puppies in all, two boys and a girl. The two boys were already spoken for, but it appeared the girl was still available.

She was cute. Very cute. The grown-up dogs were elegant and long-limbed, but the little ones were stubby and stocky. The poor mother must have been exhausted feeding her three ravenous babies. 'Our' puppy had a white diamond on her chest, and a tip on the end of her tail. Her ears and muzzle were black, and she had perfect Cleopatra flicks around her eyes. Ned had already fallen in love with her. I did wonder exactly what my cats would think of a dog, but we would have to cross that bridge if, and when we came to it.

The next day, Ned and I left Adrian at the cottage to drive back to London. I'd primed myself to bring up the subject of the knickers with Adrian when I called him that evening. But, as the conversation flowed, and I felt myself soften, it seemed totally ridiculous to jeopardise the relationship. They could have been under the bed for months, judging by the amount of dust. Antonella's even.

But still, over the next few days, I couldn't quite forget about them, or bring myself to throw them out. Instead, wearing rubber gloves, I double bagged them and dropped them behind the wardrobe.

CHAPTER 18

Antonella relented, finally, about me seeing the girls, around six months after Adrian and I had started seeing each other.

Adrian celebrated the beginning of this new stage in our lives by inviting Ned and I over to stay with him and his daughters for the weekend. It was a couple of weeks before Christmas and, between us, Adrian and I planned some nice, festive things to do together.

Penny, our fast-growing puppy, had been ready to leave her mum around six weeks after our visit. She'd been living with Adrian ever since, and Giuliana and Issy were as besotted with her as Ned was. There had been a shortlist of names, including some slightly pretentious ones; Orinthia, Tamara and Cornelia. I tried to imagine calling them out in the middle of Holland Park and refused to allow any of them. We all agreed on Penny, though the girls insisted that her actual name was Penelope.

We arrived in Westbourne Grove around teatime. Giuliana and Issy were already there and playing with

Penny in the lounge. Ned had only been to the house a few times and I was anxious he'd feel shy seeing Adrian's daughters as well as being in the new surroundings. I shouldn't have worried; he threw off his coat and immediately joined in, rolling around on the large fluffy rug on the lounge floor, and letting Penny jump all over him.

I waved over to the girls.

'How are you both?'

I asked how school was, and if they were excited about Christmas. They nodded. If Ned was more relaxed and less shy than I'd imagined, they were the opposite. As I watched Adrian open a bottle of Amarone I felt their gaze on me; half inquisitive, half something else. What was it... resentful? I hoped not, but couldn't help thinking that the six-month hiatus would prove to do exactly what Antonella had hoped; prevent a bond forming between her daughters and me.

It wasn't going to be the same with Ned. There were no barriers between him and the girls. He made them laugh. Being girls and having a very different school and lifestyle, they must have seemed very exotic to him and vice versa. They chatted all the way through dinner, and afterwards they disappeared upstairs, Penny dutifully following them, tail wagging.

As I cleared away after dinner, Adrian came up behind me and wrapped his arms around my waist.

'Thank you for making the evening so lovely,' he whispered.

'No need to thank me, everyone just naturally got along fine. The girls seem quite relaxed about me being here.' I turned to gauge his reaction.

He blushed a little and giggled. 'Giuliana asked me where you were going to sleep earlier.'

I raised my eyebrows. 'Is it a problem, me staying in the same room? I can bunk up with Ned if you'd prefer.'

'No, don't worry, she figured it out I think, when I hesitated, and said I hadn't really thought about it. I'm just quite struck by how naïve she is.'

I'd been invited to an open studio of a photographer I'd met through Agnes, at a complex of workshop spaces in a converted warehouse in Clerkenwell. They were having their yearly Christmas event. I'd suggested it as something we could do together. Adrian had looked up Morag Skelton, the photographer, and it turned out she was an acquaintance of Antonella's. Adrian thought he might have met her. 'Really wonderful work, she's just had an exhibition at Friel.'

I'd never heard of the Friel Gallery so I Googled it and found it was just off Bond Street. I clicked on the links to recent exhibitions; contemporary Asian sculpture, Italian avant-garde abstract painting, an Austrian installation artist. Morag's high-contrast black and white photographs of brutalist architecture fitted right in. I liked them but conceptually they were nothing out of the ordinary.

I fussed around, making sure everybody had eaten enough at breakfast, and it struck me that I'd suddenly stopped feeling like a guest. Adrian and the three children took Penny out into the communal gardens and I went upstairs to have a shower.

We planned to leave at midday, and a few minutes before twelve I heard everyone come in from the garden, a babble of excited chatter and Penny barking.

As I ran downstairs I heard Giuliana ask, 'where are we going today, Daddy?'

'Well, Alex and I thought it might be nice to go and do some shopping together, perhaps you can find something nice for Mummy. But before that, we're going to a photographer's open studio, a lady called Morag Skelton.'

'A photographer like Alex?' she enquired.

'Oh no, much more successful than Alex. Morag has exhibited at some of the most prestigious galleries, like Mummy and I.'

I felt a sharp stabbing pain in my chest. I held onto the banister to stop myself falling. How could he say that? Why would he say that? Surely he wouldn't have said it if he knew I could hear, would he? Did he think my work was devoid of artistic merit because it wasn't displayed in a gallery in fucking Bond Street?

Why did he choose to answer Giuliana's question that way? Was it to undermine me in his daughters' eyes? I couldn't see how he could have had any other intention.

I had a choice. My instinct was to pack our things, grab Ned and just walk out the door, never to see him again. My second was to confront him in front of Giuliana, though even in that moment I couldn't see what that would achieve. Ned had gone upstairs to clean his teeth, and he skipped down several flights of stairs, humming cheerfully as he did so. I caught his eye as he jumped the last four or five stairs and was level with me on the first landing. He looked so happy. I couldn't bring myself to fuck it all up.

I felt like I was in a fog for the rest of the day, as if I'd taken medication that dulled all my senses. Adrian didn't seem to notice. I couldn't bring myself to say anything to him. That night, yet again, I let him fuck me as though everything was fine and dandy. Penny must have heard us because she started whining. Adrian went downstairs to quieten her. He was gone for some time and I pretended to be asleep when he came back.

The next morning he said Giuliana hadn't felt well in the night and had been sitting on the stairs outside her room when he went down to check on Penny.

'She must have heard us having sex,' he whispered to me as we lay in bed. He looked guilty.

'Is that the end of the world? She must know what adults get up to. Would she never have heard you and Antonella?'

He smirked. 'I doubt it – we didn't have sex for at least the last three years we were together.'

'Can you talk to Giuliana about it? Maybe see how she is today? She might bring it up herself.'

Even with the distance of a year or so, the memory of Ned opening the door and seeing Mal and I in bed flooded me with shame. Ned had only been four at the time and would have completely forgotten it within a matter of days. Giuliana was eleven, and I could see that last night could easily be etched on her memory.

Before we left Adrian's on the Sunday morning, he told me he was going to Paris with James, his agent, later in the week. He'd just completed a few commissions, and wanted to show these to a couple of clients he had there, and to a few galleries on the Left Bank where he had previously exhibited. The trip was as much about schmoozing them. I imagined he'd take them for a pre-Christmas lunch too.

Adrian travelled to Paris with James and, apart from the odd text, I didn't hear from him much for the next few days. The 'successful photographer' comment niggled away at me. I called Agnes one afternoon, ostensibly about a job, but I needed to get it off my chest.

'Oh, come on, that's ridiculous. What's his problem?'

'When I relay it back, it sounds like it could have been a joke. But it wasn't, the tone, it was just... I don't know, really weird.'

'Are you sure he's the right man for you, Alex? He sounds like an idiot.'

'I know; most of the time it's great. And he seems to get on well with Ned. And Ned absolutely loves his daughters. I just have to weigh up the pros and cons and be pragmatic. If I held out for the perfect man, I'd be on my own forever.'

And anyway, I thought I'd found the perfect man; Mal. And look what happened there.

I told Agnes about all the other minor incidents; the 'stubby' leg comment, the knickers under the bed. It all sounded so petty, as isolated incidents, but it was the intention that really hurt.

'What's the sex like? she asked.

'It's good. Pretty good. A bit brutal at times. Sometimes I can't sit down for a day or so.'

'Jesus Alex, are you serious?' I could imagine her expression was somewhere between alarm and envy. 'Is he...?'

'Well endowed? Average, I'd say, but very vigorous. I've started buying those cool pads you put on kids' foreheads when they have a temperature.'

We laughed. 'Listen, you've told me how charming and handsome he is and all the rest of it, but that comment... be careful,' she added before saying goodbye.

Her words bounced around my head for the next couple of hours. Adrian had texted me earlier to say he was taking a client out for dinner at eight. As I left the house to pick Ned up from after-school club, I checked the time on my phone; just before seven in Paris. I tapped his name on my phone and heard the long beeps of an overseas call. My heart pounded.

'Alex, darling, how are you? I'm just leaving the hotel... can I call you later?'

'No, I just wanted to say hello. I know you're meeting Monsieur Berthaud later.'

'What have you been up to today?'

'Oh, just work. I'm on my way to pick up Ned.' My throat felt dry. 'Listen, Adrian, something's been troubling me for a couple of days.'

'I thought something was off. What is it?'

'Do you remember on Saturday morning, when we were getting ready to go to Morag's? I was upstairs, and Giuliana asked you where we were going later.'

He stayed silent. I could hear the Paris rush-hour traffic in the background.

'Well, I didn't know if you knew I heard, but you said to her "Oh, we're going to see a photographer, much more successful than Alex."'

'Alex, what are you talking about?'

'Are you telling me you don't remember?'

I heard him snort. 'Have you been drinking?'

'You said it, Adrian. I heard you, plain and simple. I have no idea whether you knew I'd hear, or whether what you said was purely to belittle me in front of your daughter, or to undermine me, or to tease me or something. Perhaps to signal to her that you didn't think I was as creative as Anton—.'

'Alex, this is pure fantasy. You've imagined the whole thing. I really haven't time for this nonsense. I'll call—'

I wasn't going to give him the pleasure. I hung up first.

Ever since he was born, Ned had a calming effect on me; nothing else mattered in comparison. Within seconds of spotting him, playing football with all the other boys in the main school hall, I forgot about Adrian. We went home and cooked dinner together, and read a few chapters of his book before I tucked him up in bed.

Adrian send me a grovelling email that night, but I didn't see it until the next morning. He didn't apologise, I wouldn't have expected him to, but he told me how happy he'd been since we'd got together, how I'd given him a new lease of life. He said he knew he wasn't perfect, but that I was making him a better person.

'I love you, Alex, with all my heart,' he added at the bottom. I remembered that first time he told me, when he looked in pain as he said it, as though falling in love was a terrible burden.

I left it a few hours before replying, keeping it short, not quite forgiving him. And over the next few days, before he arrived back from Paris, I did miss him. I could never feel lonely with Ned around, but I missed having an adult conversation over a glass of wine in the evening. Even just the physical presence of him next to me when I woke, the warmth of another's body, his breath on the nape of my neck.

I also had to be realistic; I was now well into my forties. I'd been internet dating for a couple of years before I met Mal, but increasingly I knew, as my age increased, I was going to be a less attractive prospect for men my own age, who were generally looking to meet someone 15 years younger.

I'd had fun in those couple of years, but dating hadn't resulted in anything serious, anything that could have remotely turned into a long-term relationship. When I first started seeing Adrian I'd been so hopeful, it had felt so solid because I could see us being together, into the future. And now I had to admit, even though part of me still yearned for Mal, I had so much more history with Adrian.

CHAPTER 19

I've always loved having parties, or rather the idea of having them. The reality is a little different. But the organising? That's the best bit. Since Ned came along, we'd had a yearly bash for his birthday, and that more or less satisfied my desire.

But leaving south London after twenty years felt too momentous not to mark. I'd talked to Adrian about it and he was up for it, especially as it would be an opportunity for him to meet more of my friends. I mentioned the idea to a few people and, before I knew it, I'd set a date for the party; a week before we were due to move.

Work was busy, and I'd started packing, so party planning was sidelined. On top of that I was feeling lousy. I had a persistent sore throat and a urinary infection. I put it down to not enough sleep but my GP insisted on investigating the cause.

I felt unprepared as I picked Ned up from school on the Friday afternoon and we went food shopping for the party the next day. I didn't even have a list so I filled the trolley with anything that sprang to mind – meat, vegetables and fish for the barbecue, salad, humous, crisps, balloons and streamers.

My phone rang as I was adding beer to the already overflowing trolley.

'Hello... Alexandra Kendrew? It's Sarah Davies from the surgery.'

'Hello, speaking.'

'I have the results of your tests, Alexandra. I'm sorry, but they were positive for gonorrhea.'

My mouth went dry and I felt myself redden as I noticed the hot dog rolls were getting squashed underneath the boxes of Staropramen.

'Miss Kendrew, are you still there?' I could hardly hear what she was saying, blood was rushing in my ears.

'Er, yes, that's... are you sure?' I couldn't bring myself to say out loud the name of an STI in the middle of East Dulwich Sainsbury's.

'Do you have any idea who you might have caught it from? All your sexual partners should also be tested, and treated if they prove to be positive. People can often have it without showing any symptoms; that's one of the reasons it's so easily spread.' She stopped, thankfully.

'How... how long does it take to...'

'The incubation period? In men, it's quite soon, two to five days, usually. In women, it's longer. More than half of women don't show any symptoms. You could have been exposed to it months ago.'

We drove straight to the surgery. There was frozen food in the boot that would be completely thawed by the time we got home, but there was nothing I could do about that. I wanted the antibiotic injection as soon as possible.

'So, you're not able to tell me how long ago I caught this?'

Doctor Davies answered the question I was really asking. 'You need to contact any sexual partners you've had, within the last year at least.'

There was only Adrian. It was at least eighteen months since my crazy few months after Mal dumped me. I needed to speak to Adrian, but the party was not the time.

I was slightly irritated that Adrian didn't offer to help get ready for the party, but he arrived with his daughters early the next morning. Now that Antonella had softened her stance, he'd invited the girls, as well as his brother Peter and his family. He soon got to work in the garden, setting out chairs and tables, and Ned, Giuliana and Issy blew up balloons and decorated the garden with streamers.

One minute we were waiting for anyone to arrive, the next we were inundated with guests, and I gradually let myself relax and enjoy myself. Ned went round with my phone, taking snaps from the unflattering viewpoint of a six-year-old; from that angle virtually everyone had a double chin. I seemed to only manage brief chats with everyone as I handed round plates of crostini and cupcakes.

I'd half planned to give a little speech, though I hadn't thought what I might say, and hoped Adrian would do it instead. As the afternoon slid into evening, and evening into night, the idea seemed less and less appealing. Everyone was having a nice time; the music was loud and the booze was flowing. Dermot, an old friend I'd met when we shared a house in Brixton twenty years earlier, and who I could rely on to get blind drunk, was arguing loudly with Nicole about Nietzsche.

I'd stayed fairly sober for most of the party but, as a result, felt strangely removed, like I was observing everyone else. I hadn't invited Ingrid, mainly because I didn't think she'd come, but I missed her presence; it was never a proper party without her. I opened a beer, and then another, and then moved onto whisky.

Jess's daughter Millie tugged on the back of my dress to tell me she was hungry. I looked round to see what was left on the table but almost everything was gone, apart from a large bowl of couscous salad my neighbours had brought, and a few beheaded cupcakes. I found an unopened pack of fish fingers in the freezer and Jess, Nicole and Ruth set about making fish finger sandwiches for all the kids. They wouldn't let me do anything.

'Don't be daft, we've got this,' they all seemed to say in unison. I felt a pang of sadness that I would no longer be seeing them every day at the school gates.

I hadn't seen Adrian for hours. I glanced around the lounge but couldn't spot him, and then looked in the garden. He was there, deep in conversation with Dan, a guy I'd met when I first started dating and we'd kept in touch as friends. I'd invited him, hoping I'd be able to play cupid and get him together with Marta, one of the mums at school. I'd seen them talking earlier. I went to join Adrian, but on the way I was grabbed by someone for photos, and then a few people started to leave, and I was on the verge of tears saying goodbye to people and hugging them, and at the same time, trying to reunite them with their child's scooter.

In the kitchen Jess and Nicole were interrogating Dan; why didn't he have a girlfriend? Jess couldn't believe how much he looked like Lee Mack, and told him so, vehemently and repeatedly. Nicole sat staring up at him, like she'd suddenly found her true love. I couldn't see them together; I thought Marta was much more his cup of tea, but what did I know? I'd failed miserably to matchmake all my life. I just needed to leave them to it.

I'd lost Adrian again and glanced around looking for

him – I hoped he was enjoying the party. I was sure he saw himself as being a few rungs above me socially, money helped as well, of course. We did live in very different worlds, but my friends were successful too – even within Ned's class, there was an actor, a playwright, a child protection officer, a theatre director. As a photographer, I considered myself to be very low down that particular ladder. The comment he'd made a few months before, about me being an unsuccessful photographer, had hurt. A lot. Meeting all my friends, getting to know them, perhaps he would realise the gap between us wasn't as great as he'd assumed.

Dan was trying to leave but was very drunk. Nicole hadn't given up on the idea of accompanying him home; her Ned was already staying the night with us. I booked an Uber for Dan and, as he fumbled around in his bag, checking he had his wallet and house keys, he handed me a card he'd forgotten to give me earlier. The message was really sweet, saying he'd really miss our chats over coffee. I hugged him.

'We're not going to be far away... even if west London feels like a different planet to me. I'd love you to come over and bring a bit of south-east London sparkle.'

Nicole didn't want to miss out on the action and threw her arms around both of us.

'Dan, your Uber is here,' Adrian said, breaking up the impromptu love-in. Nicole looked at Adrian with disdain; she was not one for forgiveness. I'd done a good job of keeping them apart since the evening at hers. Nicole returned her attention to Dan, whispering in his ear. He looked terrified; I briefly thought about intervening, but she looked like she was on a mission. She'd grabbed her bag and was trotting after him. I went out too, partly to ensure they got into the cab without falling over.

Adrian followed me out to the car. 'What does she think

she's doing? He's far too good for that tart,' he muttered, not making any attempt to stay quiet.

'Leave it,' I whispered, throwing him a warning stare. I ran ahead to say goodbye to them both. Nicole was already staggering back from the cab, towards Adrian.

'You mess Alex around, and I'll kill you,' she said, squaring up to him. 'I mean it, I'll fucking kill you.'

I stepped in between them. 'Come on darling, it's fine.'

We hugged. She smelt of gin and the woody Jo Malone scent I'd bought her for Christmas. My left ear got caught in her chunky metal necklace. Out of the corner of my eye I saw Adrian storm back towards the house.

'He's a complete cunt, Alex,' she said, bumping her head as she got into the car beside Dan.

Everything that could go wrong did go wrong on the moving day. No-one heeded my request to not park in front of the house, so the removal men had to carry everything to the lorry, six or seven houses down. The cats were completely freaked out by all the activity, so I locked them out in the garden to avoid scaring them any more. When I did eventually let them in, Marmaduke hid under my bed, and scratched my arms to shreds when I pulled him out, peeing and shitting all over the floor.

Angie, one of the mums from school, came to the house and wanted to take photos of us all before we left, even though she'd taken about a zillion at the party. I looked like shit, having been awake since four, and shouted at her.

On top of that, Adrian hadn't offered to come and help and I was too proud to ask. When Ned and I arrived at his around teatime, I was hot and sweaty and smelt of disinfectant and cat piss. The car was jam-packed with my most treasured possessions, Ned, the cats and my cameras.

We parked on the drive and Ned ran towards Adrian and Penny. I followed them inside and gently put the cat boxes down on the kitchen floor. Penny's instinct was tweaked and she immediately came over to investigate. I don't think I'm exaggerating when I say Marmaduke's box jumped three feet in the air. The door of the cat box fell off as it landed and he ran out, into the hall and up the stairs.

'God, I need a drink,' I said wearily to Adrian.

The first few weeks were strange. Ned and I had been to Adrian's so many times, I thought it would immediately feel like home. I'd expected him to be welcoming and loving, but he wasn't. I assumed he'd understand that I might occasionally need help with Ned; taking him to school, or reading to him at night. But he didn't.

There was one afternoon, a few weeks after we moved, when Adrian arrived home after a few days away. Penny was beside herself. She was still in the habit of peeing every time she got over-excited. Penny followed Adrian into the kitchen. I got a floor-cloth and hot water to clean up the puddle in the hallway. Ned must have heard the commotion and, as I wiped the floor, I heard him run to join Adrian and the dog in what I imagined was a group hug. I was so happy that they were enjoying a moment together like that; Penny would hopefully be the catalyst that helped form the bond between Ned and Adrian.

My joy was short-lived.

'Will you get off and let me say hello to my dog in peace.' His tone was abrasive, his words chosen to be hurtful.

I don't think he knew I overheard him. I don't know

why I didn't confront him then, other than a desire to not upset the apple cart so early on in our life together. Instead I waited for a few minutes, and then went to find Ned who was sitting watching TV. I hugged him and told him I was sorry that Adrian had shouted at him. I expected him to be upset but he seemed to have forgotten it already.

A few days later, Adrian announced he'd invited a client, Larry, and his wife over for dinner, an American hedge fund manager who'd bought a few of his landscapes. Adrian had presented me with the menu he wanted me to cook. It had taken the whole day to prepare everything, on top of curing a whole salmon several days before. At the time I'd quite enjoyed the preparation but Adrian had pissed me off when he breezed in an hour before his guests were due to arrive and took over, and then took all the credit. I'd given the cats and Penny a tiny bit of the salmon earlier that afternoon, and when he got it out of the fridge, they all must have sensed they were going to be in luck again, sitting patiently by his feet in a row by the kitchen sink. I went upstairs to change.

That evening, whether it was on purpose or completely subconscious, Adrian didn't fill my wine glass the entire evening. He averted his eyes from my initially enquiring gaze the first few times he'd filled everyone else's. This turned to quiet rage. He knew I couldn't question him in front of his guests or walk out. At the point where I was ready to explode, I stood up and reached for the bottle which had been strategically placed far enough away from me, and helped myself.

'Oh, I'm sorry darling, did I miss you out that time?' he quipped.

I gave a wry smile when Larry's wife Monica thanked me

at the end of the night. I figured she'd been in the same situation and knew it had been me who'd done all the work.

That night, as he lay in bed, naked with his arms resting behind his head and with a waiting but dwindling hard-on, I stood towering over him, fully clothed.

I was ready to accuse him of not filling my glass all night, but I remembered I hadn't seen Marmaduke since before Monica and Larry had arrived. 'Have you seen Marmaduke at all?'

He looked up from his book. 'Marmaduke – which one's that?'

'The ginger one, of course.' I had thought he only pretended to dislike my cats but I was beginning to think I was wrong.

'Not since I stood on him. He's so stupid, he got right under my feet in the kitchen. I think he ran out into the garden.'

'You stood on him, for crying out loud. Why are you...' I stopped myself. Instead I slammed the bedroom door and ran downstairs to the garden, shaking a packet of cat treats which caught Maisy and Penny's attention instead. Finally, Marmaduke emerged from under a rose bush. I checked his paw; he didn't seem to be limping, but the next morning I took him to the vets to be safe.

Adrian's laissez-faire attitude to pet care also extended to Penny. For his birthday I bought him some chocolates from Melt on Ledbury Road. After sampling a few, he left the box on the bookshelves above the sofa in the lounge. 'Don't leave them there – Penny can easily reach them and dark chocolate is really dangerous for dogs – it damages their liver.'

The next morning I came down to find the box on the floor, chewed and empty. Adrian was insouciant, waving away my claims that he'd been negligent. I took Penny to the vets who must have thought me the worst pet owner in the world. She was given apomorphine to make her sick. When I picked her up later that afternoon, she still had the runs, poor love.

It became the new normal. He assumed I would just accept the way he was; the honeymoon period was well and truly over. I didn't accept it; I just wracked up all the shitty things he did.

I rang my mum, not something I did more than once every few months, and heard myself saying how wonderful everything was. Had I told her the truth, I knew what she'd say, because she'd said it to me before, about Sean.

'Well dear, you've made your bed.'

PART II

TWO YEARS EARLIER

CHAPTER 20

July had started cold and grey, but by the beginning of the second week it turned unusually hot. At night we lay under a single sheet, the windows wide open. Adrian and I had been living together for almost a year. I still wasn't used to sleeping in the same bed as someone else. I used to swap sides in the middle of the night, moving over to a plump, cool pillow. Now Adrian occupied that territory, and I resented him for it.

The bed always smelt of male skin, male sweat. I changed the sheets once a week, sometimes more. He slept on his back. At first I'd found his rhythmic, if not exactly quiet, snoring reassuring. In the first months I would rest my head on his chest as we fell asleep. Inevitably I would still be awake as he descended into unconsciousness and I would extricate myself from him, and move over to my own side.

Every morning around five he would get up to use the bathroom; find me a middle-aged man who doesn't. He would come back to bed and spoon my body, a drop or two of pee caught between his skin and mine. He'd listen for my breathing and fall into line with it. After being woken at 5am I rarely managed to go back to sleep. I would lie awake, pretending, breathing gently and evenly so that he could follow. But more than that; to avoid a conversation with him, or, heaven forbid, to have sex.

It was one of those mornings. Penny whined downstairs, so I slipped away from him when I could tell from his breathing he'd gone back to sleep.

I padded downstairs, wearing a thin cotton dress; my attire for taking Penny out into the garden. It was the first full summer we'd lived with Adrian and, as the mornings started ever earlier, the first bright rays of light reached corners of the kitchen that for most of the day were in deep shadow. The house was positioned in more or less the same direction as the Gipsy Hill one, with the kitchen facing east. I couldn't tell whether the similarity was comforting or the exact opposite. I fed the cats and Penny, then opened the patio doors, taking my laptop with me. I liked to make the most of that time, before anyone else was awake, before I had to make breakfast and organise Ned and Adrian.

I sat on the top step of the decking and, as the laptop glowed into life, I took in the garden, all bluish, viridian shades in the early morning light. There was a gentle breeze that bent the wall of young bamboo stalks along the right side of the garden. I felt a thrill up my spine and down my arms as the cold pricked my skin, giving me goose pimples.

I'd been cleaning up fifteen or so shots of a gorgeous open-plan studio in Spitalfields. I was given the job by an architect friend of a friend who in turn had been commissioned by a sculptor. She wanted to turn two floors of a former warehouse into a live-work space.

A wonderful job that had turned into a nightmare, with the woman changing her mind every five minutes, not agreeing the budget, not paying... John the architect was ready to throw the towel in, but somehow managed to get it finished. Though the relationship between him and his client had all but broken down.

The sculptor refused to let him have the place photographed.

'Fuck that,' John said, in a protracted text conversation we'd had about the job. 'I'm sorry to ask, Alex, but can we go and do the shoot really early one morning before she gets there? And before she remembers I've still got keys and demands them back?'

I'd agreed, with a disclaimer. 'That's fine, John, but I've had quite enough conflict in my life over the last few years. She's not going to barge in and throw all my camera equipment out the window, is she? Maybe me too?'

The enormous windows should have afforded us plenty of natural light, but a 5am shoot, even in July, relied heavily on it being a bright, sunny morning. It was cloudy and, on top of that, the windows faced west, so I had to use flash. By seven the cloud had thinned, allowing moments of bright sunshine to bounce off the windows of the building opposite and filling the studio with sharp, almost eerie, silver-white light and dark grey geometric shadows. It worked brilliantly, but I was in constant fear that Scary Sculptor, as she'd become known, would turn up and go nuts.

I liked working quickly – it forced me to make decisions based on instinct. In addition, the light was constantly changing. I said to John I might need to do quite a bit of work afterwards to balance the colour and light. We needed to make sure we got all the shots done as it was highly unlikely we'd get another chance. I couldn't guarantee I'd managed to take the perfect exposure for each shot, but I knew from looking at the screen on the back of the Canon they were going to make a very nice set – not just for the architect but for my portfolio too. It was just after eight when John agreed to do one last shot; half past, and I was running down the street to my car, tripod and lights weighing me down, hoping I'd reach it before the traffic warden.

The retouching had been time-consuming. Not difficult work, but tedious and repetitive, and it was difficult to stop my mind wandering. I wanted to get it all finished though. John wasn't paying me a huge amount, and I was probably spending more time on the Photoshop work than the job warranted, but I wanted them to be perfect, as much for me as the client. And it gave me an excuse not to spend the evenings with Adrian. Once Ned was in bed I went back to my studio in the basement and sat with a glass of red wine, making tiny adjustments to the curves, cleaning up reflections of my lens in shiny metal surfaces. I'd save four or five versions. To the casual observer they looked exactly the same; some were slightly warmer, some with a tiny amount of noise added for texture. I'd sent John a set of low-res JPEGs the night before and I was keen to see if he'd replied. I really wanted him to like them.

I searched through my emails down to ones sent the night before, not long after I'd sent the files. He might just have sent a 'thanks, Alex, will look in the morning' reply. But before I spotted his name, my eyes focused on another. MALCOLM RUSSELL. In caps. I couldn't quite believe what I was seeing. My eyes were tired after five hours' sleep. I rubbed them and looked back at the screen.

How many times had I willed that name to appear? How many times had I hoped he'd email, or call, or text? Sometimes I'd found myself picking out the letters that made up his name from others, as if stringing them all together was some kind of subliminal message from him.

A few months before, on a cold, grey February afternoon, I'd typed in the name of a client whose surname was Mallinson and Mal's email address had come up as a suggestion. It had crossed my mind then, that I could send him an email pretending I was sending it to Karen Mallinson. My mouse hovered over his name for twenty seconds before I realised how pathetic that would be, how sad he would think I was, seeing through me immediately. I dismissed the thought and it never surfaced again.

Sitting in the garden of Adrian's huge stuccoed villa in west London at six in the morning, my life didn't resemble the one I'd had the last time I'd seen Mal. My heartbeat had increased so much that I could feel blood vessels pounding in my ears. What if I clicked and deleted it, or clicked and somehow sent a blank reply? He'd think I was an idiot. I could hardly bear to see what he'd written. My hand trembled as I clicked on the email.

Hi Alex, I've just noticed a message you sent me on Facebook, ages ago! I'm so sorry not to reply earlier. I hope things are still going well for you and that the move to west London you mentioned has worked out as well as hoped – you deserve to be happy. Best wishes, Malcolm.

PS You may not remember but we met for coffee at the Ritzy Cinema in Brixton and we both loved Nick Cave. His new album is fantastic... but of course you'll already know that!

My eyes filled with tears, so that the whole laptop screen blurred. I hadn't noticed Penny coming to sit next to me, but I was slowly aware of the familiar warmth of her body against my thigh. I looked down at her, wiping the tears away, and she looked up quizzically, whining gently. I tickled her under the chin, working down her throat to the rough

little whirls of fur on her breastbone. I bent my head down
to her so that we touched noses, and she flopped down on
the decking next to me, resting her chin on my lap, folding
her elegant limbs to the side.

I felt numb. There'd been no great declaration in his
message, just an acknowledgment that he'd received mine.
Did I believe Mal? That he hadn't seen it at the time? Not
really. I had sent the message to him a year or so after
meeting Adrian, when we'd first started talking about living
together. I'd been so excited and had skipped home to south
east London, full of ideas about how I'd make the house feel
like home, how Ned would love having the huge bedroom in
the converted loft near his two new step sisters' rooms.

I'd gone onto Facebook and near the top of the newsfeed
there was a panel entitled 'People you may know' – Mal was
the first. At the time, seeing the tiny profile photo of him, I'd
felt a sharp stab in my chest. I'll send him a message. Just a
'hi, how are you? So funny, you came up as 'somebody I
might know' on here. I'm really happy, met somebody new,
hope you and Louise still blissfully happy too'. That kind of
thing. Did I hope he'd be happy with her? Not really. If I'm
honest, looking back, a part of me hoped he'd get in touch
straight away and tell me how thoroughly miserable he was,
how it was all totally over with Louise, how they now hated
each other. But I hadn't got anything back. A couple of days
later I was absolutely sure I'd never hear back from him and
I forgot about it. The cheery message I'd sent could be
remembered as just that, not a cry for help.

I walked aimlessly round the lounge, catching my reflection in the mirror above the fireplace. My face looked simultaneously pinched and saggy from lack of sleep, my eyes red
and puffy. I read the email twenty times, perhaps more,
searching for something positive to hold on to. If a tiny

flicker of acknowledgment of the closeness we'd had formed in my thoughts, it was extinguished by reading it again.

Penny looked at me expectantly; I grabbed her lead and left a post-it note on the kitchen table. *Just gone for a run, back at seven. Taken Penny.*

We took our usual early morning route – three miles, through Holland Park -- but afterwards I couldn't remember any of the details. Instead, playing over in my head, the words Mal had written in his postscript. *You may not remember but we met for coffee at the Ritzy Cinema in Brixton.* How the fuck could he think I had forgotten?

CHAPTER 21

The reply from Mal had taken a year and a half, so I was determined not to reply too quickly. Would I reply at all? I was still trying to figure that out as I made an espresso after lunch and sat down to drink it while I re-read the message.

With a vague idea of wanting to sound indifferent, but knowing I'd probably fail, I started typing. *Hi Mal. Don't worry, I wasn't really expecting a reply. And I just wanted you to know that I'd managed to dust myself down and start again. I was very upset when you told me Louise had been in touch and that you didn't want to see me again, but it shouldn't have come as a surprise. I hope you're both happy together. I suppose the other reason I sent it was to try and avoid you getting in touch – I didn't want you turning my life upside down by hearing from you out of the blue. Sorry if that sounds harsh but it's true.*

Ned and I moved in with my new man, Adrian, about a year ago. I'm really happy, very busy with work, Ned loves his new school, Adrian is wonderful (you'd like him I think – very clever, interested in history, politics, theatre) and loves me. But there are times when I'm convinced the whole idea of long-term monoga-

mous relationships is deeply flawed; men and women are fairly incompatible, I think. I wonder sometimes if I might be happier on my own, with the occasional romantic interlude via a dating site. Take care, Alex.

A couple of hours later, I had a reply. *I'm so pleased it's worked out for you... Adrian sounds great. It didn't with Lou and I, and I'm angry with myself that I didn't accept that a lot sooner.*

He said he completely agreed with my comments about long term monogamous relationships. *Not many people are as honest... that's one of the things I liked about you.* He thanked me for being so understanding and asked if I thought it would be appropriate to become Facebook friends. He added a PS. *Do you like The National? Over the last few years, they've become my go-to band.*

The timing was cruelly ironic. When I sent the Facebook message to him, I had been completely in love with Adrian. Or at least I thought I was. We had still been in that dreamy period when it was impossible not to tear each other's clothes off at every opportunity. That was a distant memory though – I was aware I had put on a brave face in my reply to Mal. I told him I loved The National, and Matt Berninger's baritone. *If I close my eyes I can imagine him standing behind me, singing softly into my ear. Of course it helps he's a babe!* I agreed to being Facebook friends, as long as he promised not to laugh at my pictures, and ended it with a line about his team having a good season. I'd never had much interest in football but, after meeting Mal, I always listened more intently when Arsenal were mentioned on the radio.

Ten minutes later, he replied. *Blimey, Alex, I'm just remembering how well we clicked... do you remember that morning at the Ritzy Café? And then I lost my nerve and ran back to Louise. I think I've pretty much given up on the idea of anything long term... I'm too set in my ways for a start!*

I heard Adrian walking around in the hallway and, to avoid seeing him, I went into the bathroom with my phone and replied to his email. *I've locked myself in the loo! One of the problems with living with someone is not having the opportunity or privacy to email an old flame...*

I continued writing, now and again listening out for Adrian. I said I couldn't believe that it hadn't worked out with Louise. How I'd imagined them living happily ever after.

I told him I'd settled into the West London way of life quite well, but that it felt completely different to Gipsy Hill.

When I confirmed him as a friend on Facebook, I clicked on 'photos of Mal'. The first that came up were a few at Arsenal matches, some with Ewan, but it felt too intrusive to go digging through his past, recent or ancient. It also occurred to me I might come across some photos of him with Louise and I couldn't face that. When he'd come up as someone I might have known a couple of years ago, I did go digging around. I'm not proud of it. I clicked on his 'friends' list and saw there was a 'Louise Russell'. She had that elfin look – quite pointed features, choppy blonde bob. She couldn't have possibly looked more different from me. I immediately regretted looking for her. I'd never be able to forget what she looked like.

It seemed that Mal had taken the opposite approach; he'd looked at all my photos. *You and Adrian look very well suited... he's a lucky man! Strange seeing you in your photos, having a glimpse into your world after so long.* He added a PS, quoting Pulp's lyrics about Ladbroke Grove in the song "I Spy".

It was so bizarre to hear him saying all that, after years of silence, after so long hoping he'd be in touch. Nothing. If he had, not long after I'd sent him the message a few years back, perhaps I wouldn't have agreed to move in with Adrian. Perhaps I would have dumped him and gone running after Mal. I replied. *Such a brilliant song, Cocker at his vitriolic best.*

Tuesday became Wednesday, Thursday turned into Friday. The days had become meaningless. Time was defined by the space between messages. On Thursday Adrian left to supervise the hanging of his new exhibition at a gallery in Bath. He was staying at his cottage in Wiltshire. It was a relief not to have him around.

Ned was happy at school. It was the last few weeks of the summer term and in Year Two everything was still quite relaxed, though I knew Year Three was likely to get more serious. His class had had a couple of trips – Natural History Museum and London Zoo – a fun end to the term but I'd failed to volunteer to help and felt guilty about it. I tried and mostly succeeded to limit the amount of time and energy I spent thinking about or writing to Mal while Ned wasn't at school. But it hadn't been my most productive few days, workwise, or my most engaged as a parent. Both made me uneasy. I didn't want the messages to end, the frequency or length, but I knew at some point they had to.

After I'd taken Ned to school, I replied to Mal's message from the night before. He'd told me about his son, Ewan. He was now fifteen and had got into acting at school and at a local arts centre. He was just about to play Lysander in their production of A Midsummer Night's Dream. *Ewan sounds lovely – just thinking Ned (and actually my newly-acquired step-daughters too) would think he was the coolest thing on earth! It's so nice to be in touch. PS I haven't looked at your Facebook page yet. I fear I may burst into tears!*

An hour or so later, Mal replied. *Don't worry, I've aged a bit, these last few years. PS Yes it's lovely to be in touch.*

Mid-morning I made coffee and sat on the steps into the garden, replying to him on my phone. *I will have a look at your pics – I'm sure you'll still look every bit as lovely which will be the problem! And also, just as you said about seeing a window into my life that you didn't know much about, I imagine I'll see the same. Would be nice to see pics of Ewan too – I'm sure he's every inch the budding actor. And he's fortunate to have a dad who looks a bit like David Tennant – a future Doctor Who, perhaps! Ned is seven – he's grown up a lot in the last few years.*

Ten minutes later, I heard back. He told me he had meetings until mid-afternoon and then was going back to Brighton on the train. He finished with a PS. *Yes, I take hundreds of photos of Ewan... he went through a shy phase around fourteen but it didn't last long!*

I was experiencing a strange mix of excitement and regret as a result of being in touch with him. But I didn't know where the conversation was going. I was very aware that, so far, I hadn't told Mal I was unhappy with Adrian. Part of me was worried that if I did, he'd get cold feet and it would be over. I was waiting for Mal to expose his feelings, give me a green light, or a red one. For the time being, I had to keep it light. I replied.

I have thousands of photos of Ned too – I'm usually behind the lens so there's not many of me. It's lovely to see how they grow over time. Ned's changed physically quite a lot recently – taller, his face has matured and the gaps between his baby teeth are now huge. Still my baby though!

Half an hour later, he wrote back. *Feeling the effect of a glass or two of bubbly... it was a colleague's birthday so a little party in the office. Don't I remember you getting me quite tipsy one evening?*

Was that a green light? Perhaps. Still, I wasn't going to take any chances. *Yes, I did get you tipsy but should have sent you home after the wine and before the whisky. I had a line from Suzanne Vega's "Marlene on the Wall" playing in my head... do you know the one? Something about not giving the goods away too soon?*

I tried to picture him on the train to Brighton as he tapped his reply into his phone, looking a little the worse for wear, his tie and top button loosened, five o'clock shadow, those cute crows' feet appearing as he read my reply. Yes, that completely worked for me.

CHAPTER 22

S unday morning. I didn't hear back from Mal the night before, and I was determined not to keep checking.

Ned woke up and wanted to play football in the garden. We were capitalising on Adrian not being around; kicking a ball was outlawed as well as hanging out the washing.

Ned begged me to join him, so I grabbed his spare football and tried, for the first time in my life, the art of keepie-uppies. Three was about my limit at first but then I got into more of a rhythm. Ned stopped and watched me. 'Seven, eight, nine... Mum, you're really good at this. Can we do a video?'

I fell to pieces in front of the camera, five being my best score. Instead I filmed Ned who thrived under the added pressure. After he reached thirty a couple of times, he ran into the kitchen to get water.

I left my phone in my studio and didn't look at it until mid-morning. Mal had sent a message an hour earlier.

That made me laugh, Alex. It was a long time ago, that night at yours...

I sent a quick reply. *Yes, quite a lot of water under the bridge.* I called Ned back in for lunch, and reminded him there was a small piece of homework to do – I'd found the sheet folded up at the bottom of his book bag entitled 'What I liked about our trip to London Zoo'.

As Ned sat drawing giraffes and penguins at the kitchen table, my mind drifted. I needed to talk to Mal, be upfront, let him know what was going on. While Ned was still fully consumed with writing about the zoo, and with me dipping in occasionally when he needed help spelling 'tortoise' and 'komodo dragon', I emailed Mal.

There's something I need to tell you. I've been putting on a brave face, about Adrian. Not long after we moved in together – a matter of days if I'm totally honest – I knew I'd made a terrible mistake. It's a year ago – I've been hoping things would get better, give things a chance to develop, for him to form a bond with Ned. But if anything it's getting worse. I think it's having a detrimental effect on Ned too – the exact opposite of what I was hoping for. It's like Adrian was putting on an act – pretending to be someone he thought I wanted him to be – until we moved when he realised he didn't have to make any effort. He's arrogant, pompous, self-important – not three traits you actively seek in a partner. I've rented out my house, I would dearly love to move back and pick up our life where we left it, but Ned is now very settled in his new school and it seems very selfish to move back. Blimey, such a mess. I remember once you describing your life had been a bit of a car crash – mine's become a pile up!

It took him a couple of hours to reply. I was anxious to see how he'd react to my news. *Oh no, Alex, I wasn't expecting that. I'm really sorry. It sounds like you've invested so much into your relationship with Adrian – and he's taking you for granted. Sounds very complicated though. Wanna chat on the phone? You can tell me all about it.*

I also had a text from Adrian – he was coming back from Wiltshire later that evening. I knew he'd expect dinner when he got home, and I prayed that he'd arrive after Agnes and her kids had left.

We'd arranged to meet Agnes in Hyde Park. Before we left to meet her, I sent Mal a reply. *A chat would be lovely. How about tomorrow morning?*

We met Agnes in the Diana Memorial Garden. The children shrieked and yelled and jumped off the side of the pirate ship into the sand. Her daughter, Bea, was a year older and her son, Jem, a year younger than Ned. The afternoon was one of the very first times we'd been able to sit and chat; before that Jem had been too little.

'Things haven't improved?' Agnes asked. Whenever I could, I'd still orchestrated shoots to take place at hers. Neither Agnes nor Adrian were the type to play happy families in order to avoid an awkward situation.

'He gets annoyed with Ned all the time, even when he's not doing anything wrong. He wasn't like that when I met him, around the time of the college reunion. Not until we moved here. I think he's always had this aloof thing going on, like he thinks he's just that bit more cultured and intellectual than everybody else. A few friends have said he looks down his nose at them. I can see it. I suppose when I met him, I thought it was attractive – his painting, his stature, his confidence – he was so unlike Sean.'

'Can't you just leave?'

'It's not that simple. Ned's made new friends here, he likes having a dog and a big garden. Adrian has promised to build a treehouse at the bottom of the garden... not that it's materialised yet.'

After a couple of hours at the pirate ship, much dissection of our relationships fuelled by several trips to the kiosk for coffee for us and ice cream for the children, we left the playground to stroll around the main park. The kids reclaimed their bikes that were propped against the tree we'd been sitting under. Bea, a year older than Ned, was very confident on hers, Jem still had stabilisers on. Ned was in between, and I imagined didn't want to be shown up by me helping him. As Bea tore off, Jem trundled sensibly along, looking back and grinning at his mum, proud of his achievement. Ned was disgruntled at having to wear his helmet, elbow and knee pads, and wobbled jerkily from one side of the wide path to the other, somehow managing to avoid any collisions with pedestrians walking the other way.

'Can you come back with us and have tea?'

'Sure, I just need to get back by eight-ish, seeing as it's a school night. When is Adrian back?'

'I don't know, probably eight or nine, I guess. I'm dreading it even more than usual.'

'Why's that?'

I gave her a potted history of the email conversation with Mal. I'd talked to her about him hundreds of times over the last few years, and she'd always been sympathetic, but I was pretty sure she thought I was nuts.

We picked up a bottle of white wine on the way back to the house. Since moving to Adrian's, impromptu get-togethers with friends had been few and far between and I relished the opportunity. For a while at least, having Agnes and the kids round would help me forget what a shit-show my life had become.

As soon as we arrived back the children ran out into the garden with Penny. Agnes opened the wine and poured us a glass each. I made some pasta and salad, Agnes set the table, and we called Ned, Bea and Jem in. They were a little hyper, shrieking, standing on chairs so they could reach the bread. It was absolutely perfect timing for Adrian to arrive home. I didn't hear the door, but Penny must have; she raced along the hallway to meet him.

'I didn't realise we were having a dinner party,' he said, accusingly, as he stood in the doorway. No 'hello', no 'hey, great to see you again, Agnes, how's things?'. But then again, I didn't reciprocate. Only Penny was pleased to see him.

He was wearing his favourite stripy tanktop; mustard and dark green stripe, several sizes too big, the yarn unknitting itself along the bottom. It made him look ridiculous.

I had to say something. 'You remember Agnes, don't you? I spend more time with her than I do you. And this is Bea and...'

Adrian turned round mid-sentence and disappeared into the hallway.

'We should make a move. Come on – Bea, Jem, eat up,' Agnes said, glancing sideways at me, gauging my reaction to Adrian's arrival back.

'No, take your time, it's fine. See what I mean? Have you ever met anybody quite as rude? I'm so sorry.'

'Don't worry, you know me. It's water off a duck's back, that kind of thing.'

'That's not the point. I've never been so off-hand when his friends turn up, which they do...' I added under my breath 'all the fucking time.'

I took a large gulp of the white Rioja. 'And he expects me to be the perfect hostess and rustle up a three-course meal.'

Agnes leant into me, resting her chin on my shoulder and whispered, 'You need to get out, hon.'

CHAPTER 23

Adrian didn't come downstairs that night, after Agnes and the children had left and Ned had gone to bed. I was thankful to avoid an argument. I couldn't face sleeping in the same bed as Adrian, not now, possibly not ever. I'd already made up the spare bed and, after taking Penny out into the garden at around eleven, went up to the spare room on the top floor as quietly as I could.

The next morning, after arriving back from dropping Ned at school, I only had twenty minutes before Mal was due to call. I'd been hoping Adrian would go out so I could relax while I was talking to Mal. Unless he did go out, Adrian would be in his studio at the bottom of the garden but, even so, I wouldn't necessarily hear him come into the house. I knew I'd constantly be on edge if there was a chance he'd be able to overhear me.

Having charged my phone, and not wanting to have to talk face to face to Adrian, I left the house with Penny. We walked eastwards along Westbourne Grove with the intention of picking up coffee. Eventually, having passed a few places with a huge queue, the Ottolenghi on Ledbury Road was almost empty.

Just as I was paying, Mal called. Even though I was expecting it, the shrill ring, up to maximum volume so I didn't miss his call, made me jump and I spilled half my coffee down my jeans.

'Let me sort you out with another one.' The young American woman who'd served me waived away my claims of responsibility.

'Hello you, what are you up to?'

'Oh, just scalding myself on hot coffee, how about you?'

'Well, I'm coming up to town on the train; bit of a late start but it was a busy weekend. I've got back-to-back meetings all afternoon so I'm not going to feel too guilty. So what's going on with you and Adrian? I was quite shocked when you told me it wasn't great. It all sounded idyllic up until then.'

'Yeah, I know, I put a positive spin on things when we started emailing. I just thought we'd exchange one or two messages and that would be it. There was no need to tell you everything had gone pear-shaped; I wanted to retain an iota of dignity if I could.'

Mal laughed. 'At our age, I think any dignity has long since dried up, my age anyway. I haven't forgotten you're a little younger than me. Looking good still, Kendrew, from what I saw on Facebook.'

'I can't bring myself to look at all your photos yet but, yes, in the ones I've seen...' I took a sip of coffee. 'So what happened with you and Louise?'

'Well, you know what it was like with us. She just kept going back to Stewart. It was like she was taunting me. On Facebook -- she was always a big fan of Facebook -- she'd post loads of photos of them together; having a romantic break in the Maldives, or nipping over to Paris for some shopping. I'm sure she only posted them to piss me off.'

'But there must have been something addictive about seeing her photos too, was there? Like you couldn't look away.'

'Yeah, totally. But, I dunno, I remember I got a birthday message from her, six or seven months ago. We weren't seeing each other, she was back with him, but she'd kept texting me, wanting to hook up. And then when she got in touch on my birthday, I saw the day before she'd posted photos of her and Stewart, all loved-up, having Sunday lunch in a country pub. I met her a few days after and some-thing had changed... in me, her too I think, but she persuaded me to try, one last time. It just felt wrong, meeting in hotels. That connection had gone. It felt toxic, sordid even.'

'I empathise. I'm sorry. So what now?'

'Oh, Alex, you know me. I've got Ewan, Arsenal, my mates, music. I have very little to complain about really. And you know, I'm sure you've worked it out for yourself – I'm just too selfish to have anything meaningful.'

'Well, 'meaningful' is hardly a word I'd use to describe my relationship either. Adrian came back from his place in the country but I've moved into the spare room. I can't bear the thought of his skin touching mine. Even his breathing annoys me, his smell, the way he turns over in bed.'

He didn't reply. After a few seconds I realised he must have lost a signal. I tried him but it went to voicemail. A minute later he called back.

'Sorry about that, we went into a tunnel.'

'I was just describing how much I hated sharing a bed with Adrian.'

'Yeah, I think I heard most of that. Blimey, it's that bad?'

'Yeah. I had a friend, a really old friend that's also an important client, over yesterday afternoon, after we'd been to the park with our kids. He just blanked her.'

'And it all started to go wrong as soon as you moved in?'

'Yes. But even before there were moments when the veneer wore thin and he showed his true self, but I thought it was the other way round – ninety-eight per cent benign. Nobody is entirely good, or entirely bad, are they?'

'That's an interesting thought, you're probably right. And instead he was ninety-eight per cent bad?'

'You got it in one.'

Penny and I has reached the café at the Serpentine. I'd rarely seen this part of the park so quiet. It was still early, not quite eleven. The lake was perfectly still, the sun glinting off it and giving the light a strange, hyper-real edge. In an hour the lake would be thronging with tourists and locals alike, in the blue pedaloes hired by the hour. The perfect spot for a selfie.

Penny was pulling me towards the water's edge, showing a little too much interest in the Canada Geese and swans – she wouldn't come off well in that encounter.

'So, can you extricate yours...'. I'd lost him again. We were walking round the end of the lake, past the café. I knew Mal would arrive at London Bridge soon, and our chat would end. I needed to get home and do some work.

Mal called again a few minutes later.

'Hey, sorry, it's such a pain, losing signal on this route.'

'I wanted to say how much I've enjoyed getting your messages. It really has been the highlight of every day, but I know we can't keep it up forever. What do you want to do? Could we meet up, perhaps?'

'Sure, that'd be nice. Let me have a look at my diary, I can give you a couple of dates. Sometime later this week?'

'Yeah, sounds great.'

We said goodbye. I stared at my phone; call with Malcolm Russell, fifty-four minutes, finished. A cocktail of emotions swirled together in my mind. Elation; expectation of what might follow. Sadness; as in his emails, there had been no great declaration in our chat that he wanted anything to happen between us.

His voice, so familiar yet I'd forgotten how he really sounded. He'd always had a way of making our phone calls very intimate in that brief period three or so years ago. We'd talked for hours on the phone a few times, before he'd dumped me. A couple of times he'd called totally out of the blue, just to say hello, just to hear my voice, he'd said. And, as he explained in an email a few days before, he felt like he'd known me longer than he had. That had to count for something, didn't it?

I felt deflated as I walked back to the house. The knowledge Adrian would be at home not helping. I was relieved to find his car was gone when we got back.

There had been a line drawn, after talking to Mal, and I imagined it would bring the email correspondence to a close. In a way it would be a relief. I needed to concentrate on work. The following week I had a shoot with Agnes art-directing; a catalogue job for a furniture retailer. There was a lot of organising to do before that.

Adrian was still in comedy sulk mode and I didn't think it was entirely down to Agnes being there on Sunday afternoon, more about the situation as a whole, and a realisation that the relationship had crossed a line. Not having children together, we didn't have that joint investment, the glue that bonds couples even if eventually it comes apart, like a photograph coming loose from its page in an album, the sticky squares drying out and turning to dust.

That evening, after getting Ned into bed and washing up after dinner, I sat down at my desk. I told myself it was to do an hour or so of work before bed but also I wanted to reply to the email Mal had sent earlier. Adrian was sitting at my iMac, on Facebook. He barely looked round when he heard me come into the room, Penny trotting behind me.

'What's going on?'

'I can't get a signal in the studio. We need to get onto BT – the Wifi is pathetic and I pay a fortune for it.'

'Did you not think it appropriate to ask me first, before you used my Mac?'

'No, I didn't. You haven't got anything to hide, have you?'

'That's not the point.' I knew I said it with a fair amount of vehemence, which he would probably interpret as a guilty conscience. I hoped I'd hidden my email app. Fuck. I had no way of knowing – even if it was hidden now, he could have done that. Why had I not been more careful? He clicked the browser window closed, stood up and, without looking at me, stormed out of the room, slamming the door behind him, leaving Penny whining. She hated us arguing.

I knew he hadn't logged off from Facebook. He never did. As long as I didn't log into my own account from the same browser, I'd be able to access his. I wasn't proud of it, but I knew there might be messages there that could be useful to me, especially if he found out about Mal.

I could hear the Newsnight theme and Kirsty Wark's voice from the TV room. Turning off the iMac, I grabbed my handbag and was quietly walking up to the spare room when Adrian appeared in the hallway. I could tell he'd been drinking. His cheeks were flushed and his eyes had that faraway look he had when he was well on the way to being pissed.

'Are we going to bed?'

I didn't answer until I'd reached the second-floor landing. 'I'm sleeping in the spare room.'

'Oh, that's fucking wonderful,' he said, walking into the kitchen, probably going back to get another beer from the fridge.

I turned off the light. I'd held off looking at Mal's Facebook photos, but now that we'd talked and were probably going to meet, what harm could it do? I flicked through his albums; holidays with Ewan, Arsenal matches, gigs. I was actively avoiding any with Louise, and quickly scrolled past any with women in. I sent him a reply.

Finally had a quick look at your Facebook – Ewan looks very grown up, very sweet. You've still got it, but I didn't cry!

I was exhausted after lying awake for most of the previous night. I quickly fell into a feverish, dream-laden sleep. I always found being in a different room disorientating – perhaps that was the reason I'd woken up. Moonlight flooded in through the skylight and, as my eyes adjusted, I remembered I wasn't lying next to Adrian. Yet I was aware of him; his smell, his breathing. I jerked my head round – he was kneeling on the floor by the bed, his hand between my legs, a finger or two working their way inside me.

'What the fuck are you do—'

He put his other hand over my mouth, at the same time holding my head against the pillow.

'Get off me!' I shouted, though it was muffled. I jerked my body from side to side so that he lost his hold on me.

He leant down so he could whisper in my ear. 'No. I'm going to fuck you up your cute, tight little arsehole and you're going to enjoy it.'

I could smell his breath; familiar, disgusting, beer mixed

with mouthwash. When he couldn't be bothered to brush his teeth, he'd just have a mouthful of it.

He pulled the bedlinen to one side. I was wearing an old, loose t-shirt, nothing on my lower half. He rolled me onto my front, pushing my head down into the pillow. With the other hand he held one of my thighs as far away from him as he could. A sharp snap of a tendon or muscle made me cry out loud. He pushed my face further down into the pillow. I kept writhing around to stop him. I was strong, but he was stronger. I knew he'd get what he wanted eventually.

When I felt his grip move from my neck to my thigh, I moved my head a fraction of an inch so I could breathe. I still resisted him by writhing around, but he fell on top of me, realising he could use his weight to stop me moving. I knew my resistance would be pissing him off. Either that or it would be a turn on. He had his full body weight on top of me and my ribs felt like they would crack. I could hardly breathe. I didn't know what was worse; letting him anally fuck me or the fallout from not.

'Get off me.' I kept repeating it, half whispering, half growling. I didn't want to wake Ned up.

He tried to get inside me but kept swearing under his breath. I could tell his hard-on had disappeared. We often had anal sex, usually him wanting it. Always, actually. I agreed when we'd already been fucking and if I'd been drunk, more relaxed, otherwise it was too painful. He'd always asked me if he could before. He would be hard, near to coming, and I said yes, knowing it wouldn't last very long. But he'd drunk too much this time and with me resisting, it wasn't going to happen.

He staggered off the bed, his watch grazing my neck as he pulled his arm away. 'You cunt.'

It wasn't clear if he was addressing himself or me.

CHAPTER 24

I didn't know what to do. What happened; was it enough to report him to the police? Or would they just tell me to go away? On the way back from dropping Ned at school I rang the managing agents to see if I could break the lease so that Ned and I could move back to Gipsy Hill. I suggested I could pay the family a couple of months' rent if they moved out in the next month or so. They said they would try but couldn't guarantee anything.

I saw I had a text from Mal. *I'm glad I've still got it! Perhaps you didn't cry because you now know what a nightmare I'd be in a relationship... discuss!*

I decided to call him. Seeing his name on my screen still shocked me, even though it had happened a few times now, it still felt surreal.

'Hello you, everything okay?' He sounded mildly concerned.

What could I tell him? I didn't want to sound hysterical so I tried to keep my voice even.

'Not really. Last night he tried to rape me.'

I didn't give him time to respond. 'He's in a complete

sulk because I've moved out of the bedroom. He got drunk last night, realised I wasn't coming to bed, and—'

'Wait, has he done this before? You sound quite calm, considering... too calm.'

'No, not really. I mean, he has forced himself on me, occasionally. But not with the strength he used last night. Anyway, he couldn't keep it up, he'd drunk too much.'

'That's terrible, you have to go to the police.'

'No, I can't, I've thought about it, but...'

'What are you doing today? I'll come and see you.'

'There's no need, I'm fine.'

'No. Listen, I don't have any meetings, after one starting in about ten minutes. I could meet you somewhere at around one?'

'Okay. How about the King's Road?'

'Great. The bar at the Royal Court?'

I came off the phone and looked in the mirror. In my twenties an up-all-night look the next day added a certain element; dark circles under the eyes equalled up-all-night drinking or dancing or fucking. That was long gone. I looked terrible.

What was I going to wear? I thought it was likely we'd meet at some point over the next few weeks and I had a few outfits in mind. A red wrap-around dress – too flirtatious, considering the conversation we'd had earlier. A floaty, low-cut white shirt I'd imagined pairing with leggings and strappy mules – not right either. I had a shower, washed my hair, and, as I was drying it, decided on a pair of slim-fitting suit trousers and a silky black blouse.

By the time I'd finished getting ready, I didn't have much time. Driving would be quicker than getting the tube. Adrian's car was parked in the driveway. I assumed he was out. I went back into the house to check I'd turned my Mac off, and that I hadn't left any evidence. Penny sat looking expectantly. She'd come to school with me, but she would have to wait until I got back for a proper walk. I left a note on the kitchen table. *Penny needs a walk.*

I'd had a Sharon Van Etten's *Tramp* playing in the car for the last few weeks. I've always adored the second track of the album, 'Give Out'; I turned the volume up and sang along, the pertinence of the words sending a shiver up my spine. Mal *was* the reason I'd move to the city.

I arrived at the theatre with five minutes to spare. In the toilet the artificial light confirmed my fears; I looked tired and stressed. I was looking thin though. I hadn't eaten much over the last few days. That was a consolation.

I found a table that I hoped would be quiet and give us some privacy. Watching the stairs made me nervous so I checked my emails instead. Just as I was scrolling through them, I became aware of someone slowly walking towards me. Mal.

I stood up and we kissed, very gently. We locked eyes and I felt tears forming. I hugged him before they could escape.

'It's so good to see you.' The understatement of the century.

We pulled away, loosely holding each other's fingers.

'Looking good, Ms Kendrew,' he said, his gaze moving slowly down.

'You too,' I replied, blushing.

'What can I get you?' he asked.

'A double espresso would be perfect, thanks.'

'Nothing changed on that front, then?'

'Nope.'

As he stood in the queue, I was able to get a good look at him. I suspected he'd have done the same. He had been the object of my desire for so long, I knew it was bizarre, ridiculous even, that I had spent so little time with him. I tried to remember what he looked like undressed, during those few minutes in my bedroom, all those years ago. His frame was more wiry than I remembered. As he reached into his back pocket of his trousers to get his wallet, his open jacket revealed a long and lean torso. I wondered if he always wore fitted shirts to show it off.

He caught me gazing at him and winked. Not enough men wink these days. He smiled. I smiled back, blushed and looked down at my phone.

He came over with the drinks. 'So, last night? I still think you should be contacting the police.'

I retold the events of that night in more detail than I had over the phone but kept it quite sketchy. He didn't need to know everything.

'I've calmed down a bit now. I was very scared, even more so when I realised he couldn't get it up. I thought he might take it out on me in other ways.'

'That's really troubling. You're not going to stay with him, surely?'

'I'm trying to get the Gipsy Hill house back. I've got tenants at the moment. It's going to be expensive and difficult to break the tenancy agreement. But not impossible.'

'So what's his back story, Adrian? He sounds like he's got one.'

'Well, it's interesting. He had a very humble upbringing. Dad who left when he was a baby. He's got an older brother and sister. His mum was left to bring up the kids on her own. They lived on a council estate in Swindon. I've never met his sister, but his brother Peter is a lovely guy. He sounds like he grew up on a council estate in Swindon – you know, no airs and graces. He's very down to earth, he's a teacher, nice partner and kids. But Adrian has this weird, pseudo-posh thing going on. I think he went to art college and reinvented himself. From his voice, you'd think he'd grown up with a silver spoon in his mouth, completely different from Peter. He sold all his records when he was nineteen. I think he liked all the usual stuff for that time – The Smiths, REM, The Cure – he decided classical music was the way forward.'

Mal sat there looking bemused.

'He must have had some XTC if he grew up in Swindon,' he added.

'Yeah, probably.'

It was one of the things I loved about Mal – his encyclopedic knowledge of pop and rock trivia.

'I hate him already, and not just because of XTC.'

Mal took a few sips of his latte. 'Why do you think last night happened?' he asked, catching my eye.

'It's all about control with him. He wants me to behave in a certain way; tending to his every need; be submissive, cook for him every night, be at home when he wanted me there. When we first got together he kept buying me clothes, designer stuff, the kind of thing I'd only buy myself once in a blue moon. I thought he was treating me, to show how much he loved me, but I soon realised it was more about him wanting to decide how I looked all the time. I didn't want to dress like I spent every day having lunch with friends, or going to galleries'.

'What an arrogant shit. I hate him even more than I thought. What has he said to you? Has he apologised?'

'I haven't seen him. He's kept a low profile. Apologising really isn't his style.'

'How well does he get on with Ned? He must sense something is going on between you.'

'A few months ago he dreamt Adrian tried to kill me.'

Mal looked up from his coffee. 'Jesus.'

'I know, that's pretty extreme. Ever since, once or twice a week, Ned's woken up at some point in the evening and come down to check I'm okay. It's very sweet but he shouldn't need to worry about me, not at six years old. Adrian has totally failed to develop a relationship with Ned, that's been the main problem.'

'Have you talked to Ned about moving back to Gipsy Hill?'

'Yes, I asked him if he'd like to. He thought about it for a few seconds and then said, "I like it here." He's made lots of friends, he's settled at school. I don't know what to do.'

'But if you did move back, he'd just pick up where he left off, wouldn't he? With friends and school?'

'I'd hope so, but it's a worry, in case he doesn't.'

My voice wavered. Mal was sitting close to me, our thighs touching. He reached a hand over and squeezed mine.

God, I'm sorry, it sounds like a terrible situation. I wish I could help.'

'Didn't I say my life sounded like a pile-up in one of my messages?' I rested my head on his chest, and he wrapped his arm around me.

'How about something stronger?' he asked.

I nodded, reaching for my bag. 'Yeah, my turn though.'

'Not a chance, Kendrew. Red?'

'You choose.'

I watched him queue again, that long and lean frame twisting under the suit as he leaned against the bar. How was it that I had been obsessed about him for so long and I couldn't really remember what he looked like with no clothes on?

I glanced at my watch; it was nearly four. I would have to leave soon if I was going to pick Ned up from after-school club. I texted Denny to see if she was free.

Mal came back with two enormous glasses. I'd forgotten to remind him I was driving.

We chinked.

'So, the conversation's been rather one-sided. What happened with you and Louise?'

'Oh, you know, I've told you all of it, really. It just got toxic, and I've got too old and selfish to really have a proper relationship.'

'Do you miss her?'

'That's a good question. The affair caused so much aggro. Over time I came to the conclusion I was happier when I was on my own, or with Ewan. And since his mum and I split up, I've never forgiven myself that he was caught in the crossfire as badly as he was. I've had to compensate for all the damage I did. I can't blame anyone else.'

We were sitting, our heads almost touching, talking quietly, the subject matter still sensitive. To onlookers, we must have looked like we were having an affair.

'But it sounds like your relationship with him is very solid. And he's a happy kid. You've got a lot to be proud of.'

Mal had this way of becoming a little embarrassed when I complimented him. His cheeks coloured ever so slightly, he looked down, eyes shaded by lashes. Those bloody crows' feet.

'I don't know. I wish I'd done things differently.'

'In what way?'

'I wouldn't have had an affair for a start.'

'You would have just left Mel, asked her for a divorce?'

'Yes. It would have been less painful. Anyway, it's pointless thinking about how that would have panned out...'

'And has there been anyone since?' I looked at him intently. I wanted him to be honest, and not say something just to stop me getting hurt.

'Well, there was someone at work. She's a lot younger. We kind of fell into it. She'd broken up with someone – classic rebound. It was kind of fun, but we both knew it wouldn't last. On the upside for her, she changed departments as a result and it was a promotion, so it was all okay in the end.'

This stung more than it should. I looked down, not wanting him to see my eyes fill with tears.

'Alex, I'm sorry, I...'

'It's okay. I knew you wouldn't have been living the life of a monk. It's an effective litmus test – you know you still have feelings for someone if the thought of them fucking someone else really hurts.'

There was an awkward silence for a moment while I looked down, embarrassed that I'd got upset.

'So what are you going to do next?' he asked, changing the subject.

'The only option is to move back to Gipsy Hill as soon as we can. I still don't know when. A month or so, maybe more. I've been wondering if I could keep Ned at the same school and travel across town every day, perhaps until the end of the summer term.'

'What do you want to happen with Adrian?'

'I want out. I was stupid. I thought I'd fallen in love with him. I think after you, I just wanted to have something concrete. He seemed to really want me too... perhaps we just got carried away. Plus the shared history we'd had when we were at college. It was foolish, looking back.'

'Do you love him?'

'No,' I said, more emphatically than I meant to. 'Within a

few days of moving in with him I realised I didn't. And it was like he thought, "well, she's here now, I don't need to make an effort". As well as all the controlling stuff, it's like being married to someone from the 1950s. Who expects dinner on the table at seven every evening these days?'

'He's not going to tonight,' Mal smiled as he looked at his watch.

'Fucker.'

I told Mal I'd tried to organise a babysitter and checked my phone. Denny had replied; she could pick up Ned but was only free until eight to give her time to get back to south London.

It was surreal, sitting there with Mal, after years of thinking I'd never see him again. He looked at me in the way he had when we had first met, in the Ritzy café. He was a typical 'bloke'. I'd never met anyone like Mal before and when I first met him, it felt good, different, to be with someone who loved football and going to the pub with his mates, who might choose a holiday destination because of its beaches and weather rather than its architecture and culture. Not in a million years would Adrian be described as a 'bloke'.

We talked about both our sons; what they were doing at school, what they were into, how both of them had a confidence we didn't have when we were kids. We talked a lot about music.

'Have you seen 'Call Me By Your Name?' God, I was never a Sufjan Stevens fan before but I've gone and bought everything he's ever done.'

'Yeah, great film... I'll never look at a peach in quite the same way again.' We both laughed. 'Visions of Gideon is really beautiful, they all are, but his best song is 'All of Me

Wants All of You.' I reached over and kissed him. 'Let's watch that film together sometime.'

The conversation moved on to work. I talked about how it had been increasingly difficult to get good freelance jobs, how everyone these days could take a photograph. 'Why would anyone pay someone to take them when you can do them yourself on your phone?'

Mal told me how he'd grown to hate his job, that the only reason he was still there was because his financial commitments were sky-high. He paid a fortune to his wife; maintenance and her mortgage. 'My affair cost me a lot more than just a crap marriage.'

The daylight that had flooded the space from the glass bricks in the ceiling had dissipated. Only the far end of the bar was illuminated in its orange glow. Time was running out. I didn't want the evening to end, especially when there was no guarantee I would see Mal again.

Mal insisted on walking me back to the car, even though I protested. All the shops were closing, apart from the odd café, and the Kings Road had fallen quiet. We turned off, down leafy side streets where commercial properties quickly made way to terraces of manicured red-brick mansion blocks. I'd left the car next to a little park though hadn't made a note of its name. I didn't want Mal to think I was an idiot and not remember where. It was a mixture of relief and sadness when we turned a corner and I spotted the black railings next to where I'd parked.

'Well, this is me.' I glanced through the window into the back seat. 'New car, still messy,' I added, remembering how embarrassed I'd been when Mal had walked me to my car on our first date.

'You should see mine after Ewan's been in it. Discarded Coke cans and McDonalds wrappers everywhere.'

There was a silence for a few moments, the first since we'd met three or four hours earlier, as we stood a few inches apart.

'Well, this has been fun,' he said, possibly to prevent the break in conversation becoming awkward.

Before I had a chance to answer he leant in and kissed me. Gently. His kisses were always so gentle, more sensuous because of it. He put his arms around my waist and I instinctively wrapped mine around his neck, running my fingers through his hair. Three or four times we parted and then came together, becoming more urgent each time.

I ran my hand up between the silky lining of his jacket and shirt, my fingers running over his back and shoulder blade. I held him, my head resting on his shoulder. 'You know, there's not a single day gone by that I haven't thought about you.'

Not always good thoughts – I kept that part to myself.

'I'm not worth it, Alex. You must realise that. I'm just a bit of fun.'

'No you're not. I mean, not that you're not fun, but...' I kissed his neck as we continued to hold each other. 'Every day.'

Eventually we loosened the embrace. I looked at him, needing to gauge his reaction. It was hard to tell. He'd always looked at me in a way that made me feel wanted. But I needed him to know I wanted him too. Our gaze held until he glanced down, that signature blush colouring his cheeks.

I opened the car door. 'I can't give you a lift home?'

'I'm in diametrically the opposite direction to you,' he answered. 'And you need to get home to your boy.'

'Well, let's stay in touch, huh?'

'Yeah. See you soon.'

I sat gathering my thoughts for a moment as I watched

him walk across the road, round a corner and out of sight. I started the car, setting off in the same direction he'd gone. As I turned into Smith Street, my phone lit up with a message. Denny. I stopped in the middle of the road, checking no-one was behind me. *Don't worry about rushing back – don't need to leave until 10-ish, Dave is going to pick me up. Take your time, darlin', you deserve a bit of fun.*

I glimpsed Mal from the back, between parked cars. I saw a gap on the left side of the street. I swerved into it, lowering the window. I didn't think he'd spotted me – he looked lost in thought.

'Cab for Mr Russell,' I called out of the window. He laughed.

'Get in. I don't need to be home. Denny can stay with Ned for a couple of hours. And anyway, I'm not ready to say good night.'

He sat down in the passenger seat and closed the door. When we kissed a few minutes earlier, it had been restrained; a goodbye kiss. In the car, it quickly escalated – our mouths wrestling, his hands on me, mine feeling his chest and torso. My hair fell into my face and I had to push it away to stop it getting caught up as we kissed. The space was limited. It was both restrictive and exciting.

'I've got an idea.' I smoothed my hair and clothes, started the car. Mal leaned back in the seat, his arm resting behind my neck.

'That sounds intriguing.'

The traffic was light along the Kings' Road, round Sloane Square, down towards the river. The bridge looked picture-perfect, arcs of twinkly lights rising to the middle of the bridge and falling away on the other side.

Mal moved his hand down to rest on my left knee. As he

began to move it up my thigh, he asked where we were going.

'Almost there.'

Over the bridge, I took the first turn right, through the heavy iron gates into Battersea Park. Under the avenue of horse chestnuts, it was quiet, the light underneath them inky blue.

The car park was almost empty. We parked away from the path that ran along the riverbank. A Wandsworth Council van drove slowly along the road towards the main gates.

He kissed me, more urgently than earlier, holding my head and pushing me towards him.

'Let's move to the back seat,' he whispered in my ear.

Mal got out and came round to the driver's side, opening the door for me and taking my hand. We kissed again, his mouth moving down my neck. I ran my fingers through his hair as he unbuttoned my shirt – one or two, just enough to expose my bra. He kissed me there, expertly unfastening the strap at the back. I reached down to unbuckle his belt, the clasp on his suit trousers, feeling his hard-on, silky and smooth underneath his briefs.

'Wait Alex, are you sure about this? After last night?'

Mal lay on the back seat.

'I've never been more sure about anything.'

I knelt down and took him in my mouth. I broke off to catch my breath and to look at him, holding his gaze as I took his erection in my hand. I ran my fingers up and down, coming back to the head, rubbing it with my thumb and squeezing before I sucked him again.

'God, you're good at that,' he half whispered, half groaned. I don't remember either of us saying another word.

He pulled me up, out of the footwell. We kissed again. And then we fucked, still three-quarters dressed. Dishevelled, hot, sweaty. He held my hair, just tightly enough for it to be sexual, gentle enough for me to feel desired and womanly. I loved the way he kissed me, the way he looked at me.

As I drove Mal home, I resisted the temptation to ask what he was thinking, what might happen next. The roads were quiet and, as we drew closer to Herne Hill, I was sad that the journey had been short. The time I was spending with Mal was drawing to a close with every green traffic light.

CHAPTER 25

The next morning I felt like I might have dreamt the whole thing, had I not felt a little bruised. No message from Mal, but I wanted to break the silence with something light and breezy, and to communicate that I had no regrets. *Those few hours were the most fun I've had in a long time. Thank you. I could taste you on my lips all the way home...*

Half an hour later, Mal replied. *Yes, a lot of fun... probably just as well you have tinted windows in the back of your car... Fancy getting together again soon?*

I hopped and skipped on the way back from school after dropping Ned. How things would progress, I didn't know. What was going to happen with Adrian? I had no idea how I was going to extricate myself. But I knew that my relationship with him had turned sour before Mal had reappeared on the scene. I found I kept justifying it to myself, just as I knew I would have to with everybody else. But for the moment, I just wanted to savour the excitement of being back in touch with Mal.

Before I picked up Ned from school, I bought a bunch of

peonies from the flower stall outside the tube station and popped round to see Itsumi. I met her shortly after we'd moved in with Adrian. She lived seven or eight houses away and was often watering her front garden as I walked to school with Ned and Penny in the morning. We had started to say hello to each other and quickly became friends. Itsumi – pronounced 'it's me' – was Japanese, in her seventies, and I loved that her hair was a different colour every time I saw her.

Her house was modern, probably built in the 70s. It was ugly, she was the first to admit it, but she'd allowed ivy to grow all over it, small patches of red brick only visible here and there.

Itsumi made green tea, and we sat drinking it from delicate black bowls on her small balcony.

'So, what's happening with Adrian?' she asked, with steady glaucomic eyes.

'Oh, it's not great.' I smiled weakly. I didn't know whether to talk about Mal. 'But Ned is very well, I know he'd love to see you.'

'I'd love to see him too, pop round any time with him, he's such a joy. I wish Haruto and Naoki were closer.'

She had two sons – Kenzo was the eldest and lived in Paris with his French wife. He'd produced grandchildren – Haruto and Naoki. Itsumi adored them and often hopped on Eurostar to visit. Ned was almost exactly the same age as Naoki, and I hoped it was a comfort spending time with Ned, rather than making her feel even further away from her grandchildren.

'I'll bring Ned round any day you like. How about Friday?'

She nodded, and I willed myself to remember to write it

down in my diary later. Despite Itsumi's years, I was much more likely to forget.

My breezy, short reply when she asked about Adrian had not put her mind at ease. When I was getting ready to leave, she asked me again and I gave her a summary of recent events, leaving out the attempted rape. She'd only met Adrian a couple of times and was far too polite to criticise him. But I knew she was alluding to him when, one morning a month or so earlier, we bumped into each other in the park and she started to tell me about her husband, Takehiro. He had been emotionally abusive, and capitalised on the clearly-defined gender roles in Japanese society, as well as the general male chauvinism of 1970s England.

She said she'd always hoped Takehiro would change, and that she stayed with him while the children were growing up in the hope that he would. Finally, he divorced her to marry his twenty-something PA. Itsumi had her own career as a translator and I think her family had been wealthy so she didn't rely on her husband financially. She walked away without fighting over the family home or maintenance for the children.

'I was free of him, Alex, you must do the same before Adrian kills your spirit. That's what men like him want.'

She was right, I just couldn't see it, and no-one else had the guts to tell me. I'd only known her a matter of months but I felt closer, more able to confide in this elderly Japanese lady with violet hair than to anyone else.

Mal and I meeting brought about a change in pace in our communication. The long emails stopped, and we moved to short texts and daily phone calls. Sometimes he'd call on the train home after evening drinks with colleagues or an Arsenal match.

Mal was spending the weekend after our meeting down in Brighton with Ewan. I hadn't seen or heard from Adrian for days, but one morning he texted me to announce he was going to Paris to discuss a potential exhibition at a gallery on the Left Bank. *Like I give a shit*, I thought to myself as I deleted the message.

My usual routine had been skewed with everything that was happening with Mal. I tried to organise a few social things for Ned over the weekend – having a friend over or meeting in the park. But I wanted to spend some quality time with him too.

I hadn't looked at my diary all week and I felt a stab of guilt mixed with slight annoyance when I got a text from Caroline to see if it was still okay for her to come and stay at the weekend. I hadn't contacted her since Mal had been back in touch. *Can't wait to see you all!* she'd said at the end. I couldn't cancel at the last minute, so I texted her back to tell her Adrian was away and asked if she might like to come another weekend soon so she didn't miss him. *Oh, no, don't worry, I don't mind at all. That means more time with you and Ned!*

I didn't know if I should mention what was happening with Mal to Caroline. She would be quietly judgmental about it, I was sure. I would just have to see how it panned out. Last time she'd stayed, there had been a few awkward moments. It had been a couple of days after my birthday – she'd come armed with flowers and prosecco. Adrian had seen my birthday as an excuse to bring a case of Bolinger up from the cellar, transferred all twelve bottles to the wine fridge, and we, or rather he, had been working his way through it.

'Let's open a bottle,' he announced, after we'd said our hellos, with a vaguely stiff hug between him and Caroline.

'Oh, I brought one with me,' she piped up.

I can't remember his exact words but it was his expression that said it all. He was as much of a snob about wine as he was most things – supermarket prosecco versus Grande Année was no contest as far as he was concerned. Though most people would have graciously accepted the gift he did not feel such niceties need apply to him. Caroline just stood there, looking deflated and embarrassed as he'd picked up the bottle she'd brought and dismissively placed it on the side. I grabbed it.

'I'll put it in the fridge and we can have it once it's chilled,' I added breezily, throwing an accusing glance at Adrian.

During that same weekend, thankfully, there was an evening when Adrian had taken his daughters out for dinner. We'd been to the park with Ned and he'd fallen over and scraped his knee. After cleaning it up we'd abandoned the idea of going out to eat and, as I chopped vegetables for cooking, Caroline sat on a stool next to me while Ned watched TV.

'So what did Adrian buy you for your birthday?' she asked at one point.

Adrian had an infuriating tendency to tease. Nothing was ever straight-forward, and no comment or compliment could be taken at face value. Over the couple of years we'd been together, he'd often bought me elaborate gifts, not just for birthdays and Christmas, but randomly. Over time, it dawned on me the gifts – a dress or necklace – were often given just before a private view or an important dinner and he would expect me to wear them. It took me a while to realise the timing was calculated. He wanted everyone to see them and comment on them and I would have to be endlessly grateful.

For my birthday, he'd bought me a car; a huge Audi built like a tank. He was embarrassed to have my ten-year-old Golf on the driveway. He thought I'd sold it, but I drove it back to south-east London and left it there with a couple of hundred quid in cash in the glove compartment. Someone had once said to me 'Always be ready to get away if you need to.' I'd taken that seriously. I always had some cash stuffed into a shoe box when I lived with Sean, before that too.

I'd had to follow clues that finally led to the car. They were all written on postcards – some were red herrings – some were little messages telling me how much he loved me, or did I realise there were still five rooms in the house where he hadn't fucked me yet? I had to collect the post-cards, all depicting famous paintings by artists he admired. I felt like I'd tackled an assault course at the end of it. He'd been very proud of all the planning and insisted I kept all the postcards as a memento. They were propped up against the mirror above the fireplace in the lounge.

I told Caroline the story. She sat goggle-eyed at the lavishness of it all. She peeked a look out of the window at the car. 'Sandy, you're so lucky!'

I raised an eyebrow. As I started frying onions and garlic, I saw her reflection in the fridge door, wandering round the lounge, studying photos on bookshelves and Adrian's paintings on the walls.

I took a gin and tonic through to Caroline and saw her standing with the postcards in her hand.

'Oh, no, please don't read them, some of them are quite...' I blurted out as quickly as I could, lunging forwards, ready to snatch them away.

Rude, I would have added, too late to stop her turning beetroot.

'I'm going to fuck you in every room in the house, and I want you to dress like this,' he had written on the back of a postcard of Edouard Manet's *Olympia*. Attached to it was a black velvet ribbon, like the one Olympia was wearing around her neck. On the ribbon was a small silver key and at the end of the note was the line 'find the keyhole for this to discover a secret hiding place.'

It was a bit over-the-top but I knew that kind of thing appealed to him and I'd played along. Some of the postcards were simple declarations of love. Another, on the back of Berthe Morisot's *Julie Manet and Her Greyhound Laertes,* were promises to capture mine and Penny's likeness in oil as Morisot's daughter had been with her dog.

There was one gynaecological description of me on the back of a postcard of a pencil sketch by Egon Schiele entitled *Woman Masturbating*, in the kind of detail I would never be able to verify unless I took some selfies.

For Caroline's imminent visit, I was prepared to go to great lengths to avoid a similar incident.

CHAPTER 26

I decided to keep quiet about the situation with Adrian, not to mention Mal and, depending on how everything panned out, tell Caroline more the next time I saw her. She arrived late on Friday evening and, after I'd put Ned to bed, we settled down on the sofa with a gin and tonic, easing into the comfortable, familiar way we had with each other.

I'd hoped Adrian's absence would dispel any interest in him, but Caroline kept bringing him up in conversation. I answered her questions with a short explanation and changed the subject, hoping she'd take the hint. When she didn't, I stood up and used getting dinner ready as an excuse to count to ten and calm down.

It worked. As I stood in the kitchen, I mentally listed a handful of questions about her family that would require long answers. When she joined me a few minutes later, I was ready.

'So, how's your mum doing?'

'She hasn't really begun to recover, to be honest. She's been prescribed sleeping tablets, and she's having counselling. I think sometimes she's more traumatised by the divorce than his death.' Caroline looked close to tears.

I went over to give her a hug but realised my hands were covered in garlic. I washed them first, by which time the moment had passed.

'Really? That's quite... why do you think that? I thought they'd separated quite amicably.'

'I thought so too, the whole family did. It seemed almost too easy. It wasn't until afterwards... do you know he had an affair?'

'Your dad? No, I can't believe that. He...'

'Didn't seem the type?'

'Yes, I guess that's what I meant.'

'He'd been seeing a woman on his rowing team. She was younger, twenty years or so. We didn't have proof until...'

She'd hesitated, even before we both heard Ned stumbling down the stairs. I rushed into the hall to meet him.

'Are you okay, Mummy?'

'Of course, sweetheart, what's the matter? Did something wake you up?'

'I had a terrible dream again.'

'What kind of dream? Not a nightmare?'

'The same one...'

I whispered, not wanting Caroline to overhear. 'Adrian wouldn't do that, darling, we've talked about this, haven't we?'

'I saw him hurting you the other night. And there were some photos on the computer this afternoon.'

I froze, panic rushing into my thoughts. Ned looked up at me, hoping I'd have some explanation. I pulled him to me, wrapping my arms around him, his head resting against my stomach. I reached down and asked as gently as I could, 'What did you see him doing to me?' Even before the words had come out of my mouth, I knew the answer. I flinched in preparation, holding him tighter.

'It was in the middle of the night, not in your bedroom, in the room next to Guiliana and Issy's room. I woke up and needed a wee so I went to the toilet and that's when I saw him. He had his hand round your throat. I thought he was going to kill you, Mummy. I moved away from the door so he wouldn't see me, and then you shouted at him and he stopped.'

How on earth could I explain that? He was sobbing, his face buried in my t-shirt. I picked him up, like I had when he was a toddler, his head snuggled into my neck, legs wrapping round my hips. I felt his hot tears trapped between his skin and mine.

'We were just having a game. He was tickling me.'

He lifted his head to look at me. I flinched as he studied my face, on some level knowing I wasn't being truthful. His crying stopped instantaneously, in that way only children can manage.

'You were playing a game?'

'Yes, sweetheart, we were.'

'It didn't look like a game. You kept telling him to get off.'

'That's only because he was squashing me. Don't worry about it, darling, I'm completely fine.'

His eyes were red-rimmed, cheeks flushed and streaked with tears, hair in full bed-head mode. I felt terrible lying to him, even worse that I'd been able to so easily, but the reality? I couldn't have explained it at his age. We hadn't ever got onto the subject of sex, though I knew that wouldn't be far off. I hoped by the time it did, this incident would be well and truly forgotten about and he would never make the connection.

I carried him back to his room. I could feel his body

relax and take on the weight of sleep. I pulled up his duvet, putting his favourite cuddly sheep next to him.

'Night night, Mummy,' he said, already half asleep. I was relieved his anxiety seemed to have lifted. I waited for a few minutes – I missed watching him sleeping. I'd forgotten Caroline was there until I heard her on the landing.

'Is everything okay?' she whispered, perhaps not as quietly as she could. The sound caused a tiny reflex in Ned – the Moro – a slight lifting of the arms. Even at seven, Ned still had it, very slightly, when he was falling sleep. It was so sweet, the last trace of babyhood.

'Yes, he just had a nightmare. He's gone back to sleep.'

We went back downstairs.

'I need a drink.' I went to the fridge – there was only a glass or so left in the wine bottle. 'Would you like this? I need something stronger.'

I took the glass of white wine to her. 'There's something I need to do, I'll only be a few minutes.'

'Okay. I'm catching up on Springwatch anyway, don't worry about me.'

I went to my Mac and opened up iCloud. Ned and I had been looking at the films of his keepie-uppies earlier. He'd also wanted to see photos of when he was a baby. Most of the ones I'd taken had been on my Canon and, terrified of losing them, I'd stored a copy on iCloud as well as external hard drives and my iMac. Recently, I'd accidentally integrated my iCloud account with Adrian's. It must have been something to do with us being on the same package, perhaps it happened automatically. When Ned and I had been looking through all the photos earlier, I'd seen some Adrian's daughters must have taken on his phone. I'd dragged him into the twenty-first century, kicking and screaming when I bought him an iPhone for his birthday.

He was still resisting, but his daughters were encouraging his foray into technology.

I opened up iCloud. My password loaded automatically. I was going to have to change that. I clicked on 'Photos'.

There were dozens of shots taken two days earlier – I had to scroll down quite a way to see them all. All taken in Paris, Rue de Rivoli. I recognised the hotel. Adrian had taken me for a weekend a few months after we'd started living together. It was not far from the Champs-Elysées; some rooms overlooked Le Jardin des Tuileries. The style was very traditional, all Louis XVI furniture, gilt mirrors, chandeliers, and parquet floors.

Taking a large swig of whisky, I opened the first thumbnail. It was of James, Adrian's agent, with his arm round a young girl; classically French, dark-haired, high cheekbones. She looked like she might be in her mid-teens and was dressed in a pale pink camisole top and tight jeans, her hair tied in a high ponytail.

The first dozen or so were of James and the girl drinking champagne and laughing. They reminded me of the shot that was all over social media of Prince Andrew with the young girl Jeffrey Epstein had introduced him to. Very respectable, apart from the fact the girl was undeniably young enough to be his daughter. The next group were of Adrian, with the girl, and then another around the same age. The next girl was blonde and looked drunk or stoned, her expression blank, eyes unfocused. The next row of thumbnails showed the girls undressing, the last few out-of-focus close-ups of indeterminate areas of flesh.

Further down were videos. I opened one at random. It showed James on the bed with the two girls. The blonde was sitting on his face, the brunette vigorously giving him a blow job. I recognised Adrian's laughter. As he moved closer to the bed, James' groans became louder, the image blurring and refocussing as Adrian crouched down to capture what I imagined was the money shot. I didn't need to see that. I paused the film, took photos of all the thumbnails on my phone, showing the date and location. I emailed myself a couple of the videos, and then downloaded everything onto a USB stick, and shut down the computer.

The Springwatch credits rolled as I joined Caroline on the sofa.

'Everything okay?' she said, looking mildly concerned as she turned the TV off.

'Yes, I'll tell you about it in the morning. Nothing to worry about.' I smiled weakly. 'Caroline, you didn't finish telling me about your dad.'

'Oh, don't worry, Mum will be fine in time.'

We spent the next morning shopping along Westbourne Grove and having lunch. My deal with Ned was that we did grown-up stuff in the morning. In the afternoon he could practice cycling without stabilisers again and then we'd see a film at the multiplex at Westfield.

When we arrived back home around eight, I knew something was wrong. Adrian's car was parked next to mine on the drive and the lights were on in the lounge and the bedroom. I ran up the steps to the door and tried to open it – the key jammed. I hammered on the door and, when nothing happened, called Adrian's number. I could hear the phone ringing inside the house but it went to voicemail. Penny started barking on the other side of the door. I tried to calm her, letting her know it was me, but this made matters worse. She yowled and sniffed at the bottom of the door before barking again.

I looked down at Ned and Caroline – both looked confused.

'Can you just walk round the block for a minute?' I said, as calmly as I could.

Caroline frowned, but nodded in agreement. As they turned to walk the way we'd come, Ned looked over his shoulder at me, but his gaze suddenly moved to the lounge window. Adrian had appeared, a sardonic grin forming. He mouthed through the glass, 'Sorry, changed the locks.'

His eyebrows lifted as his grin broadened into a laugh, just for a moment before he composed himself. There was a glint in his eye; something I'd seen many times, often when he thought sex was on the cards. I'd found it cute, sexy even, in his own, buttoned-up kind of way. Now I just wanted to punch him.

'Let me in, you cunt,' I shouted, knowing that Ned was possibly still in earshot. Not a word I used often but it was wholly appropriate for Adrian.

He kept the grin, but slowly shook his head, and mouthed 'no'.

I turned away from him and dug around in my bag for my phone. I opened my emails, and scrolled down until I found the few I'd emailed to myself the night before. At random I chose one, downloaded the mp4 file, clicked play and stretched my arm out towards the window to give him a better view.

The grin faded, replaced momentarily by confusion, embarrassment, and finally anger. He disappeared from view and a few seconds later the door opened, Penny yelping with delight that I was finally being let in.

'Family Sharing on iCloud, not a good idea when you're shagging underage girls.\

'They weren't underage.'

'They said that, did they? Or their pimps? What's the French word for pimp?' I was quite enjoying this.

'What do you want?'

'I'd have thought that was obvious. Don't even think about coming back here, until we've moved back to Gipsy Hill. I'll let you know when we've left. Unless you'd like me to show these videos to the police…?'

CHAPTER 27

Mal was understandably reluctant to come to the Westbourne Grove house. 'I don't want Adrian turning up while we're in bed, and he decides the only appropriate response is to cut my penis off with a bread knife.'

He had a point. Going to Mal's, where he rented a room from his colleague, wouldn't have been appropriate either. Even though Sally was often away at the bank's head office in Frankfurt, she didn't always let him know if she arrived back a day earlier than she'd expected.

Instead, we got into the habit of meeting in hotel rooms, usually during the day. Mal would book a few hours out in his diary, a few days ahead and then book the room.

We'd only had sex once – in the car in Battersea Park. It had been unbelievably exciting, because of the situation and the unexpectedness of it all. What if, in the cold light of day, or even the soft, warm, flattering light of a plush hotel room, he found my forty-something body with all its flaws unappealing?

The first afternoon we met at a hotel, as the hours before

disappeared, fear took over, and I felt sick with apprehension. Are they the same thing – fear and excitement? I wanted it to be perfect.

The first few times were a little too rushed. We were constantly aware of the ticking clock, foreplay all but dispensed with.

Over time, we slowed down. A few hours before we were due to meet one evening, I sent him a text. *I'm going to undress you slowly, one button at a time. Next, I'll lead you over to the bed... and ask you to lie down on top of the towels I've already put there. I'm going to massage you... your back first. I'll sprinkle more oil between my palms and sweep them over your chest and shoulders, one moment pushing down with all my strength, the next gliding my fingertips lightly along the sides of your torso. Next, I'll work down your legs and ask you to turn over. Do you think at that stage there might be any part of your body that requires special treatment...?*

He replied a few minutes later. *OMG, Kendrew, how am I supposed to present the latest growth figures to the board now?!?*

We talked about having a weekend away together. He understood it was difficult with Ned. Towards the end of September, Mal suggested I go down to Brighton to stay for a night, as a compromise. *Wednesday night?* he asked me in a text, the weekend before.

I replied, panic rising in my chest as I searched around, thinking who could look after Ned. *Yeah, sure, sounds great.*

I was on the verge of asking Sean if he could come, when I remembered Caroline had offered to stay. She needed to use up some holiday as the photo library were about to upgrade their website and there wouldn't be anything for her to do while it was happening.

Wow, that would be fab, if you're sure you haven't got better things to do than look after a nutty seven-year-old!

She replied. *Nope.* Followed by smiley and sad face emojis.

In the morning, I finished off a shoot at Agnes'. The traffic was a mess on the way back to Westbourne Grove and I arrived home with minutes to spare before Caroline was due to arrive. I threw toiletries into a small travel bag and rifled through my wardrobe as I cleaned my teeth.

We met Ned as his class spilled out into the playground and, as we walked home, he told us about the afternoon's lessons. Maths, followed by art. He loved his new teacher, Miss Flitlock.

I showed Caroline where everything was for supper, and reminded Ned which drawers his clean uniform was kept in.

I hugged Ned, told him to be a good boy for Auntie Caroline. She followed me out into the hall.

'Nice dress, where's that from?'

I followed her gaze down to my feet. My running shoes were turquoise with magenta flashes and resolutely did not go with the geometric black and white dress I'd hastily chosen. I'd never mastered the art of driving in heels so I'd put on trainers for the drive. Women in smart work clothes and trainers had become such a look, but not the one I wanted for that evening.

'Shoot, I've forgotten to pack any shoes for later.' I ran upstairs and grabbed a pair to change into when I got to Mal's. I did one final sweep of the bedroom. I hadn't allowed time to do anything with my hair, so I grabbed a butterfly clip and twisted my hair into a bun in the hope that by the time I got to Brighton, it might have a bit more body. Back downstairs, I ran into the lounge and hugged Ned who was cuddled up on the sofa, watching kids' TV with Penny and the cats.

'Remember sweetheart, be a good boy, okay? I'll see you

after school tomorrow.' I kissed him on the top of his head and he briefly tore his gaze away from the screen.

'I will Mum, have a lovely time with your friend.'

In the hallway I hugged Caroline. 'Thank you so much, I owe you!'

I picked up my overnight bag.

'Have a great time, Sandy, I'll text you and let you know how Ned is.'

The traffic through town was hideous but I made up time on the motorway. I hadn't had any messages or calls which was a relief and, as the traffic slowed to a crawl as we neared the junction with the A27 on the outskirts of Brighton, I reached into my bag to get my phone. I could get myself to Brighton without needing satnav but my knowledge of the centre of town was too sketchy to find Mal's flat. I felt around but couldn't detect anything phone-shaped. Someone beeped me from behind; the cars in front had nosed forward.

When I reached Preston Park, I turned off the main road and stopped to search properly, but my phone wasn't there. I'd put it in my bag, I was sure of it. Could I picture doing it? Not quite.

I spotted a petrol station and pulled into one of the parking spaces at the side, away from the pumps. I ran into the shop and asked the cashier if there was a payphone. He looked at me as though I was mad.

'I've left my phone at home, can you think of anywhere I could make a call?'

'You can use mine, if you're quick and not calling Australia.'

He handed it to me and I tapped in Adrian's landline number. Caroline picked up after the first few rings. 'Hi, it's me, I've been really stupid and left my phone at home.'

'Yes,' she replied. 'I heard it ring a while ago. It was charging in the kitchen.'

Shit. 'Okay, can you do a couple of things for me? Can you go into my texts and find Mal's address? He sent it to me last night, there should only be a few messages after it.'

I heard her putting down the handset as she picked up my mobile. 'You haven't got a security code on it?'

'Er, no, Ned's always locking us out by using the wrong number so I thought it was less hassle not to have one.' I found a pen in the front of my bag and scrabbled around looking for a piece of paper but couldn't see anything so when she started reading out his address I wrote it on the back of my hand.

'Thanks,' I said. Just one more thing – can you text Mal and let him know I haven't got my phone and that I'm going to be a bit late? I should have been at his half an hour ago.'

'Sure, I'll do that now. Oh, by the way, Adrian's here, he said he was just picking up a few things… is that okay?'

'No, it's—'

'I don't know how long he's been here. I think he must have arrived when we went to pick up Ned, I didn't hear him come in after that. The door into the garden was open and he just wandered in.'

'He's got a key to the communal gardens at the back. Don't worry though, thanks for letting me know. I'm not going to stress about it now.'

'Okay, have fun, I'll text Mal now.'

I thanked the guy in the petrol station and got the road atlas out of the boot. I found the Brighton page – Brunswick Square, luckily, was right on the edge. I just had to keep driving until I hit the seafront and then head west.

I found a parking space, sprinted along one edge of the square and reached his flat.

I pushed the front door when the buzzer sounded. Mal called down to me from the top of a rectangular staircase, five stories high. The stairs were wide and shallow, with a thick royal blue carpet that looked like it had been vacuumed five minutes earlier. Mal ran down to meet me halfway and I apologised for being late.

'No need, you've made all the effort,' he said as we held each other for a moment, our mouths instinctively finding each other's. We kissed like teenagers.

His hallway was filled with all my favourite cooking smells; basil, garlic, onions sweating in butter. The ceiling heights were typical of Regency properties and everything felt spacious and airy. He was on the top floor and had a panoramic view of the sea, even though he was at the far end of the square. He led me up to a small roof terrace where he'd set a table.

I'd never been a huge fan of Brighton, or any seaside town for that matter, but as he went back down to the kitchen to make us a gin and tonic, I surveyed the skyline and thought, from this perspective, I could change my mind.

Mal's kitchen was to die for; stainless steel surfaces contrasted perfectly with painted brickwork, a good range oven with plenty of expensive copper-bottomed pans and matching utensils hanging above it. While he stirred stock into the risotto, I sat on a bar stool with my G&T.

'D'you know, if someone had told me six months ago I'd spend an evening sitting in Malcolm Russell's kitchen watching him cook me dinner, I'd have told them they were nuts.'

I remembered how, that first afternoon we met in the Royal Court bar, I'd studied his frame as he queued for drinks, and tried to conjure up in my mind what he'd look like undressed. Those moments in my bedroom, three or four years ago, before Ned had interrupted us, had been fleeting after all. Now, I knew every inch, what his hair and skin smelt like, the position of every mole on his torso and back, how his limbs felt long and lean next to mine.

We ate on the roof terrace, in the late September evening sunshine, but dusk descended quickly and a chilly breeze picked up. We moved downstairs, and he led me into the lounge.

'Why don't you choose something to listen to?'

'No, I can't do that, not with you. Play me something I don't know you like. No, I've got a better idea... how about the first single you ever bought. And then we could have a chain... one song follows on, somehow, from the next.'

I saw a flicker of something move across his face that I hadn't seen before. 'A challenge. You're on.'

He picked up a remote control and subtle pale turquoise lights twinkled into life on the stack of Cambridge Audio Hi-Fi separates on the bookshelves behind the sofa. 'And then you can play something I don't know you like. Brandy or whisky?'

'You're asking a fellow Scot.'

'Okay. Laphroaig, Glenlivet, Lagavulin, Balvenie, Craigellachie...?'

'I've never tried Craigellachie.'

As he disappeared to get our drinks and the first few bars of "Young Americans" filled the room, I couldn't help but sashay in time to the sax, gravitating towards Mal's bookshelves by the window. He had a huge collection of crime fiction and thrillers, organised alphabetically, though the largest sections were devoted to Scottish novelists – Iain Banks, James Kelman, Val McDiarmid, William McIlvanney, Ian Rankin, Ali Smith. Two or three shelves of non-fiction, mainly economics and finance but some history too.

On the other side of the room the mantelpiece was crammed with photos in matching silver frames, mainly of Ewan, either on his own or with Mal. At one end was a photo of Ewan with his mum. It would have felt intrusive to look too closely so I turned away and let out an involuntary shriek when I spotted one of me at the other end. We hadn't taken many photos of each other, but there was one evening in a little bar in Clerkenwell when we'd been in the mood and happily snapped away, like we were on holiday. I had the corresponding photos of Mal on my phone.

I didn't notice Mal walking up behind me with the drinks; I was looking at one photo of Ewan and Mal stretched out on sun loungers, smiling up at the camera. Ewan must have been about seven or eight.

'He was quite little there. He's a few inches taller than me now.'

'He's so sweet. I can really see you in him.'

'Yeah, even more so now. Luckily, he has his mother's brains and common sense.'

We clinked whisky glasses.

'So, Kendrew, your turn on the juke box.' He passed me his phone.

'Okay, no pressure.' I thought for a moment – where to go from "Young Americans"? But then I remembered the premise. I typed 'Martha and the Muffins' into the search button at the top of the Spotify screen.

'This is the first single I bought. I played it over and over again. I drove my mum mad. I just loved that intro... still do.'

'Pretty cool... you must have been about ten or eleven?'

'Yeah, about that. I was in the car with my dad, driving through the Cairngorms to go fishing early one morning when I heard it on the radio. I was instantly hooked; I wrote down the name of the band and the title on my hand and took the bus into town with the contents of my piggy bank to buy it the next day.'

He bent down to kiss my temple. 'Cute.'

I handed him his phone. 'Your turn, baby.'

He took a large gulp of whisky and closed his eyes, resting his head on the back of the sofa for a moment. 'Okay, I remember taking the bus into town to buy this...'

A guitar intro began that I recognised but couldn't place until the vocals came in. 'Steve Harley & Cockney Rebel... cool! When did this come out?'

'It must have been 1974 or early 1975. What were you listening to then?'

'I seem to remember "Save All Your Kisses for Me" by the Brotherhood of Man being played on the radio a lot in the mid-70s. I'm not going to subject you to that though!'

I scrolled down the list of the various 7-inch and 12-inch versions of The The's "Uncertain Smile" until I found the one from the album, the one with Jools Hollands' incredible piano solo. Every time I heard the first few bars played on the xylimba – an African percussion instrument Matt Johnson had picked up in a famous music store in New York – a shiver ran up my spine.

'The link is the word 'smile' from "Make Me Smile". Without doubt, my 12-inch of this would be one of the possessions I'd risk my life to save if the house was burning down.'

'God, I love this song as well.'

'I have great taste... well, in most things.' I got ready to leap away as he grabbed me. I shrieked.

'Everything apart from men?'

'Yeah, well, it's taken me over twenty years but I think I've finally found my match.'

He kissed me. 'Ditto.'

I kissed him back. 'So where do you go from "Uncertain Smile"?'

'I'm taking the double word link. The The to Talk Talk; "It's My Life".

'Another great choice, Mr Russell.' I took a sip of whisky. 'Okay, when I was about seventeen or eighteen, I went to a brilliant club. Friday was alternative night at the Kirk. Coach loads would travel in from Leeds and York... even Newcastle. The DJ always played Talk Talk. And this...'

'"Just Like Heaven". I queued all night outside The Kilburn National to see The Cure when I first moved to London. That must have been in the early nineties.'

'Okay, I saw The Smiths at the National – 23rd of October, 1986. *The Queen is Dead* tour, absolutely brilliant gig, one of the best nights of my life, save for a few notable exceptions spent at Highbury.'

The opening bars of "There Is a Light That Never Goes Out" filled the room.

'Yeah, I think this is my favourite Smiths song too. *The Queen is Dead* c*a*me out when I was in my first year of A-levels.'

'Ah, yes Kendrew, I always forget you're a wee bit younger than me.' He smiled. 'Where next?'

'We had a record player in the sixth-form common room. *The Queen is Dead* was probably the most played album at the time. I took in *Steve McQueen* by Prefab Sprout in an attempt to attract the attention of Simon Nash who'd just joined the sixth form.'

My finger hovered indecisively over the tracks of the album, but then I remembered one killer line from "Goodbye Lucille One".

'Did it work?'

'Did what work?'

'Did Simon Nash fall at your knees?'

I laughed. 'No, quite the opposite. He went out with my best friend instead.'

'Ah, I can see that cut quite deeply.'

I feigned a pained expression. 'I'm just about over it... so where are we going next?'

'So, their biggest hit was "The King of Rock 'n' Roll", right? So I'm taking us to the actual King.'

As the opening bars of "Always On My Mind" drifted out from the speakers, Mal took my hand and led me into the middle of the room. His arms enveloped my waist, mine instinctively wrapped around his neck.

We kissed; slowly, gently, swaying in time with Elvis, smooching as though it was the last song of a school disco.

'You were always on my mind,' I whispered, my voice wavering, tears blurring my vision.

Mal kissed me again, inching down my neck, pushing away the shoulder strap of my dress, dipping into my collarbone.

'I made a terrible mistake, three years ago. I was stupid to run away like I did. I'm not going to do it again'.

CHAPTER 28

M al was half dressed when I opened my eyes. He'd made coffee and the aroma drifted towards me from the tray he'd left at the bottom of the bed. A jingle from an unfamiliar breakfast radio programme drifted through from the bathroom. I glanced at Mal's alarm clock; just before seven.

'Hey, sleepy head, how are you?'

'Good, thanks, my head's a bit fuzzy though. How much whisky did we get through last night?'

'Yeah, me too, a shower helped though.' He sat down and kissed the top of my head, before buttoning up his shirt.

'I need to get the 7.50 to London Bridge so I'm going to have to leave in a minute. Is that okay? You can take your time. I've left the spare set of keys in the kitchen – you can lock up and give them back to me when I see you next.'

'Lovely, thanks.' I leapt out of bed and threw my arms around him. He was perusing a huge selection of blue and grey ties in a shallow drawer. 'Thank you for a wonderful evening, it was really special.'

'It was. No need to thank me though, you're the one

who's made all the effort, coming down here, organising childcare and everything.'

We kissed, his arms around my naked waist, my hands wrapping around his torso. I ran my fingers through his hair.

'I've never seen you fresh out of the shower before. I could get used to it,' I whispered in a low voice.

'And I'm not accustomed to having a naked woman in my bedroom; I could get very used to that too.'

We said goodbye. I wrapped a towel around me and watched him from the window. He hurried along the street and then turned the corner into the road at the top of the square and disappeared from view.

I called home from Mal's landline to check everything was okay. Caroline said Ned was fine and had eaten breakfast. She'd text to let me know when she'd dropped him off at school, even though I wouldn't get the message until I was home. She'd left my phone charging in the kitchen. I asked her about Adrian, and she said she'd only seen him once again that evening. Half an hour after she'd first seen him he told her he'd collected everything he needed and was leaving.

I had a shower, filled Mal's dishwasher with the breakfast things, and did a sweep of the flat to make sure everything was tidy.

When I got home, my phone screen was full of messages and missed call alerts. I replied to Caroline. She'd dropped Ned off at school and I thanked her for looking after him. I texted Mal to let him know I'd got home safely, and to thank him again for an amazing evening. I called Agnes to see if all the recent shots had been approved, and if there were any I needed to do more work on. She said there were a couple where her clients thought they needed to be lightened and she'd email me the details.

I felt fuzzy for the rest of the day, a result of too much whisky and too little sleep. A Diet Coke would get me through. As I worked on the shots for Agnes, I kept myself going with flashbacks from the night before. Funny things Mal had said, long gazes held during a particular song we both loved, realising it was the first time we were listening to it together. Moments of pleasure.

I picked Ned up from school and, walking back with him, I realised I hadn't had a reply from Mal. I checked to make sure I had sent my message – yes, it was delivered, though the box was green where it would normally have been blue. I never understood why sometimes text were sent as iMessages, sometimes not. I'd leave it a while and send him another message to check he was okay.

As the evening went on, I became more anxious. I texted Mal and then called. It just went to answerphone; this is the Vodafone messaging service... blah, blah, blah. I kept it brief. Hoped he was okay and not too tired and that work had been okay. Thanked him again.

Nothing.

I couldn't sleep that night, not for more than an hour at a time, in feverish, dream-laden snatches. I took my phone to bed and checked to see if Mal had replied every time I woke.

When I came back from dropping Ned at school, I saw Mal's keys in my bag, mixed up with my own. What could I do with them? Send them back, with a pleading letter, asking what I'd done wrong? For a moment I thought I could drive back down to Brighton and let myself in and wait for him. Confront him. Yes, that's what I'd do... if I was a bunny boiler.

I'd wait a few days. Surely he'd get back in touch. Maybe Ewan had been taken ill. Or his mum – she lived in Worthing now, he'd told me, and was in her early eighties. She'd always been so strong that he found it very difficult to accept that she was getting frail.

I waited a few days. A few days turned into almost a week. I promised myself I'd wait until the following Tuesday to get in touch again. I only had Mal's personal email address. I could look up his bank email on their website but that didn't feel right, and I was sure that would piss him off. Clearly he was already pissed off with me. I pleaded in the email for him to tell me what I'd done wrong. Was it because I'd arrived late that evening, and on reflection he'd decided an unreliable girlfriend wasn't what he needed? Or perhaps the closeness, the acknowledgment that this was becoming something serious, had freaked him out. *I can't see myself getting involved in anything long-term again*, he'd said soon after we were back in touch. I made a list of all the things we'd said that evening in his flat. All the songs we'd listened to. The sex, for fuck's sake. How could he possibly want to break up after that?

Nothing the next day.

On the Wednesday evening, a week exactly after we'd been together in Brighton, I did what I feared most; I checked my social media. I knew the answer already. Facebook, LinkedIn, Instagram; he'd unfriended me, disconnected, unfollowed. That was it, everything I needed to know. Perhaps I'd never know why. Just as it didn't completely make sense when he broke up with me three years earlier, how could I even begin to understand now? After everything he'd said? 'I'm not going to let it happen again.' I can remember how he looked at me, how he pronounced every syllable.

CHAPTER 29

The weeks went by. The pain numbed a bit and, anyway, I knew I couldn't fall apart. I had Ned to think about, and work. And finally I got word from the estate agents that the tenants were moving out. They'd found somewhere they liked that was 'much more suitable anyway,' the estate agent told me several times, and were leaving the following Saturday.

I went into overdrive, organising a removal lorry for the following week. One morning after dropping Ned at school, I drove to Gipsy Hill and cleaned the house from top to bottom. By the end of the day my t-shirt and jeans had a scattering of pink splodges where I'd dropped bleach.

Walking back to the car, I looked down at the pavement, to avoid catching the eye of anyone I knew. That day would come when I had to face their pitying glances. 'Alex, I'm so sorry it didn't work out. We've missed you. No, it wasn't stupid at all. You were really brave to do something like that.'

I didn't tell anyone about Mal. Not Caroline or Agnes or Ingrid. I would, in time, but I was too heartbroken. At least if I knew why he'd broken up with me, it would seem less pathetic. I would seem less pathetic. Perhaps he had gone back to Louise again. It seemed like the obvious answer.

The only person I told was Itsumi. She nodded sagely when I told her. She said she saw how miserable I'd been with Adrian, and how Mal getting in touch had transformed me.

'You're a clever woman, Alex. And strong. Don't waste your time and energy on men who don't appreciate you.'

I collapsed into her arms, sobbing. 'You're right, I know. It still hurts though, like somebody's stabbed me in the chest.'

'Yes. It will fade; I know you'll be fine.' She smoothed my hair, and I closed my eyes.

She smelled of roses from her garden and smoky tea. I felt an odd sensation from this woman, something I had never really encountered; she was maternal. My mum had never really taken to parenthood, and I think my own approach to parenting was a reaction to that; to be as least like my own mother as possible.

Over half term a few of Ned's friends invited him over for play dates in the afternoon, and I found myself alone, unable to stop myself from thinking about Mal. A dozen times I picked up the phone and my finger hovered over his name in the contact list as my heart pounded in my chest. Every time I thought of the call going unanswered yet again and diverting to voicemail.

The moving date came, and I was relieved that for the next few days I would have something to think about, something that would exhaust me physically and mentally. By early afternoon the lorry was ready to go, and I locked the door without giving the house a backward glance. I would text Adrian, but not for a day or so, in case there was anything I'd forgotten. The bastard could wait.

I'd given the removal guys keys and the lorry was at least half emptied by the time we arrived back at the house. Our neighbour across the road, Sam, spotted us and invited Ned over to play with her boys. We hadn't spoken since we moved, and I felt guilty I hadn't stayed in touch. She'd been really supportive when the graffiti appeared on the front of the house. Some neighbours would have gone through the roof about it but she downplayed it completely.

'We'll catch up... come over for a glass of wine soon, huh?'

No fishing for details. Now we were back, I needed to foster friendships with people like her.

The next few months disappeared as we settled into life back in south-east London. I knew some people would gloat. A few did, but on the whole they were people who had proved not to be such good friends anyway.

A month after we'd moved back, I texted Adrian to tell him we'd gone. I was being a bitch, yes, but he deserved it. I didn't tell him I'd changed the locks; he could work that out for himself. I left the car he'd bought me on the drive. I toyed with the idea of selling it and pocketing the cash, but it would have felt like dirty money. I still had the videos from the Paris hotel room up my sleeve.

Christmas came and went. We were invited to parties, and it felt like we'd been wholeheartedly welcomed back into the fold. It felt good.

Ned kept in touch with his Westbourne Grove friends on Skype and once a week we had one of his friends over, or we went to see them. When he had a play date, I'd go and see Itsumi. I was very aware that so much of our conversation was about my disastrous relationships. I tried as much as I could to turn the conversation round to her and her sons; one lived in Hackney and seemed to be perfectly happy in his relationship, and didn't cause her any trouble. She worried about the older one, Kenzo, more. She told me he had always been the more difficult child.

She'd been to stay with them in Paris at Christmas and said she was aware there had been a bit of an atmosphere between Kenzo and his French wife, Juliette. Sure enough, he'd called Itsumi a few nights earlier to say they were splitting up. His wife said he spent too much time at work and she felt neglected. I wondered if Kenzo had taken up one of his adopted country's pastimes and was having an affair, but I didn't want to ask Itsumi that question.

'Are you going over to see them?' I asked.

'Do you think I should?' She perked up. I don't know how Kenzo's wife viewed her mother-in-law, but I couldn't imagine anyone could possibly dislike Itsumi, and it wasn't in her nature to interfere.

'Gosh, I don't know. I guess it depends what stage they're at. Perhaps you could suggest going over to look after the children while they take a few days away together to try and work things out. But if they're way past that...'

She called Kenzo as I got ready to leave to pick up Ned. I'd only ever heard her speaking in Japanese a couple of times; hardly any of the sounds were familiar, the structure of the words or sentences. I could tell it was animated though, and argumentative, from her exasperated expression, but she came off the phone looking happy.

'What did he say?'

'He's resigned to the fact that they're separating, but he

hasn't completely lost hope. He agreed to let me come and stay, and he'll offer to take Juliette away for a few days.'

'That's sounds pretty positive. We can organise the tickets now if you like, or just let me know when you'd like to travel.'

I'd helped her with the Eurostar website ever since she mistakenly booked a return journey a month too late. I told her it was very easy to do and that I'd done it myself, so we usually sat down together.

'And I'll come and water your plants, of course.'

'Oh no dear, don't worry, it's too far for you to come now. When you were a stone's throw away it was—'

'It's no trouble... I can run over every morning, after I've dropped Ned at school.'

She opened her mouth to protest but knew she wasn't going to win the battle.

'I've got your keys, and your instructions for what to water, and how often.'

It was incredible that she trusted me with her beautiful garden, full of exotic and rare plants. I had warned her I was the least green-fingered person in the world.

We hugged. I always felt like a giant in comparison to her tiny frame, but she was stronger than most women half her age.

Itsumi texted me the next morning to say she'd like to leave from St Pancras the following morning if there were tickets available. I dropped Ned at school and logged onto Eurostar's website.

I picked up my phone to double-check what time Itsumi said like to travel and an unknown mobile number appeared on my screen. There was always the possibility of someone getting in touch about work.

'Hello?' I said.

'Alex.'

My heart started pounding. Even in those two short syllables, I recognised the voice.

'Yes.' My voice wavered.

'Jesus, Alex, I don't believe it. I thought you were dead.'

'What d'you mean?'

'I had a text, months ago now, from Adrian. It was the day after you'd come down to Brighton. He said you'd been killed in an accident on the M23, driving back to London. On no account was I to get in touch with Ned, or come to the funeral, or...'

'What, are you...' I didn't know how to finish the sentence.

Mal filled the silence. 'Adrian... he told me you'd been killed. Made it clear it was my fault, because you'd been travelling back from seeing me, that I'd left Ned without a mother. And I was wracked with guilt about it... you know me, haven't been to church for thirty years but that Catholic blood still courses through my veins. I went to Confession last week.' He paused and I heard him take a long drag on a cigarette.

He'd told me before that he only smoked about three times a year, but I was guessing this conversation might warrant one of them.

'So... how did you find out I wasn't dead?' I tried to keep my voice as even as I could. Waiting for a response from him, I heard the London traffic outside his office; a distant police siren, a black cab's engine labouring close by, dropping someone off at the bank's entrance.

'It was after Confession. I just felt this heavy dull ache, you know? I realised I just needed to know what happened, who caused the accident, if anyone else had been hurt or killed, that if I didn't I'd never find any peace. So I started researching all the accidents on the M23 that day; local websites, Sussex and Surrey council's, the police. There was nothing, not that included a dark grey Q7 anyway. Then I started looking on the M25, the A23—'

I interrupted. 'I called you though. And emailed. And texted. Dozens of times. I stopped because I realised you were obviously angry with me and if I kept on it'd only make it worse.' My nose started to fizz as my eyes filled up. 'I thought perhaps you'd decided to go back to Louise again, and that you thought cutting it off without explanation was the kindest way.'

'Bloody hell, Alex, what do you think I am? We had such a wonderful evening, when you came down, I'd have been a total bastard to cut it off after that.'

I hesitated. *Because you've got form in that department?* That would have sounded mean and resentful. 'I know.'

I'd gone over the details of that night in Brighton so many times; why could I not recall all the facts? 'How did Adrian get hold of your number? Did he call you at work?'

'No, he texted me. I've got a mate who works for the Met. I asked if he could track the number for me. He found out it was a prepaid mobile, no contact details, or at least not real ones.'

'Adrian bought a burner phone? Jesus, I've heard it all now.'

I could hear Mal's footsteps on the pavement, echoing, and the traffic noise fading. 'Remember, that night, you left your phone at home.'

Details returned to me in waves.

'Adrian must have got hold of it. He came to the house, Caroline told me, to pick up some paint and a few canvasses he was working on. I'd left it charging in the hallway.'

'That makes sense, he must have got into your phone.

Since I found out there was no road accident, I've been calling your mobile but it doesn't connect. I figured your number might have changed. But according to your website, it hadn't. So I'm using my mate's phone... my number must be blocked.'

I walked downstairs to the kitchen. 'Is there any way I can find out? It was too late for coffee; I poured myself a large glass of red wine.

'Yes, look at your blocked numbers.'

I clicked on Settings.

'There are three numbers; two mobiles and a Brighton landline.'

CHAPTER 30

I tsumi took the train to Paris. The following day I ran to Westbourne Grove to water her plants after dropping Ned at school. It was around eight-and-a-half miles, further than I normally ran but it felt good to push myself. My treat at the end was breakfast at Ottolenghi's.

As I left the café to walk to Itsumi's, I spotted Penny on the other side of the road, but she'd seen me first. She was yelping and pulling Adrian into the road towards me, and he had no choice. She'd managed to get free of her collar before when she was determined to get away. He scowled at me as Penny jumped up, her front paws landing gently on my chest, and she tried to lick my face.

'Hello sweetheart,' I said to her, tickling her under the chin. Her tail wagged side to side and she let out a classic sighthound yowl. I kept my gaze firmly on her as I calculated my best response to Adrian.

Eventually I looked up at him to break the silence; he wasn't going to start the conversation. His frown had made way for a curious smirk.

'You look well, Alex.'

'I am, thank you. And deliriously happy...'

'...with Mal,' I couldn't stop myself adding. 'So your attempts to break us up by telling him I was dead have failed completely.'

'I have no idea what you're talking about.' His expression changed only a notch towards incomprehension before he feigned concern. 'Honestly Alex, I think you need help.'

'You have a very selective memory.'

He stood there; motionless, emotionless. Penny started whining – she'd never liked it when we argued. I bent down to stroke her. I kissed the top of her head and looked up at him. 'Go fuck yourself, Adrian – I never want to see you again.'

Tears blurred the busy street as I walked away. The thought of never seeing Penny again was heartbreaking. I knew it would be for Ned too, but cutting loose from Adrian was more important.

On the walk to Itsumi's, I blocked his numbers on my phone. In her small, neat garden, I carefully followed her instructions for watering each treasured Acer. They were a riot of colour; pistachio, mustard, orange, magenta, and every shade in between. I'd arrived at her house in a rage after the confrontation with Adrian. I knew being there would calm me. I made tea, using a few spoonfuls of the lightly smoked blend she mixed herself.

Perching on the edge of a large wooden planter, I weighed up my options about Adrian. He'd gone to such crazy lengths to break off communication between Mal and I, but I suspected the police wouldn't take that very seriously, even the claim I'd been killed in a road accident. The attempted rape would be. And the under-age girls? I had all the videos at home on a USB stick. Surely they would have to look into them. But they took place in Paris. I'd watched enough police dramas to know that would blur the boundaries about who should investigate.

I glanced down at my empty tea bowl and, though I wasn't superstitious, willed the tiny leaf fragments at the bottom to form themselves into some sort of sign. Adrian was a coward. Part of me figured he would just let me get on with my life. But the other part knew I'd always have a nagging doubt. He might be spineless, but he was also stubborn and wasn't happy when things didn't go his way. He also had money, and that worried me.

I set the burglar alarm and locked Itsumi's front door, then searched for local police stations on Google Maps. Kensington looked closest of the ones still open.

When I arrived, the front counter was quiet. Tuesday mornings must be a good time to report a crime. I gave my details to the young woman behind the glass screen and she told me to take a seat.

A female officer, Sergeant Neilson, took me to a small room. She asked if I'd be happy for the interview to be recorded. The word 'interview' made it all seem very serious and official – there was no going back. She typed in my name and contact details, as well as Adrian's, into her laptop.

'I know this can be very difficult, madam. Take your time.' She sat back and smiled sympathetically. 'For the moment, I don't need too much detail, just the main facts.'

Fuck it, I thought, I don't have anything to feel guilty about. First I told her about the night Adrian tried to rape me. Then the videos and photos I'd seen on our iCloud, and added that my seven-year-old son had been the first to see them. I showed her the few videos I had saved on my phone and told her I had all of them backed up at home.

'One more thing... I caught Gonorrhea from him,

shortly after one of his trips to Paris. In the videos, it doesn't look like him or his friend are wearing condoms. So he was putting the health of those young girls at risk, as well as mine.'

I paused while the officer typed a few words.

'That's it, that's what I came to report. But he was so controlling, so undermining of me. All little things that would seem petty if I told you now, but...' I trailed off. 'And after we'd split up, he found out I'd started seeing an old boyfriend. He tried to finish the relationship. He went into the contacts in my phone and changed the numbers.'

The Sergeant was typing something on her laptop keyboard. When I paused, she stopped and looked at me. 'So that when you called your boyfriend, it went to him.'

I nodded. 'And he sent Mal a message saying I'd been killed in a car accident, and that on no account was he to go to the funeral.'

Sergeant Neilson went back to her laptop, typed a few words in and then searched through the results. 'Did Mr Evans previously live in north London?'

I nodded. 'Islington. Barnsbury. Somewhere round there.'

'Someone reported him for soliciting underage prostitutes, three years ago. And of coercive control. But then the charges were dropped.' She looked back at the screen. 'Antonella Evans... is that his wife?'

CHAPTER 31

I dropped Ned at school and drove to Brixton, just as I had all those years ago when Mal and I first met. I arrived at the Ritzy Cinema almost an hour early. I'd brought my laptop so I could do some work while I waited, but I knew it would probably be futile; I wasn't able to concentrate on anything. Earlier, Ned caught me staring into space while I made his packed lunch. He shook my arm. 'Mum, are you okay?'

He'd recently dropped 'Mummy'. He was growing up, still my baby though.

'I'm sorry darling, I was miles away.'

I needed to get a grip, but I knew that wouldn't happen until I'd met Mal.

I stared through the glass doors at the deserted square outside the cinema. One old lady, undeterred by the heavy rain, fed the pigeons from a bag of white sliced bread.

A figure appeared in my peripheral vision. Mal was early too, walking towards me, his raincoat soaked, underneath it a mid-blue suit I hadn't seen him wear before. He looked tired and pale.

We held each other for a long time. Instinctively, we turned our heads and kissed. When we broke off, my sight was clouded by tears. He was crying too.

'They're going to ask us to leave and get a hotel room,' I whispered into his ear. I felt him breathing in deeply.

'You smell good,' he said. 'You've lost weight.'

'I know. I haven't felt much like eating. How about you?'

'I've been drinking too much, again. We've had quite a tough time at the bank too. It's been a difficult few months.'

'I'm sorry.' I wiped away the tears rolling down my cheeks. 'How's Ewan?'

'He's good, thanks.' He took off his raincoat and we sat down. 'He's rehearsing with the local drama group. They're putting on Doctor Faustus in a month or so. And their pantomime was fantastic – Mother Goose – he played Jack. He was brilliant. Look, I've got a few photos.' He got out his phone. 'Here he is.'

'Ah, cute, love his costume.'

Ewan was wearing multi-coloured checked trousers, a white shirt with voluminous sleeves and a red waistcoat.

'He hated it, of course, but he's smart. He knew the costume designer went a bit over the top but he took it on the chin.' Mal paused. 'And Ned?'

'He's good too. To start with he was upset to leave his new friends in Westbourne Grove but we've been back to see them once a week or so. And I've promised to build a tree house in the back garden to placate him a bit.' I looked at Mal and tried to keep his gaze but tears blurred my vision again.

'You didn't really think I was dumping you?' He looked at me with a pained expression. 'After that night?'

'I know, it didn't really make sense but...' I hesitated, trying to summarise my thought process. 'We're not as young as we were. By the time people reach their forties, they're very stuck in their ways. Life's complicated, and we've both got commitments, our children, work...'

I took a sip of water. 'I figured after that night you thought something more serious might develop and decided that was going to be a lot of hassle, that it would impact too much on the rest of your life. I mean, you more or less said that's why you didn't want to get involved when we first met.' I let him process that for a few seconds. 'And then factor in that, again, we're in our forties... I wish my body looked like it did when I was twenty-three, but it doesn't. I thought you might have just decided—'

'Hey, come on, that's not fair.'

'You told me you had a fling with a thirty-year-old. I was just being very practical, presenting myself with all the possibilities.'

'Well, it's all academic now anyway. What are you going to do about Adrian?' he asked, sitting back in his seat.

I told him about the videos I'd found on iCloud, and that I'd bumped into Adrian and Penny when I was in West-bourne Grove, watering Itsumi's plants. 'He was so fucking arrogant, on the spot I decided to go to the police. His ex-wife reported him for coercive control before they separated, but dropped the charges. They've taken the underage sex allegations very seriously but the fact that it happened in France muddies the water a bit. And because of the...' I flushed as Mal caught my eye. 'They're recommending I apply for a court order so that he can't come anywhere near me.'

'That sounds really positive. Is that what you want?'

'I don't want to ever see him again. I want him to face justice for the girls in Paris, but that's not my battle. I have to rebuild my life in Gipsy Hill with Ned and repair all the damage I've caused by uprooting him.'

I went to the bar to get coffee and tried to think of a diplomatic way to ask him how we were going to move forward. When I sat down, Mal beat me to it.

'I know if I asked you, you'd be able to tell me, give or take a few weeks, how long it is since we first met here. So here's an idea... why don't we do all the things we would have done then, if I hadn't been such a dick and gone running back to Louise?'

'You mean, like going for proper dates and stuff?'

'Yes.'

'Okay. Where do we start?'

He got his phone to check his calendar. 'I've got loads of tickets for gigs; let's go together.'

'Sure. Send me a list and I'll put them in my diary and organise a babysitter. And what about meeting Ned? Do you fancy doing that?'

'Of course. And I want you to meet Ewan too.'

'You're serious?' I looked at him intently, not allowing him to break my gaze, little dimples on either side of his mouth appearing. He nodded.

'Yes. I'd be crazy to fuck this up again. It's got to be all or nothing. Let's start off gently, introduce our boys to the idea. Ewan's old enough to understand that me having a girl-friend doesn't mean I love him any less.'

'And I think Ned is still young enough to know that he's the most important person in the world, and that his mum having a boyfriend isn't going to change that.'

Mal walked me back to the car and this time he didn't let his embarrassment stop him; he kissed me, in broad daylight, as the rain soaked us both.

.   .   .

I felt invigorated and focused, much more able to concentrate on work. I paid for a LinkedIn subscription and emailed my CV and portfolio to some potential clients, something I'd been putting off for months.

'Ned, I've got something to tell you,' I said, as casually as I could, one teatime.

He looked up from his bowl of pasta. 'What is it mum? Are you okay?' A note of concern flashed across his face. I must have looked serious. I held his hand and smiled to reassure him.

'Yes, completely. It's just that I wanted you to meet someone, a friend of mine...'

'A boyfriend?'

I blushed. 'Yes, I know it's not long since Adrian and I separated... well, he isn't a new boyfriend, I've known him for quite a long time. But at the time he decided he didn't want me to be his girl—'

'I'm cool with that, mum, don't worry. Anyway, I've got a girlfriend,' he said nonchalantly, piling his fork with fusilli.

'What?'

'Freya. She just started in our class.'

I remembered. One day a couple of weeks ago when I'd dropped him off in the playground. All the kids had been swirling in and out of groups of parents on their scooters, but he'd stopped and was staring at this one girl who was patiently waiting in the line with her mum.

'Okay, good to know. Well, erm, I was thinking I might ask Mal round for dinner one evening. And he has a son too. He's a bit older than you. I thought we could make carbonara together, seeing as it's your favourite. What do you think?'

He took the empty pasta bowl over to the sink. 'Yeah, sounds cool.'

I texted Mal to organise a date for him and Ewan to come round and we decided on the following Saturday afternoon.

By the time the doorbell rang, nerves were getting the better of me. I hadn't really thought what it might be like to meet Ewan. It had been mildly excruciating meeting Adrian's daughters, and then Antonella's intervention ensured I never really formed a relationship with them. Boys were straight-forward, and I had more experience dealing with them. Ironically, I found girls much more alien.

Ned rushed to open the door, but the lock was too stiff for him. Ewan was holding a bouquet of spring flowers and Mal had a bottle of red wine under his arm, and a large plastic bag.

'Please, come in, it's so lovely to meet you, Ewan.'

We all hesitated in the narrow hallway. I shook hands with Ewan and Mal did with Ned. Mal and I both decided to compromise with a kiss on the cheek but aimed for different ones and banged noses instead. Mal handed the plastic bag to Ned.

'This is just a little something for you, Ewan helped me choose it.'

'Wow, thank you, can I build it now?' Ned said, opening the bag, his eyes popping; it was a large Scalextric kit.

'I'll help you,' Ewan added, following Ned into the lounge.

'Not on the rug though, Ned, otherwise you'll lose bits of it, and I'll end up standing on them in bare feet again.'

I walked through to the kitchen with Mal.

'Phew, so far so good,' he whispered, holding me round the waist. 'It's good to be back here.'

'It's like a dream come true. I hope Ewan's okay with it.'

'He's fine, don't worry.'

I glanced towards the boys, as subtly as I could. Ned, of course, was completely uninhibited. Ewan wore the self-consciousness of a shy teenager, but was managing pretty well, considering. He had the same physique as his dad; tall and lean, and already an inch or so taller. His hair was dark brown and full. I momentarily wished I'd met Mal when he was younger, before he'd become a silver fox.

While we ate, I asked Ewan about school and the drama group. Over the course of the evening his shyness fell away and I felt my own nervousness abating. He had a party to go to and they left around nine so that they'd be back in Brighton by eleven.

Mal texted me to let me know they'd got back safely. *You get the thumbs up from Ewan... this is verbatim: Wow, Alex is really nice, like a million times nicer than Louise. And Ned is cool too.*

Ned also liked Ewan, but I made a conscious decision not to make too much of it. Ned had loved meeting Giuliana and Issy too. I was very aware that things could go pear-shaped again.

CHAPTER 32

Nicole had her 50th birthday coming up and was having a party at the pub. I wrestled with the idea of bringing Mal, partly because I felt I might be judged. To most people it was only five minutes ago that I left to live with Adrian. Did I care? Mal said he'd love to come and meet some of my friends, so I stopped fretting about the positives or negatives.

The party kicked off around three in the afternoon. I dressed down, not wanting to compete with the birthday girl who, uncharacteristically, had gone all out. She was wearing a silky top, perfectly cut trousers and heels. Miraculously, after our leaving party, Nicole and Dan had got together, and though I knew from his updates that the relationship was tempestuous, they were still very much an item. I caught his eye at one point; he mouthed 'see you at the bar in fifteen.'

The pub was open plan with a large, enclosed garden. The kids had been invited too, so they played Man Hunt, allowing the parents to relax and drink large glasses of Viognier and pints of IPA.

I'd been anxious about what Mal would make of my friends. Ruth was the first person I spotted.

'Hey, chick, you look amazing! So glad you're back. What happened?' She couldn't help but glance at Mal.

'Ruth, let me introduce the famous Malcolm Russell.'

He looked at me sardonically.

'The Mal...?' she asked, looking back at me.

'Yep.'

Ruth and I had met up in town a few times, and she'd been over to the house in Westbourne Grove. I hadn't mentioned the problems I was having with Adrian at the time.

'It all went wrong, Ruth... Adrian turned into a monster. And on top of that, he didn't make any effort to form a bond with Ned. Quite the opposite.'

'Oh Alex, I'm sorry. I always thought he was...' She broke off, presumably reassessing whether it was sensible to slag my ex off in front of my new boyfriend.

'An arse?' I filled in the blank.

'Something like that.' She turned to look back at Mal. 'Anyway, you make such a lovely couple... what do you do, Mal?'

I turned away to check on Ned. He was in the garden, jumping off the climbing frame with a few other boys. On the whole he'd settled in really well, but I was aware that a year was a long time in the life of a seven-year-old; friendships had shifted, new alliances made. I spotted Johan, Ingrid's son, in the crowd, and wanted to be aware of any problems. I spotted Ingrid too. She'd unfriended me on Facebook at some point but I suspected she'd have found out we were back. I hadn't made any effort to get in touch with her and felt guilty about it. And then felt angry with myself for feeling guilty.

Mal was deep in conversation. I wondered if they'd got on to his favourite subject; Ruth and her husband were both ardent Gooners.

There were enough people mingling that the slide from one conversation into the next was completely natural. I chatted briefly to Nick, another dad at school I knew vaguely. I couldn't place him to start with, or him me, but then I remembered I'd sold him some baby stuff at an NCT sale a few years earlier. He'd beaten me down on price, the stingy bastard. He was fun though, and a terrible flirt.

I looked around for Mal, hoping he wasn't being flirted with. Several of the mums from school could have won an Olympic gold in it. I saw Ingrid in the crowd, headed to the bar, ordered a single shot of Glenmorangie, downed it in one for Dutch courage and walked towards her.

She gasped when she saw me. 'Alex, wow, I heard you were back but I didn't know whether to believe it.'

We hugged, squeezing each other tight.

'I've missed you, Ingrid.' I looked at her, my eyes welling up. I meant it.

'Me too. All that stuff between the boys...'

'Look, they've forgotten it.'

Johan and Ned were in a queue of mostly boys, walking up the slide and jumping off the top.

'Fresh start, eh?' she asked me.

We clinked glasses.

'I'll drink to that.'

She introduced me to Anneka, her youngest. She had her mother's blonde hair with a hint of red from her dad.

'How's Jim? Is he here?'

'Later, hopefully. There's some family emergency. You know what his mother's like, always some catastrophe in the offing.'

'Yeah, I do. Didn't she throw her toys out of the pram once because he refused to drop everything and drive up to change a fuse or something? Johan was a few weeks old?'

She snorted. 'If anything, she's got worse.'

I'd always felt sorry for Jim; a high maintenance mother and partner was a lethal combination.

'So Alex, what happened?'

I started telling her what had happened with Adrian, but Anneka pulled at Ingrid's top. 'I want Johan.'

We took her out into the garden to play with the bigger kids, and stood watching her as we talked.

'And Mal is the guy from all those years ago?'

'Yes, d'you remember that morning we went to the soft play centre and I told you he'd dumped me to go back to his girlfriend?'

'That was a couple of years ago at least, I was just about to have Anneka.'

'Yeah, I know. Well, he got in touch again, and by then it had all gone horribly wrong with Adrian. Mal was my knight in shining armour.'

I couldn't quite bring myself to go and find him to introduce Ingrid. My fears about him falling in love with her were as real as they had been three or four years earlier.

I went to the bar to get drinks and couldn't see Mal anywhere inside. He wasn't in the garden either, so I went to the front of the pub and looked outside. He was leaning against a tree trunk, talking on the phone. He looked agitated, angry, and was smoking. I couldn't imagine who he could be talking to that would cause that reaction. Louise, perhaps, or his ex-wife. I didn't want him to catch me spying on him, so I turned away and rejoined Ingrid in the garden. Twenty minutes later, he'd disappeared from the front of the pub. I searched the pub and then called him, but his phone went to voicemail.

I didn't hear from Mal for the rest of the weekend. I tried to call a few times, and texted, but eventually I gave up. A few days later, he finally got in touch. *Hi Alex*. I knew things were bad when he started a text with my name. I braced myself.

Thanks for your messages. Hope you're both okay. Bad few days since I left you in the lurch. The board rejected the proposals I presented last week. All about money, of course, they don't want to spend any more now in order to save money later. I feel very low... never really suffered from depression apart from the odd spell that doesn't last more than a few weeks. I appreciate you've been through all this with Sean and I have no desire for you to repeat the experience. I'm determined to come through but finding it very tough. I haven't felt this bad since my marriage finally broke down. I'll call later. Sorry for being so useless; you don't deserve it.

That must have been the problem when I saw him on the phone at Nicole's party. But with my limited knowledge of how the financial world operated, it seemed odd that any problems couldn't wait to be dealt with until the start of the working week.

I remembered that Ruth's husband was a financial journalist. It felt wrong to go snooping around but I didn't have a choice. I texted her to ask if she'd mind just having a word with John to see if he knew about any plans at Schwarz-Müller to restructure, if anything had been leaked to the press, or if there had been any adverse financial news about them. I told her Mal had left the party early without saying goodbye. *I'm really worried about him. The pressure seems to be*

*getting too much. I know I don't need to mention it, but I'd be
really grateful if John could be as discreet as he could.*

I jumped five feet in the air when Mal called later that
evening. I pressed the green button but felt choked into
silence. I waited for him to speak.

'Alex, I'm so sorry. How are you?'

I was half-way through a glass of Pinotage and took a
large swig. 'Erm, okay, I don't know what to say.'

'How is Ned?'

'He's fine, thanks. Ewan?'

'Yeah, good too.'

'So, what's happening?'

'Not much more than I said in my text, really. There was
another board meeting this morning. I presented a revised
proposal that doesn't go as far as we'd initially recommended but I think it'll be rejected too.'

'This isn't an attempt to push you out? You're not
thinking about jumping ship?'

'Yes, both. I have my allies at the bank, but I've put a few
noses out of joint over the years. I've got a call booked with a
headhunter tomorrow, and I've got a mate at another bank
who's seeing what he can do. All very hush-hush.'

'Well, you don't need to worry about me; the world of
corporate banking is a million miles away from photography.' I paused to have another mouthful of wine. 'I
remember you said your position is so specialised that
within each organisation, there won't be more than one or
two people who do what you do. So it's not going to be very
often that positions come up?'

'As usual, you've got my career issues in a nutshell.'

'You could become a photographer... you can be my assistant.'

'Sounds irresistible. What's the starting salary?'

'I'll have to get back to you on that.'

He told me he hadn't left the flat in days and was living off Deliveroo takeaways. He finally acknowledged that eating stuff from jars in the fridge with mould growing on the surface wasn't a sensible option.

'So I've been working from home, but I had to go into the office this morning for the board meeting. And on the train home this nutty woman sitting opposite tried to strike up a conversation.'

I laughed, and took a sip of wine. 'I don't blame her... she probably saw you didn't have a wedding ring on and thought she'd try her luck.'

He snorted. 'Yeah, well, I think she might have already done that. She claims I helped retrieve coins she dropped on the floor in Pret last week. I only vaguely recall it happening; I wouldn't have been able to tell you what she looked like afterwards.'

'Blimey, let's hope you haven't just got yourself a stalker,' I said without really meaning it.

'Yeah, that would be just my luck. Don't worry, I'm being paranoid. Jesus, I'm sorry you're having to deal with this. You're a tough cookie, Ms Kendrew. But I'm very aware you don't need any more stress in your life, especially after Adrian. What do you want to do?'

'You make me very happy, you know that. You make me feel alive, like nobody else I've ever known. Let's try and find a way. You have to be honest and upfront with me though. I didn't know you were struggling so much. You can talk to me, I hope you know that.'

'I do, I'm just embarrassed, I suppose. It's not easy laying yourself out to be scrutinised.'

'I'd never judge you though.'

'I know you wouldn't.'

We agreed to meet at lunchtime the next day. We had a picnic in a park near the bank's offices. The weather had become unseasonably warm and I wore a thin dress and sandals, in contrast to all the women walking past in regulation navy trouser suits and heels.

We were packing the food back into the cold bag when one of Mal's work colleagues spotted us. He'd been very careful not to talk about the problems at work. Lots of banks had offices in Canary Wharf and any information about one that wasn't common knowledge was ammunition for another.

'Alex, you remember Phil from the Agnes Obel gig at the Roundhouse?'

Mal had got tickets before we'd been back in touch; so had I. He'd invited Phil, I'd taken Agnes, and we'd laughed that, other than the 'Agnes' on stage, she was probably the only other one in the building. I didn't remember much about Phil, other than that they'd been at university together and now worked for the same bank. He seemed very straight and a bit dull, in comparison to Mal anyway, but I'd wanted to show interest. In the bar beforehand, I asked what he did at the bank, but Mal cut in. 'Oh God, don't get him started... we'll miss most of the gig.'

After that, I'd asked Phil what the nineteen-year-old Malcolm Russell had been like. 'Oh, much like he is now. Supported the wrong team, drank too much beer, always got the pretty girls.' There had been a slight grimace from Mal when Phil said that, and I wondered if their friendship was entirely harmonious.

'Yeah, hi Phil, how are you? Mal's been telling me all about the problems at—'

Mal cleared his throat and squeezed my arm. 'Yeah, that was a great gig. We'll have to go to some more.'

Phil was involved in the restructuring work so why did Mal interject like that? Was it all top secret? We stood in silence, and then all three tried to break it at once, Phil a nanosecond ahead.

'Well, I should leave you lovebirds alone to enjoy the rest of your lunch. Great to see you again, Alex.'

'You too, see you soon.'

Mal didn't talk about the encounter as he walked me back to the tube station. I figured there must be some tension between him and Phil as a result of the difficulties at the bank, maybe as far back as the gig at the Roundhouse. I didn't want to push him into telling me, especially when I wouldn't really understand it anyway.

Later that day Ruth called me to say her husband hadn't heard anything about restructuring plans at Schwarz-Müller per se, but that there were always merger rumours and the share prices often soared or fell in accordance.

'I hope that's all good news,' Ruth added. 'It's all mumbo jumbo to me, Alex... John said Schwarz-Müller AG's share price had been increasing for the last three weeks. He said that's the opposite of what you'd expect if a major restructuring was in the offing.'

I let this simmer. I couldn't bring the subject of the restructuring up with Mal. I knew nothing about it, but he would be angry if he knew I'd been digging for information, especially with the help of a journalist. I hated the idea of him bottling it all up and feeling depressed but I'd just have to bide my time, wait for him to tell me, and be as supportive as I could when he did.

PART III

NOW

D C Noble led me past the other patrol cars and armoured vans in the enclosed car park, towards the station's entrance.

'This is Alexandra Kendrew,' she announced to the two uniformed officers behind the desk. From their expressions, they must have assumed I was drunk. 'Arrested for the attempted murder of Malcolm Russell, 46, of Marlowe Road, SE24.'

'Mrs Kendrew, my name is Sergeant Gibson, I'm one of the custody officers.'

I wasn't sure what I was supposed to say or do so I nodded and looked down at my feet. Sergeant Gibson, a woman roughly my age with a neat, dark brown bob and sharp features, turned to DC Noble. She listened to Noble describe what had happened at home earlier.

'Mrs Kendrew,' Sergeant Gibson began, 'we are detaining you for questioning, and to allow a thorough search of your property, in your absence, to be carried out in order to obtain evidence. Do you understand?'

I nodded again.

'I'm going to book you in now,' she said, glancing at her watch. 'DC Noble, can you take Mrs Kendrew to room C5 or C6?'

Noble led me along a corridor. The doors were mainly open and the rooms reminded me of a GP's surgery. She turned into one room and asked me to sit, closing the door behind her.

DC Noble logged in to the computer on the desk, opened a cupboard labelled 'Clothing – Female' and pulled out a handful of plastic bags. She put on some plastic gloves, uncuffed me and carefully helped me out of my dressing gown, trying to prevent the sick from getting everywhere. Still, a few tell-tale orange lumps landed on the floor.

'Can I keep my underwear on?' I asked.

She shook her head. 'It all needs to be taken as evidence.'

She helped me into a blue t-shirt and sweatpants, then bagged up my clothes and watch. She picked up the phone on the desk and asked for a custody assistant to come to the room. A minute later Sergeant Gibson knocked on the door and came in.

'We're fairly quiet this morning, for a change. I'll take Mrs Kendrew down to the custody block.'

DC Noble left the room with the evidence bags. I felt like I'd be more able to communicate with Sergeant Gibson about Ned, perhaps because she was nearer my age and may have had children of her own. DC Noble had been at the house, and seen Ned, yet I hadn't felt any compassion or empathy from her towards him, maybe she was too young.

I cleared my throat, not knowing exactly what I was going to say. 'Sergeant Gibson, can I please talk to somebody about what's going to happen to my son? There's been a terrible mistake; I haven't done anything.'

I waited for her to respond. She asked me to sit down.

'I need to sort out someone to look after my son, before school finishes. He's only seven.'

'Did the arresting officers take any details from you?' she asked.

'Yes, a few, but it didn't seem to me like they were going to make him a priority. But he is to me; I'm all he has. Please, you have to understand, I need to know what's going to happen to him.'

Sergeant Gibson glanced at the computer screen. 'It's just after eight. Your son will be finishing school at around three?'

'He finishes at three-thirty, but goes to after-school club until six-thirty.'

'Good, that gives us a little more time to organise something. Who else would be able to look after him? His dad?'

'I don't want him to, he's the absolute last resort.' I retraced my thoughts from earlier, trying to work out who would be the best person to look after Ned.

I just didn't know if I could trust Sean to be stable and calm. Any stress always sends him over the edge. If that happened the situation could get a lot more complicated; the care system could become involved. I couldn't bare that happening to Ned.

I decided on Agnes. She'd known him since he was a baby. I knew she'd be busy though, with work and her own kids. Perhaps she'd be okay for a few days but if I was in here for longer? I'd have to rethink.

'Can you call my friend Agnes Brewer, please?'

The officer nodded. 'What's her number?'

'God, I don't know it. They're all on my phone. Nobody knows anybody's number anymore, do they?'

'You'd be surprised. Young men know their mum's,

usually. Did DS Lambert or DC Noble take your phone earlier?'

I nodded.

The officer picked up the phone on her desk again and asked one of her colleagues to bring down my mobile. 'We only need it for a couple of minutes to get some contact details.'

A young male officer came down with the phone in an evidence bag with my name, date of birth and a case number added in large, blue capitals. Gibson scrolled down my contacts list. She wrote down Agnes' number and then called it from the phone on her desk. She left a message, giving her name and explaining what had happened to me, and that I was hoping she'd be able to look after Ned. 'If you could call me at Brixton Police Station as a matter of urgency, I'd be very grateful,' she added at the end.

'Right, let's start with a bit more information about your son. What school does he go to?'

I gave her the details of the school, his name, his teacher's name. She said she would get in touch with them herself.

'Now, as well as your friend Agnes and the school, is there anybody you'd like to be informed that you're here... friends? Family?'

'No, I just need to organise my son's care. My babysitter Denny came to look after him earlier, when I was arrested, and to take him to school. I don't think she'll be able to look after him for very long but she might if all else fails. I just need to make sure Ned is looked after.'

'Okay, let's find Denny's number too. What about his dad; did you say he's not around?'

'Yes. No, he's not around.'

'We should probably contact him anyway. Does he see your son much?'

'Not really; he has serious depression.'

'Fair enough, in that case we'll contact him only if we need to.' Gibson typed a few sentences into a section of a document on the screen. 'Let's get started with all the admin. Are you feeling better now? You can see a doctor.'

'No, thanks, I'm not ill, I was only sick because I was in shock. But...' I sighed and hesitated for a moment. 'This is all a complete nightmare. I didn't do it, what they've arrested me for. I'm so worried about Mal; I'd never do anything to hurt him.' My stomach clenched as I conjured up his face in my mind's eye. 'If I can organise my son's care, I'll feel a whole lot better.'

Ned was going to be so confused, so worried. I remembered how he'd felt a year ago with all the uncertainty when I broke up with Adrian, how he'd dreamt about Adrian trying to kill me. I needed to push those thoughts from my mind. Focus.

'I have a friend who's a solicitor; can I call her too?'

I remembered that there was a mum at school, Greta, who was a lawyer. Property, I thought, but she posted on Facebook a lot about human rights so I could have been wrong about that. She wouldn't be able to represent me, but she might know someone who could.

Sergeant Gibson took my details, filling in sections of the form on the computer screen. The keyboard made a hollow clunking sound. As if encountering the Qwerty layout for the first time, she entered the information one finger at a time.

She photographed me from the front, both sides, head and shoulders, full body. I must have looked like shit; not a trace of make-up, unshowered, Croydon facelift.

Next, she took me into an adjacent room to take my fingerprints. I was watching police dramas from twenty years ago; it wouldn't have occurred to me that they were no longer taken by pushing each finger into an ink pad.

We returned to the previous room where a woman doctor was waiting to take a blood sample. Sergeant Gibson swabbed my hands and mouth, scraped under my fingernails, and took a few hairs. Everything was bagged up and labelled.

She then took the name of the solicitor I knew; Greta Mayhew. I couldn't remember if I had her as a contact on my phone, but she was easy to find online. I'd only ever talked to her a handful of times; standing watching our kids stomping in the paddling pool in the park up the hill, and once in the Costcutter at the end of the road. She was a single mum too, and we'd joked about being terrible parents, getting home to find the fridge empty and having to pick up something last-minute for our children's dinner. Maybe a packet of fish fingers and some frozen peas, along with a bottle of the least offensive white wine they had on offer in the chiller.

Bizarrely, when Mal and I became Facebook friends a couple of years ago, the colleague he rented a room from, Sally, had come up as someone I might know. Both he and Greta were friends of hers. Small world. Even during those short encounters with Greta, I got the feeling she was someone worth getting to know. She had gravitas, authority, she seemed like a proper person. We'd moved to Westbourne Grove before I'd had a chance to foster her friendship.

The male officer who had brought my phone down reappeared in the doorway. 'Can I have a word?' he asked Gibson.

While they murmured in low voices, I searched around in my brain thinking for someone else who might be able to look after Ned. I thought about his friends' parents, and who would have the capacity to look after another child, if only for a few days. There was Nicole, but she worked full time. Ingrid, but things had never been quite the same with them after falling out about Ned not choosing Johan for his football team. Though us moving to west London had distanced the boys, Ned said they had started to play together again at lunchtime.

As they were talking, my phone on the desk lit up; the screen was full of message alerts but it was too far away for me to read the senders' names. People were going to start wondering where I was if I didn't respond. My next shoot, due to start on Thursday. It was the least of my worries, but still; I put my head in my handcuffed hands.

'What's the matter, love?' Sergeant Gibson asked. Love. It was comforting, in a situation like that, for someone to use any form of endearment at all.

'Oh, it's work. I've got a job starting the day after tomorrow. It's only just occurred to me.'

'You're starting a new job?'

'Oh, er, no, I'm a photographer, freelance. It's just for a few days, starting on Thursday. But I'm really going to be in the... trouble... if I don't do it. It's the least of my worries though.'

'You never know, you might be out of here by then.'

I looked at her blankly. I didn't believe her any more than she did.

'Any ideas about who else can look after your little boy?'

'Yes, I was thinking but I've only drawn blanks. I don't want to impose on friends who already have too much on their plates. Please, just give me a minute. I'm sure I can think of someone.'

She nodded as she sat down and started to fill out more sections of the form on her computer screen.

'And your work; the job you talked about? You're only supposed to have one phone call, strictly speaking. But your situation is a little unusual. If you give me a name I can call someone to let them know you're in a bit of a fix.'

I gave her the name of the architect, John, who had asked me to take some interim photographs of his new build in Dalston. Gibson started searching through my contacts for him.

I dismissed the idea of getting a friend with kids to look after Ned -- too much extra work they could do without. So I took the opposite approach; couples who didn't have children. Were there any for whom the idea of looking after a child wouldn't be a terrifying prospect? I drew a blank.

Single people; would they be better? There weren't many I could think of, they'd all run a mile. Itsumi would be delighted to look after him, but she was too elderly and frail to deal with a nutty seven year old boy for more than a few hours. Also she'd worry if she knew what was happening to me.

Then suddenly, it occurred to me; Caroline. If she had a few days' notice, and it would be the weekend by then, she could come down from Cambridge. She'd looked after her sisters' children when they were little. And she'd looked after Ned the night I'd gone down to stay with Mal in Brighton; she'd offered so many times to look after him, I felt a bit mean that, until that point, I hadn't taken her up on the offer.

'Yes, okay, as well as Denny, could you also contact Caroline Wilson? She's an old friend, she lives in Cambridge, but with a bit of notice, she might be able to come down and look after my son.'

'That's fine, I'll get in touch with both of them, Mrs Kendrew.'

'Actually Sergeant Gibson, it's not Mrs. I'm not married.'

'Miss Kendrew then?'

'I guess so. Or Ms. Mrs; it's just sounds a bit strange.'

'Fair enough. I'll make a note on the system. I'll call your two friends. Denny and then...' she looked down at the notes she'd made on a sheet of paper on her desk. 'Caroline Wilson.'

'That's it, thank you very much.' I smiled weakly, tears pricking the back of my eyes. 'You know, I didn't do this, there's been a terrible mistake.'

She half smiled, reaching out and placing her hand on top of mine. 'If you didn't, then there's nothing to worry about, is there?'

After the admin was complete, I was taken down to one of the cells. Gibson led me through the main corridor with around a dozen heavy metal doors on both sides, unlocking a barred gate which led to more.

'These cells are just for women; they're a little more pleasant as a result,' she added.

I didn't need to ask why. Walking past the men's cells, there had been an overwhelming cocktail of smells; stale BO, piss, sweaty feet, disinfectant.

We turned a corner and towards the end of the shorter cul-de-sac, she opened the door of one cell.

The only natural light came from a panel of glass bricks towards the top of one wall. The walls were painted in sunshine yellow gloss. It was ugly but, I guessed, easy to wipe clean. The minimal light coming from outside was supplemented with a harsh strip on the ceiling. Built out of the wall, below the glass bricks, was a low bed with a thin blue plastic mattress and pillow, and a couple of folded fleece blankets.

'Sit yourself down, love,' Gibson said. She explained to me what would happen next; as soon as a legal representative was appointed, her colleagues would interview me, in the presence of the lawyer.

'If your friend doesn't call us back soon, we can appoint a duty solicitor for you, unless there's someone else?'

'How long will you need to wait before doing that?'

'It depends where DS Lambert is with the enquiry. I'm sure he'll want to interview you as soon as possible. The duty solicitor scheme is very good, but there's no pressure to agree to take one.'

'Okay, hopefully Greta will get back to me. And can you also check if my friend Agnes has called back?'

CHAPTER 34

I sat down on the hard, blue mattress, my head falling into my hands, eyes closed. I couldn't take it all in. What had I done yesterday that could have led the police to thinking I'd tried to kill Mal? It didn't make sense. He'd come over the night before; Sunday. I hadn't been able to get a babysitter that night and he was still very conscious of not spending too much time with me. He wanted to make sure Ned felt he had plenty of his mum's undivided attention. I'd accepted that, understood it. Cosy evenings with the clichéd bottle of red and a Netflix boxset were infrequent.

I felt there was something on his mind that night. I'd asked him about the work situation and he said that it had calmed down. The board were considering the restructuring plans and weren't going to make any rash decisions.

It wasn't until the next morning that I plucked up the courage to ask him if there was anything else. He told me that a few nights earlier Louise had been in touch with him. At least he was upfront about it, when he finally spilled the beans. I asked him if he was going to get back in touch. The quick flush of pink I knew so well spread over his cheeks as he told me he'd agreed to meet her for a coffee, just to tell her he was seeing me and that he was happy, and that he wasn't going to go back to her. I'd taken it at face value. Things had been great between us, there was no need for me to feel insecure.

'Why do you have to see her though? Why can't you just text her?' I'd asked, as he left for work. He didn't really have an answer. I'd left it at that, but felt a coldness from him that day, in his one word replies to my texts. The night someone had tried to kill him, I'd called to apologise. He hadn't replied so I left a message. When he didn't reply then, not even a text, I texted him back, asking him whether he'd arranged to see Louise. Asking; well, accusing, you could say. It wasn't going to look good from the police's point of view.

My heartbeat was irregular and jumpy. I could feel the start of a caffeine headache coming on, not caused by too much coffee but a lack of it. I tried to concentrate for a moment on my breathing. One, two, three – in, one, two, three – out.

Gibson came back to the cell a few minutes later.

'Right, Alex, your friend Agnes has called us back – she's got her elderly mother staying with her and said it would be difficult to have Ned to stay.'

I remembered her mum was due to visit, I just hadn't realised it was this week.

'So, you need to think of someone else. What time does school finish again?'

'After-school club finishes at six-thirty but I try and pick Ned up before six; he doesn't like being the last one there. Please could you just try Denny and ask if there's any way she could look after him for a little longer? And tell her I'll pay her for her time.'

'Fine. Why don't we have a back-up, just in case? I've also put in a call to Caroline Wilson, just waiting for her to get back in touch.'

'Someone as well as Denny and Caroline?'

'Yes, if you can.'

She locked the heavy metal door behind her again, multiple bolts clunking into place. I looked round the room properly for the first time. It was airless; no wonder the cells smelt so bad. There was a two-foot wall that jutted out to make a separate area for the metal toilet and small basin. For a moment as I sat down to pee. I was self-conscious, before realising how ridiculous that was, in the circumstances.

Gibson came back fifteen minutes later, pulling down the small hatch in the door for a moment, before unlocking it. 'Okay, love, your solicitor friend hasn't called us back yet, but DS Feddersen is very keen to interview you as soon as. There's a duty solicitor upstairs at the moment, dealing with a couple of kids from the Tulse Hill estate who've been arrested on drugs charges. Would you like to see him? He's very nice; Mr Chowdhury.'

'Sure, whatever is going to get this sorted out sooner.'

'I'll ask him to come down to one of the interview rooms. If it happens that your lawyer friend gets in touch, that's fine, the duty solicitor can brief him or her.'

She locked the heavy door again. I could hear several doors further back, along the main corridor, being opened and closed too. Voices raised, trainers squeaking on the rubber floor, the dull thud of shoulder against the corridor wall. I could picture new residents, the kids from the Tulse Hill estate for instance, putting up more resistance to their incarceration than I had done. I'd been as meek as a lamb, frozen by fear, but now I worried I hadn't been vocal enough about my innocence and that would go against me, somehow.

I couldn't sit still. My mind had was in overdrive. Top of my list of worries – what was going to happen to Ned. What if nobody could look after him and he was put into care? I couldn't let that happen. I would have to agree to Sean staying with him if there was no other option.

I paced the room; three steps one way, right turn, two steps, right turn, three steps, right turn, two steps. And repeat. I must have done this a hundred times when I glanced up and saw the camera, fixed to a corner of the wall just below the ceiling. Suddenly I felt self-conscious; would I look like a crazy person pacing the room like that? I stopped mid-step, standing in the middle of the room, staring into space. How could I stop myself losing my mind? Never mind appearing like a mad woman to anyone watching the CCTV at the custody desk, there was a possibility I might actually become one.

I heard the metal gate that separated the male and female cells being unlocked and then locked again. A moment later the hatch was lowered for a few seconds and then the door unlocked, opening out into the corridor. A young male officer who I hadn't seen before came into the cell.

'Mrs Kendrew, I'm Jason, one of the DDOs here.'

He had a badge with his name and rank but he was too far away for me to be able to read it. I must have looked at him blankly; he explained. 'I'm a Dedicated Detention Officer... DDO for short. I've just called your friend Denise Coleman. She's agreed to look after your son until tomorrow evening. She has some family issues so it will be difficult to continue to do so after then.'

I sat down and my head fell into my hands. 'Okay.'

'But I've also talked to Caroline Wilson; she's organised taking a few days off work. She'll drive down from Cambridge tomorrow evening and can stay until the weekend, if we still need her. Sergeant Gibson has filled me in a little about your situation; she's gone off duty now. She asked me to suggest you consider your ex-husband taking over the care of your child from that point onwards.'

The radio on his belt crackled into life; he listened to his colleague and then turned to face me again. 'Your solicitor is just being briefed by colleagues. After that he'll come down and tell you what he knows so far. Once he's done that, you'll be interviewed by DS Feddersen and DC McMenemy.

'What about DS Lambert? He arrested me; will he not interview me?'

'DS Feddersen, I believe, was one of the officers who attended the crime scene earlier today so he has a better handle on the situation at present.'

Crime scene. God. Part of me hadn't quite accepted that this wasn't just someone's very sick practical joke.

The officer led me past all the other cells to one of the interview rooms. Already seated was a young guy in a trendy suit. I was almost old enough to be his mother.

He stood up and shook my hand. 'Hello Mrs Kendrew. I'm Ashok Chowdhury, from Aldridge and Kemp on Walworth Road. I've been briefed by Lambeth Police about your case... you're still looking for representation?'

I nodded. He pulled a seat out from the table for me.

'So, I've just talked to the officers, the ones who attended the crime scene...' He looked down at his notes. 'A ground floor flat, Marlowe Road.' He looked up at me again. 'What do you know about the events of last night?'

'Nothing, I wasn't there. All I've been told is that somebody tried to kill Mal, my boyfriend, and that the police think it was me.'

'Where were you last night?' he asked.

'At home, from about six when I picked up my son from after-school club.'

'How old is your son?'

'Seven.'

Chowdhury made some notes and then looked up at me. 'A seven-year-old child isn't old enough to be an alibi, I'm afraid. Were you with anyone else last night?'

'No. I did have a text conversation with Mal, Malcolm Russell. He didn't reply but I think... I thought... he could have been at a friendly at Arsenal and that's why he didn't reply.'

Chowdhury wrote this down. He had a beautiful silver Caran d'Ache fountain pen. His hand was full of flourishes, a style which didn't lend itself to quick note-taking.

'I'll tell you what I know. Malcolm Russell, lives on Marlowe Road, SE24, attacked at his home last night at approximately 8.30 pm.'

I shook my head. 'I've never been to his flat, not inside anyway, I've dropped him off and picked him up there in the car a few times. He rents a room from a colleague, I think she's called Sally... I've never met her before.'

'His colleague, as you say,' he looked at the previous page of his notes to check her name. 'Sally Dowell, let a woman into the flat. The woman called herself Alex Kendrew. She said she'd been in the area and wondered if Mal was free to have a drink. She said the woman had looked a bit surprised to see Sally at the door, and stumbled over her words, like she was a bit embarrassed to be there.'

The solicitor turned the page. 'This was, as far as Sally Dowell can remember, about seven-thirty; she was about to go to her book club at a pub nearby. She was already a little late, so she just allowed the woman into the flat, got her a drink of water, and left her to it. Sally told the police last night that she hadn't met you before, though she knew all about you, being his girlfriend and everything. She'd seen a few photos of you on Malcolm's phone, but that's all. As far as she could tell, the woman at the door was the person she said she was – you – she had absolutely no reason to think otherwise.'

'But it wasn't me.'

'If it was, you need to tell me. I'm not going to be able to defend you properly if I don't know the truth.'

'I realise that. But it wasn't me. Apart from someone telling them it was me, have the police got any evidence that I was there?'

'Not at the moment, from what they're telling me,' he replied.

I stood up and started to pace the room.

'But what about Mal? Has he not spoken to the police?'

'Mr Russell is in an induced coma. He was stabbed in the abdomen. Only one quite deep wound, as far as the police know. The hospital aren't giving them much information. He underwent emergency surgery in the early hours of the morning.'

I stumbled over to the table, grabbed the back of the chair with both hands, my legs collapsing beneath me. 'It can't be him. There's got to be a mistake.'

'I can see this has come as a huge shock, Mrs Kendrew. You need to think about who would want to do this to you. If you don't have an alibi I need to present the police with some evidence that someone is trying to frame you. Is there anybody who dislikes you enough to want to do that?'

'Do you mean low-level dislike or full-on hating my guts? There are a few of both.'

Ashok Chowdhury raised an eyebrow. 'I'd concentrate on full-on hate initially.'

'My ex, Adrian – Adrian Evans. About eighteen months ago, when our relationship was pretty much over, he tried to rape me, anally. Around the same time I found videos on our iCloud account of him in Paris, with underage prostitutes. I went to the Kensington police station to tell them. He was arrested and questioned about my rape and also about the underage prostitutes.

I stopped to take a sip of water. 'But because that happened in Paris, and no-one knows for sure if the girls were underage legally, or just, you know, very young, he wasn't charged. Not yet anyway.'

'What have the police at Kensington station told you,' Ashok asked.

'About the Paris investigation?'

'Both,' he added.

'The Parisian police are trying to track down the girls. The French and UK police are still arguing about who will eventually charge him but that will only happen if they find enough evidence against him, and he's so unbelievably arrogant I'm pretty sure he thinks they won't and it'll all be dropped.'

'But if that's the case, why would he wait a year and then try and frame you, when in all likelihood he could get off anyway? And your rape... was he charged with that?'

'Yes, they took it very seriously, but I didn't go to the police straight away so there wasn't any physical evidence.'

'Why didn't you go to the police immediately?' Ashok enquired.

'To be honest, I just wanted to forget all about him.

There was a court order; he couldn't come anywhere near me. But a few months after the attempted rape, and discovering the Paris videos, I found out that, months before, he'd got hold of my phone and texted Mal... he told him I'd been killed in a road accident. He changed the numbers so that when I tried to contact Mal it went to him instead.'

'Woah, that's pretty out there.' Ashok made some more notes. 'Okay. And you have evidence of that?'

I nodded. 'But I can't absolutely prove it.'

'Okay, I'm not saying he's not involved but the year-long gap worries me. Anyone else?'

'There's my other ex, my son's father. He's seriously depressed, but I can't see him being involved. Though, a few years ago, quite calmly one morning, at the end of one of our daily arguments, he said "you know Alex, I could quite happily kill you now".'

Chowdhury started writing again.

'Were you worried? At the time?'

'No. I mean, maybe a little. He's a big, strong man. I'd have had no chance if he'd meant it. It was more because we'd got to the point where we hated each other so much, things like that were very easy to say.'

'Did you respond when he said that?'

'Only with a look of disgust.'

'What's his name... I don't think you said?'

'Sean Moran. He lives with his mother, just outside Oxford.'

'He's not looking after your son at the moment, right? You don't have joint custody?'

I shook my head. 'My friend Denise Coleman is looking after him, at our house. Or she will be once she's picked him up from after-school club later.'

He continued to make notes; a large, ornate 'D' and 'C' at the start of each name.

'I'm going to be honest, Alex, it's not looking good. We're going to have to find some concrete evidence that your ex was involved or they'll pin an attempted murder on you. Of course, it will be a lot worse if Mr Russell doesn't pull through.'

'I realise that.' One thing occurred to me. 'Have the police interviewed Mal's colleague... the one he rents a room from?'

'They did last night, at the crime scene. She was traumatised, understandably, to find Mr Russell at their flat, covered in blood and unconscious. She's been staying with her parents in Kent, recovering. I understand some officers were going to travel down there to interview her fully this morning.'

'But if she saw me, in person, she'd realise it wasn't me who stabbed Mal.'

Ashok looked down at his notes.

'Without doubt there'll be an ID parade. Sally Dowell will be shown around eight or ten video clips, you being one of them.'

'What if she picks me out by mistake? God, what if she's behind it and she's setting me up? I know that sounds crazy. She came onto him at a work Christmas party, and they ended up going home together, though it didn't go any further. Relationships between colleagues were frowned upon by the bank. But I think there's a good chance she might still have a bit of a thing about Mal.'

'Did Mr Russell tell you that?'

'Yes, ages ago, years in fact.'

'Have you got it in writing... in a text or email?'

'No, he just told me one night when she came up in conversation.'

'That's a shame.' He made more notes.

'Can you think of anyone else?'

'Not at the moment.'

'I'll go and talk to the DS. When they're ready they'll interview you in one of these rooms. I'll be there with you. They'll ask you a lot of questions. Try to stay calm and stick to the facts. Let's not make any wild accusations that we won't be able to back up with evidence at a later date.'

Chowdhury rose to his feet and put the notes away in his leather briefcase.

'Would I be able to talk to my son on the phone? Just so I can explain to him what's happening?' I asked.

'I don't think at this stage they'll allow that.'

'Yes, I thought that would be the case. I just need to know he's been picked up from school and is being looked after. Can you ask though... please?'

CHAPTER 35

A wave of exhaustion hit me. I fell back onto the sticky plastic mattress and pulled my knees up to my chest.

I needed to write down my thoughts. I rang the red buzzer next to the door. A few minutes later, Jason, the DDO came back, pulling down the small hatch before opening the door.

'Oh, I'm sorry, I just wondered if it was possible to have some paper and a pen?'

'What for?'

'I just want to get some thoughts down. Would that be possible?'

'Yes, but not right now. DS Feddersen is ready for you in one of the interview rooms.'

He led me out of the cell, closing the door behind him. A colleague in the same kind of uniform, a woman around thirty, was waiting at the metal gate. She unlocked it and they led me through the corridor, past the men's cells. I heard crying; high-pitched, almost like a howl, from one cell. From another, on the opposite side, a banging on the door in response. 'Shut the fuck up, will you? Or I'll break your fucking neck.'

The air was dank, stale; the way it is in summer after weeks of hot weather. The undeniable aroma of coffee drifted from a stairwell that led up to the ground floor. God, I needed caffeine. We passed the room I'd been in earlier, to another almost identical one.

Chowdhury was sitting at the table with his notes in front of him. Standing opposite him were two officers I hadn't seen before; a man and a woman. She was short and pear-shaped, with a neat, sensible haircut. The man was tall and lean, around my age, had a long face to match his height and cropped blonde hair that made him look, at a glance, ten years younger.

'Please sit down, Mrs Kendrew,' the woman said. 'I am DC McMenemy, my colleague here is DS Feddersen; we are the Senior Investigating Officers on this case. Also present is your solicitor, Ashok Chowdhury, who has been appointed for you. We will be videoing this interview, in line with normal procedures in cases of this nature.'

McMenemy stood up and checked the camera propped on a tripod in the corner of the room. She returned to the table and pressed a button on a black box which looked like an old-fashioned video recorder. A couple of buttons lit up.

'Alexandra Kendrew, you have been arrested on suspicion of the attempted murder of Malcolm Russell. You have told my colleagues, DS Lambert and DC Noble, when they arrested you at your home this morning, that you were not involved. Have you anything you want to say regarding that?'

'Yes, it wasn't me, I wasn't there. I have no idea why somebody would try and frame me, but that is what's happening. You have to believe me – this is crazy. I would never do anything to hurt Mal. I love him. We've been through so much—'

'But you sounded quite angry in your text messages with him last night?'

I sighed. 'An old girlfriend of his had been in touch and he hadn't categorically said he wouldn't see her. I was just a bit annoyed about it, that's all.'

'And Mr Russell finished your relationship some time ago, is that right?'

'Well, yes, a long time ago, origi—'

McMenemy didn't wait for an answer. 'And was that the same woman he'd been in touch with? Surely that would make you quite angry, feasibly you could have been angry enough to do something quite drastic?'

'No, of course—'

Chowdhury interjected. 'Please DC McMenemy, can you let my client finish her response before you ask another question?'

She nodded and smiled slightly. Feddersen spoke up for the first time.

'Mrs Kendrew, we need to establish where you were last night, from around 5 pm until 10 pm.

'Actually, I'm not Mrs, I'm Ms.'

McMenemy made a note with a hint of a smirk on her face. I couldn't shift from my mind the notion that I'd met her somewhere before.

'Ms Kendrew, please continue.'

'I picked my son up from after-school club. The school is virtually opposite so I'd have got there just before six and been home a few minutes after. Before that I'd been working at home, doing some retouching on screen.'

Something occurred to me. 'The times of the Photoshop files will verify I was at home. And after I made tea for my son, Ned. After we'd eaten he watched something on TV and I did a bit of work before getting him ready for bed. After that I went back upstairs to my studio and continued working.'

'We have all your computer equipment; we'll check that.' She sat back in her seat. 'So, let's go back to your relationship with Mr Russell. You had found out he had been in contact with his ex-girlfriend...' McMenemy looked down at her notes again. 'Louise Russell.'

'He'd had a text from her, or a voicemail. He hadn't heard from her for ages, and they'd both agreed that their relationship was over. That's partly why he got back in touch with me. He'd finished our relationship, three years ago, because she'd got back in touch then. There was a bit of a pattern in her behaviour.'

I paused and glanced at my solicitor. 'Look, she had more reason to attack him than I did; perhaps she's trying to frame me. She must have found out he was seeing someone else, on Facebook, or through mutual friends.' As I added this, I turned to Chowdhury. He closed his eyes slowly, with an almost imperceptible shake of the head. I took from that he thought I'd gone off-piste enough for the time being. I turned back to the officers sitting opposite and dropped my gaze.

'You don't have a very public relationship though, do you? Looking on your social media, there doesn't seem to be many posts where Mr Russell is mentioned? Only a couple of photos. And the same with him. Nobody would've been able to ascertain from your social media that you were together.'

Anger rose up through my body and flushed my cheeks. 'His profile photo on Facebook is of us together... that's pretty public, isn't it? Neither of us are the type to splash hundreds of selfies of us together on Facebook or Instagram. You know the kind of thing; here we are in a cocktail bar thirty-four floors up the Shard. Look, everyone, Mal is taking me to Paris for the weekend... aren't I lucky? It's not anyone's business what we do.'

'Do you talk to your friends about him? Do his friends know about you?'

'Yes, some. A few of my friends have met him, and my son has. I've met his son and a few of his friends.

'He has children?'

'Yes, one; a boy, Ewan. He's sixteen; he finished sitting his GCSEs in June. I've met him a few times.'

'Only a few; isn't that a bit odd?' McMenemy asked.

'No, not really. When he's not staying with Mal he lives in Brighton with his mum. Mal always felt he'd done enough damage to his son by having an affair and destroying the marriage. He didn't want Ewan exposed to any more carnage.'

'That's understandable,' Feddersen added.

Chowdhury looked up from his notes. 'I don't really understand where this line of enquiry is going. We've established my client has a relationship with Mr Russell. Any problems you are insinuating they have, are fabrication. Ms Kendrew does not have a motive for attacking him.'

'Thank you Mr Chowdhury, we just need to be certain of that,' McMenemy said. 'It will help your client's position if you are able to present any evidence you can gather about any other person or persons who might have a motive.'

Chowdhury leafed back through his notes. 'Ms Kendrew's ex-partner had a motive. He was jealous that she'd rekindled her relationship with Mr Russell and took extreme steps to break them up.'

'Such as...?' McMenemy looked at me suspiciously. She was one of those women who hated women like me.

Ashok continued. 'My client has told me that approximately a year ago, Adrian Evans interfered with her phone, changing contact details, and sent a message from a prepaid mobile phone to Mr Russell. It said that Ms Kendrew had been killed in a road accident. Ms Kendrew went to report this to the police approximately six months ago when she found out he was behind it.'

'Which police station did you go to?'

'Kensington. We lived... he still lives there, Westbourne Grove. Kensington was the nearest station. There were a couple of other reasons I went to report him... he tried to rape me one evening. Around the same time, I found videos on our Family iCloud of him having sex in a Paris hotel room with young girls. I was in two minds about whether to report these, but finding out he'd split Mal and I up was the final straw.'

McMenemy's expression softened a fraction. 'And what happened as a result? Was he charged?'

Ashok explaining the situation, referring to his notes from earlier; why I hadn't gone to the police about the attempted rape immediately, the situation in Paris and the waters being muddied because the alleged crime happened in France.

McMenemy and Feddersen exchanged glances.

My solicitor broke the silence. 'Have your colleagues interviewed Sally Dowell yet? My client is aware that Ms Dowell and Mr Russell were romantically involved, briefly, five or six years ago.'

Feddersen turned to face him. 'A further interview has been conducted with Ms Dowell. We haven't watched it yet but we will once this interview has been completed. As soon as she's able, Ms Dowell will be shown a video ID parade.'

'I suggest we terminate this interview and reconvene later,' McMenemy added.

Ashok asked if he could use the room so he could interview me further and they agreed. As the detectives opened the door, he asked 'Can you give me an indication when the ID parade will take place?'

'We're keen to do that as soon as possible, before Sally Dowell's memory of last night begins to fade,' Feddersen replied.

Before they left, I had a question I needed to ask. 'Can you tell me how Mal is? Mr Chowdhury said you'd told him he'd been put into a coma and that he'd had surgery. Is he going to be okay?'

'We aren't able to tell you anything at the moment. If there are any significant changes, for instance his medical situation deteriorating, or improving, we will tell Mr Chowdhury.' McMenemy gave a tight little smile before she moved her shoulder away from the door and let it slam closed.

Ashok sat down at the table. 'Okay, Alexandra... do you prefer Alexandra or Alex?'

'Alex is fine, thanks.'

He got up and walked over to the door and put his ear to the wood to check if he could hear anyone on the other side. He returned to the desk and leaned forward, dropping his voice to a whisper. 'The police are not permitted to record any conversation we have, but them overhearing something is a different matter. Let's keep our voices low, just in case. I've had instances where clients have become irate and landed themselves in trouble.'

I nodded my understanding. 'Okay,' I whispered back.

'The information they get from your computer may be the key. You didn't leave the house at all after you returned back with your son at around 6 pm?'

'That's right. I put the recycling out at one point, I can't remember when exactly. I was working in my studio. One of my neighbours might have seen me; my desk is next to the window.'

'I'll make some enquiries about that.'

'Do you have a car?'

'Yes, it's parked just a bit down from the house, I think.'

'Is there CCTV in your street?'

'I don't know, there's one camera right at the end, above a bakers' on the corner with the main road. I've no idea how much of our road is covered by it, if any.'

'Let's hope it does, and that it shows you didn't leave the house, apart from taking your recycling out,' he added with a note of optimism.

'What else will the police be looking at to find evidence I was at Mal's flat? It doesn't take a genius to see they're going to be trying to prove my guilt rather than my innocence. What about DNA at Mal's flat?'

Ashok sat back. 'Well, a key witness thinking it was you is our main hurdle. The ID parade will be our chance to disprove that. They'll be having any DNA samples found at the scene analysed and it'll take at least 24 hours to get the results. Obviously they will also look extensively at your phone. How do you communicate with Mr Russell?'

'Text message usually.'

'And do you talk on the phone?'

'Yes, apart from clients, he's probably the only person I regularly call, or who calls me. We speak at least once a day.'

'The police will be checking the cell site data for your phone for last night, and over the last week or so, I imagine.

Of course, you leaving it at home, they would say, doesn't prove you weren't responsible. You could have left it there on purpose.'

'I might have made calls or sent texts though, during the evening; I couldn't have done that if I'd left it at home and I was several miles away, trying to kill my...' I couldn't finish the sentence.

'I'll raise that with them if it comes up. Unless they think you might have an accomplice who could have used your phone.'

'This is just crazy. What kind of parent would leave a seven-year-old at home on his own? Surely they'd take that into consideration, wouldn't they?'

'Yes, but you could have had someone look after him. I'm just playing devil's advocate here. Or gone out once he'd gone to bed. They're going to try and paint you in as bad a light as possible.'

CHAPTER 36

B ack in the cell, I was amazed to find some A4 sheets of paper and pen had been left on the bed. While everything was fresh in my mind, I needed to write it all down. I made three columns; name, reasons for, reasons against.

First; Adrian. In the 'Reasons For' column, I made a list.

1. Jealousy.

2. Payback for underage prostitutes and rape charge.

3. Coercive control?

And the 'Reasons Against'.

1. Does he have the balls?

What about Sally? When I'd mentioned to Ashok that she'd had a thing for Mal, I didn't realistically think she was involved, but now I thought about it more, it started to make sense. What if Mal and Sally had a fight; suppose she'd come onto him again and he'd turned her down? She'd got angry with him, it got out of control. They were in the kitchen; she saw a knife and in a moment of madness picked it up and stabbed him. She panicked and fled the scene.

Perhaps it was only later she worked out she could

frame someone else and I was the first who'd come to mind. She wouldn't have meant to kill him, wouldn't have even meant to hurt him. She thought she'd killed him when she'd fled the house. She thought he was dead; couldn't feel a pulse, saw all the blood, and jumped to conclusions. Then, if he was dead, if she was found guilty, not of manslaughter on the grounds of self defence but murder, the penalty would be much greater. She realised she could push the blame onto someone else. She decided to return home and call the ambulance, telling them she'd just found him, stabbed and unconscious.

Why hadn't it occurred to me before? If she was responsible, there must be dozens of inconsistencies in her account. Had she gone to her book club; did the police check? How did she behave? She would have had to change her clothes. Did the police check she didn't throw any away? Or were they so intent on finding me, they didn't explore any other possibilities?

I scribbled it all down, not in nice, neat, succinct bullet points like I had with Adrian, but in one big, almost illegible scrawl. I paced the room, reading it, looking for holes in my theory. It could be her. Still, if it wasn't and she could prove it, I'd be back to square one, and Adrian would be the only other possibility.

Who else? Louise? Did she really have a motive? I had no idea. He could have lied about their recent conversations. Perhaps there was more to it than he'd admitted. If she'd got in touch with him, as he said she had, I understood why better than anyone else. We just got each other, Mal and I, right from the word go. The way he talked to me, looked at me. Whether he meant to or not, he always made me feel like I was the only woman in the room. He made me feel special, wanted, alive, like no-one had ever done. After all the years they were together, I imagine it had been the same for Louise.

She had to be on the list. I needed to make sure Ashok mentioned it to Feddersen and McMenemy. They could have her phone checked, or his; substantiate what had been said between them recently.

'Reasons For'

1. Jealousy.

2. Not used to being rejected.

'Reasons Against'

1. Their on-off relationship, why different this time?

Who else? The more I tried to search around in my mind, the more impenetrable it became, like fog descending in ever-denser waves.

I leant back against the wall, closing my eyes, willing myself to relax and clear my head. Breathe. I counted to one hundred, two hundred.

I stood up, stretched, suddenly aware that my muscles ached from inactivity. I walked around the cell in a clockwise direction; three steps, right turn, two steps, right turn; a small rectangle the size of a dining table. I started slowly, no quicker than a fast walk, but gathered pace a little and found a rhythm. My body took over, and before I knew it, I felt calmer, my mind almost free of thought.

After a few minutes, I became aware I was measuring it. Runners are obsessed with noting the length, time, speed, though I knew it would be wildly inaccurate. I counted the laps. Ten steps per lap. I guessed each lap must have taken about four seconds. I got to about seventy and started to feel dizzy; the lap so small, it was almost like going round in circles. I changed direction to counteract it, and then again when I got to one hundred and forty. I made little calculations in my head; seventy laps at four seconds each, that was two hundred and eighty seconds, nearly five minutes.

Halfway through the third anti-clockwise set, I lost count and my mind drifted back to Mal. I had to know if there was any new information. I decided to do seventy more laps, then I'd press the red button and see if there was news.

Each time I passed the bed, I read glimpses of the list I'd made. Adrian, Sally and Louise; that's as far as I'd got.

I tried to think who else might have a grudge against me. Even a small one, low-level. What about some of the men I'd dated? Maybe someone I'd dropped like a hot potato? That period where I went a bit crazy after Mal; most of them had ghosted me, not the other way round. Then with a speed that hit me like I'd run into a lamppost, I remembered one. I'd blanked him from my memory so completely, I couldn't even remember his name.

I could, unfortunately, remember his spectacularly bad hygiene problem. And then, though nothing was ever proved, there had been the word BITCH sprayed on the front of the house. What was he called? I felt nauseous as I conjured up his face. There was nothing outwardly ugly about him, it was just because of what happened, the night he came round. I wasn't proud of myself for letting it happen but I put it down to experience, moved on and forgotten about it.

It was the needy texts afterwards that made the whole idea of him repulsive. I'd had one email from him I didn't read and after that I'd added his email address to the junk folder and never checked to see if there had been more. He hadn't called my landline, or turned up at the house, the only possible options left, so I assumed he'd decided to leave me alone.

Zeiss. That was his profile name. A German lens manufacturer, adored by nerdy photographers. And he was definitely one. I still couldn't remember his real name.

I hadn't worried about him after that. The word BITCH
on the house? I'd never found out who did that. He'd used
that word in one of the last messages; *You know, women like
you are such prick teases. I hope you get what you deserve, you
little bitch.* The message had been a few months before the
spray paint appeared on the front of the house. I'd called the
police about it; they'd taken my details and I'd given a short
statement. I'd never heard back from them, and I'd assumed
they hadn't taken it seriously.

I slowed my running pace, came to a halt, picked up the
sheets of paper on the bed, and started a new list entitled
'low level'. I added 'Zeiss' in the name list.

'Reasons for'

1. I dumped him.

2. Ignored threatening messages.

3. Blocked his number.

4. BITCH.

He knew where I lived… he could have followed Mal one
morning when he left the house.

'Reasons against'

1. Had left me alone afterwards, must have got the
message. Or so I thought.

As I finished writing, I heard the metal gate between the
male and female sections being opened; it was Jason.

'Alex, I need you to come up to the custody suite so we
can video you for the VIPER.'

I stood up. 'Who will be there when Sally Dowell
watches all the clips?'

'A senior officer, not one working on the case, and your
solicitor; he called to say he's on his way back. Also your

lawyer friend, Ms Mayhew, called earlier; she said she has a friend who'd be able to represent you. Either she or he will call us.'

I thanked Jason for letting me know. He handcuffed me and led me out of the cell. Just as he was locking the door, I remembered the notes I'd been making and asked him if I could take them with me to show the solicitor. He agreed. He took me into the VIPER room; I'd been expecting a normal video camera but instead there was a large grey metal box, somewhere between a regular photo booth and an airport security scanner. He sat me down in front of the camera, a white background behind me. I could see my reflection in the lens of the camera; I was almost unrecognisable from the normal Alex Kendrew; fully groomed, hair and make-up done. In the small black circle, I was unsmiling, frowning. I looked tired, heavy lidded, stern; it could have been my mother staring back at me.

When Jason was satisfied with the VIPER, I was taken back down to one of the interview rooms where Ashok waited for me.

'Alex, how are you feeling?'

'Not great. I haven't been told anything at all since you left earlier. I don't know how Mal is. Or where they're at with their enquiries. I feel completely at sea.'

He looked down at his notes. 'Okay, this is what they've just told me. Malcolm Russell is still in an induced coma after surgery. The doctors will probably try and bring him out of that tomorrow or the day after, depending on how his body is responding to the medication. He'll be on heavy-duty painkillers; morphine, something like that. And antibiotics to stop infection taking hold. He's had a blood transfusion too; he lost quite a lot of blood during the attack.'

For a few seconds I had to fight to breathe. 'Ashok, I didn't do this. The police seriously think it was me?'

'I don't know to be honest. Sally Dowell is coming in to view the video IDs shortly, and she'll be interviewed again while she's here. If she picks you out--'

'But it wasn't me. What if she makes a mistake? It's her word against mine. I've been thinking... she might be trying to set me up.' I passed my notes over the table to Ashok. 'I told you Sally and Mal had a bit of a thing, years ago. He's rented a room from her for four or five years. They've both been single on and off. Perhaps she wanted to rekindle it and he knocked her back.'

'Okay, I can't see why that would make her want to try and kill him though.'

'No, neither do I, unless she was really obsessed with him and couldn't bear the thought of him being with someone else,' I added. 'But you could say exactly the same about his ex-girlfriend, Louise Russell. Or me.'

CHAPTER 37

I stared at the wall of the cell, the glass bricks above the bed casting a long, skewed diamond of light onto it. Sally Dowell must have already arrived at the station; perhaps she had already determined my fate. Was it a good idea to conjure up in my head the possible outcomes? She picks me out. Mal doesn't pull through. She's adamant it was me. I'm charged with murder. There's no evidence to show I didn't do it. By default I'm found guilty. What would happen to Ned? If I didn't get out and Sean was his main carer until adulthood, what chance would he have to be normal, happy, well-adjusted?

What if, even if I got out and everything was fine, this incident was enough to trigger something in Ned's young, malleable brain? What if he became stressed and anxious as a result – not just now, not just for the next few months, but forever?

Somewhere in the middle of these potential scenarios, some fight or flight response must have sparked in my brain; my breathing short and sharp, my heart racing, palms suddenly sweaty. It couldn't happen, could it? There are miscarriages of justice all the time; of course it could.

My heart pounded in my rib cage. I felt light-headed. I stumbled over to the wall, reaching out both hands to steady myself, and rested my forehead against it. The painted brickwork was rough and sharp in places, but cool.

I couldn't allow myself to think it would all be okay. Imagining Sally upstairs not picking me out, and somehow, miraculously, being allowed to walk free. No, I had to be prepared for the worst.

An hour or so later, Jason came down to my cell. I knew it was him from the way he shook his bunch of keys before unlocking the metal gate in the corridor. Ashok was with him.

'Alex, come through to the interview room please,' Ashok asked.

'Why, what's the matter? What's happened?'

Jason ushered me through to the interview suite; Ashok closed the door and sat me down at the table.

'Sally Dowell has just seen the video identification parade. She picked you out, with very little hesitation. That's quite unusual. I'm sorry, Alex.'

'What does that mean?' I felt like I'd been punched.

'There's a good chance they will charge you, if the Crown Prosecutor thinks their case is strong enough.'

'But it's just Sally's word against mine. Especially taking into consideration what we know about her. What about the other evidence? CCTV, for instance? There's no concrete evidence I was there, is there? If she's framing me, of course she's going to pick me out.'

Jason knocked on the door.

'DS Feddersen is ready to interview you, Ms Kendrew.

Mr Chowdhury, I can only give you another couple of minutes.'

Ashok glanced at me.

'Let's just go now,' I said. 'If I'm done for, I'd rather just get it over with.'

Feddersen and McMenemy were already seated in an interview room. The room must have very recently been occupied by another interviewee; the stench of male body odour was so acrid and acute, it made my eyes sting.

McMenemy went through the procedural stuff. Why I was there. My rights. Reminding me that the interview would be videoed. She noted the time and date as she pressed a button on the black box that sat on the table.

I felt sick again; a combination of my situation and the fetid atmosphere. 'Can I have a glass of water, please?'

Feddersen nodded, looking at the large glass window. I hadn't realised earlier, but there must have been an observation room on the other side. He read out all those present. 'For the tape, Alexandra Kendrew, can you please confirm that neither the officers present nor any other investigating officer has discussed the case with you since the last interview this morning?'

I nodded. 'That's correct.'

'As you'll now be aware, Sally Dowell has positively identified you during the video procedure. What is your response to that?'

'She's wrong, I wasn't there. She's never met me. And I think there's a possibility she might be behind this; what if she stabbed Mal because he'd turned her down? She lost her temper and now—'

Ashok interjected. 'My client has, as you know, pleaded her innocence, from the moment she was arrested. As we mentioned earlier, Ms Kendrew has reason to believe Sally

Dowell may have cause to frame her, in an attempt to cover up her own reasons for wanting to harm Malcolm Russell.'

The door opened and an officer came back with a jug of water and plastic cups. McMenemy and Feddersen looked at each other as I filled the cup, gulped and refilled it. I guessed they had worked together for so long they were able to communicate telepathically. McMenemy looked down at her watch.

'I suggest, Mr Chowdhury, that you provide us, by nine tomorrow morning, concrete evidence that supports Mrs Kendrew's claim of her innocence and the possible implication in this crime of these other persons.'

'We will, thank you. There is also my client's ex-partner, Adrian Evans. Surely your colleagues at Kensington police station will be able to verify what Ms Kendrew has told you.'

'We are waiting to hear back from them.'

McMenemy leaned over to the black box on the desk and pressed the stop button on the camera.

The two detectives stood up to leave the room. I turned to ask them the question I had already asked several times. 'Can you please tell me how Mal is? Is there any...'

'We don't have any more news at present. If we do, as we told you, we'll update Mr Chowdhury,' McMenemy said as she stood up and followed Feddersen out of the room.

Chowdhury turned to me. 'Okay, we're going to have our work cut out to get anywhere in that time. Let's concentrate on Sally and your ex, Adrian Evans. What do you know about her?'

'Nothing really, other than she works at the same bank; Mal is often at the flat on his own because she spends at least half the week at their head office in Frankfurt. I've never met her, as I said. I've never been to her flat. I've dropped Mal outside a few times, and picked him up. He seemed quite reluctant for me to meet her. I didn't really question it.'

'But he talked to you about her?'

'Yes, a few times. Just in passing. I think they were quite good mates. I never got the impression anything had happened between them, after the night at the Christmas do. He said he thought she fancied him a bit, but they're colleagues so it wouldn't have been sensible to get involved. I'm sure if he'd been uncomfortable living there, he'd have moved out; it's not difficult to find spare rooms to rent in London.'

'Why do you think she might be responsible for this if, so far, she's had a very normal platonic friendship with Mr Russell?'

'Well, there was a bit of an odd situation about a month ago. Mal and I had used the 'L' word for the first time.' I felt myself reddening, telling this stranger about a middle-aged relationship; it must have seemed faintly ridiculous to him. 'The night before, when he'd taken me out for dinner. You know, it's one of those milestones in a relationship, the first time you say that you love someone.'

Chowdhury smiled and nodded, prompting me to continue.

'This one evening, we'd been talking on the phone. He often sat in his bedroom when he called me as he couldn't get much of a signal in the kitchen. And his bedroom was more private; it wasn't his flat after all. In the kitchen he'd opened a bottle of wine to let it breathe and when he'd been gone a while, Sally had poured a glass for him and brought it along to his room. The door was slightly ajar. We'd been talking a bit, you know...'. I paused as I felt myself blushing again.

'He said he knew she was outside the room because he'd

heard her footsteps in the hall. He went to the door and saw her there. He rang off to check she was okay. He was a bit pissed off she'd been listening, though he realised it wasn't intentional. If Sally's got a thing about him... I can totally understand where she's coming from. He's a great guy.

'I know they went out for a drink after work sometimes, and to the cinema, that kind of thing. I never felt threatened by that. The only thing that did occur to me was that she might be worried he'd move out to come and live with me. That wasn't going to happen but she wouldn't have known that.'

'Feddersen and McMenemy didn't interview her after the ID; she was visibly shaken and just wanted to leave. I'll put pressure on them to call her back in as soon as possible. I'm sure they'll have asked what her relationship with Mr Russell was like, but they may have only touched on it.'

'What if I'm wrong? If she's not involved, and she just made a mistake with the video ID? What about any other evidence? Were they pinning their hopes on a positive ID?'

'I don't know.' Chowdhury sat down and opened the clear blue plastic wallet containing his notes. He leafed through them until he came to a page covered in his florid hand. His choice of stationery – the Ryman wallet and his beautiful fountain pen – couldn't have been more incongruous. Perhaps the pen had been a gift. Or the wallet had been grabbed from his office, last-minute.

'This is what I imagine they're concentrating on. CCTV on your road. And Mal and Sally's. Scene of Crime officers will have been at their flat all day. House to house enquiries; again, in both locations. Your house will have been searched, top to bottom. There would have been a lot of blood at the crime scene. If you'd been there, it's almost certain a piece of your clothing would have traces of

Malcolm Russell's blood on it. You could have thrown every-thing away, of course, if there are large council bins on the street nearby, outside shops or restaurants, for instance. They will have searched those to see if they'd been dumped, near the crime scene and your house, though anybody would be pretty stupid to do that round the corner from their own home.

'Your phone will have been checked, it's extremely likely they'll still be working through that, as well as the cell site analysis for the night of the attack. Emails. All the corre-spondence with Malcolm Russell. Your social media. The files on your computers.'

'Will you be shown the findings?'

'Not in full, no. They will at some point disclose infor-mation, but only to back up their case against you.'

'What about character witnesses, friends, neighbours, that sort of thing? Anybody who knows me would back me up. They know, especially my best friends, that I adore Mal, that I'd throw myself in front of a bus to save him.'

He shook his head. 'Most of that won't happen unless you're charged. An attempted murder case won't go to court for at least four or five months, same if he dies and it becomes a murder charge. That will give them time to put together the best possible case against you. Let's not go there now.'

Chowdhury thought for a few seconds. 'Actually, while any memories are fresh in their minds, I'll knock on the doors of your neighbours, see if they remember seeing you last night. Are there any you know particularly well?'

'The ones directly opposite, number three. Robert and Sam. They've got boys a little younger than my son. We've been over to see them a few times. Playdates, that kind of thing. And they've been over to ours. I know most of the others, to say hello to, anyway.'

He made some more notes, turning over to start a new page.

'D'you think they'll charge me? Is Sally's positive ID enough? What if there's no evidence that I'm guilty; nothing at my house or in the car, or at Mal's flat?'

'It depends. The Crown Prosecutor will have the final say.'

'What if I'm charged, and they realise it wasn't me after all. Can I be uncharged?'

'The charge can be dropped, yes.'

'God, it's just such a foreign world. You know, I must have walked past this station dozens of times. I came in once because my car was broken into. They must have thought I was nuts to think they'd investigate it. Never in a million years could I have imagined I might one day end up here.'

Ashok tidied his papers back in the wallet and stood up.

'And Adrian; are you going to look into him at all? I haven't spoken to him for months.'

'I'll check they're following up with Kensington station. As far as we know it was the woman who Sally let into the flat that stabbed Mal. It's perfectly feasible for someone, out of jealousy or anger, to hire a contract killer. Adrian Evans has plenty of money?'

I nodded.

'So if he wanted to get rid of his partner's bit on the side without being implicated at all, he has the means. As with Sally Dowell, we have to put together any evidence that demonstrates the traits you say he has if we're to have any chance of Feddersen and McMenemy investigating him. Is there anything else you can tell me about him?'

'There's plenty. He got jealous for the most ridiculously

small reasons. He felt threatened by my relationship with Ned, my son. I've never met anyone as arrogant or pompous. He's a psychopath, I'm sure. Aren't one per cent of the population? He's not at the Charles Manson end of the scale, but still. He's entirely incapable of empathy.'

'And he knew about your affair with Mr Russell?'

'Well, it wasn't an affair because our relationship was well and truly over by the time Mal was back in touch with me.'

'But you said just now Adrian was prone to jealous rages?'

'Yes, he was, and a control freak. When I went to Kensington station they told me his ex-wife had reported him before they divorced – for coercive control.'

'Okay, that's really useful, I'll dig a bit further. Do you think she'd back you up?'

'I don't know, probably not; she withdrew the accusation, but I think that was because she realised if Adrian was in prison, he wouldn't be earning any money, and she'd got very used to spending it. She hated the fact he'd started seeing someone else. She stopped their daughters having anything to do with me when we first got together.'

'Okay, good to know. I might try her anyway... what's her name?'

'Antonella Evans. She's a fine art photographer, she has a website... I don't know for sure, but her contact details might be on it.'

I'd quite successfully managed to block Adrian from my mind. But now that door was open, I remembered something. 'I've just had a thought... the underage girls in the videos... their faces are very clear in them. A few years ago, before I saw the videos, I found some underwear, under the bed at Adrian's cottage in Wiltshire. I was horrified at the time... I didn't know whose they were or how long they'd been there. I took them, double-bagged them, and put them behind the wardrobe—'

'You think the underwear might belong to one of the underage girls?' Ashok looked sceptical.

'I'd totally forgotten about the knickers. At the time I felt compelled to take them... I don't know why. But because they're well wrapped up, do you think the police might still be able to take a DNA sample?'

'I don't know. They're at your house?'

'Yes, behind the wardrobe, in the bedroom on the top floor at the front of the house.'

Ashok added to his already copious notes. 'I'll tell McMenemy and Feddersen, see if they'd take a DNA sample. If anyone comes forward in Paris, they could try a match. It's a long shot.'

'Yeah, I know. Worth a try though.'

Ashok nodded. 'Okay, going back to Sally Dowell... we need to find a way of discrediting her if we can. As well as your neighbours, I'll go and talk to hers; see if anyone remembers hearing her arguing with Malcolm, or seeing them together. I'll check her out online too; see what her professional status is like, what kind of friends she has, see if it all adds up. I'll find out if there's any appetite for Feddersen and McMenemy to interview her as a suspect. At the moment, that's all we can hope for. But I'll talk to them about Adrian first – we need to concentrate our efforts on him with Sally as a back-up.'

I nodded. A wave of exhaustion hit me. My eyes hurt. I had a raging headache. I felt like shit.

Ashok started a new page. 'You said Sally is friends with Malcolm Russell on Facebook?'

'Yes. She comes up as someone I might know occasion-ally. She's a friend of another friend too. Greta Mayhew.'

'Can you give me your log-in details? If I can access your account, I might be able to get some information about her. Depends what privacy settings she has, obviously. Have you any idea what she does at the bank?'

'No. But my friend she knows is a lawyer – Greta – maybe Sally is in the legal department at the bank. I think Mal and Sally are connected on LinkedIn too.'

He made a few notes, and I wrote down my log-in details for Facebook and LinkedIn.

'Something else; I don't know if it'd be useful. Sally was on dating sites too, when I met Mal. That was four years ago, but as she's single there's a good chance she'll still be on one or more; these days most people who use dating sites are on a few at a time. I don't know if it might uncover something about her that might help.'

A thought rushed into my head. 'The paintings... oh my God, Ashok, I've been really dumb. Adrian painted young girls... he has some of them on the walls at home.' I remem-bered the lurch of envy I felt when I saw them, visiting Adrian for lunch the first time.

'What are you saying?' He looked confused.

'The girls in Paris... perhaps they came over so he could paint them. He has a larger studio at the cottage in Wilt-shire.' My mind was racing ahead. 'If he painted them, he'd have had to organise dates for them to sit for him. He'd have emails, photos. He keeps meticulous records of all his refer-ence material. That could be how the underwear ended up under the bed.'

Ashok added a few bullet points at the bottom of the page entitled 'Adrian'. 'Okay, I'll talk to McMenemy and Feddersen about that too. If they get a search warrant for him, they'll be able to see if there's any correspondence with the girls... the French police will be able to cross-reference names.'

Ashok put his notes away. 'I'll see you in the morning, Alex. Keep thinking, but get some sleep. And stay positive, okay?'

CHAPTER 38

B ack in the cell, I collapsed on the narrow mattress, bringing my knees up to my chest. The foetal position had always felt comforting for me. It must have been for Ned too. Ever since he was a few months old he'd fallen asleep like that.

I needed to focus. There must be some way I could prove my innocence. If only Mal would regain consciousness. But what if he had no recollection of that night? Wasn't it true that after a traumatic event, sometimes people lose their memory of it, as a coping mechanism? What if he couldn't remember anything about that night, but everybody told him it was me who had stabbed him, and he began to believe it, began to remember it that way?

Suddenly the lights went out. It had been dark when I'd been brought back to the cell, it must have been after midnight. Tomorrow I'd be interviewed again; I needed to be firing on all cylinders. And perhaps miraculously I'd be able to talk to Ned on the phone. I needed to sound upbeat for him, and not the emotional wreck I'd turned into.

At the other end of the corridor, the clanging of cell

doors and distant voices was strangely comforting. I fell into a deep, feverish sleep. I dreamt almost continuously, the classic, recurring dreams. The kind I always had when I was anxious. Variations on a theme; being on the outside of a tall building, often in a precarious position but without any sensible explanation why I was there.

That dream segued into another; realising suddenly I needed to catch a flight with almost no hope of getting to Heathrow in time, but doggedly trying to get there, regardless. It came to an abrupt halt when I fell on the concrete floor of the cell, covered in sweat. I landed on my right side, hitting my cheekbone, shoulder, hip. I ran my fingers over my cheek; my skin was grazed and no doubt I'd develop a spectacular bruise. I wanted to cry.

I hauled my body up to a sitting position and leant against the side of the bed. From the light, I guessed it must have been almost dawn. I spotted the paper and pen on the floor beside me. I closed my eyes, composing in my head what information would be most useful to give to Ashok.

I tried to summarise what I'd written about Sally, Adrian, and briefly, Louise. Jealousy; I'd written it down as a motive for all three. Is that what drove humans more than any other emotion? Or was there something stronger? There must be. But what? And who could be driven by it to the point of trying to kill Mal?

Fear, anger, guilt, shame, disgust; the words catapulted around in my head.

I went over to the hand basin in the corner of the cell and cupped my hands to drink some water. I ran it for a minute, waiting in vain for it to turn cold, gave up and splashed it over my face and neck. I bashed my bruised cheekbone against the tap as I straightened up.

I felt my cheek again, running my wet fingertips over it

as gently as I could, and comparing it to the left side. It was hot and swollen. There was a mirror, of sorts, above the basin; a thin sheet of metal, covered in scratches. I couldn't have used it to draw eyeliner flicks but the reflection was sufficient to see I looked like I'd just had a couple of wisdom teeth extracted.

I walked back to the bed, picking up my notes, willing them to be more comprehensive and coherent than I knew they were. I needed to lengthen the list of possible suspects, even if they were longshots.

I searched around in my head, going through all the people Mal knew. What about his wife? He wasn't divorced but he'd mentioned recently she wanted to start proceedings now Ewan was sixteen and old enough, she thought, to deal with any fallout. It must have been seven or eight years since she'd thrown Mal out, when she found out he was having an affair with Louise. Good on her, I'd have done the same. Perhaps she still felt aggrieved, or she'd found out that any potential divorce settlement wouldn't be as generous as she'd hoped and she was angry he wasn't giving her more. He hadn't talked about it, and I didn't want to know.

Could it be her? But why would she try and frame me? She probably didn't even know anything about me. If anyone, she'd want to get back at Louise.

I added her name. What was it? It took me a few seconds of churning through my mental contacts list before I could grasp it. I was sure it had been quite like his.

And what about Louise's husband, Mal's cousin; Stewart? Mal had only mentioned him once or twice. Every time Stewart and Louise had split up, she went back to Mal. Stewart and Mal must hate each other now, even though they had been very close. I knew absolutely nothing about

Stewart, but he had a motive to want Mal dead, perhaps more so than Louise or Mal's wife.

Mel, that was Mal's wife's name. Melanie Russell.

My list was getting longer. And still, there was something looming at the back of my head I couldn't quite put my finger on.

What about Mal's other friends? I'd only met a handful; a couple of his workmates, and one of them he'd been at university with, Phil. He was a nice guy, if a little dull, in comparison to Mal anyway. He'd come to the Agnes Obel gig at the Roundhouse.

A few hours later, Sergeant Gibson opened the small hatch in the door.

'I've got some breakfast for you, Alex'. She unlocked the door and placed the tray next to me on the bed. 'What have you done to your face, love? It's all swollen.'

'I fell off the bed in the middle of the night. I must have turned over in my sleep.'

She looked concerned. She'd probably dealt with many attempted suicides.

'It was an accident, don't worry, I wasn't trying to hurt myself.'

'We've got a first aid box upstairs, I'll get some Savlon for you.'

'Thank you.' I glanced at the tray; porridge, some fruit, tea. 'I just wondered... I asked one of your colleagues last night if I might be able to speak to my son on the phone. He wasn't really able to say yes or no.'

'He's still being looked after by your friend?'

'Yes, at home. I just need to know he's okay.'

'I'll see what I can do. Your solicitor's called to say he'll

be here around eight-thirty; DS Feddersen is going to interview you at nine.'

'And what time is it now, please?'

'Seven, give or take a few minutes.'

'Okay, thank you.' I sighed in resignation. 'Is there any
chance I could have a shower? It sounds dumb but it'd just
make me feel a bit more human.'

'Not at the moment, love, mornings are very busy.' She
walked over to the small basin and tested the liquid soap
dispenser to check it wasn't empty. 'I know it's not ideal but
I've known women – men don't usually bother – to have a
full body wash in the basin. You can block the plughole with
some loo paper, temporarily. I'll see what I can do about
getting you a shower later.'

'That's very kind, thank you.'

'Don't forget to eat,' she said, standing in the doorway.
'Keep your strength up, eh?'

'Can you please ask if there's been any news about Mal
Russell too? I'm so worried about him.'

She nodded and smiled before locking the door.

Sitting on the bed drinking the tepid, milky tea, I went
back over the notes I'd written. There was something I
hadn't allowed to rise to the surface, something about Mal.
What was he not being totally upfront about? I couldn't put
my finger on it. There was the whole situation with Louise,
but was there something else?

I worked backwards, through the months. July, June,
May. April – the heated conversation I saw him having on
the phone outside the pub at Nicole's party. And one
lunchtime when I'd taken a picnic and met Mal at Canary
Wharf. We'd bumped into Phil; the atmosphere between
them was palpable.

As I sat on the hard, concrete bench, the edge digging in

to the tendons at the back of my thighs, I tried to imagine what significance that might have, if any. The bank Mal worked for was German, though a lot of their business was based in the UK. They'd been hit badly by the economic crash of 2008, and in the intervening years had struggled to get back to a level comparable to before. Mal's department, ironically, had grown, becoming more prominent within the business, and he'd been promoted. It occurred to me that perhaps Phil's had seen the opposite. Just suppose he'd taken risks, got involved in some dodgy deals, and Mal was too, somehow. Or Mal had found out and was going to dob him in it, whistle-blow. Perhaps Phil was behind all of this. I knew Mal had told Phil about me very early on. He'd been one of the friends he'd shown my profile to.

Someone tried to kill Mal because of dodgy dealings at the bank? It seemed too far-fetched. But suppose Mal had found out Phil was doing something illegal. He threatened to expose him. Phil retaliated and refused to back down.

I began scribbling down a few notes about Phil on the low-level list. Was this low-level though? How did it compare to Adrian, or Sally? Or Louise? Would the police even entertain the idea of investigating anyone else? And what if Sally and Phil were working together?

CHAPTER 39

Ashok told me Feddersen and McMenemy had postponed my interview because they hadn't yet been able to talk to Sally Dowell.

'She's keeping a very low profile. She's not at home, or at her parents' in Kent. She's got her phone switched off too. Feddersen called her parents earlier; her mother asked that her daughter be given some time to recover from everything she's been through. After all, she did discover Malcolm Russell at her flat; that would be a huge shock for anyone.'

'Or given some time to concoct a story in case the police start to suspect her.'

'Well, I've just talked to McMenemy. She didn't say it outright, but I think they're pretty convinced she had nothing to do with it. They've seen dozens of these kinds of incidents; they get an inkling, a sixth sense almost, when someone is lying, or telling the truth for that matter. Her and Feddersen arrived at the scene less than half an hour after she called the police. They said she was in total shock. That's quite hard to emulate.'

'But she could have been in shock if she did it, too. So we

just wait until she resurfaces?'

'Unfortunately. I'll keep asking them if they've had news. Shortly, the Chief Superintendent will come and ask a few questions, mainly just verifying your identity. I'll argue that, with a lack of any concrete evidence, you should be released on bail but it's unlikely they'll allow it, even taking into consideration that you're the sole parent of a young child.' Ashok opened his briefcase and took out his notes.

'Were you able to find out anything about Sally?'

'There's nothing unusual on her social media. She's usually fairly active on Twitter, with personal and professional accounts. Facebook; the last time she posted anything was Monday morning. I searched for profiles of women called Sally on five or six dating sites. There were about two hundred in total. There weren't any photos I could match from her Facebook or Twitter and the dating sites, so it was nigh on impossible to work out if the dating profiles were hers. Then again, I can't imagine many people use the same photo on their LinkedIn and Tinder profiles.'

'I did. I hate photos of myself. Most photographers are the same. What about Adrian?'

'There's absolutely nothing online about his arrest for using underage prostitutes. I've looked on French news sites too. That suggests he's got a good lawyer on board who's managed to keep his name out of the press.'

'He's had to take a few clients to court over the years; his lawyers are in Holborn... three names, Napier, I think, is one of them. He uses a PR agency too, for his work.'

'And he has an agent, James Marlowe... do you know anything about him?'

'He was with Adrian at the hotel in Paris. They've always gone on business trips together. At first I took it at face value. For a while I even wondered if they were having an affair. But, no, it's simpler than that; they both have a thing about young girls.'

Ashok looked suitably disgusted. 'I also drove to Adrian Evans' house in west London last night, to see if there was any sign of life, but no-one was at home. Then I tried to call him. His mobile went to voicemail. The ringing tone sounded like he wasn't in the UK.'

'Wouldn't they have seized his passport when he was arrested?'

'Possibly. I could be wrong about the ringtone, but if I'm not, he could have breached his bail conditions. So you think he travelled to France specifically to have sex with young girls?'

'Yes, I didn't know that until late in our relationship. I was so naïve. At first I believed him when he said they were going to visit galleries, or spending a few days touring vineyards.'

'How did you find out?'

'To start with, I'd had a bad case of conjunctivitis that wouldn't clear up with the usual eye drops. My GP was concerned about it and took some swabs. It turned out I had gonorrhoea.'

'From him?'

I nodded. 'He accused me of getting it from someone else. I had a sexual health test when I started seeing him. He told me he hadn't slept with anyone other than his wife in fifteen years. I hadn't had any other partners, so I knew he was lying, I just couldn't prove it.'

'Did you accuse him?'

'Yes, but he just denied it. Then I went to James' home in Surrey and talked to his wife. I'm not proud of it but I taped the conversation on my phone. She's a total sap; she knew James started seeing younger women, around the time she was pregnant with their second child. He explained it was an addiction and that he was seeking help to deal with it... yada, yada, yada.

'By chance I found photos and videos on our family iCloud account; of Adrian and James in a hotel room. I Googled it; the legal age of consent in France is 15, but using a prostitute under the age of 18 is illegal. There were two girls in the film; they both looked like they could be fifteen but not eighteen. He'd used his phone to film it.'

Ashok summarised everything in bullet points in his notes. I waited for him to finish before I continued. 'I'd bought him an iPhone because he had this ridiculous, ten-year-old Nokia; I'd text him and he wouldn't be able to read the message if it was longer than twenty words because the technology was so out of date. It hadn't occurred to me that I'd be able to access his photos and texts. Actually it was my son who did, when he went onto my computer to see some pictures he'd taken on my phone, he came across the Paris videos.'

'And did you confront Adrian?'

'Yes. It all happened around the time he found out I was back in touch with Mal. I told him he was a hypocrite. That was the night he tried to rape me. He couldn't keep it up because he'd drunk too much but he blamed me for being frigid. It was the final straw.'

'Have you still got the tape you made when you talked to James Marlowe's wife?'

'Yes, it's still on my phone and I made copies.'

'I wonder if they've come across it.'

'It was over a year ago. I copied it onto my Mac so they could easily find it. It's in my Admin folder on my iMac, along with all of Adrian's videos.'

'Good, that's really going to help us.'

'Did you talk to any of my neighbours?' I asked.

'Yes, a few. Some weren't at home. The family directly opposite, Rob and...'

'Sam.'

'Yes. Sam had a vague recollection that she saw you come home with your son at around six but she said you often arrived home at the same time and she couldn't say with absolute certainty she saw you on Monday afternoon. Rob wasn't at home but I left my card and asked his wife if he could call me if he remembers anything. Nobody else could give me anything concrete, with times.'

The air felt heavy, the warmth of the day had built up and managed to seep all the way down to the basement of the station.

'And Sally's neighbours?'

'I only stopped for five minutes; that's all the time I had. I didn't get an answer on one side but on the other are a young family. If this afternoon was anything to go by, any noise from Sally and Mal would have been more than drowned out. I'll try again tomorrow though, or later this evening if I get a chance.'

'Do you think the police will treat Adrian as a suspect when they hear all this? If pursuing Sally is off the table for the time being?'

'From what you've told me, they have to pursue him. If he's broken bail conditions, that alone will be sufficient for him being arrested. I'm worried about his passport though; if his was retained, he must be travelling under a false name. That could mean it'll be difficult tracking him down.'

I nodded. 'There's also someone else you could look into. One of Mal's work colleagues, Phil. He's in a different part of the bank. The two departments' aims are diametrically opposed, from what Mal told me.' I remembered what

I'd written in my notes. 'Just suppose Sally is in on it too – her and Phil are working against Mal?'

'That's going to cause us quite a lot of trouble. A big, powerful organisation like a bank isn't going to offer up any information at all.'

'If there was some hush-hush deal going on, isn't there a chance nobody there would know anything about it anyway?'

'Maybe. Do you know Phil's full name? We can at least start some enquiries.'

'No, I don't. But I'm sure he'll be a friend of Mal's on LinkedIn or Facebook. If you log on as me, you could look at his friends or connections.'

Ashok nodded slowly. 'Okay. I'll see if I can catch Feddersen or McMenemy now, talk to them about Adrian, see whether they've heard back from Kensington.'

'Have you still got the notes I gave you?' I asked.

'About Adrian? Of course, they're just here.' He flicked back to the pages I'd scribbled on the day before.

'It's not Adrian… there was someone else. A guy I met briefly a few years ago, on a dating site. He was threatening in some text and voicemails – he called me a 'little bitch' for leading him on and then turning him down. And then a few months later the word 'bitch' was graffitied on the outside of the house. I don't know if it was definitely him—'

'Wait, have you mentioned him here?'

I tried to read my almost indecipherable writing upside down. 'Yes, just briefly. I still can't remember what he was called but his dating profile name was Zeiss.'

'You want me to look into him?'

'Maybe. I've just got a nagging feeling he might be involved. I've managed to forget all about him. Or at least I had.'

CHAPTER 40

Fatigue took hold, and it wasn't until Gibson was standing over me, shaking my shoulder and shouting at me that I finally woke. 'Alex, your son is here. Come on, I've got an interview room for you. He's waiting upstairs.'

I stumbled to my feet, my head heavy, my sight blurred from sleep. I hated the thought of him seeing me look dishevelled and dirty. 'Can I just splash some water on my face?'

'Of course, be quick though, we don't want to keep him waiting.'

Peering in the scratched metal, makeshift mirror above the basin, I smoothed my hair down in an attempt to look less scary and more normal.

As we climbed the last flight of stairs up to the ground floor, I could hear Ned and Denny talking and laughing further along the corridor. Gibson uncuffed me before she knocked on the door.

'Mum, you're here!' Ned got up and leapt into my arms.

'Oh sweetheart, it's so lovely to see you. How are you?

Let me look at you... I think you've grown in just the last few days.'

We hugged, his little arms wrapped around my neck, his legs around my waist, just as he'd done hundreds of times.

Denny's concerned expression quickly faded. I closed my eyes and breathed him in, burying my face in his hair, its familiar smell so comforting that tears pricked my eyes. I had to wipe them away so that he didn't notice me crying; I didn't want him to be upset that I was upset.

'How has school been? Have you been working hard?' I asked, as cheerily as I could manage. 'What lessons did you have today?'

'We had Literacy this morning. And PE. We were practicing for sports day tomorrow.'

God, I was going to miss it. I'd missed it last year too because I'd been on a shoot and couldn't get away.

'Mum, what have you done to your face? It looks sore.' He reached out a hand to touch it. Denny glanced at me, enquiringly. I smiled back to reassure her. She was mouthy; if anyone was going to make a complaint about police brutality, it was Denny.

'Oh sweetheart, nothing. I just fell off the bed and bashed my face. It doesn't hurt very much. Sports Day – that's exciting, you'll do so well, I'm sure. What was your favourite race when you practiced today?'

'The three-legged race was really fun. Johan was my partner. We came second in the first race but then we came last the second time because we were laughing so much we fell over.'

'I can picture you doing that. I'm hoping I can be there, but if not, you'll tell me all about it?'

'Yes, mum. What are you doing here?'

'Oh, I won't be here for very much longer, darling, don't

worry. Somebody said I did something bad, but I didn't do it. I've just got to find a way to show the police that I didn't. I'll be home before you know it. And you've got Auntie Caroline coming to stay with you tonight?'

I looked over at Denny. 'Is that still happening?'

'Yes, I talked to her earlier. She's in Cambridge, have I got that right? Or is it Oxford?'

'Yes, Cambridge.'

'She's leaving work at five, and hoping to get to yours by seven.'

'That's good news. Has everything been okay?'

'Yeah, fine, don't you worry. He's been good as gold. He's not worried, I don't think anyway. He's asked a few questions, but he seems to be doing fine.'

'Oh bless him. I've been so worried. Thank you so much for looking after him. I knew he'd be very happy with you. I'll pay you for your time though, when I get out.'

'Don't be silly, I won't hear of it. Anyway, hopefully it won't be too long until you're out. What's happening? Are they telling you much? When Dave was arrested – do you remember – that girl said he'd assaulted her boyfriend? It was all dropped in the end. They kept him in the dark while he was in here though.'

Denny was south-east London born and bred. She pronounced 'girl' like it had a 'w' in it. Ned, even with a spell in upmarket west London, did too. I felt mean picking faults – Denny had saved my bacon so many times. Never quite like this though.

We both looked over at Ned as he started chatting to the young officer guarding the door. His responses were monosyllabic. Ned asked him, amongst other things, if he was hot in his uniform, to which he replied, 'yes, a bit'.

'I've met Caroline a couple of times, haven't I?' Denny

screwed up her nose as she added, 'She's the slightly spinstery one of your friends, isn't she? A bit prim and proper.' Denny paused. 'Listen to me, that's so rude. But you know what I mean.'

'You're right, Den, I'd never thought of it, she's too young to be a spinster, really, but I think she's been single for so long...'

'Well, I'm sure she'll have a lovely time with Ned. I'll be around, I can pop in and check they're okay. I've got Martine coming with the baby, I know I'm going to have my hands full, but I'll be walking past your house a couple of times a day; I'll have to walk the dogs.'

'Thank you, Den, that's very kind.'

The door flew open. McMenemy. 'What on earth's going on?' She glared at me, Ned and Denny, and back to me.

Sergeant Gibson appeared at her shoulder. 'DC McMenemy, I'm sorry. I'm responsible for this. Miss Kendrew has been apart from her son for so long, I thought it was best for him if he was able to see his mum for a few minutes.'

'Well...' She didn't quite know what to say. 'We're going to the magistrates court now, to extend your custody period. I'm sorry to be breaking up this happy family reunion.'

What a cow.

I ran towards Ned and hugged him. 'Don't worry, darling, I'll be home soon. Be a good boy tonight for Auntie Denny, and then Auntie Caroline tomorrow. Promise?'

'Of course, mum. I love you.'

'I love you too, more than anything in the world.'

'More than anything in the world.' He kissed my cheek, so gently it made me cry.

Denny hugged me too, the smell of cigarette smoke so strong in her hair it made me gag. 'Look after yourself. It'll all be fine, okay?'

CHAPTER 41

The euphoria I felt at seeing Ned subsided faster than I could have imagined. Perhaps that few minutes with him, cut even shorter by McMenemy, brought my incarceration into even sharper focus, my desire to be back at home with him in inverse proportion to the likelihood of it happening.

The trip to the magistrates' court was surreal. Jason and another DDO, a woman, handcuffed me and led me through the station to the enclosed car park, and stayed with me in the van.

The court hearing lasted around half an hour. Ashok cross-examined McMenemy, arguing that the only piece of evidence was circumstantial.

'Sally Dowell has never met my client, Alex Kendrew, and the entire case against her is based on Ms Dowell's positive ID. In Ms Dowell's statement she clearly admits that the time the two women were talking was very brief and she did not get a very clear look at the woman. Indeed, the woman, according to Ms Dowell, was wearing sunglasses for almost the entire time. Miss Dowell has mistakenly identified my client; she has now disappeared and is not returning calls. I would say this is the behaviour of someone trying to implicate another person in a crime.'

The judge, a woman in her early sixties, looked like she was wavering, but McMenemy hit back, saying that there was plenty of evidence but they needed more time to examine it all, and that they were still waiting for DNA tests.

The judge granted the extra 36 hours, taking me up to Friday morning. It was already 36 hours since I'd been arrested and had felt like a lifetime. Could I stay sane, locked up for another day-and-a-half?

Back in the cell, I saw that someone had left a pencil drawing on the bed. Ned must have brought it with him; it was of him, me, the cats, Penny. Green grass below us, a strip of blue sky above, sun in the corner, yellow rays emanating from it.

I could still detect the faint aroma of Ned's hair and skin on my t-shirt, but I knew it was fading and would soon be gone altogether. I sat on the bed, holding the drawing against my chest and let my body fall backwards, barely registering the jolt of pain as my shoulder blades hit the brick wall.

Jason opened the hatch. 'Mrs Kendrew, please come with me to the interview suite.' He led me back to one of the interview rooms where Ashok was waiting with a stony expression.

He pulled out a chair for me. 'Alex, I'm sorry we didn't get the outcome we wanted at court.'

'Don't worry, you did all you could. I thought the judge was going to release me at one point.'

'Yeah, me too.' He smiled momentarily. 'I'm afraid Mr Russell's condition has deteriorated.'

My stomach lurched, my legs threatening to buckle under me. 'Are they going to let us know what's happening? How serious it is?'

'I'm sure they will. But for now we need to concentrate on your position. Feddersen and McMenemy are ready to interview you now. Have you had any more thoughts?'

'Not really. My son came to see me earlier, and with the court hearing I've been a bit preoccupied. But it was a weight off my mind, seeing that he's okay.'

He nodded. I guessed he was too young to have children yet; he might not understand fully why it would have been so important for me to see him.

McMenemy took the lead in the questioning, as always; I wondered why. She was the junior of the two, a Constable whereas Feddersen was a Sergeant. Younger, definitely, by ten years or so.

'Alexandra Kendrew, we are resuming our interview from this morning at 9.09 pm. You will know that Malcolm Russell's condition has deteriorated during the day.' She sat back, waiting for my response. I stared ahead, unable to focus, picturing Mal in an intensive care bed, surrounded by tubes and drips and computer screens.

Ashok cleared his throat to prompt me.

'I can't bear the thought of him being in hospital, unconscious, of course. But it doesn't matter how long you hold me here, I'm not going to admit to something I didn't do.'

The two detectives sat in their chairs, expressionless.

'I adore Mal, he's the best thing that's happened to me in a very long time.'

Ashok sat forward in his chair. 'Apart from Mr Russell's condition, are there any developments you're able to share with my client and I at the moment?'

The two detectives exchanged glances, before McMenemy continued. 'Our technical support have been investigating your desktop computer, Ms Kendrew. It appears there was a 45-minute gap between saving two Photoshop files. There isn't any other activity on the computer within that time; emails sent, for instance. That would give you sufficient time to drive to Malcolm Russell's flat, attack him, and drive home again.'

McMenemy broke off for a moment and looked down at the loose A4 printouts she had in front of her.

'According to Google Maps, the quickest route by car from your home to Marlowe Road is sixteen minutes. I think early evening, the roads would be pretty clear, and you could probably cover that distance in ten.'

I looked at Ashok.

'What time did it occur, the forty-five minute gap?' he asked.

'One file was saved at 7.52 pm and the next at 8.34 pm.'

'I would have been putting Ned to bed. His bedtime is 8 pm, a little later sometimes. And then filling the dishwasher, probably.'

'And your son doesn't emerge from his room after bedtime?'

'I read to him, or he reads to me, for about fifteen minutes, usually. It's normally lights off by 8.15 pm by the time we say good night. It's rare for him to get out of bed after that, unless there was something wrong; if he's poorly or something.'

'But you could have done his bedtime routine a little earlier. He wouldn't have necessarily known, would he?'

'He's got a clock by his bed. Most seven-year-olds can tell the time,' I said with a hint of sarcasm.

'But you could have changed it, so he thought it was later than it was.'

'For a start, I wouldn't leave my son at home in bed on his own at night. I always get a babysitter if I go out.'

'The owner of the corner shop, just on the main road, forty or fifty metres from your house, has seen you in his shop, several times, in the evening. Late evening, ten or ten thirty; your son must have been in bed then?'

'Yes, a handful of times at most, when I've realised we don't have any milk, just before bed. The shop doesn't open until nine in the morning, too late to get milk for my son's breakfast. I wouldn't have left the house for more than five minutes. The shop is less than a minute's walk, it's literally round the corner.'

'A lot can happen in five minutes though. The start of a house fire, say, or a burglary. Or your son could have got out of bed for some reason and found you weren't there.'

I felt my throat tighten, tears threatening. How dare she assume I was a bad mother.

'That's totally ridiculous. As a parent you have to weigh up situations, and the risks involved. I decided, on those occasions, that my son having porridge in the morning was better for his overall health and wellbeing than the possible risk to it of a mad axe-man murdering him in his bed in the intervening five minutes.'

McMenemy remained expressionless. 'But surely, if you're happy to risk leaving him for five minutes, what's to say you wouldn't also calculate the risk of leaving him for forty-five minutes to be sufficiently small?'

'Well, I didn't, and no, I wouldn't.'

'And your mobile phone...' McMenemy returned to her

notes. 'Similarly, no activity between around 7.30 pm and 8.30 pm. The cell site analysis shows the phone was turned on during that time, and didn't leave the triangulated area around your home. You could have left it there on purpose. You sent a text to Malcolm Russell at 8.47 pm. "You okay? You haven't returned my calls. You've decided to meet Louise?" That's what you said. There were several others earlier in the day, in a similar vein.'

Ashok interjected. 'Doesn't that prove my client wasn't responsible? Why would she send a text shortly after she'd visited him? She would have had the opportunity to ask him that question face to face.'

Feddersen shifted his gaze from Ashok to me. 'Or you could have sent it in an attempt to shift the blame away from you.' Feddersen spoke for the first time.

'I know my response to Mal being in touch with Louise again must make me look a bit jealous. He dumped me when she got back in touch with him, years ago. I just didn't want it to happen again.'

Ashok glanced over at me and rested a hand on my forearm. 'I take it you don't have any evidence showing my client was even in the vicinity of Malcolm Russell and Sally Dowell's flat the night in question, never mind actually inside it? No CCTV in Marlowe Road? Or on Dulwich Road at one end or Railton at the other? ANPR of her car in the area?

'No evidence that Ms Kendrew even left her home that night. What about public transport? Did Ms Kendrew use her Oyster card that evening? On a bus or train? It's nigh on impossible to travel in London using cash these days.'

McMenemy turned to Ashok. 'Let's take this outside. Interview suspended.' She reached over to stop the video recorder, gathered her papers and stormed out of the room.

Ashok and Feddersen exchanged a glance that I couldn't read.

'We'll just be a minute,' Feddersen said to me as he held the door open for Ashok.

I was left alone for what seemed like hours. Ashok came back on his own, looking mildly euphoric.

'What happened? I said, wondering how he could possibly seem so upbeat in the circumstances.

'I just drilled them to tell me what actual evidence they had. They're still studying CCTV from the area, and public transport but they haven't found anything significant yet.'

He sat down and got his notes out.

'Herne Hill station; Railton Road would be the obvious route between there and Malcolm's flat. The attacker must have arrived at some point. DNA – they're still waiting on the results but they should get them back tomorrow.'

I ran the top of my thumbnail across the fleshy part of my index finger. 'What about at mine? Is there any CCTV that would show I didn't leave the house?'

'There's a block of flats opposite. I talked to some of the residents when I was there yesterday; a few years back, there was a spate of vehicle thefts in the block's car park.

I changed hands; my right thumbnail was short and stubby. Manicures were never on my list of priorities; I felt across the deep ridges that had formed unnoticed. 'I remember. The council installed a few CCTV cameras as a result.'

Ashok nodded. 'Yeah, I saw them. It's highly likely one of them will cover your house. McMenemy and Fedderson didn't even know about them.'

'Anything else? What about Sally? I asked, hopefully. 'And Adrian?'

'They're still trying to locate Sally. I think they're regretting not putting any restrictions on her; as a result, she's not breaking any law. Her phone and online activity are now being monitored.' He flicked back a page.

'They're also trying to track down Adrian. Whatever happens, as it appears he's breached his bail conditions on two counts, he'll be arrested as soon as they do.'

As Ashok stood up, I had a thought. 'Can you call Greta Mayhew? She's my lawyer friend I called when I was first arrested. She's also a friend of Sally Dowell. If she knew how serious the situation was, she might be able to talk to Sally, make her see sense.'

Without warning, McMenemy and Feddersen walked back into the room, and resumed the interview. McMenemy looked angry, as though she'd had a bollocking. She was wearing a V-neck t-shirt and her decolletage looked flushed, the way mine did after a couple of glasses of red wine.

Ashok broke the silence. 'In the current position, with no actual evidence to show that my client was in the area of the attack on Monday night, none at all, I urge you to consider releasing my client on bail. Being away from her son has caused her a great deal of anxiety, and it would be in his best interests to have his mother back home with him.'

CHAPTER 42

Drunken shouting, swearing, banging on metal doors and the blood-curdling screeches of one man provided a strange lullaby.

'Alex, we've had a busy night, but things have calmed down a bit now. You can have a quick shower if you want.'

For a moment I couldn't tell if this was just the next episode in another bizarre dream. No, it was Sergeant Gibson, true to her word.

Gibson ushered me along the corridor. Singing belted out from another cell in the women's section.

'We're so lucky to have our very own Beyoncé with us tonight,' she joked, as several bars of the chorus of 'Girl On Fire' were repeated, as if the singer got half way through one line, forgot and started again. I thought better of telling Sergeant Gibson that it was Alicia Keys who sang it.

The shower cubicle was utilitarian and could have been cleaner, but the water was deliciously hot. I stayed under for as long as I thought I could without annoying Gibson. On the way back to the cell, my fellow inmate was still belting out 'This girl is on fiiiiiii-aaaaaare, this girl is...'

'Cut it out, Janie, will you?' Gibson shouted through the hatch. 'It's the middle of the night, love.'

'Is she a regular?' I asked.

'You could say that. She's harmless, as long as she's had her methadone. And she has, as far as we can tell.'

That wasn't as reassuring as Gibson must have thought it was.

'Her social worker will be here in the morning, and she'll be back out on the streets again. She's safer in here, away from her dealer and pimp. Same bloke, no doubt.'

Gibson watched me as I sat down on the bench. 'Try and get a bit more sleep if you can'. She locked the door, but then opened the little hatch. 'I nearly forgot, we have a limited supply of toothbrushes and toothpaste; most blokes can't be bothered to clean their teeth, but I figured you might.' She handed them to me. 'Might make you feel a bit more human.'

'Thank you, Sergeant Gibson, you're so kind. And for organising for Ned to visit earlier. I hope you didn't get into trouble for it.'

'Don't worry, it was all fine.' She smiled before closing the metal hatch.

I cleaned my teeth and lay down on the bed. Janie next door could still be heard through two closed metal doors; 'This girl is on fiiiiiii-aaaaaare, this girl is on fiiiiiii-aaaaaare.'

Rather than lying there, becoming irritated by the noise, I just let it wash over me, trying to imagine how out of it she must have been. From the other end of the corridor, a male voice bellowed, 'Shut the fuck up, or I'll break your fuckin' neck.'

'You shut the fuck up too, you cunt,' she replied.

After that, she returned to her singing, not quite as loud as before, and at one point she started slurring her words. A few minutes later she was silent. I must have fallen asleep; Gibson woke me with some breakfast and told me she was about to go off duty. I asked her if there had been any news from the hospital about Mal.

'Not as far as I know. I'll ask the other officers at the desk to let you know if they hear anything. DS Feddersen's been here for a couple of hours working on another case; once he's dealt with that he might want to see you again.'

I sat on the floor with my back against the wall, my legs bent, the sheets of paper resting on my thighs. I tried to write down my thoughts but couldn't focus. My eyes felt heavy and I imagined were red and puffy. The temptation was to close them and think of nothing, to try and wipe it all out, just for a few minutes. But I needed to stay positive. I got to my feet and started running round the cell, like I had the previous day. Was that yesterday or the day before? I couldn't remember; the days had begun to meld into one another. The day I was arrested was Tuesday, the day Ned came to see me was Wednesday. Was that only yesterday?

Thirty laps in, I heard voices in the corridor, and the squeak of the hatch being opened. 'Mrs. Kendrew, you've got visitors.'

The DDO took me along to the interview rooms. The air was filled with a familiar perfume; citrussy, light, modern. Sitting at the table was Greta and a man about my age; I recognised him, though it took a few seconds to remember where from.

Greta hugged me and the scent I'd detected in the corridor enveloped me. 'Alex, I'm so sorry it's taken this long to see you. Your lawyer messaged me again last night. I called Martin... Alex, this is Martin Hathaway; he's a defence lawyer. He's the husband of a very good friend of mine. We were all at university together twenty-odd years ago.'

He was one of the men I'd slept with after Mal had dumped me. The one I'd met for a drink, and, after a lot of sexting, at a hotel on the south bank for sex. Great sex. He obviously didn't recognise me, or if he did, he kept quiet.

I wanted to reply to Greta, and say, *yes, I know all that, except he's called Neil, not Martin*. Instead, I shook him by the hand. 'Pleased to meet you.'

'I was going to be here this morning anyway; I've got a client who's about to be charged. When Greta called me, I said I'd meet her and come and see if there was anything I could do to help. You've got a brief? How's he doing?'

'I think he's doing alright. It's difficult to tell, I don't have anything to compare him to.'

'What's happened so far?' Greta asked.

I told her everything I knew about Monday night, and Sally positively identifying me in the video parade. 'But she's mistaken. And now she's gone to ground. The police are convinced she wasn't involved but I think there's a possibility she's trying to frame me, or at least blame me because I'm an easy target.'

'And how is your boyfriend?'

'Still in an induced coma. He needed emergency surgery. He hasn't regained consciousness yet, and they told me last night his condition had deteriorated.'

Martin, aka Neil, got out his phone and made a few notes on it. 'How long have you known Mal? Do you know him well?' he asked me.

'Yes, I've known him for four or five years.'

'How do you know him?'

I exchanged glances with Martin; perhaps he had begun to remember. He might not have recognised me, visually. I must have looked a million times more attractive, the night we met at the hotel. But my voice was quite distinctive. Suddenly I had an idea.

'I met him online. We chatted for a while. He told me he was in an open relationship. Actually, so open that he no longer slept with his wife. He was experimenting with... what's the modern word for swinging... polyamory, that's it. He said his wife wasn't interested in him sexually any longer, that she was perfectly happy for him to meet other women. Anyway, we met for a drink one night at a pub, and then we...'

I stopped myself; not to save Martin's blushes, or mine, but Greta's.

'Then we started dating.'

By the look in his eyes, he'd got it, I could tell. He knew I was sparing him... did it occur to him he might have to give something in return?

I remembered Martin had told me he mainly represented 'real' criminals; murderers, terrorists. I imagined he spent a lot of time in places like Brixton police station. Would he have some sway here?

'So, can you tell me where the police are so far? And what has your brief been doing?' Martin asked, his voice wavering slightly. He was obviously used to holding court, but this situation had thrown him.

I sat, resting my head on my hand for a moment, trying to summarise it all in my mind.

'There's been no evidence, CCTV or anything, that shows I was there. I was at home with my son Ned who's only seven, so too young to give me an alibi. I'd been doing some work that evening, while making supper and getting Ned ready for bed. There was a gap of about forty-five minutes between files being saved on my computer, and the police are accusing me of leaving Ned at home on his own, driving to Mal's and stabbing him, and then driving home again, all in the space of three-quarters of an hour.'

'It sounds quite thin, the evidence against you, apart from the ID. Are there any other suspects?' Martin asked.

'A few. My ex-partner, who knew I'd started seeing Mal again. Mal's ex-girlfriend. A work colleague of his. Even Sally. I'm sorry, Greta, I know she's your friend, but the fact that she's done a runner makes me think she might have set me up because she's jealous or something.'

Greta's expression sat somewhere between concern and incredulity. 'I've tried calling but her phone's been switched off. I've left a couple of messages. I really can't imagine she's involved.'

'But neither am I.'

'I know, Alex, I didn't mean you were, I'm sorry. Martin, what can we do?'

'What has your brief been concentrating on so far?' he asked me. 'What's his name?'

'Ashok Chowdhury. He works for one of the 24-hour law firms, in Camberwell, I think. He's been trying to find witnesses, my neighbours for instance, who might be able to say I was at home all evening. It's a long shot. It's the positive ID that's stuffed me. Ashok was banking on me not being picked out. Sally did though, very quickly, without any hesitation. He said it was quite unusual; in most cases, people take a while poring over the videos, watching them again and again.'

'Yeah, that sounds quite strange. How many times have you met Sally?'

'Never, that's the weird thing. The ID was the day after the attack. The police wanted it to take place as soon as possible so her memory didn't fade.'

A cheery burst of The Liquidator filled the room.

'Sorry, that's my phone,' Greta said. 'Will you excuse me for a moment?'

I wouldn't have had her down as a Chelsea fan but her son had recently started playing football with a local team in the park on Sunday mornings.

Greta left the room. Martin leaned over the table towards me. 'Thank you,' he said, finally.

'What, for not dobbing you in it? I didn't particularly want Greta to know I was the kind of woman who meets strangers in hotel rooms for sex either.'

He half smiled. 'I'll help in whatever way I can. I'll talk to the detectives in charge, see how closely they're tracking Sally. Even if she's not involved, she may have implicated you for her own reasons. Alternatively, she may have just panicked in the video ID; shock can affect people in strange ways. She could be charged with perverting the course of justice if she doesn't get in contact with them.'

I shook my head. 'The trouble is, they think it's me, so it seems they're not really putting in much effort finding anyone else.'

'Who's in charge?' he asked.

'McMenemy and Feddersen. McMenemy seems to be leading, though she's quite a bit younger than him.'

'Yeah, I know them. There's been a push to use more junior detectives in serious investigations. McMenemy's worked her way quite quickly up the ranks; she seems to get results and that's good for Lambeth's performance stats.'

Greta came back into the room after finishing her call at the same time as Ashok arrived with coffee.

'Ashok, this is my friend Greta who you messaged last night, and her friend Martin Hathaway who's also a defence lawyer.'

The two men squared up to each other for a moment before shaking hands. I hoped Ashok wouldn't feel like his nose had been put out of joint.

'Alex was just putting us in the picture. I'd like to help in any way I can.'

Ashok put the coffee down in front of me. 'I've just seen Feddersen in the corridor. Malcolm Russell had a good night; his condition has stabilised. They're going to start reducing his sedation.'

'God, that's such a relief,' I said. Tears pricked the back of my eyes. 'What happens now?'

'We just have to wait and see. It might take a couple of days for him to regain consciousness. We need to hope there aren't any other setbacks. And there's no guarantee he'll remember anything; we have to accept that's a possibility.'

'Is there any news about Sally Dowell?'

'Not that they've told me. They're going to keep quiet about Mr Russell's condition improving. They wouldn't tell Sally about it yet, even if they could contact her.'

While the two men were talking, my mind drifted back to Sally. What was she up to? Surely she must know that she'd be found out if Mal regained consciousness. I remembered something.

'Her dating profile username – I think it had her actual name in it. I know, in the circumstances, she's unlikely to be checking her messages. But her profile might... I don't know, give away some information. Is it worth checking? It was 'Sally can wait,' from 'Don't Look Back in Anger,' something like that.'

'Gosh, I had no idea she was dating.' Greta looked shocked.

Martin got his phone out. 'Okay, I'm Googling "Sally in song lyrics". "Don't Look Back in Anger", number one, then

"Lay Down Sally" – Eric Clapton, "Mustang Sally", "Ride Sally Ride", "Long Tall Sally", "Sally Cinnamon" – The Stone Roses.'

'That's it, I'm sure; Sally Cinnamon. Though it was a long time ago, when Mal told me about her dating. She might have changed it by now.'

I gave Martin the name of the dating site; the same one we'd met on when he was pretending to be Neil. I was impressed we both managed not to blush.

'Got it. Sally Cinnamon, forty-three years old. Lives in Brixton. Single. Doesn't want children. Looking for a man between forty and fifty. *Up for all sorts of adventures*, she says. Logged in yesterday.' Martin showed me the profile picture.

'I don't really know what she looks like. Is that her, Greta?'

'Yes, that's Sally. It's a bit strange that she logged in yesterday.'

'But if she was in the middle of conversations, or had arranged to meet someone, she might just have logged on to say she couldn't make it. Will the police be able to log in and read her messages? Or any other sites... Facebook perhaps?'

'I don't think they have so far; they'd need a warrant to access anything other than public information. There's been no need so far as she's still not a suspect. I'll go and talk to them now,' Ashok said, standing up.

Martin looked up from his phone. 'What about her home? That's been searched, it was the scene of the crime, right? What about her computers?'

Ashok answered. 'They haven't mentioned to me anything about Sally's devices. They've examined Malcolm Russell's phone so I suspect they have his computer too.' He made a note. 'I'll check.'

Before Greta and Martin left, I asked her if she could call

home and talk to Caroline, and pass on a message to Ned that I loved him. She agreed. 'Don't worry, we're going to get to the bottom of this, and get you out of here. Okay?'

The same DDO led me back to my cell. The gate between the male and female sections was open; the first time I'd seen it like that. I realised why when we passed through it; I could see there were two paramedics in a cell just along from mine. I caught a glimpse of a woman's body, unresponsive, her eyes gazing into the distance, foamy blood trickling from her lips. I couldn't tear my gaze away from her. The officer put himself between me and the scene.

'Into your cell please, Mrs Kendrew.'

'Is she going to be okay?' It must have been Janie from the night before.

I was left alone in the cell, listening to the sounds of the paramedics trying to revive her. 'Stay with us, Janie, can you hear me?'

I sat down on the narrow bed, eyes closed, head in my hands, but still I had the image firmly printed in my memory; her body supine, the foamy blood coating her lips.

My stomach lurched. Mal; the detectives told me, had lost a lot of blood. He must have looked the same; grey, life-less. I felt a numb heat travel up my spine and through my skull, blood rushing in my ears. My vision wavered. I closed my eyes for a second to concentrate; I knew I was moments from fainting.

CHAPTER 43

M cMenemy looked impatient. We'd hardly sat down when she pressed the buttons on the video camera control panel on the table.

'When I was at your home earlier, I had the distinct feeling I'd been there before, Mrs Kendrew. Have you had any dealings with the police in the last five years or so?'

I'd given up correcting 'Mrs'.

'Yes, only once, about four or five years ago. My ex-partner, Sean Moran, my son's father, is seriously depressed. He tried to hang himself at home. He'd taken a handful of paracetamol tablets, then tied the rope to the stair banister, before kicking away the chair he'd been standing on.'

That's where I recognized her from. Two police officers had come to the house, a man and a woman. I paused, assessing how much detail I should give them. 'The banister couldn't take his weight; it broke, sending him crashing to the floor. It was about two in the morning; the noise woke me up. He'd left a note at the top of the stairs. I ran downstairs and found him, and called an ambulance. The paramedics rushed him to hospital, and afterwards he was assessed by a psychiatrist. The police arrived shortly after they'd left for the hospital. They questioned me.'

McMenemy looked intently at me. 'I think I was one of the officers.' Leaning in to whisper to Feddersen first, she left the room.

DS Feddersen continued the questioning. 'Mrs Kendrew, we've been looking further into your phone history; with Malcolm Russell, but also with Adrian Evans.'

'Have you been able to locate Mr Evans?' Ashok asked. 'Or Sally Dowell?'

'I'll come to that. About a year ago it appears you broke off contact with Mr Russell, or he did with you. Do you remember?'

'Yes.'

'Would you like to expand on that?'

'It was around the same time that I found the videos of Adrian with the young girls in Paris. I went to stay with Mal in Brighton, just for one night. I had a friend come to look after Ned.'

I took a sip of water. 'It was the first time in months Mal and I had been able to spend the night together. Mal was very reluctant, understandably, to stay at Adrian's. On the journey down to Brighton I realised I'd left my phone at home, so I couldn't contact Mal during the journey.'

I cleared my throat and had another sip of water. 'I texted Mal to let him know I got back safely the next morning but I didn't hear back from him for the rest of the day. I just thought he was in a bit of a strop and it would pass. Mal left his flat in the morning and everything was fine, great in fact. He'd never been sulky, or stroppy but I'd arrived nearly an hour late and I thought that might be the reason. I called him that evening; it just went to voicemail.'

'Did he reply the next day?' Feddersen asked, sitting back in his chair.

'No, I didn't understand why. Still nothing the day after that. I couldn't sleep, worrying about it all. I texted again, called again. Then I just got this weird inkling that he was cutting off all ties. Sure enough, I went onto Facebook and saw that he'd unfriended me, same on LinkedIn.'

I paused, trying to make sure I was including all the important points. 'And then about six months later Mal called me. He said he got a text the morning I'd left him in Brighton, from Adrian, saying I'd been killed in a road accident driving back on the M23. On no account was he to get in contact again. He wasn't welcome at the funeral.

'Mal said he was devastated. Eventually he went to Confession, hoping that would help him, but it only made him realise he needed to find out what happened. He got in touch with Sussex and Surrey police... there was no accident.'

'Did you confront Adrian Evans?' Feddersen asked.

'No. It felt much sweeter revenge for us to just be together, and to not have allowed Adrian to mess it up between us for good.'

'So, you didn't go to the police about it?' McMenemy asked.

'Not at first. But then I bumped into Adrian; I was in Westbourne Grove to water my friend's plants while she was away. He completely denied it. He was so smug and arrogant that, on the spot, I decided to report him for the attempted rape and the underage girls.'

Ashok looked bemused. 'This puts Adrian Evans much more firmly in the picture for Malcolm Russell's attempted murder, surely?' He went back over the notes he'd been writing. 'Have you located him?'

'Not yet. We now know his passport was seized so he hasn't been able to leave the country. We've been trying to find him, and all the necessary measures to do that have now been put in place, across the UK.'

I remembered something. 'I think he mentioned once he had another passport. Ireland were playing one afternoon in the Six Nations; his mother's Irish by birth.'

'We'll get in touch with the Irish embassy,' Feddersen said.

'So where does this leave Ms Kendrew? Surely this throws a different light on everything. Adrian Evans' behaviour must strike you as very extreme, and specifically designed to finish my client's relationship with Malcolm Russell.'

'I agree, but until he's in custody, I can't allow Mrs Kendrew to be released. Or alternatively, if Malcolm Russell regains consciousness and confirms your client's innocence...'

McMenemy came back into the room, clutching six or seven sheets of A4 paper that looked like they were fresh out of the printer. Everyone looked at her expecting her to speak but she sat down and remained tight-lipped.

Ashok tried another tack, directing his question at McMenemy. 'Have you viewed the CCTV footage from the camera in the car park opposite my client's house?'

'Yes. Mrs Kendrew's house is covered by one of the cameras but it's very small in the frame.' After a few seconds she added 'we're having the images enhanced.'

'Can you see my client leaving the house at any point?'

'I can't say with absolute certainty. Shortly after 10 pm she put out a bag of recycling, as she stated. I visited the house earlier. Ms Kendrew, you could have climbed over the fence, and through neighbour's gardens, into the grounds of the sheltered housing centre that back onto your garden.'

'To avoid being picked up on a camera that I didn't know existed?'

She retorted, 'The fence was broken, as though someone had recently climbed over it.'

'There was a man trying to escape a gang and the police, a few months ago. He climbed over neighbours' gardens and then tried to get in through our kitchen door. I called the police but you never came to investigate. I can't have been high priority enough; you know, a woman on her own with a young child, and a potential madman in the back garden. He probably broke the fence.'

Was McMenemy's expression one of slight embarrassment? Momentarily, perhaps. She leafed through the A4 sheets.

'As I thought, I was one of the officers who attended after your ex-partner's suicide attempt. Looking at my notes from the time, I'd written that you appeared to be very angry.'

She paused. 'Anger – that's not an emotion most people would display after their partner had attempted to kill themselves. Sadness, guilt, grief; having witnessed many people in that situation, those emotions are a more natural, more likely, reaction. Though you displayed none of them. I thought at the time, and think now, that you displayed your true character that night; heartless, cold, and selfish.'

I put my head in my hands; she had no idea. Ashok interjected. 'DC McMenemy, unless you were in her position, you have no right to assume how she would feel, or how she would react in the circumstances.'

'I'm going on the reaction of your client that night, as I witnessed it. And I can only surmise that exactly the same set of traits came into play on Monday night. You were furious, finding out, as you did, that Malcolm Russell had agreed to meet his former girlfriend, his cousin's wife. You allowed that anger to take over and you planned to kill Mr Russell in cold blood, with an equally cold heart.'

'That's not true. But on the night Sean tried to kill himself, I was angry, very angry. By that stage in our relationship I'd tried everything, every approach to try and get him to go and get help. I was sick of him being depressed all the time, never doing anything, the inertia. In a way it would have been a relief if he'd succeeded, but not for a second did I want him to die. I didn't want my son to be fatherless. I was angry because he'd decided it was acceptable to try to commit suicide in the family home, where we would have found—'

McMenemy raised her hand to stop me. 'There was a large amount of zopiclone, a common medication for insomnia, in your blood on Tuesday morning.' She held my gaze. 'I put it to you that you were attempting to overdose, having begun to feel remorse for attempting to kill Mr Russell. That doesn't quite sit with your claim to be protecting your son. If you'd succeeded, he would have found you the following morning, surely.'

'That's just... I'd taken two tablets, at two in the morning... less than four hours before you arrested me. I hadn't heard back from Mal. I couldn't sleep because I thought he was breaking up with me again. I couldn't take it.'

My chest tightened. Tears pricked my eyelashes, and spilled out, down my cheeks, falling onto the table. I wiped them away.

McMenemy sat back, folding her arms; she was almost enjoying herself.

CHAPTER 44

I couldn't get out of my head how vitriolic McMenemy had been. How she'd assessed me on the night Sean tried to kill himself. Is that why she'd had it in for me all along; subconsciously she remembered me? In all the interviews, she seemed as though she'd already made up her mind that I was guilty; she was like a dog with a bone.

Feddersen had wrapped up the interview, after McMenemy's onslaught. Walking back to the cell with me, Ashok said he got the impression Feddersen thought she'd overstepped the mark, but couldn't admonish her in front of us.

I knew I should feel more positive with the imminent questioning of Adrian and Sally, but being closer to a resolution was even more frustrating. I couldn't sit still. My train of thought veered off in a different direction every three seconds. Adrian – it must be him. Why though? Was jealousy enough? A moment later, I turned my attention to Sally. Same question. Or what if it was Mal's work colleague, Phil, possibly with Sally's help, who'd stabbed him, when some multi-million, dodgy deal at the bank had gone badly wrong?

I lacked the energy to run round the room; two nights with hardly any sleep, I felt broken, physically and mentally. I rested heavily for a minute against the brickwork until the rough edges dug into the flesh on my upper arm and I had to shift my weight.

Being completely helpless; that's what I found so hard. That, and being apart from Ned. It was Thursday afternoon, wasn't it?

I wondered what Ned would be doing. I tried to picture him at after-school club. The little kids had the end playground all to themselves, so the bigger ones didn't knock them over; their games were all a bit too rough. Not that Ned minded. He was fearless, always had been. Next year, after the summer holidays, he'd be moving up to the next group, playing with the big kids. Would I ever see him at school again? I didn't dare think about it.

I lay down on the bed and, as I moved my hand under the pillow, I came across Ned's drawing. I looked at the figures, the individual marks, wondered what he'd drawn first, pictured him sitting at the kitchen table with his pots of assorted pens and pencils we'd accumulated over the years.

The cells were deathly quiet. Surely I wasn't the only person there. People had come and gone, this was my third day, after all. I guess most people are usually only under arrest for a matter of hours before being released or charged. I was in limbo, suspended in time. I hated it.

Eventually I ran out of energy to stay awake. I was woken by the metallic screech of the hatch opening.

I sprang upright, head heavy and mouth dry. 'What's happened?' I asked the DDO through the small window in the door. He took me through to the interview rooms where Ashok was waiting.

'Okay Alex, a couple of things. The police were granted

permission to track Sally Dowell's phone. They've seen some activity today; she used it for a short time, before she turned it off. They weren't able to locate it exactly because the coverage is pretty sparse. It was down on the Kent coast; Rye, Hastings, somewhere around there.

'Greta left several messages, like she said she would, so let's hope Sally has heard or read them. Greta and Martin are driving down to Kent to see if they can talk to her, make her see sense.'

Ashok paused for a moment. 'There was also news from the Irish embassy; Adrian Evans' Irish passport is under his mother's maiden name – Hegarty. He used it to travel to Paris over a week ago. Lambeth CID are really over-stretched at the moment so they can't send anyone to Paris, but they've been in contact with French police.'

He flicked through his notes. 'There's a strike amongst public sector workers in France. Police aren't striking but they're also at full stretch with rallies all over the place; Paris, Lyon, Marseille, Nantes... and on top of that, alleged terror alerts that have proved to be false, but that they've had to investigate.'

'Shit, why hadn't I remembered about the other passport sooner?'

Ashok looked up and smiled. 'Don't beat yourself up about it, Alex. It might not have made any difference. And now you've remembered, it's given us our first definite lead.'

My mind felt fuzzy and disorganised as I processed the new information. 'Okay, so if he left London a week ago, he could have organised a hitwoman before he went, and left before so that he wouldn't be implicated?'

'Whatever happens, he's broken his bail conditions, so the Met are putting a lot of pressure on the French to find him. There's been a search of guests' names, staying at hotels within Paris. There aren't any matching either surname.'

'He always stays at Le Monet, near the Louvre,' I said. 'I don't know for sure, but it looked like their rooms in the videos he filmed with the young girls.'

'He wouldn't go back there though, the hotel wouldn't allow him to, surely.'

'He spends a lot of money there. And he's arrogant enough to think he can do what he likes.' I rested my head on my hand, digesting everything. 'Any news on Mal?'

'He's remained stable and they're reducing the sedation, though there seems to be no definite timeline for him coming out of the coma. McMenemy is itching to interview him though, she'll be keeping in close contact with the hospital.'

Ashok placed a hand on my shoulder. 'We're going to get you out, Alex, don't worry.' He smiled. 'Listen, I've got to take my girlfriend out tonight or I'm going to find myself suddenly single. Let's hope we have some good news in the morning.'

'Thank you, have a nice time this evening.' I was growing to really like him. 'If you get a chance, would you mind just calling home and having a quick chat to Caroline, my friend? Just to check everything is okay? And to thank her, and to tell her to say to Ned that I love him.'

'Sure, see you in the morning.'

It was completely dark when the hatch was lowered again and I was taken back to the interview room by a DDO. Martin Hathaway was there.

'Alex, I'm just back from Kent. Greta and I were trying to track down Sally Dowell; we went to visit her parents to see if they could talk some sense into her. I've tried to call your brief but his phone just goes to voicemail.'

I nodded. 'He was taking his girlfriend out this evening. He said he didn't think anything would happen tonight anyway. Have you got any news?'

'There was an ANPR call out for Sally Dowell's car. She was picked up on the M25 by a routine patrol car, not far from her parents' in Sevenoaks. She must have decided to go back to see them. She's being brought in for questioning.'

'What, here?'

He nodded.

'Is she under arrest?'

'Not at the moment. That might change, depending on how the interview goes.'

'Does she know Mal might regain consciousness at any time?'

'I don't think they'll make her aware of that, if they can help it. Greta has asked me to represent her.'

'But wait, if she finds out he might regain consciousness, would that make her more or less likely to come clean?'

'I don't know. Greta's gone home. I'm going to be in a difficult situation, one I know is all my own doing.'

'We had an agreement. If she tells you something that implicates her and at the same time exonerates me...'

He nodded and sat down next to me. 'Yeah, I know.' He turned to look at me and I resisted looking back at him for a few seconds; I knew what he was about to say. 'So what happened with us?'

'You don't remember?'

He shook his head.

'We met at a hotel and had sex. Really great sex, actually. I was on a bit of a bender, to be honest. I'd been dumped by

Mal and was desperate to meet someone else. Classic on-the-rebound stuff.'

'And then what?'

'Nothing. I didn't hear from you the next day, I didn't expect to. It was all pretty self-contained.'

'Jesus, what a dick.' He looked down at the floor, his cheeks reddening, before looking up at me. 'No hard feelings?'

'I had fun that night. I think there's always been, and still is, maybe... some unwritten rule that women shouldn't really enjoy sex. That it's something done by men to women, that we're not an eager participant but a vessel to be used. I think some women propagate that idea. Maybe not the younger generation, those in their twenties now, I think they have a better balance.

'But women my age; they use sex as a weapon. They don't seem to enjoy it, just tolerate it. I'm not like that. That night at the hotel, I was in control as much as you. I used you as much as you used me.'

'Yeah, but still, I owe you.' He stood up to go.

'I know.'

I t was a busy night in the cells; lots of coming and going. Banging on doors. Shouting. A constant stream of noise. Instead of being irritated by it, or frightened by my close proximity to violent drunks, it was strangely comforting. It allowed me to shut off and not think about everything else. I just needed a break; from myself and my thoughts.

The lights dimmed at some point. Listening to the commotion outside the cell had lulled me into a kind of meditative state, not asleep, but not fully awake either. It was like my brain had gone into energy-saving mode.

I don't know whether it was the grey light of dawn that woke me, or the dull ache coming from low in my stomach. As I turned to lie on my side, I felt a tell-tale trickle run down my inner thigh, only stopping when it reached the plastic mattress. Would Sergeant Gibson's emergency supply of toiletries extend to tampons? It seemed ridiculous to buzz the desk to ask for some. I'd just have to wait and hope it was Gibson or another woman doing the breakfast rounds.

I curled up in a ball, holding my lower stomach. The period pain, for a while, trumped everything else.

It must have been a few hours later that Sergeant Gibson gently roused me from my semi-sleep. She told me Ashok had just arrived as the detectives needed to interview me again. I asked Gibson if she had any tampons and clean clothes. She said she'd see what she could do.

Ashok looked tired. He had a cardboard tray from Caffè Nero in his hands.

'Thanks for the coffee... how was your evening?' I asked, after taking a gulp of espresso.

'Alex, Malcolm Russell died in the early hours of this morning, without regaining consciousness.'

I sat, staring at him; I had no idea how long for. Eventually I let out a huge sob, tiny spots of coffee flying across the table. All the strength in my muscles seemed to dissipate at once and I sank to the floor.

Ashok knelt on the floor next to me, gently shaking my shoulder. 'Alex, are you okay? Can you hear me? Do you need a doctor?'

'I'm okay,' I replied. I couldn't summon the energy to move. Tears rolled over the bridge of my nose and over my cheek. I'd been so convinced Mal would pull through, especially after the improvement in his condition yesterday. I felt anger; at him for not pulling through. Anger towards the medics for not keeping him alive. But mainly I directed it at myself. If Sally hadn't let the woman claiming to be me into her flat, he would still be alive.

Ashok's phone rang; he looked down at me and when I nodded to let him know I was okay, left me to continue his conversation in the corridor. I could hear him talking about Belmarsh and whether his client was too young to be prosecuted in the criminal courts.

When he came back he helped me off the floor and into a chair. I didn't seem to have any control over my limbs and, sensing I might fall again, he stood behind me, holding my shoulders. He slowly let go of his grip and sat on the chair next to me.

'I'm really sorry Alex, but they're going to rearrest you, for murder.'

I stared at him, heat rushing up through my body. I opened my mouth to respond but nothing came. He held my hand.

'There are a few other developments I need to tell you about. Sally Dowell's been questioned too, but only briefly. She arrived at the station last night, and five minutes in, she had a panic attack. She was taken to King's College Hospital just before midnight, and has been there ever since. Doctors seemed to think she was suffering from some sort of post-traumatic trauma, a reaction to witnessing the attack.'

The news allowed me to deflect my inner rage towards Sally instead. 'I don't buy that for a second. She's not going to be released from hospital and then walk free, is she?'

'No, she's wanted for questioning... she'd be arrested if she failed to attend.'

'Does she know Mal is dead?'

'I don't think so, not yet. And Adrian Evans; his where-abouts are still unclear. I gave McMenemy the details of the hotel, but I don't think she's had any luck tracking him down. According to Eurostar his return ticket is for this evening. If he hasn't been in contact with the UK police before then, they'll have a team at St Pancras to meet him off the train. From what McMenemy said, it's likely he'll become their main suspect.'

'So, if Adrian used a contract killer...' I paused. 'Do the police have much information about them?' I was thinking out loud. 'Do they know how normal people go about finding one?'

'My firm's been involved in a few cases where contract killers have been used; usually it's drugs-related. It's well known that hired killers advertise on the dark web. If the police have information about that, they're going to protect their sources and keep it very close to their chests.'

Feddersen opened the door, looking a little flustered and out of breath. Since McMenemy had taken the lead, I hadn't really got a handle on him as a person or a detective.

'Alexandra Kendrew, I'm arresting you on suspicion of the murder of Malcolm Russell.'

He paused for a moment and reached over to press the buttons on the video machine, glancing at his watch, and starting the recording with the date, time, stating who was present, and repeating his previous words.

'You do not have to say anything. But it may harm your defence if you do not mention when questioned something which you later rely on in court. Anything you do say may be given in evidence.'

Feddersen broke off, watching intently for my reaction. I nodded, looking at him, blurred through tears.

'What happened? At the hospital?' I asked, meekly.

'We don't know yet.'

Many times over the last few days, I'd pictured Mal, lying in a hospital bed with tubes attached to him, an oxygen mask, a monitor beeping to his side. I don't know why I'd insisted on forcing myself to do it, but on some level, I thought it would make the situation less surreal.

Now all I could imagine was his body lying flat on a hospital trolley; his lean torso, sprinkled with moles down the middle, concave and still; his face, chiselled and expressionless; his pale Scottish skin even paler.

A primal noise, somewhere between a groan and a scream, came from deep within me. The detective and Ashok sat in embarrassed silence while I tried to compose myself. It slowly dawned on me that my best hope of proving my innocence had died with Mal.

Feddersen waited for a few seconds before continuing. 'There will be a post-mortem, of course. I've just got back from King's College Hospital where I interviewed Sally Dowell.'

'Has her condition improved?' Ashok asked.

'Yes, the doctors seem to think she'll be fine after some rest. However, they've also carried out a psychiatric assessment of—'

I had to interrupt him. 'That's ridiculous. She's set me up, disappeared, hampered police enquiries, yet she gets the kid-glove treatment. Won't she be charged with anything? She can't be absolutely sure it was me at the flat that night – she's never met me.'

'Finding Malcolm Russell as she did would have been a huge shock to anyone. Her behaviour over the last few days may have been the result of some kind of post-traumatic stress.'

What if Martin Hathaway had already met with Sally, and bearing in mind the fact I could blackmail him, together they'd come up with this post-traumatic scenario that stopped her having to admit she hadn't seen me that evening? I couldn't talk about it in front of Feddersen; I'd have to wait until I was alone with Ashok.

There was a pause as Ashok made some notes, then cleared his throat. 'So, whatever happens, there's likely to be a delay in moving forward with Sally Dowell. Are there any new developments concerning Adrian Evans?'

'No, Mr Evans still hasn't been in touch with us. We're

waiting for the hotel, Le Monet, to confirm whether he's been staying there.'

'But his lack of co-operation, his failure to respond when you've contacted him, you must deduce from that he has something to hide, surely?' Ashok added.

'We've been granted a warrant to search his home, and access to his phone and online activity. He will be arrested for breaching his bail conditions, and questioned.'

A few hours later, I was taken back to the interview room where Ashok was waiting.

'Okay, some news. They're also going to question Phil Hughes, Mal's colleague. Now it's a murder investigation, they're trying every possible line of enquiry. You've met him, haven't you?'

'A couple of times, they've known each other for years but now work...'. I stopped mid-sentence, my chest tightening. '...at the same bank. He was on the low-level list of people I thought might be involved.'

Ashok looked back through his notes, trying to find the lists I'd made only a few days ago. It felt like months.

'We didn't pursue it because we concentrated on Sally and Adrian. Did you have any idea what the issue was between them?'

'No, but it's been going on for a few months. They're in different departments in the bank, with opposing aims, from what Mal told me. I guess Phil was involved in something dodgy and Mal was trying to stop him.'

Ashok nodded. 'I'll see what impact this has on your position. It might take several days to make any progress with the bank. Your custody period will be up tomorrow morning. Unless they charge you before then, they'll have to release you.'

He turned to another page in his notes. 'And I've just seen McMenemy upstairs. They haven't been able to interview Sally Dowell yet but they've pressed for that to take place this evening, pending another assessment. They've been looking at her online activity. On Tuesday morning, she looked at your profile on Facebook, and quite a lot of your photos. She'd deleted her browsing history on her laptop afterwards but I doubt she'll have known information is held by internet service providers. I'm surprised McMenemy told me, but it's good news.'

'So, she looked at photos of me just before the ID parade?'

'Exactly. It doesn't prove she was responsible for the attack, but it does throw doubt on her positive ID of you.'

'Just while I remember something. Sally's lawyer is now Martin Hathaway, the guy you met yesterday, or was it the day before? He came in with Greta Mayhew. I didn't say anything at the time but I had a very brief fling with him, four or five years ago; I met him on a dating site. He'd been cheating on his wife, and Greta is a good friend of hers. At one point there was only him and me in the interview room; he wants to keep it quiet but he knows I've got him by the balls. He promised if there was something that came to light that put Sally in the picture, or alternatively, cleared me, he would tell us.'

'Do you trust him to keep his word?'

'Not entirely. Don't you think this Facebook lead might be a useful bargaining tool though?'

'It's a grey area. In court, if the prosecution's case rests on a positive ID and the witness has checked social media for images of the suspect, it would be inadmissible. Sally Dowell probably won't know that.'

'Will McMenemy mention it?'

'I think it'll depend how the questioning goes.'

'Is there any way Sally Dowell can be forced to realise she was wrong about seeing me? Would the police consider her and me meeting in person?'

'I very much doubt it. They'd say that she would have the opportunity to do that at the trial.'

'But that would be months away. She'd have completely forgotten the details of that night by then. What the woman looked like, what her voice was like. Is there anything we can do? Can we use our trump card with Martin Hathaway?'

'Leave it with me.'

CHAPTER 46

I 'd grown to hate my cell. The yellow; it was so ugly. There was no warmth in the colour, it was too acidic. The police must have used it because yellow is supposed to be a mood lifter but, for me, it was the polar opposite.

And the silence. I don't think I'd ever gone for so long without listening to music. Now and again a few bars, or a line or two of lyrics from recently-released songs, would float into my head, mixed up with all the other shit. But they were replaced by others with which I had a longer, deeper history.

Nick Cave. A shared devotion had been one of the hooks when Mal and I first started chatting, all those years ago. Cave used the word 'babe' in his songs, and, almost in tribute, Mal often used it in his texts to me. We'd listened to Cave's entire back catalogue together. Not just listened – reviewed, dissected, intellectualised, whilst cooking, eating, drinking, driving, fucking – he'd been the soundtrack to our relationship.

"Green Eyes". One night, only a month or so before,

quite drunk on red wine and whisky, we'd been sitting in my kitchen listening to Nick Cave, singing along, each taking a part.

We'd been so happy that night, so content.

'This song could be about you,' he'd said, pouring us another nip of Lagavulin.

'My eyes aren't green, they're a nondescript bluey-greeny-grey,' I'd replied.

'I need a closer look,' he'd said, as he leant in to kiss me. Still basking in the rosy glow of being newly in love. Crazy, considering we'd met years before.

Recalling this moment, I slumped to the cell floor, a paralysing, wrenching ache in my chest. We were still no closer to finding out who killed him, three days later. I needed the police to find out who did it so that I could get out, but more than that, to have some kind of resolution.

Back in the cell, Sergeant Gibson had left a change of clothes and a couple of panty pads. I hadn't used them in over twenty years and I shuddered at the prospect, but they were better than nothing. I stripped to wash. The smell of dried blood on my inner thighs, sour and metallic, transported me back to being thirteen, at school, still coming to terms with frequent, sporadic, heavy periods.

The sun shone through the glass bricks above the bed, falling onto the centre of the concrete floor. The forty-nine small squares, slightly skewed, had an ephemeral beauty as the light faded for a few seconds and then returned.

I felt hypnotised, watching the diamonds wane and reappear, some angles becoming sharper, others less so, as the pattern moved imperceptibly slowly onto the wall. One of the myriad reasons why being held in a police cell was so disorientating was not having any idea what the time was.

The clean clothes helped lift my mood a little. My back ached from inactivity. I stood up and stretched. I went back to walking round the cell to clear my head, gradually increasing the pace; seventy laps clockwise, seventy the other. When I'd got into a rhythm, I let my mind drift to Ned; what would he be doing? It took a few seconds to remember; Sports Day. God, how could I have not thought about it until now? That was yesterday, wasn't it? How long had I gone without thinking about him? I didn't even ask Ashok to call home and check everything was okay, and to ask how it had gone. What kind of mother was I? A fucking terrible one.

I came to a halt, sadness and anger overcoming me. I flinched. Would Caroline have thought about putting sun cream on Ned before Sports Day? Given him enough to eat in his packed lunch? Would she have taken some photos? If I ever got out, I promised myself, I'd never ever miss another sports day.

A few hours after dawn, Sergeant Gibson came down to the cell to tell me Ashok was waiting for me. I went over to the basin and splashed water on my face, though it made little difference; I felt completely broken.

'I got a call from Feddersen about 20 minutes ago. There's been some news,' Ashok said.

'About Adrian?' I asked.

Ashok shrugged. 'That's my assumption.'

Feddersen rushed in, and pressed the buttons on the video machine, hastily recording the time and date. 'As Mr

Chowdhury has probably told you, there have been some significant events overnight.' He looked down at his notes. 'Firstly, Adrian Evans was arrested last night at St Pancras International and has been questioned at Kensington police station.

'His computer equipment and phone are being examined. The information Mrs Kendrew gave us about his attempts to sever ties between her and Mr Russell concerned us sufficiently to suspect he may be involved. He's also breached his bail conditions for the alleged underage sexual activity in Paris.'

'And what about Sally Dowell?' Ashok asked.

'We have yet to interview her fully. The psychiatric assessor gave her the all-clear last night and she was allowed home. She's coming into the station for questioning this morning.'

'What time will that be?' Ashok asked, glancing sideways at me.

'We've asked for her to be at the station at eleven, though we'll allow her solicitor some time with her first.'

Something occurred to me. 'Has she been told that Mal has died?'

'We haven't had any contact with her, but his death has been reported by London-based news organisations and local radio, as well as some nationals, so she may well know by now.'

Would the news make Sally more or less determined to stick to her story? It could go either way. Somehow I needed Ashok, with Martin's help, to make her realise she was wrong.

Feddersen cleared his throat. 'Philip Hughes is also being questioned by our colleagues at Bethnal Green police station, together with a number of other employees at

Schwarz-Müller AG, some very senior. It appears an internal investigation into possible insider trading at the bank had already been initiated, though we don't at this stage know if Malcolm Russell or Philip Hughes were known to be involved.'

Feddersen started to stand up. 'I think that's everything I can tell you for the moment.' He reached over to stop the tape.

I'd been back in the cell for a couple of hours when Sergeant Gibson came down, explaining that she had to handcuff me because Ashok was waiting upstairs.

'Why upstairs?' I asked. She shrugged in reply.

The ground floor of the police station was quiet; Ashok was sitting in the room where I'd seen Ned and Denny a few days earlier.

I sat down expectantly, and waited for him to speak. He didn't. I looked around the room in an exaggerated manner to see if there was some clue I'd missed.

I piped up, 'What's going on?'

'Shhhhh,' he said quietly, resting his hand on mine.

'What is it?' I whispered back; he didn't answer for a few seconds.

'Sally Dowell's coming in to be interviewed by McMenemy. Martin Hathaway is meeting with her half an hour before it starts.' He glanced at his watch. 'Any minute now.'

'And what, we're going to ambush her?'

'Something like that.'

'So, what do you want me to say?'

'Nothing, just leave it to Martin and I.'

Ashok stood up and opened the door a few inches to check if he could see or hear anything, and shut it again.

'What will McMenemy ask her? Will they tell her Mal's died?' I whispered.

'Yes, they will. They'll be looking closely at her reaction, just as they did with you. Her disappearance, and all the post-traumatic stuff...' he tailed off; we could both hear voices in the corridor.

He leaned in closer, and lowered his voice another level. 'I'm hoping, for your sake, that face to face her demeanour will give her away. If it does, that will give them sufficient reason to treat her as a suspect rather than purely a witness.'

Outside in the corridor, we heard Sergeant Gibson talking to Martin Hathaway, telling him which room was free.

'Come on.' Ashok pulled me up and opened the door.

'Thanks, we're finished,' Ashok said to the young officer Gibson had told to guard the door. We could see Martin disappearing into one of the interview rooms further down the corridor.

Ashok almost broke into a run, taking me with him, and stopped when we reached the open door. 'Martin, I didn't know you were going to be here today... Oh, I'm sorry, I, er...'

I held back so that Martin and Sally couldn't see me but Ashok grabbed my arm and thrust me into the doorway. I couldn't help but look straight at Sally. She looked tired, dressed in a smart if unflattering suit with a t-shirt underneath the jacket, her curly hair unruly. She stared back at me, tightening her jacket around her.

'Oh, Ashok, I'm...' Martin began.

I lurched forward towards her, partly thankful that Ashok was still holding my arm; if not I might have throttled her. 'I'm Alex Kendrew. I've never seen you before, Sally, and you've never seen me either. You made a mistake about Monday night; it was someone else who came to your flat.

I'm devastated about Mal's murder, as you must be, but you have to tell the police you were mistaken.'

Ashok pulled me back. 'Alex, that's enough.'

Sally stumbled out of her chair towards Martin, turning to him. 'She said Mal's murder... he's not dead, he's in hospital, he's going to be fine.'

Martin stepped forward. 'Okay, Ms Kendrew, my client is here to speak to DC McMenemy. Ms Dowell hadn't yet been told about Malcolm Russell.'

'Well, she needed to know sometime. I didn't kill him. Unless she wakes up and realises she's made a terrible mistake, I'm going away for a very long time, for a crime I didn't commit. You need to make sure she does that.'

I held Martin's glance for a few seconds before he turned towards the door, and I felt Ashok's hold on my arm tighten. McMenemy was standing there.

'Mr Hathaway, Mr Chowdhury, can you explain what's going on here, please?' she asked. She was almost visibly shaking, her anger barely contained.

The two lawyers looked uncharacteristically flustered for a moment. Martin stood up straight, as if expecting a bollocking, but it was Sally who spoke first, looking from me to McMenemy.

'She just said Mal is dead... is that true?'

Martin spoke up. 'Ms Kendrew was passing the room with Mr Chowdhury as we were arriving. It was extremely unfortunate. I'm sure Mr Chowdhury was just about to return to the cell with his client.'

McMenemy strode forward and grabbed my arm.

'That's enough.' She turned to the uniformed officer guarding the door. 'Please take Ms Kendrew back to the cells.'

I couldn't stop myself. 'I've been here for three days. I

didn't have a chance to see Mal before he died because of that, and I'll regret that for the rest of my life. I know you looked at photos of me on Facebook... why did you do that if you were sure you knew it was me?'

'It's not her.' Everybody turned towards Sally. 'This isn't the woman who I let into the flat. She was wearing sunglasses, for most of the time. But her voice – your voice – it's completely different. You have a slight northern accent, not much of one, but the woman on Monday night... she definitely sounded southern. You just said 'chance' with a short 'a'; she said something, the woman at the door, with a long 'a'.' She looked at each of us in turn. 'I grew up in the Midlands; I pronounce words with a short 'a' too.'

McMenemy had a file in her hands, and tried to leaf through it but it was too full and a handful of A4 sheets fell to the floor. She bent down to pick them up. Ashok helped her.

I closed my eyes, my head falling backwards. I couldn't quite take in what was happening. The only sound was the crisp, quick movements of McMenemy flicking through her papers.

'Ms Dowell, I'm just looking at your statement here, the one you gave at the scene on Monday night. You said Alex Kendrew said she was just passing and wondered if Mal was free to go for a drink.'

Sally was nodding impatiently. 'Yes, that's it. Passing. She pronounced it like it had an 'r' in it.'

CHAPTER 47

Even after Sally's admission that it hadn't been me at the flat on Monday night, I had to go back to my cell while McMenemy and Feddersen decided what to do with me.

A couple of hours later, Sergeant Gibson came down to the cell, and told me they'd dropped all charges. I couldn't believe it. I almost hugged her.

The release process was quicker than I'd imagined, though still laborious. All the contents of my handbag had been placed individually in small plastic bags and recorded and I had to sign for everything. Ashok arrived back at the station to take me home. Sergeant Gibson explained it was likely Feddersen or McMenemy would need me to update them several times a day.

'I hope you settle in quickly at home. I'm sure your son will be over the moon to have you back.' She paused, lowering her voice, and bending down towards me. 'I shouldn't say this really, but I always thought you were innocent.'

I smiled. 'Thank you. You've made my time here much more bearable; you've shown genuine kindness towards me.'

'Take care of yourself, love.'

Ashok's progress through south London was swift, a few miles above the speed limit. In Herne Hill, seeing a green light ahead, without slowing he made a huge right-hand curve to get through in time; a bit reckless and, I realised, exactly what I did at the same junction.

We parked and walked up the inclined street towards the house. Ashok went ahead of me and knocked on the door. No answer. He knocked again, and then peered over the frosted glass panels on the bottom half of the sash window. Still nothing.

'I've got my keys.'

My hands were trembling as I reached down to put the key in the Chubb lock. More than anything else, I'd wanted to be at home, back to some kind of reality, and now it was happening, it felt utterly surreal, like I was an actor playing a part. My heart thumped in my chest.

At once I could detect Caroline's sweet, floral perfume. It was both comforting, familiar as it was, but strange. It was so unlike anything I'd wear myself, for my house to smell of it was slightly disconcerting.

'Caroline?' I called up the stairs. 'We're back. Are you there?' I thought she might be in the bathroom and hadn't heard the doorbell.

'I'll call her,' I said to Ashok, reaching in my bag for my phone, before remembering it had been out of battery when I'd been given it by Sergeant Gibson.

'I've got Caroline's number – I'll try her,' he said.

I walked upstairs, calling in case she was on the top floor and still hadn't heard. I plugged my phone into the charger in the hallway.

Ashok called up to me. 'I've just called Caroline and it's gone to voicemail. I'm sorry Alex, I need to get to going if that's okay – can you try her in a few minutes?'

'Yes, of course, thanks. I'm going to call Ned's school and let them know I'm home.'

'Let me know how you are, okay? I've got a court hearing but I'll drop in to the station afterwards and find out what's happening with Adrian Evans and how the interview went with Sally. There might be some news from Malcolm's work too.'

There was an empty, dusty space on my desk where my iMac should be. Though I knew I probably wouldn't get much work done over the next few days, I called down to Ashok.

'Ashok, do you mind finding out when I might get my computers back?'

'Sure. They've got no need to keep them. I'll ask when I'm at the station; they should be able to return them later today, Monday latest.'

When Ashok left, I stood in the hallway, not knowing what to do first. School; that was my priority. I called the main reception number.

'Oh, hello, it's Alex Kendrew, Ned Moran's mum, he's in Miss Marsden's Year 2 class. You probably know I was arrested a few days ago, and Ned's been looked after by friends. I've been released though, the charge was dropped. I just wanted to let you know I'll be able to pick him up as usual after school.'

There was silence for a few seconds apart from the sound of a computer mouse being clicked. 'Oh, actually, I'm just looking at the register. He hasn't been in today. There's a note on the screen, just give me a moment to read it.'

While I waited, I set about making myself coffee. I

emptied and refilled the water reservoir, filled a cup to flush out any old water. Making espresso was a ritual, like rolling a joint.

'Right, Alex, I'm just reading here that Caroline Wilson talked to Miss Marsden yesterday afternoon. It says she was concerned Ned was suffering from all the upheaval. She's taken him to her parents'.

'Oh, okay. I'll call her, thanks.'

I took my coffee up to the studio and scanned shelves of boxes labelled 'admin'. I finally came across the box I was looking for; eight or nine old diaries, all with a piece of ribbon holding the separate leaves together. One of them had an address book at the end. It was almost completely out of date now, apart from the addresses of friends' parents. I leafed through the fragile pages until I reached the 'W' pages. Mr and Mrs Wilson, Caroline's Mum and Dad.

'Hello, you've reached Mary Wilson. I can't talk to you at the moment but please leave a message and I'll return your call as soon as I can. Speak to you soon.'

Speak to you soon. Caroline finished every phone call with those words, every email and text. She must have got that from her mum. I felt a pang of longing; longing to see Caroline, longing for us to go back to how we'd been. I knew she disapproved of the way I lived my life. The last few days would have given her even more reason.

I ran upstairs to my bedroom; the cats were in their usual spot at the foot of the bed. The girl curled up on her left side, the boy on his right, mirror images, yin and yang. They opened their eyes and raised their heads for a moment, in muted approval that I'd finally returned home.

I grabbed some clean underwear, my favourite pair of jeans and a t-shirt. On top of the chest of drawers was a framed photo of Mal. I'd taken it at an all-day festival we'd been to. He was holding his plastic pint glass, emblazoned with the festival's logo. It had been at the end of May; we'd been so happy together. I felt choked, my nose tight, tears pricking the back of my eyes. I thought about putting the photo away in the top drawer but couldn't. I wasn't ready to come to terms with the fact that he was gone.

I ran down to the bathroom and peeled off the clothes I'd been wearing in the cell. I was going to put them all in the bin. I showered quickly; it would have been delicious to stay under the water, but I needed to get up to Cambridge and see Ned. I tried Caroline's mum again, this time leaving a message, saying I was driving up to Cambridge to pick up Ned.

Ashok had given me the address of the police pound in Charlton before he left, where my car had been taken. Despite the plentiful zero-star reviews describing three-hour waiting times, I was driving away in under an hour. Sitting in almost stationary traffic on the Blackwall Tunnel approach, I got a text from an unknown number. *Adrian's been arrested. Assume you know. He asked if I could look after the dog last week when he went to Paris. He was supposed to come and get it this morning. I'm going to take it to the kennels near us unless you pick her up. Antonella Evans.*

I knew Ned would love to see Penny. I texted Antonella back to ask for her address. Thirty minutes later, I knocked on the door and could hear Penny's high-pitched bark, some way back in the house. Antonella appeared in the hall, her small, expensively-dressed frame unmistakable even when distorted through the floral pattern of the door's frosted glass panels.

Her face was expressionless when she opened the door,

but gave way to the merest hint of satisfaction as she took in my image. I knew I looked like shit.

'I'll get the dog.' That's all she said. I stood on the doorstep waiting. Penny's excited barks became louder, and a moment later they were accompanied by the familiar clatter of claws on wood as she bounded along the hall, and launched her front paws up to my chest, and with a well-practiced move she had licked my entire face in a split second.

Antonella had Penny's basket, and in it her food and a squeaky toy. She dumped it into my arms. She was already closing the door and I had to tilt my head towards the still open portion to be heard. 'Thank you for looking after her, I appreciate it. I know you're not a fan of dogs.'

'No. I'm not. The girls have enjoyed her being here though.' Her expression softened a little. 'What's happening? With Adrian I mean. If he goes to prison... well, that's going to be disastrous. For me, and the girls.' She didn't need to explain. Almost as an afterthought she added, 'but he doesn't have the wherewithall to murder anyone, least of all your bit on the side.'

Through the few inches of open door I glanced around her hallway; gilt mirrors, wall-hung Middle Eastern kilims, the modern yet ornate chandelier, unlit but with chinks of sunlight hitting it from the back of the house, prisms of rainbow colours travelling through the glass and onto the ceiling. After taking in the scene, my gaze came to rest on her.

'You make me sick. I know you withdrew your allegations against him. You didn't have the guts to go through with—'

She shook her head. 'You're right. I was a coward. But I had my daughters' futures to consider. Can you imagine how people would treat you if they knew your father had a conviction for having sex with underage girls?' I could see her point. 'He's a nasty, jumped-up, arrogant shit. Alex, I'm sorry, I made a very clumsy attempt to warn you off him, at the reunion. Do you remember? And by insisting the girls couldn't see you; I thought it would be enough of a spanner in the works.'

My mouth gaped open; did I believe her? I remembered that fleeting conversation when I was leaving the restaurant. I'd put it down to being nothing more than sour grapes on her part. Penny started whining at my side.

'Well, in that case I must thank you, but I wish you'd tried a bit harder.' With that she closed the door. Penny looked up at me, searching my expression for some explanation. 'Come on, let's go.' I realised I didn't have her lead. I held her collar until she was safely in the car but I'd have to use my belt later. She dutifully hopped onto the back seat.

I'd made the journey to Caroline's mum's house dozens of times since I'd known her, but not for seven or eight years at least, not since her dad had died. The last time I'd been pregnant with Ned.

Ned. What was he going to think? He'd seemed completely fine the afternoon he'd come in with Denny, but it worried me that Caroline had thought he was suffering from the upheaval. If that was the case, how would he react to seeing me? Would he be tearful? Or angry that I hadn't been there for him? He seemed so grown up these days, I forgot sometimes that he was only seven.

As I drove slowly into Caroline's mum's driveway, I was relieved to see two cars parked, somebody must have been home. I left Penny in the car; Caroline's mum had cats and I wanted to avoid any impromptu chase round the garden.

Mary hugged me when she opened the door. I must have

known her for twenty years or more, but she never looked a day older. As always she was perfectly turned out, with a neat grey bob, linen trousers and a Breton-stripe t-shirt. She was so nice and kind, totally unlike my own mother. I'd always been slightly envious of Caroline and her stable, loving upbringing, even if it might have been a shade dull.

'Oh, Sandy, come in and sit down. You look totally exhausted. I can't believe what you've been through. I've been reading about it on the internet. I'm so sorry. You're in the clear now though?'

'Yes, for the time being. They've arrested my ex-partner, Adrian. He didn't do it, but they think he hired someone to kill Mal.'

'Oh gosh, how awful. Do you think he did?'

'It's really complicated. I don't know to be honest. I just know it wasn't me.' I looked behind me to see if I'd missed Caroline's Mini in the drive. 'Are Caroline and Ned out somewhere? Her car's not here.'

'Oh, she's taken him to our cottage on the north Norfolk coast. You've been there, haven't you?'

'Yes, a long time ago.' I sighed. The last thing I needed was another long drive. 'Do you mind if I go up there now? I'm so desperate to see Ned. I know Caroline was only thinking what's best for Ned but really we just need to try and get back to some kind of normality.'

'Yes, it might be difficult getting hold of her to let her know you're coming. We got rid of the landline there a few years ago as we were hardly using it and it seemed like a waste. And the mobile signal isn't great there. I think some networks are better than others. David always tried...'

She froze. I hadn't seen Mary since before David had died. 'He used to say holding his phone out of the bathroom window upstairs did the trick. He would sometimes get one or two bars of signal if he waved it around a bit. That was a good few years ago though, of course, but I'm not sure the coverage on the coast is any better now.'

'These days it's hard to just be left alone; it must be nice to not be contactable for a few days.'

'Yes, I totally agree with you.'

'I'm going to go up there. I'll leave a message for Caroline on her phone and hopefully we can meet up, at the cottage. Can I take your address in Norfolk?'

'I'll write it down for you.'

CHAPTER 48

In my haste to get to Norfolk, I'd forgotten to set Google maps on my phone with the postcode. Now I was on the road I didn't want to stop again so I followed my nose. I turned the radio to 6Music; Shawn Keaveny almost lulled me into thinking it was just a normal Friday afternoon.

The distance up to the north Norfolk coast was further than I'd imagined; it was past three in the afternoon by the time I left Fen Ditton – it would be around five by the time I reached Caroline and Ned. I wanted to take him home. It would be a late night but at least he could sleep in the car.

As I neared the coast, the small, narrow roads criss-crossed the flat landscape, so I added the postcode of Mary's house into the map app on my phone to avoid going round in circles, or, more accurately, triangles.

Holme Next The Sea looked familiar as I turned off the main coast road. As well as writing down the postcode which Mary had told me covered half the village, she'd drawn a little map. Their house was called Windy Ridge, with a sign on the gate. Penny realised we were visiting someone and hopped into the front seat and back again, tail wagging, looking around and whimpering slightly.

I found the house and drove slowly along the drive, just in case Ned ran out in front of me suddenly. I let Penny out and immediately she started barking and running round the house. I imagined Ned would hear and come running out, recognising her bark.

The house was large – detached and modern, probably seventies, red brick with a steep, large roof and a stone gable end. I knocked on the door but there was no reply. I walked round to the side of the house and looked through the lounge window, feeling a stab of sorrow when I saw Ned's toys, neatly stacked in the middle of a large rug.

Penny jumped up at the window, leaving tell-tale paw marks on the glass. Nose to the ground, she travelled round the house, first clockwise, then back again, and then into the main garden at the side of the house.

Penny must have picked up a trail on the grass, a fox or cat, perhaps. She was making the classic sighthound yowl, nose in the air, mouth slightly open. I knew it well, she made it when anyone – Adrian, his daughters, Ned or me – arrived back at the house after an absence. Five minutes or five days, it made no difference. I was always amazed at how strong the pack mentality was in her.

I ran up the garden, following her as she trotted ahead, sniffing the bottom of the small gate that led to the beach. After not having a phone for those days in the cell, it was comforting to feel the heavy rectangular weight of it in my jeans pocket. As I walked I called Caroline's number again; it went straight to voicemail. I sounded out-of-breath, the sea breeze whipping my voice away in gusts every few seconds. 'Hello my lovely, I hope you got my messages earlier. I'm in Holme. I've been to the house. Have you gone for a walk with Ned, or out for tea somewhere? Call me back if you get this. See you soon.'

There was a strip of gorsey land between the garden and the sea, dotted with small, hardy-looking trees and shrubs. Penny found the sandy gravel path that twisted through the sand east and west. Out to sea, the water was surprisingly blue.

Thin cloud swept across the sky, interspersed with vapour trails chaotically crossing the pale blue expanse. A stretch of salt marsh was broken here and there by inlets of water, glinting in the sunlight.

Penny had her nose to the ground, tail wagging, whining a little, following a circuitous trail for a few seconds then changing direction completely. She looked up now and then to check I was still there, and then continued her work. I'd often thought how exotic it must be for a dog to come somewhere completely new, where all the animal smells would be fresh and unknown.

She let out a yowl and darted off between clumps of marram grass. She was looking behind her but I knew I was slowing her down. I began jogging. I didn't have proper trainers on, just Converse, not brilliant for running. I upped my pace, but didn't have a hope in hell of catching her. She was running at full pace now, her tail all I could see above the grasses. I willed her not to catch a rabbit or a bird, or send a small child flying.

I stopped when I heard a message alert on my phone; it was Ashok, just checking I was okay. I texted back to say all was fine. *In Norfolk, at Caroline's mum's place by the sea.*

Ahead of Penny I could see some people, just dots, groups of them moving along the path. The gravel made way to a wooden boardwalk, mostly covered with dry sand. Even with the layer of wire, twisted into small hexagon shapes against the weathered wood, it wasn't easy running terrain.

The path climbed through a small wood of conifers, and continued to a stretch of isolated sand dunes, circled them and ran over the top of the highest one. From here I could see further, the people no longer dots. A retired-age couple dressed in rambling gear with a white terrier trotting along by their feet; a family of four, two children, one a little older than Ned, one a year or so younger.

I saw Penny approaching the rambling couple. She was a lot bigger than a terrier and often looked at them with mild amusement when they yapped furiously round her feet. She was quicker than them too, much quicker. She stopped for a moment, the two dogs greeting each other in the customary way. But she resumed sniffing the ground, and continued in the same direction as the scent she'd been following.

And then I realised... Ned. She'd almost reached him and Caroline. My boy. I sprinted the last three hundred metres; as I reached them, Ned was already crouching down and hugging Penny, letting her lick his face.

My legs couldn't carry me fast enough and at one point I stumbled on a piece of rock jutting out on the path, steadying myself mid fall. 'Ned, Ned, sweetheart.'

He hadn't noticed me, so deliriously happy to be reunited with Penny. But when I called he ran the last twenty metres and I swept him up in my arms, tears filling my eyes so that the whole scene was a blur of ochre, pale green and dark blue. He wrapped his arms round my neck and his legs round my waist, just as he'd done when he was a toddler. 'Sweetheart, I've missed you so much.'

'Mum, you're here. I've missed you too. Have you been at the police station all this time?' he asked.

'Yes, honey, but it's all fine now. We're going home.'

He buried his head in my hair and I held him tightly to my chest. Caroline was standing a few feet away, giving us a moment alone.

'Caroline, what can I say? Thank you so much. How can I ever repay you?'

She came over, wrapping her arms round both of us. 'Don't mention it, you'd have done the same for me, I know that. I've been so worried about you. They've released you... what's happened?'

I waited for Ned to run a little way ahead with Penny so that he wouldn't hear. I told her that the police couldn't find any evidence I'd been at Mal's flat that evening, and Ashok and Martin's plan to orchestrate my coming face to face with Sally. 'But the detective in charge is pretty convinced Adrian is behind it; they've arrested him. I had to dish the dirt on him and the underage prostitutes.'

'You think he did it?'

'To be honest I don't know. I mean, I didn't realise he hated me enough to frame me for murder, but then I also didn't realise he hated me enough to try and split Mal and I up by telling Mal I'd been killed in a car crash.'

Caroline stopped and looked at me, confused. 'What? I don't understand... he did what?'

'Oh, I must have forgotten to tell you. He got hold of my phone and changed all my contact details for Mal, blocked his actual numbers so that Mal couldn't call me, and then sent a text from a pay-as-you-go phone to tell him I'd died in a road accident. Pretty messed up.'

'How did you find out?'

'Mal couldn't come to terms with it all. He got in touch with the police to find out more about the accident. Except there wasn't one.'

'Oh, well, it's very lucky he found out.'

'Yes. If I hadn't, I'd have never seen Mal again. Though right now, part of me wishes he hadn't; at least he'd still be alive.'

'He's dead?' Her face turned pale.

'Yes, last night. They said his condition had improved, and that they were going to reduce the sedatives. I don't know what happened. It's...' my voice tailed off; every word that sprung to mind to describe how I felt was completely inadequate.

'I'm so sorry, Sandy, I can't imagine how you must feel.'

I started crying, the wind whipping my tears away. 'It hasn't hit me yet. It will, I'm sure, but the last few days have felt like I was inhabiting somebody else's nightmare. I'm still living it now.'

'And how did they treat you, at the police station?'

Oh, not great. But I guess even with a murder charge, a middle-aged, middle-class white woman is going to get treated better than a seventeen-year-old black kid caught dealing crack cocaine.'

Ned was running around near the edge of the water with Penny, shrieking with delight. I noticed with a sinking heart that Caroline must have taken Ned to the barber. His hair had grown quite long and his curls had looked so cute. Now he had a short back and sides, all neat and tidy. And he was wearing new pale blue and white striped t-shirt and matching shorts that looked like they'd come from Petit Bateau. Caroline must have struggled to find anything clean and bought something; I was sure he'd had an overflowing laundry basket before I'd been arrested.

'It's been so sweet, spending time with Ned, we've had a lovely time together.'

'I'm sure you have, thank you. I'd really like to take him

home this evening though. We need to try and get back to normality.'

We started walking back towards the cottage. She stayed silent. I glanced across at her and noticed her face had fallen. 'Oh, but we've made cupcakes together. Can't you stay tonight and leave in the morning?'

I looked at her. How could I say no when she'd done so much for me?

CHAPTER 49

Returning to the cottage, we settled into a bizarre domestic situation. Caroline continued to play 'Auntie' and I felt like a convalescent, while Ned happily played with his toys, regardless. It was a cliché that boys didn't show their emotions as much as girls. I didn't think it was necessarily true; from when he was a baby, Ned had been very cuddly and I'd always encouraged him to talk about how he was feeling.

I'd always thought that because it had mostly just been him and me, we'd had a special bond. Part of me was relieved that he didn't seem affected by spending the best part of a week away from me. The other part worried that it was some coping mechanism and that it would come out as a more deeply-buried trauma further down the line.

I was desperate for a drink after the week I'd had, but for some reason I didn't feel comfortable asking Caroline if I could have one. I was sure she thought I drank too much, always had, ever since college, especially on top of other facets of my personality that were in complete contrast to her own. So it was with a false nonchalance that I answered when she asked if I'd like a gin and tonic. 'Oh, yes, that'd be nice. Let me do that,' I said, standing up. I remembered Caroline's less-than-generous G&Ts. Had anybody else ever used the width of a finger as a measure?

'Oh no, you relax, I'll do it.'

I would have to make up for my forced sobriety when I got home. Caroline was cutting slices of lemon in the kitchen.

'I'm going to pop out for a minute,' I told her. 'I need to talk to my lawyer and the DS in charge to let them know everything's okay, but I can't get a signal in the house. I had one for a while out on the coastal path earlier. I'll walk back along the beach, take Ned if he wants to come.'

But Ned was engrossed in an episode of Shaun the Sheep. Penny's ears pricked up, noticing me reach for my bag, she sensed a walk might be on the cards.

I kissed Ned on the top of his head and told him I'd only be a few minutes, then walked down towards the coastal path. I held my phone in front of me, waving it at arms' length, left and right, up and down. Nothing.

The sunshine was still strong, our shadows elongated and sharp against the sand path, beautiful in their strangeness. I took a few shots on my phone, just in time before Penny took off, trotting ahead. As I looked back at them, eight or nine tiny thumbnails appeared on the screen.

It had been over a week since I'd taken any photos. There were a few out-of-focus selfies of Ned's chin, taken in our kitchen, a screen shot of some train times, a couple of The Flaming Lips on stage at Brixton Academy, one of Mal watching them whilst holding both our pints. We did this thing at gigs, it had become a tradition; one of us would hold both drinks at the end of a song so the other could applaud.

Mal. My beautiful, funny, clever Mal. We'd never go to a gig together again. I came to a halt. My legs, unable to hold me, gave way, and I sank to the ground.

Penny realised I wasn't moving and trotted back towards me. She waited patiently, first sitting, then gracefully lowered her chest to the ground, resting her chin on her left paw. I staggered to my knees. Still no signal. We continued walking, retracing our steps from earlier. As we approached a copse of fir trees, I had a short burst of iPhone message beeps, falling over themselves to arrive first. I checked the screen; three missed calls from Ashok, Martin Hathaway and Feddersen. And texts from Agnes. I clicked the voice-mail button.

'Alex, it's Ashok, thanks for your message; let me know what's happening, and if you're coming back to London tonight.'

'Hi, it's Martin Hathaway. Just to let you know Sally Dowell's been interviewed by McMenemy. We've been going through CCTV footage from Monday night to see if she can spot the attacker. They are also trying to create an EFIT-V image but it's taking a while to get anywhere. So nothing definite yet but I'll keep you posted.'

'Ms Kendrew, it's DS Feddersen. Adrian Evans was inter-viewed this morning by our colleagues in Kensington. He's facing new charges relating to breaking bail but so far is denying all knowledge of the attack on Mr Russell, but we'd expect him to do that. Either myself or DC McMenemy are going to interview him later today, and we're looking at his phone and online history for the last few weeks.'

He paused for a few seconds, as if distracted. 'I'll let you know if we have any news. I've informed Cambridge Constabulary too, but I'd be grateful if you could update me. We've had the full forensic test results back from the crime scene. Other than those of Malcolm Russell and Sally Dowell, we have one unidentified DNA profile that isn't in the national database; it is female, and I can confirm it isn't yours.

'We can't rule out that you may be in danger. If you have any inkling that something isn't right, call 999 and give your name and mine. There's a special code – AK158 – followed by today's date.'

As I typed short text replies to all three, I became aware of someone hovering in front of me. A woman with a dog, a male Weimaraner; him and Penny were flirting outrageously. We both smiled briefly and turned to watch them.

'Your lurcher's beautiful,' she said after they disappeared into the trees. I smiled and nodded. 'Yours too, I can see mine's a bit smitten with him.'

'I'll leave you to your messages – you look deep in thought.' The woman – early sixties I guessed, maybe a little older, dressed in a fleece and nondescript jeans – smiled and turned to walk back towards the village.

I felt like I needed to apologise. 'I couldn't get a signal at my friend's house, so I came out here and then had a whole stack of messages.'

'Yes, I know, we're a black hole when it comes to 21st-century technology. I love it.'

She turned away, and for a few seconds I watched her disappear, the sleek, velvety grey hound trotting behind her, looking back at Penny, longingly.

As I began to walk back in the same direction as the woman, I realised I hadn't read Agnes' texts. *Hi, what's happening? Haven't heard back from you. Now worried. Let me know.* Followed by: *Just tried the police station – you've been released?!?*

I knew she'd be worried if I didn't reply. I texted her

back, briefly summarising the events of the last twelve hours.

The sun was still high in the sky, and walking towards it, everything was bathed in a honeyed glow. Despite this, and the news I'd had from Feddersen, I couldn't ignore an unease I'd begun to feel, a dread. What would the next few days hold for me? The next few months? Without Mal.

When I got back, Ned had joined Caroline in the kitchen to decorate the fairy cakes they'd made earlier. There were little bowls of icing, all with too much colour added to look appetising. There were little packets of sprinkles too; stars, hundreds and thousands, tiny marshmallows. Ned had never shown much interest in baking and I imagined he was humouring Caroline a little, but he seemed to be enjoying it.

'Any news?' she said, looking up, a splodge of dark mauve on the side of her nose.

I walked over to Ned and hugged him, his arms wrapping tightly around the tops of my legs.

'Mum, where did you go again?'

'Oh, I just took Penny for a quick walk and to listen to a few phone calls. Are you having fun? Let me see your cakes. Which is your favourite so far, sweetheart?'

He put his elbows on the worktop, resting his head in his hands, and concentrated on making his choice. One elbow had landed on the home button of Caroline's phone. Her wallpaper was a photo of Ned she must have taken at Sports Day; he was wearing his PE kit. I felt a flutter of unease that she would use his photo; only for a moment before it occurred to me that she didn't have anyone special of her own. I admonished myself for being so cruel.

'I think I like the blue ones best. I've made this one for you. I put little animals on them; there's a little squirrel and a dog and a rabbit. And I put some sprinkles on too.'

'Wow, it looks delicious. Can I have it for tea?'

He nodded.

'Caroline, can I make that G&T?'

'Of course, is everything okay?' She looked concerned.

'I'd had a message from DS Feddersen who's in charge of the case. Adrian's denying any involvement, though I think Feddersen's convinced he is, especially...'. I lowered my voice to a whisper. 'Because of the underage prostitutes. That's never going to throw you in a good light with the police.'

'That's good, isn't it? If they're certain he's involved?' She turned and walked towards the fridge, reached down and took out a bottle of Gordon's and a couple of mini bar-size cans of tonic water.

'Yes. And they've interviewed Mal's colleague. She's been looking through CCTV footage near the flat on the night. And they're putting together some kind of photo-fit of the woman.'

CHAPTER 50

Caroline was keen to do one last bedtime with Ned, and though I was desperate to after being apart from him for so long, I wanted to let Caroline enjoy being with him, after everything she'd done for me.

I'd been worried about Caroline for a while. She was one of my oldest friends, but there was a sadness, perhaps even a bitterness, that had descended on her in recent years. She must have come to terms with, in her early forties, that it was very unlikely she'd ever have children of her own. I knew it was one of her big disappointments in life. That, and not ever having a relationship longer than a couple of months.

I remember her asking if I could meet her for a coffee one afternoon – she'd come down to London for the day. She told me she'd been dumped by a guy who'd seemed very promising. 'I've tried to call him but his phone's going straight to voicemail... I think he might have blocked me. Sandy, can I use your phone to call him so it won't be my number that comes up? I don't understand why he's being like this.'

I managed to persuade her that wasn't a good idea. 'He doesn't deserve you,' was the best I could come up with as I hugged her.

The truth would have been too painful; she was just a bit too prim and proper. Sean had always called her an Ice Queen, but not at all like Emily Blunt's depiction in *The Huntsman*. 'Come on, she's never going to let you come all over her tits.' Crude though it was, he had a point.

Ned had a shower, and afterwards I could hear Caroline reading a chapter of *The BFG* to him. They'd been reading it at bedtime for the last week or so, and it sounded like they were near the end; Sophie and The BFG were at Buckingham Palace.

'Sandy, can you come up? Ned wants you to read the last few pages of the chapter to him.'

'Of course, I'm coming.' A minute later I was transported with Ned to Giant Country, the BFG and the armed forces in cahoots to capture all the other giants. Monday night, the last time Ned had snuggled under the duvet, me sitting next to him on his bedroom floor like any normal night, seemed like a lifetime ago.

Ned wrapped his arms around my neck. 'Love you, mum.'

'I love you too, sweetheart, more than anything in the world.'

'More than anything in the world, by a million, zillion miles,' he said.

'Sweet dreams. We're going home in the morning, so straight to sleep so we've got lots of energy tomorrow.'

'Okay. Night night.'

. . .

Caroline had been preparing a veggie lasagne and was serving up by the time I came down. She'd opened a bottle of Pinot Grigio too; not the most exciting, but it was alcohol and I would have drunk almost anything.

She filled our glasses, and we chinked. 'To happy endings,' she said, 'and new beginnings.'

'So, tell me what's been happening with you recently. I'm sorry, the conversation has rather been hijacked by me this afternoon. How's that guy you met... the quantity surveyor?' I took the opportunity to eat and drink while she talked.

'Oh, it didn't last. We had a couple of dates. He was still going online though, so I guessed he was meeting other women.'

'Well, that's kind of normal, really. The trick is to keep looking yourself, isn't it? I know it's not very romantic, but...'

I was on shaky ground, discussing online dating strategy with her. I changed the subject.

'How's your mum? She looked really well when I saw her earlier. Does she need any more treatment?'

Caroline had always suspected her mum's stomach ulcer was due to the stress of her parent's divorce, made worse by the shock of her father's death.

'She seems to be fine now – the doctor said she has to be careful and not overdo it with acidic food and drinks. Red wine is definitely a no-no as she knows that's a trigger.'

I'd drunk most of the bottle of Pinot Grigio. Caroline kept topping me up as she was talking. Several times I allowed myself to push to the back of my mind what had happened to Mal. But then I felt a rush of guilt and took another slug of wine to deaden the pain.

I felt unbelievably tired, perhaps a combination of the wine and a full stomach, for the first time since I'd been arrested. Not wanting to appear rude, I glanced at the clock on the kitchen wall when Caroline's head was turned.

I got up from the table with the empty plates and salad bowl, but my legs collapsed underneath me, the crockery crashing to the floor.

'God, Caroline, I'm so sorry; look what I've done? I feel totally exhausted. I'll clear this mess up and then I really need to go to bed. We've got an early start in the morning.'

'Don't worry at all.' Caroline jumped up. 'I'll run a bath for you. You do look shattered.'

Upstairs in the bathroom, as I undressed, I had to steady myself by holding onto the wall. Had I drunk that much? Over half the bottle, but not enough to make me feel really drunk. I put it down to the last few days and finally letting go of the tension a little.

A text alert bleeped from in my jeans pocket. Fuck, I'd forgotten to keep in touch with Feddersen or Ashok. I'd had two missed calls from Feddersen, a couple of hours ago. I pressed the voicemail button, but the signal wasn't strong enough. Feddersen's voice kept breaking up and I couldn't work out the gist, just the odd word; Sally... description... voice...

I remembered what Caroline's mum had said about her dad waving his phone out the bathroom window. I opened it, the deliciously cold air hitting my skin made me feel less woozy. With the phone held at arm's length I had two bars. I pressed the voicemail and the speaker-phone button.

'Alexandra, it's DS Feddersen again. Just wanted to update you. As I mentioned earlier, we've been interviewing Sally Dowell at length this evening. She hasn't been able to spot the woman in any CCTV yet but we've been able to work on the EFIT-V a bit more and she now thinks it's quite a good likeness.

'But, there was also been some developments with Phil Hughes, Malcolm Russell's colleague. In a series of interviews with our colleagues at Bethnal Green, he has admitted being aware of insider dealing, but is maintaining he wasn't involved. In fact, the opposite; that Malcolm Russell was, and that he'd been trying to persuade Malcolm to stop.

'He thinks a few other employees might be in on it, though he's not certain who, and denies any knowledge of Sally Dowell's involvement in the fraud. The bank's internal investigation is ongoing but at an early stage, and we're waiting to hear the outcomes of that so far.'

'And finally, Adrian Evans. DC McMenemy went to interview him in west London earlier, in relation to Malcolm's Russell's death. He has remained tight-lipped but we'll be upping the pressure on him in the morning; I'll keep you informed as best I can. We'll also distribute the description Sally Dowell has given, and the EFIT-V, to the National Crime Agency who have a database of known contract killers.'

He rang off, and I wrote a short text in reply, thinking that a phone call, with an almost non-existent signal, would be difficult, especially as it was so late.

I was putting the phone back in my pocket when I remembered he'd left two voicemails. I pressed the button again, forgetting that I needed to hold the phone out of the window and missed the start of the message. I listened to it again.

'One last thing Alexandra, I almost forgot. I don't know if it has any significance; Sally Dowell remembered something else the woman said at her flat on Monday night. She introduced herself as 'Sandy Kendrew'. Sally said she must have looked confused, because the woman then apologised and said 'Alex' instead.'

There were only a handful of people who called me 'Sandy', all of them friends from college over twenty years before. A bunch of art students who'd probably still think of me as 'Sandy' but whom I hadn't seen since we'd graduated. Why would any of them turn up out of the blue to destroy me now?

And Caroline, of course, no doubt pottering around downstairs, clearing up the mess I'd made. My arm turned limp. I watched in slow motion as the phone fell from my hand, clattering against the side of the house; once, twice, hitting a water butt before landing on the grass.

I heaved, the entire contents of my stomach filling the toilet bowl, leaving a pebble dash covering on the sides. It was blue in places and it took me several seconds to remember why; the icing on Ned's cupcakes.

I rinsed my mouth and drank from my cupped hands, splashing water on my face. In the bathroom mirror above the basin, I glanced at the door; I'd locked it.

Blood pounded in my head, deafening the internal discussion I was trying to have. It couldn't be her, could it? I went searching for clues in our conversation earlier; I couldn't think of anything she said. Did anything make me feel uneasy? Yes, but I couldn't put my finger on what.

If I was right, what were my options? If I was alone with Caroline it would be easy; I'd stay locked in the bathroom, yell out of the window and hope the neighbours would hear. Or I'd just take her on and hope I was stronger. But Ned was asleep along the corridor. I couldn't leave the house with him there, alone with her. If Caroline had been crazy enough to kill Mal, what was to say she wouldn't hurt him?

Stay or go? The decision was made for me as I heard Caroline's footsteps in the hallway below, accompanied by Penny, her claws clattering on the polished wood floor.

I ran along to Ned's bedroom, but opened the wrong door; Caroline's mum's bedroom, judging from the decor. As I turned, Caroline was there, blocking the doorway. She looked like I'd never seen her before, her expression indignant, her eyes wild and determined, as she swung a large wooden chopping board against the side of my head.

CHAPTER 51

I don't know how long I'd been unconscious. My eyelids felt impossibly heavy, and the left side of my head throbbed. My hand wouldn't move to touch it, however much I sent signals from my brain. I was lying on my side on a hard, tiled floor. I was in the bathroom.

The doorbell. Maybe that's what had woken me. I felt footsteps close by, a few feet at most, someone trying not to be heard. Was that Penny whining? Far off, outside. The doorbell rang again, but it was tentative, half-hearted, as though the person wasn't altogether sure they'd got the right house.

Ned. Where was Ned? God, it was coming back to me now. I'd been running to him when it happened.

Whoever had been at the front door gave up. Below the skull, my brain felt like someone was gently squeezing the life out of it. But at the same time, part of me was fighting, desperate to stay awake.

The door opened, so close to my head that I felt a rush of air on my cheek. I managed to open my eyes by a millimetre and saw Caroline's ankles, between her jeans and ballet pumps. I didn't have the energy to do anything, let alone fight back. Just play dead.

She knelt down on the floor next to me and started whispering in my ear. 'By now the sleeping pills will have taken hold, Sandy. Together with the wine, it'll be a lethal combination. I crushed eight tablets into the bechamel sauce; you didn't taste a thing, did you? The perfect suicide. No-one will ever suspect.'

She stopped and leaned closer, her fringe brushing my forehead. Was she checking I was still breathing? 'I want you to know how much I hate you. You've always made me feel inadequate and stupid and ugly. Well, I've got the last laugh. I'm going to be Ned's new mummy; you don't deserve to be a parent.' She sighed, indignantly. 'You can't even be bothered to take him to the barber's; his hair was so long he was in danger of being mistaken for a girl. He's never been your priority; it was always work, and then it was meeting someone new. I doubt you even know how many men you've slept with since you broke up with Sean. You're disgusting.'

Now I could remember what had niggled me earlier; the photo of Ned at Sports Day on her phone's homescreen.

She stayed there, motionless, listening for any signs of life. I desperately wanted to swallow, but knew I couldn't. The more I thought about it, the more my mouth filled with saliva. I tried to keep my breathing shallow and even, but my heart was racing. She moved a little, over to the basin and turned on the tap. I took the opportunity to swallow. She returned and started bathing the left side of my head with a wet cotton wool pad. What was the point in doing that? My lungs filled with her sweet, floral perfume that I knew so well. I almost gagged.

I'd been sick so there was a chance not all of the sleeping tablets would have entered my bloodstream.

Would the amount that had still be fatal, especially with alcohol? Stay focused, stick to a plan, I told myself. But I didn't have the brain capacity to plan anything.

Caroline shifted her weight, her knees so close I could hear the cartilage creaking.

'I'm sorry it's had to end like this, Sandy,' she continued, with a note of sarcasm. 'I'd like to say it's been nice knowing you, but frankly, that would be a lie. Not at first, not for a long time, did I realise how toxic you were, how you ruined everything for me.'

Her voice was slow and deep; it dawned on me that it was designed to be soporific. I had to keep fighting to stay awake. I drifted off for a few seconds at a time before my brain jolted me awake again, so that I only caught snippets of her soliloquy.

'... never be loved? What it's like to never be wanted? To spend your whole life... manage to keep seeing someone for a couple of... usually only two or three... And when you and Sean split... try dating. 'It'll be fun...'

I lost consciousness and when I resurfaced, the subject hadn't moved on.

'... and I couldn't believe how insensitive you were being. You'd already had... and a child. And then ten minutes after you join a dating site... interesting, handsome chaps and...' With each syllable she started jabbing my shoulder blade with a pointed finger; 'it' 'was' 'just' 'so' 'un' 'fair'. She gave a hard little snort.

'And then you met Mal. The one. You have no idea how delighted I was when, only a few weeks later, he dumped you to go back to his girlfriend. Finally, you might get a taste of what I'd been going through all these years.'

Yes, I remembered her barely-concealed glee, dressed up as concern, when I told her Mal had gone back to Louise.

'And then there's the college reunion and you bag Adrian Evans. Guess what, no longer a skate-boarding hippy, he's now a successful abstract landscape artist. Handsome and rich. He falls for you, of course he does.'

The soothing tone had segued into vitriol. As she spat the words out, tiny drops of saliva landing on my cheek kept me on the verge of consciousness.

'But it didn't matter, did it? Because, just when your perfect little world with Adrian was falling apart, Mal, your knight in shining armour, reappears. D'you know how much I've wanted that to happen to me? Some of the chaps I met... I thought perhaps they'd get in touch some day. But they never have. I'm still waiting. That only happens to women like you.

'And then, the final straw, the photos from my party. The film you'd had printed and brought up the last time you came to visit with Ned. Do you remember? You brought them because you knew there were photos of Dad in them, among the last before he left Mum, before he died.'

I searched around in my head; what the fuck did those photos have to do with anything?

'There was one photo. I don't know who took it, not you because you were in it, talking to me. Dad was looking at you; just like he did with that Elodie at the rowing club dinner. I blame you, with your come-to-bed eyes. You think you can have any man you want, even someone else's husband, father, grandfather. You've ruined my life, and Mum's.'

The birthday party. Caroline's dad had only paid me more attention because I'd told him I was pregnant, and he'd found a bottle of alcohol-free bubbly. I didn't want to make an announcement and inadvertently steal the limelight on Caroline's birthday.

I played back her words in my head. 'I blame you.' He'd lost his footing and fallen down a steep path when he'd taken Caroline and one of her sisters on a short walking holiday in the Peak District, soon after the divorce. Was she admitting guilt? Or in her twisted way, did she really think she was administering justice, then and now?

'Dad deserved it on that walking holiday. "Have you thought about adopting children, or fostering, now that you're probably too old to have your own?" How could he have been so cruel? He was missing the point completely; I didn't want anyone else's children, I wanted my own. I wanted the whole chocolate box romance, a big wedding, a honeymoon in the Maldives. Everybody else had that, why couldn't I? I didn't mean to, but he was right on the precipice, one little push was all it took.'

My mind had started to drift away but I was brought back; I thought I heard Penny barking, for a few seconds before silence returned. Caroline must have heard it too; she waited, and then began more quietly; a deep whisper, almost a growl.

'The injustice was too much, for you to live happily ever after with Mal. It was sickening. But I had an idea how I could right the wrong.' She leant closer, her breath on my cheek again. 'D'you remember, Sandy? I kept offering to babysit Ned...'

Why was she telling all of this if she knew I was going to die? What was she expecting to happen? I had to try and think from her perspective. She was expecting the sleeping pills to take hold and that I'd overdose and die in my sleep. What would she do? What would I do, if the roles were reversed?

She said she thought it would look like the perfect suicide. In that case, wouldn't she need someone else to discover my body at the same time, to ensure she didn't get the blame?

Jesus, a thought hit me; Ned. Was she crazy enough to do that? Allow a seven-year-old to discover his mother's body?

'I kept texting you to ask if you'd heard from Mal. You can't imagine how unbelievably satisfying it was to know that your perfect world was falling apart. You thought he'd dumped you, just what I'd hoped.'

Her words became incoherent noises at some point as my internal dialogue had taken over, trying to process what she was saying. It wasn't Adrian who had caused Mal and I to break up last year, it was Caroline. The night I went to stay with Mal in Brighton; she looked after Ned.

My head was a dead weight. Behind my eyes the feeling I'd had earlier, as though my brain was being squeezed, came back, much stronger. I tried to focus on the abstract, bit-mapped pattern of black and red on the inside of my eyelids. It took all my strength, but as she continued with her rant, I knew I was falling.

CHAPTER 52

I t was the cold that woke me. Wet clothes clinging to my skin. The brutal nanosecond awakening that follows zopiclone-induced sleep was familiar to me, as was the inability to recall where I was or the day of the week.

Why was I in the bath? Why did I still have all my clothes on? Why did my head feel like it was going to explode? Where was Ned? Where was I? What was digging into my back? I could feel something but I wasn't quite able to move my hand to touch it.

I'd dreamt about Mal, one of those anxiety dreams I'd had, on and off, since we'd met. But I knew I hadn't just dreamt he was dead; that fact had seeped into my bones and would never leave me.

I was lying, almost prostate, on the bottom of the bath. My feet touched one end but the bath wasn't quite long enough and my head didn't lie flat. The back of my neck ached from being in the same position for hours, like falling asleep on a long flight, head lolling forward. I propped myself up on one elbow and looked around the bathroom.

The little metal bolt on the door was locked. Had I done that? The window was slightly open and felt the chilly morning sea breeze.

Memories from the night before came back as though fed to me intravenously, drip by drip. Caroline; it was her, she'd killed Mal. But did she tell me? I searched around in my head for information. No, DS Feddersen, the voicemail. Sandy – that's how I knew. The sleeping pills. Shit, Alex, get a grip. That's why I was in the bath; she'd expected me to drown. Why hadn't I?

More sensation returned to my body, the pain in my back became more acute. Finally I summoned the energy to move my hand round to feel it. The plughole was in the middle of the bath and the flat, push-in push-out plug had come out, grazing the skin below my waist. I winced as I lightly touched the swelling.

I shivered with the cold, and the thought that if the plug had stayed in place, I would have drowned. I tried to lift myself out of the bath but the wet clothes added too much weight.

The bathroom was white, but in the corner of my eye, I noticed something out of place. I turned towards it, my neck still too painful to move it more than a fraction of an inch. Words, scrawled in red lipstick, on the tiles above the bath. 'I KILLED MAL. I'M SORRY. SANDY.'

The sound of water flooding out of my clothes almost drowned out the soft, electrical 'ding-dong' of the doorbell. Hadn't I heard it before? It was at the other end of the scale from the harsh, mechanical 'dring' we had at home. Was that what had woken me? Was I imagining it? I froze, waiting again, and knelt on the plughole to stop the water gurgling down it so I could hear better.

A longer burst followed by banging on the door. I hurled

myself out of the bath, and unlocked the door, wet feet slipping on the tiles.

'Open up please, police.' I could hear Penny barking excitedly at the door.

Thank fuck. But as I peered down I could see Caroline was already at the bottom of the stairs, looking up at me as if she'd seen an apparition, her mouth hanging open.

'I couldn't find a pulse,' she said, incredulously. I hurtled down the stairs and threw myself at her, grabbing her arms from behind. She twisted her body from side to side to try and free herself but I was stronger. I held on to her arms, determined not to let her go despite her attempts to kick and head-butt me.

The policeman shouted through the letterbox.

'You need to open up now, or I'll have to force entry. I've got your dog.'

Caroline was inching towards the back door, away from the policeman. I shouted to him. 'Help. Help. Please, you've got to help me. Just break the door down now.'

Ned appeared at the top of the stairs, still dozy from sleep and unable to comprehend the scene.

'Darling, go to the door, let the policeman in. Quick!'

He ran to the door but I knew he'd struggle with the lock. While I was distracted, Caroline managed to manoeuvre herself to one side. My arm was twisted to the point that I thought my wrist would snap. I had no choice but to let go. She bolted for the back door and fled into the garden.

I ran to the front door where Ned was still trying to unlock the Chubb key. I turned it and flung open the door.

'Quick, we've got to catch her, she'll get away.'

'Wait a minute, what are you talking about? I've come about your dog. Are you Alexandra Kendrew?'

'Yes, yes I am, but...'

'One of your neighbours found your dog in the boot of your car last night... that's an offence as it would potentially...'

Penny jumped up at me and then Ned, back to me, whining, tail wagging.

'I haven't got time to explain it all... she's going to get away. Call Brixton police station and—'

'At the station, we ran a check on the vehicle registration number... you've been in custody very recently and—'

'Tell them Caroline Wilson killed Malcolm Russell. I've got a case number; Feddersen, the DS in charge gave it to me. AK158.'

'Sounds like I'm going to need back-up.'

'Fine, but I'm going after her, unless you want to?'

'I can't run very far at the moment; dodgy knee, doctor's orders. That and a kebab belly.' He looked only slightly embarrassed as he gestured towards his paunch, two or three shirt buttons straining over it. 'There isn't much call for chasing after villains in this neck of the woods.'

'Can you stay with my son? I'll take our dog; she'll be able to pick up Caroline's scent.'

'I'd much rather you didn't do that, and you waited for the back-up instead, madam.'

'We don't have any choice.' I looked down at Ned, his bed-head hair lending a strange normality to the scene. 'Ned, darling, stay here with the policeman, he'll look after you.' He looked up at me and nodded. I kissed the top of his head and ran round to the back of the house. My phone was still there, next to the water butt. I picked it up, relieved that it still had some battery.

Penny started sniffing the ground, darting around from left to right as we joined the coastal path. Which way would

Caroline have gone? Patchy fog swept in from the sea, covering the village to the west. She would have headed in the other direction, to avoid being seen by anyone, along the coastal path.

Penny looked up at me, searching my expression for clues. I stopped for a second to hold the phone up to see if there was a signal. Nothing yet.

The mist hung low to the ground, nestled in the network of muddy inlets below the path. On the other side a large field was home to a few dozen cows, quietly grazing on the scrubby grass. The tide was out; yesterday afternoon the inlets had been full to the brim. Now the exposed banks provided a feeding ground for wading birds.

I slowed for a moment and, seeing there were two bars of signal, I pressed Feddersen's number. As I waited for him to pick up, I looked north, in the direction of the sea, but the fog was heavier further out and it would have been impossible to spot Caroline, even if she'd been only twenty or thirty metres away. Penny seemed to be following a scent. I had no way of knowing whether it was Caroline's, but my gut instinct, and Penny's, was to keep following the path eastwards. As the path rose, through the mist I could see we'd reached the sand dunes.

The strength of the ring tone wavered as I started running again. Feddersen answered on the fifth or sixth ring.

'DS Feddersen, it's Alex Kendrew. I know who killed Mal; it was my friend, Caroline Wilson, there's no doubt about it.'

'How do you know for sure?'

'Sandy. She calls me Sandy, always has done. What you said in your voicemail; it all made sense. And last night she tried to kill me with a sleeping pill overdose.'

'Where are you now?'

'On the north Norfolk coast, near her mum's holiday home in Holme next the Sea, but we're heading east... the next village along is Thornham, I think. She ran off, about ten minutes ago when a local policeman came to the door. He was going to call for back-up but we're miles from anywhere.'

'We'll get armed response there as soon as we can. Does she have a weapon?'

'Not on her, as far as I know.'

'Okay, they'll be there as soon as they can. Stay safe, don't take any risks. We might be able to track your phone; that'll help them locate you.'

'Okay, thanks, but the signal is very patchy.'

As we rang off, I spotted Penny; she'd kept disappearing as I'd been talking to Feddersen, chasing dozens of small, sparrow-like birds in every direction as they swooped low on the path, finding refuge in a cluster of spiky-looking gorse bushes every time she got too close.

I stopped for a moment, the sand dunes were raised ten or twelve metres above the surrounding area. It would have been a good vantage point, but the view was obscured by banks of heavy fog further out to sea.

I was struck by the utter silence. At home, there was always some kind of noise; the metallic squeak of the tracks over the bridge when a train passed it, a police siren or two, the sound of school children shrieking with delight at break-time.

A haunting bird call broke the silence, perhaps a bird of prey, high up in the sky. It came in short but repetitive bursts of *wheeeee, wheeeee, wheeeee*, almost like a whistle. And then, more eerie because it was impossible through the mist to work out where it was coming from, a church bell tolled. Seven o'clock.

'Morning.' A man was running up the boarded path towards me and I felt stupidly jealous of his routine start to the day.

'It's going to be a beautiful morning, once the haar's cleared.'

I called after him. 'Excuse me, did you see a woman running along here, about my age, a few minutes ago?'

He shook his head. 'I don't know for sure. Possibly. I was in my own little world, to be honest. Sorry.'

I thanked him and started running again. I called Penny away from the birds and she returned to my side, nose to the ground again. The path descended as we left the sand dunes behind us, and then turned a sharp right, away from the sea. Penny barked, turning off the boardwalk and through clumps of small, scrubby bushes. I followed her, keeping my eyes on the horizon; nothing. Penny leapt over a ditch; one of her specialities. It was too wide for me so I ran along the water's edge looking for a narrower spot to cross. I gave up, jumping far less gracefully than Penny, one foot landing in sandy mud three or four inches higher than my High Tops. She found a gap in the breakwater that stretched in both directions, made up of wooden poles positioned in a zig-zag pattern in the sand held together by a strip of chicken wire at the top.

Old posts lay abandoned to weather and grey. It hadn't occurred to me to bring anything to defend myself. I picked up a few wooden posts, discarded a couple that disintegrated when I tested their strength. I found one that felt sturdy enough, a couple of rusty nails embedded into the top.

Running on the wet sand was arduous and holding the

heavy, wet fence post slowed me down further. The fog was thick as we neared the water, and most of the time I couldn't see Penny at all, only her footprints. After we'd been running on the beach for a couple of minutes, Penny's path became interlaced with human footsteps.

I could hear the rush of the sea and, in the far distance, police sirens getting closer, I thought, but then they seemed to almost disappear as if they'd changed direction.

The fog broke for a few seconds and, for a moment, I saw her before a new bank rolled in. Caroline was at least sixty or seventy metres ahead, and Penny had almost caught up with her. She was barking, short sharp bursts, alerting me.

My legs felt heavy, but knowing Caroline was in reach, I found the extra gear I needed to speed up. Out of the mist, suddenly, she was there; twenty metres, ten. She was running, already in the sea, up to her calves. Penny hesitated until I reached the water's edge and then followed me, whining in protest.

I hit the water running, bracing myself for the coldness that for a moment took my breath away. The sand underneath was heavy, forcing me to keep each footfall as swift as possible to stop myself sinking. Caroline looked back at me, with a serene, almost amused expression. She had slowed but seeing how close I was she turned and sped up, the sea now up to her waist. I forced myself onwards, my progress slowed by the deeper water. Penny doggy paddled next to me, barking, confused.

'You're not getting away with this,' I shouted above the noise of the water. I heard sirens again, closer, competing with each other, out of synch. Two times, three times, I lashed out at Caroline with the fence post, but she was just out of reach.

'I don't have a choice. I'm trying to save myself, save myself the indignity of it all. My life has been one big round of little disappointments.'

'I'm not going to let you kill yourself. After everything you've done, you need to pay.'

'That's rich coming from you, Sandy. But it's too late, there's nowhere for me to go. I can't go to prison; what would my family say? It'd destroy Mum, after everything she's gone through.'

The swell of the water around my legs pulled me towards the shoreline and then further out. Whatever happened, whether Caroline lived or died, I couldn't go down with her. I had to stay alive for Ned.

'Your mum will find out anyway. Much better to give yourself up to the police now. Committing suicide will just make matters worse.'

'I can't let her find out. I'd rather kill myself. You're the cause of all my problems but no-one will see that. They'll just think I'm crazy.'

'You are fucking crazy.' I lunged forward, but she twisted and dived under the surface. I dived in after her. The tide must have been coming in; she was only a few metres further out and had drifted to the right. I lashed out at her legs with the wood, not managing to make contact. As she tried to make progress through the foaming water, her feet appeared near the surface. I grabbed an ankle and held on. She kicked me away, but I managed to keep my grip. Without both legs to propel her forward she couldn't move. I lunged at her with the post, again and again.

On the ninth or tenth attempt, a nail ripped through her jeans. She shrieked in agony. Blood rushed out and seeped into the sea water, dark red swirling like cigarette smoke into the grey-green, turning everything a dull orange.

I didn't have a moment to lose; while she was still reeling, I grabbed her feet and pulled her back to the shoreline. No fucking way was I going to allow her to drown in the water. She'd be seen as the victim, me the villain.

Penny yelped, darting back and forth in the shallow water as I neared the sand, simultaneously confused and excited, her instincts aroused by the smell of blood. Caroline's body was motionless. I dragged her away from the water until we reached a narrow strip of broken razor clam shells, washed up on the beach.

I shoved Caroline onto one side and slapped her back between her shoulder blades. One, two, three... I kept a steady rhythm until her body jerked back to life, the sea water in her lungs spluttering out onto the sand.

I looked up the beach. The fog hung in bands close to the ground, intermittently obscuring my view; all I could make out at first were a few figures in dark clothing. But they were moving quickly and stealthily. Stark against the bulky black uniforms was a bright yellow taser gun, held against the chest of one of the officers.

Caroline sobbed as I held her down with every ounce of strength. She wasn't fighting back; she knew it was over. I waved towards the police.

Caroline must have sensed my weight shift and the hold on her soften. I didn't notice her pick up the wooden post I'd dropped, only her arm sweep upwards in a perfect arc, as she thrust the nailed end into my neck.

CHAPTER 53

I was in hospital for ten days. Two nails were embedded in my neck, but had avoided the main arteries and veins by millimetres, I was told. I had some nerve damage that the doctors hoped would heal with time, but for the short-term was likely to give me problems swallowing. I had been very lucky.

The police arriving on the scene were confused. Two middle-aged women, both with shoulder-length dark brown hair and a slim build. One was a killer, one a victim, but which was which? At first they weren't altogether sure we weren't sisters. Caroline was conscious and maintained she was Alexandra Kendrew; the police had no reason to believe she was lying. They insisted on taking her to hospital but she tried to break free when they reached the ambulance further up the beach.

Feddersen and McMenemy drove up to Norfolk as soon as the local police had called them. They questioned Caroline. At first she refused to answer any questions, but her flat was searched and they found two phones hidden in a box of receipts. They only had messages on them from a couple of numbers; mine and Mal's. There was no doubt it was her who got hold of my phone the night I went to stay with him in Brighton.

The detectives interviewed me; this time as a witness. They told me what they found on the back of the large cork board hanging in Caroline's study; one corner of a photo had been sticking out, otherwise they may never have discovered it. Photos pinned on a wall, post-it notes on top, a few words scribbled on them. Dates, names.

There were some photos of me, but mostly they'd been defaced in some way, scribbled over, in one case the surface had been scratched away with a pin or a nail. She'd printed photos of Mal from his Facebook account. There were more than a dozen of Ned; one I'd taken of Caroline with Ned as a baby, he was teething and chewing on a piece of carrot. Her computer's search results showed she'd looked into guardianship, legal custody, adoption, and the rights of parents imprisoned with a life sentence.

On her phone, her camera roll included all the photos of Mal she'd printed out. I'd flinched once when she told me she downloaded onto her phone photos from profiles of men she'd chatted to online, even ones she hadn't even met for a date. That had struck me as odd. I'd have completely freaked out, had I found out a man had done that with mine.

Analysis of her phone showed she'd been in the vicinity of Mal and Sally's flat on the night he was stabbed. It also showed she'd been near his office in Canary Wharf, more than a dozen times. I vaguely recall him telling me some nutty woman had started chatting to him in the queue in Pret A Manger one lunchtime, when she'd dropped her purse and he'd helped her pick up the coins. He hadn't thought anything of it until, the next evening, on the train home the same woman had recognised him and tried to strike up a conversation.

I remembered all the times she'd asked about Mal. To start with, when I first started internet dating, it had been fun discussing profiles with her, sending links of them to each other, comparing notes. But, looking back, I know there was a tipping point where she'd shown too much interest, seemed to remember too much about my dates, and an undeniable flicker of satisfaction when I told her Mal and I had split up.

Why didn't I say something at the time, confront Caroline about her strange behaviour? If I had, none of this would have happened. She could have got help. And Mal would still be alive.

Caroline did start talking, after she was told the police had found incriminating evidence at her flat. They wouldn't tell me what she'd said in detail, but they didn't need to; what she'd said on the bathroom floor of her mum's house in Norfolk would haunt me forever.

A psychiatric assessment was carried out and the doctors suspected Caroline had multiple personality disorders. Her family were interviewed, and Caroline's mother, Mary, admitted she'd had concerns about whether her daughter might have been involved when her ex-husband had died accidentally. Her parents had informed her that they were separating, amicably, but Caroline had taken it very badly. When her father had suggested her adopting, she'd seen it as him being thoughtless, heartless, as though he'd already given up on her finding a partner and having children of her own.

I went to visit Mary a few weeks after leaving hospital. I was nervous about contacting her; she could have been very hostile to me, blaming me for what happened to Caroline, but I had to try.

I didn't need to worry; she was as warm and welcoming as ever when I phoned to ask if I could see her. Mary told me she had always worried about Caroline; she was the baby of the family, and seemed to be the butt of all teasing or jokey comments. Mary said she knew Caroline had always considered herself to be a bit plain. Pre-pubescent, with two teenage sisters already wearing make-up and going out with boys, whilst she wore glasses and her sisters' hand-me-downs.

I'm not proud of it, but my own vanity played a part in our friendship's dynamic. We all have our place. I thought of Ingrid and her perfect Nordic skin and bone structure. She was always above me on that ladder and she knew it.

The doctors' assessment did make sense; I had subconsciously suspected Caroline might have some kind of mental health issue. It seemed a ridiculous idea, given the mess I was making of my life, but it appeared she was living vicariously through me. If I'd been a good friend, I would have confronted her, though ironically I thought she was too fragile. Instead I'd taken the easy option, changing the subject rather than embarrassing or upsetting her. I cringed when I remembered her reading the set of Adrian's post-cards left on the mantelpiece. That would have been the perfect opportunity, but I didn't take it. Guilt came in waves, subsided and returned with even greater force.

Sean had been looking after Ned at home, and he brought him to see me in hospital. As it had been when he came to see me at Brixton police station, I found seeing Ned was bittersweet; his face was pale and he was uncharacteristically quiet and withdrawn. I vowed to myself, yet again, that I would devote every waking hour to him, to being the best mother I could be. I had made decisions in the past that I thought were in his interests, but I'd been wrong, sometimes. It was too late to fuck it up again.

I was desperate to leave hospital and when I was finally discharged, I had to wear a neck brace for a few weeks. The doctors told me I needed to be careful, not overdo things; no exercise or strenuous lifting, and no driving.

Investigations continued at Mal's bank; it appeared he was at the centre of a scheme to manipulate share prices. Contrary to what he'd told me, his friend Phil had been trying to dissuade him, not the other way round.

I felt gut-wrenching remorse for Mal's death, for Ewan being left without a father. I knew I would carry that for the rest of my life. I hadn't been responsible, but my actions had been the cause. I would have to come to terms with that.

I knew, had always known, that I loved Mal more than he did me. 'I'd cut off my right arm with a pair of rusty nail scissors to be with you,' I told him, several times. But he was planning to see Louise after all; maybe her pull on him would have won out in the end. Even if we'd stayed together, it seemed very likely that he would have been jailed for several years for his part in the bank fraud. Why he'd become involved was still a mystery.

Mal's funeral had already taken place by the time I left hospital. It took me a few months to pluck up the courage to visit his grave, at a cemetery on the outskirts of Brighton, one foggy morning in November. His birthday.

The lawn cemetery was vast; I had no idea where his grave would be. I walked around the perimeter, methodically scanning every row of neatly placed tablets, laid flat on the ground. Halfway round, I heard voices, crying; only snatches of a conversation, but it sounded like a small group of people. The sea fog had thickened and I could only see twenty metres ahead at best. I froze; of course his family would visit his grave on his birthday. I couldn't risk them seeing me. It would be a terribly sad day for all of them, and seeing the woman who caused his death would be the last straw.

My paralysis was broken by the sound of murmuring voices and footsteps approaching. I couldn't see faces but I could just make out the shape of people walking towards me. I turned and ran, heels sinking into the soft grass, but at least my footsteps wouldn't be heard on the tarmac path. I spotted the toilet block near where I'd parked and ran into it, locking myself in the cubicle at the end.

I waited an hour, feeling like a coward sitting there hiding. Car engines started up, then slowly passed the toilet block. A handful of people came into the ladies'. I caught snatches of conversation, but no mention of Mal, no Scottish accents.

I rummaged for the small flask of whisky in my handbag and took a large swig before I unlocked the toilet door. Hesitantly, listening out for other mourners, I retraced my steps and eventually came across a row of recently-placed tablets, fake grass covering the earth. Mal's was among them. I added the small bouquet of white roses to the four or five already there. I thought about reading the messages hanging from them, but couldn't. It felt far too intrusive. I wasn't family, and now I never would be.

I knelt down. The marble tablet was hard and cold, dark

grey and flecked with white. Tears rolled down my face, blurring his name, carved in a traditional typeface, elegantly sloping serifs, all in capitals. I ran my finger along the gilded letters. 'MALCOLM ALISTAIR RUSSELL. Beloved father, son, husband and brother. You will be dearly missed and always in our hearts.'

PLEASE LEAVE A REVIEW!

If you have enjoyed this book, it would be fantastic if you might consider writing a review.

Reviews help me get noticed; they can bring *Alter Ego* to the attention of other readers who may enjoy it.

Please feel free to leave a review on the website of your favourite bookseller, GoodReads or use the social media links below.

Thank you so much!

instagram.com/author_kamasson
facebook.com/kamassonwriter
twitter.com/kamasson_writer

ACKNOWLEDGMENTS

I started writing *Alter Ego* almost by accident. I emailed Faber Academy on a day when someone had just pulled out of their 'Start Your Novel In A Week' course. Without that stroke of luck, I may never have got further than the first few chapters.

I am very grateful to Graham Bartlett for his expertise in all things police-related; with his incredible knowledge he helped me understand not only what *would*, but what *could* happen.

A heartfelt thank you to fellow writer Jessica Stone, whose memoir *Craving London* will be released shortly after *Alter Ego*. It has been wonderful to share the last leg of the journey with her, swapping tips and advice during our transatlantic chats, and to have made a great friend in the process.

It was a joy to collaborate with two fantastic editors. Firstly Susan Davis who helped me to kick the book into shape structurally. Secondly Suzy Pope; as well as dotting the 'i's, she identified how the plot and characters could be further developed for the enjoyment of the reader. A huge thank you also to my dear friend Firuza Ali for being super eagle-eyed!

I'd like to give a special mention to my partner and son, for their endless enthusiasm, encouragement and patience. Thank you to Graham for filming all the fantastic footage and ads, not to mention his help and expertise with developing the plot. Thank you also to Dylan for being an Instagram ninja, the inspiration for 'Ned', and the best son ever.

Finally, I had the perfect setting in Gipsy Hill; nowhere has ever felt more like home. Thank you.

ISBN: 978-1-8382416-0-5

KAT CLUB

Join my 'Kat Club' to receive a free novella-length epilogue of *Alter Ego*, straight to your inbox on 14 December 2020.

In addition, you'll receive news and offers about new books, and the opportunity to become an advance reader.

It's completely free to sign up and you will never be spammed by me; you can opt out easily at any time.

To join the 'Kat Club' visit
kamassonwriter.com/contactkat